T0312987

THE SACRIFICE OF LESTER YATES

Also by Robin Yocum:

Fiction

A Perfect Shot, 2018
A Welcome Murder, 2017
A Brilliant Death, 2016
The Essay, 2012
Favorite Sons, 2011

Nonfiction

Dead Before Deadline, 2004
Insured for Murder, 1993

THE SACRIFICE OF LESTER YATES

A Novel

ROBIN YOCUM

An Arcade CrimeWise Book

First Arcade CrimeWise Edition

This is a work of fiction. Names, places, characters, and incidents are either the products of the author's imagination or are used fictitiously.

Arcade Publishing books may be purchased in bulk at special discounts for sales promotion, corporate gifts, fund-raising, or educational purposes. Special editions can also be created to specifications. For details, contact the Special Sales Department, Arcade Publishing, 307 West 36th Street, 11th Floor, New York, NY 10018 or arcade@skyhorsepublishing.com.

Visit our website at www.arcadepub.com.

10 9 8 7 6 5 4 3 2 1

Library of Congress Cataloging-in-Publication Data is available on file.

Cover design by Erin Seaward-Hiatt
Cover photograph © Sjo/Getty Images

ISBN: 978-1-951627-53-9
Ebook ISBN: 978-1-951627-59-1

Printed in the United States of America

To Ryan, Ashley,
and Jaclynn

Acknowledgments

I have a great agent in Colleen Mohyde, who has now put my sixth novel into print. Colleen has been a warrior on my behalf for more than a decade, and I am very appreciative of her efforts.

Lilly Golden was my editor for this novel; it was our third book together. Lilly has a deft touch and her efforts made this book better. She does an awesome job of keeping me safe from self-inflicted wounds in my narrative. Thanks to her and the team at Arcade Publishing for their support and confidence in this work. Also, thanks to Mike van Mantgem and my former *Columbus Dispatch* colleague Kirk Arnott for their work copyediting this book.

Lastly, thanks to my beautiful wife, Melissa, who is a constant source of inspiration. Her support and encouragement make the task of writing a novel infinitely easier.

In memory of the Egypt Valley Eighteen

Donna Herrick
1969–1993

Betsy Bergen
1967–1993

Identity Unknown
Died 1993

Anne Touvell
1973–1994

Angel Brown
1964–1995

Johnnie Jo Sephardic
1963–1995

Denise Brown
1971–1995

Maddie Kaminski
1969–1996

Tina "T" Pavlik
1969–1997

Teri Lynn Mason
1967–1997

Stephanie Wetzel
1964–1997

Divina Gardner
1963–1998

Gretchen Essex
1978–1999

Allison "Stormy" Wethers
1972–2000

Danielle Quinn
1971–2000

Nancy Farmer
1970–2001

Rayanne Schmidlin
1967–2001

Louise E. Love
1979–2001

Prologue

Ed Herrick was playing out the string, waiting patiently to die. He was two days past his eighty-fifth birthday when I interviewed him on the back porch of a two-story frame house that was as worn and sagging under its own weight as its owner. It was a slate gray morning, cool for June, and the leaves on the sugar maples had turned up in anticipation of the storm that would blow through the Upper Ohio River Valley later that morning. We sat on a pair of paint-starved rocking chairs and watched the waters of Wheeling Creek churn under the Blaine Hill Bridge on the old National Road. It was the house in which Herrick had been born, lived, and planned to die. He seemed to be grateful for my company, even if it was to discuss the murder of his youngest child.

Herrick had rheumy eyes and features that had been sharpened by age. Translucent skin stretched taut over hands that were flecked with wine spots and appeared to have the fragility of butterfly wings. A fine line of tobacco juice flowed like a slow leak from the crevice that stretched from the corner of his mouth to his stubbled chin. He smelled faintly of urine, the tang of stale testosterone, and the chewing tobacco that was crammed into his jaw. He called it "my last vice."

"The doctor won't let me have whiskey no more," he said, rubbing at his belly. "I got bad ulcers. You ever had an ulcer?" I told him I had not. "The doc didn't have to do a lot of convincin'. You don't want whiskey with an ulcer, I can tell you that, but I sure do miss it."

He was sickly thin, a feature exaggerated by a baggy red and black checked flannel shirt that was worn thin and white around his bony elbows and green pants that were cinched tight at the waist, the excess leather from the belt lying limp between his thighs. He had outlived his wife, two daughters, and his savings. On several occasions during our talk, his sunken eyes filled with tears and he groaned that he was tired of living and wanted "to go see Mom and the girls."

Periodically, I would lose him. His eyes would drift out over the rushing waters and focus on a time and place to which I was not privy. When he turned his head back to me, he would ask, "What was I talking about?" After one such lapse, he said, "It's hell to get old."

The death of Donna Herrick weighed heavily upon him, wearing down his bones and his will to live. He wished he could reverse time and go back and save his daughter. Not once in two decades had he stopped blaming himself for her death. It was an absurd supposition. How does one stop the wanton action of an unknown killer? You don't. But he was a father. It had been his duty to protect his little girl, and in his mind he had failed. He had held that belief since the day they had found her body, and he would surely take it to his grave. When his daughter needed him most, he wasn't there. "I buried my wife and that was bad, but nothing hurts like the pain of burying a child."

Donna Herrick had been young and a bit of a hellion with a quick smile and a lust for life. She was the youngest of his four children, a surprise that came fourteen years after the son that he and his wife believed would be their last. Ed Herrick was forty-eight when Donna was born, and by his own admission wasn't as strict with her as he had been with the older children. By the time Donna was fifteen and hitting her hormonal stride, her father was sixty-three and out of gas.

"She was my wild child," Herrick said. "She wasn't a bad girl, but ornery as all hell, always pushing the limits. When she was little, she would always fight with the boys; she was a scrapper, that one.

When she got a little older and found out she had something boys wanted, things changed. She was fearless; wasn't afraid of a damn thing. I always figured that was what got her killed." He pulled a balled-up, yellowed handkerchief from his hip pocket and dabbed at his eyes and blew his nose. "Donna always said that she wanted to be a movie star. She used to say, 'Pops, someday I'm going to be famous.' Well, she is, but for the wrong reason." He looked out over the water and slowly shook his head. "I still miss her—every damned day."

On July 17, 1993, a Saturday, Donna Herrick left her job at an automobile parts distribution warehouse south of Wheeling, West Virginia, and drove back across the Ohio River to the three-bedroom ranch in St. Clairsville that she was renting with two friends from high school. Donna cranked up a Def Leppard CD and the three young women laughed, sang into their hair brushes, made piña coladas in the blender, and smoked a couple of blunts before heading back across the river around nine o'clock to make the circuit of the clubs on Wheeling Island—the Merriment, Lou's Voo Doo, and Tin Pan Alley. Donna was twenty-three and loving life, dancing and drinking; it was another raucous Saturday night on the island. The last time her friends remembered seeing Donna, she was at the bar at the Merriment. She had a cigarette in one hand and a bottle of beer in the other. No one saw her talking to anyone particular. No one saw her leave.

She was there.

And then she wasn't.

Some forty miles to the west along Interstate 70, Piedmont Lake was overflowing its banks and spilling into the surrounding lowlands, filling the marshes and backwater inlets. These coves normally drew just enough water to create fetid mud bogs that supported little more than moss, sickly honey locust trees, and water moccasins. But after three days of rain the swollen lake had filled the back bays, including an inlet on its western edge near where Township Highway 357 dead-ends, the remainder of its southern route lost to the depths when Stillwater Creek was dammed in 1937 to create Piedmont Lake. The moss that had thrived in that dank inlet rose on the floodwaters, creating an emerald pool that shimmered when the sun finally showed itself on the morning of July 24, a week after Donna had disappeared.

It was just a few hours later when Merle Dresbach parked a Ford pickup truck that was more primer than paint along the berm of Highway 357. He and his grandson, Nick, grabbed a tackle box and two rods from the bed of the pickup and maneuvered over a sodden path that led to the water. Merle had his fishing gear in one hand and two sack lunches in the other.

By the time I started looking into the death of Donna Herrick, Merle Dresbach was fifteen years gone, having succumbed to black lung, the consequence of four decades spent mining coal deep beneath the hills of eastern Ohio. But his grandson remembered that day, if only through the eyes of a boy who was barely six. He remembered following his grandfather down the path and trying to step in the footprints left by his work boots, which seemed gigantic to him. The overgrown grass and foxtail were still soaked from the rain and they bent over the path like the arched roof of a cathedral, brushing against the young boy's face like so many wet paintbrushes. He remembered his grandfather stopping suddenly, dropping the lunches and the rods and tackle box, its contents of lures, hooks, and orange bobbers spilling over the damp soil.

"My grandpa was a pretty tough old bird, but when he saw that girl in the water, that really spooked him," said Nick Dresbach. "He didn't think I'd seen anything, but I did. I was little and there was a gap in the cattails, and I could see right through it. I saw that girl floating on the water; she was face down and her black hair was fanned out in a perfect circle. It was floating on the moss like a halo."

She was naked from the waist down and had been strangled with a dirty, rawhide shoe lace.

His grandfather scooped Nick up in his arms and ran, his diseased lungs pulling hard for air and producing a strained wheezing. Nick remembered being disappointed that they weren't going fishing and how his grandfather's white knuckles wrapped around the steering wheel as they sped to a nearby house to call the sheriff.

The sphere of interest in Donna Herrick's murder was centered in the Upper Ohio River Valley. Reporters came to Ed Herrick's house for interviews and asked for photographs to accompany their articles, and for the next week stories of her death dominated the front page above the fold. But a story works its way out of a newspaper in concentric circles, like a pebble dropped in a still pond, or a body dropped in a man-made reservoir. Other people die in car crashes, mayors and city councils clash, a highway construction worker is crushed to death in Yorkville. The latest victim is always the star. Donna Herrick's connection to an even larger evil had yet to be discovered, so the headlines faded. She was buried in a hillside plot in the Catholic cemetery overlooking the little town of Lafferty, and her life began to drift in memory except for those who had loved her.

The Belmont County sheriff assigned two deputies to the case. But where does one go when there are no witnesses and precious little physical evidence? And, after all, it wasn't like Donna was the daughter of a state senator or bank president. Her daddy had worked in a glass factory in Bellaire. As the stories disappeared from the newspaper, so did the leads into the sheriff's department, and soon Donna Herrick's file yellowed in a steel cabinet.

It would be another five months before a deer hunter found the body of a second woman, Betsy Bergen, in a thicket near the Old Egypt Cemetery. She was naked, with ligature marks on her neck and a green Christmas scarf with embroidered red reindeer lying at her feet. Then came the spring thaw and the badly decomposed remains of a third woman—to this day unidentified—was found in a stand of cattails on the western shore of Piedmont Lake near the 4-H camp. Seven months later, turkey hunters would find the body of Anne Touvell lashed to an elm tree near Egypt North Road; she had been garroted with baling wire that remained embedded in her neck.

The Egypt Valley Wildlife Area is a protected expanse of more than eighteen thousand acres in eastern Ohio. It was named for the extinct farming town of Egypt, which had grown up around a flour mill that pioneer James Lloyd erected near the banks of Stillwater Creek in 1826. The little town had a school, general store, post office, and a Baltimore & Ohio Railroad train station, but not much else. Egypt disappeared sometime in the early 1900s when the surrounding farmland, known as the Egypt Valley, was purchased by the coal companies, and the vast majority of the Allegheny Plateau was stripped away. The wildlife area was reclaimed after strip mining operations had extracted the last of the Pittsburgh No. 8 coal seam that lay beneath the surface. The dense Egypt Valley Wildlife Area horseshoes Piedmont Lake, a 2,270-acre reservoir with thirty-eight miles of shoreline.

The Egypt Valley was wild, isolated, and full of timber, brush, and concealed inlets. In short, it was the ideal place to dump a body.

It was a newspaper editor at the *Ohio Valley Journal*, Mitch Malone, who finally discovered the pattern. He began researching unsolved murders and documented eleven deaths—all women—over a five-year period. The victims, he noticed, were largely disposable members of society—prostitutes, drug addicts, petty criminals, and the occasional wild child, like Donna Herrick. He presented his findings in an award-winning series of stories in which he dubbed the killer, the "Egypt Valley Strangler." Newspapers all over the country picked up Malone's stories, and the remote Egypt Valley of eastern Ohio and its strangler became known to all.

Malone's series of stories ended, but the killings did not.

Sheriff's offices and small police departments along the Interstate 70 corridor began comparing notes and looking at old case files.

They had a problem.

The strangler continued to use the Egypt Valley as his killing grounds. Frustrated sheriffs called in the FBI for assistance, but they were no more successful than the locals. The national media descended on the little towns of Flushing, Hendrysburg, Holloway, and Sewellsville, interviewing residents. Some speculated it was a local man, a hunter perhaps, someone familiar with the woods and terrain. Others suggested an over-the-road trucker who passed through the area on occasion. In the four years after Malone's series of stories, another seven women—making eighteen in all—would be found in or near the Egypt Valley.

The murderer's ability to ply his craft with impunity was an embarrassment to law enforcement. Thus, it was with great fanfare in late October of 2001 that they announced they had their man.

This, however, did little to ease the troubled mind of Ed Herrick. He used a yellowed nail to pick at a chip of paint that was arching its back on the arm of his chair. "I'll die not knowing for sure what really happened, who really killed her," he said. "They say it was that one fella, that white supremacist boy, but I don't think they know for sure. I think they wanted to clear up all those murders, so they blamed 'em on him, and that was that. Case closed. It's important for fellas like you to find the killer. That's what you do. I don't worry about it anymore. I don't know if he did or he didn't. Either way, it doesn't bring my daughter back, does it? She's gone, and I understand that he'll be gone pretty soon, too. I suspect I'll be dead not long after that. Maybe I'll find out what really happened when I get to the other side."

⋆ ⋆ ⋆

The higher you climb in the justice system, the less interaction you have with the Ed Herricks of the world, the victims, the individuals left to pick up the pieces and whose lives are forever broken by the cruelty of others. The day I drove to eastern Ohio and interviewed Ed Herrick and Nick Dresbach was the first time I felt like I had done legitimate investigative work in the nearly three years since I was elected attorney general of the state of Ohio. I had been dealing with the so-called elite of the criminal justice system, the white-collar stuff, graft, misspent campaign funds, scams. The men—they're always men—I dealt with wouldn't sully their hands with a Saturday night special, but they had no compunction about bilking an eighty-year-old widow out of her life savings.

Losing a life savings, however, is nothing like having a cop show up at your front door and tell you that your daughter has been found face down in a lake. For that reason, law-enforcement professionals tend to dehumanize the victims. They push to the outside limits of their consciousness the photographic images of the victim's smile or tales of their tenderness. They treat their cases as if they are complicated puzzles to be solved and devoid of humanity. It is a coping mechanism that keeps them from losing their minds with grief.

I had done it many times. I immersed myself in the technical, scientific, and legal machinations of the case in order to put a man in prison or see him sentenced to death. But at some point, I would find myself across the table from a grieving father or wife seeking answers for their loss, my technical world colliding with their raw emotions.

That is why I became a prosecutor. I sought justice for those who could not fight for themselves, either because they were dead or because they were survivors thrust into the violent world of predation. Regardless of my motivations, the worst part of the job was dealing with the Ed Herricks of the world, those souls who would go to their graves with a hole in their heart as real and ravaged as one from a bullet.

As I drove back to my office that day, I was oddly rejuvenated by the misery of Ed Herrick. I had shared in his pain at the loss of a woman who would be perpetually twenty-three and full of life, and it was a reawakening. I remembered what I had been born to do, and once again my life had real purpose.

ONE

Four days earlier.

Eight weeks and one day before the scheduled execution of Lester Paul Yates.

Be careful of what you wish for in this life.

I dreamed of the day that I would be Ohio's attorney general—the most powerful law-enforcement authority in the state.

I have now ascended to the throne.

And I have never been more miserable.

From my corner office on the thirty-second floor of the Rhodes State Office Tower, the city of Columbus and the plains of central Ohio spread out before me. To the west, the Scioto River bends south and starts its trek to meet the Ohio. To the south is the state capitol building, the gray lady, and beyond that the orange neon and moving white lights of the Ohio Theatre marquee. I was at my office each morning by seven and frequently drank my first cup of coffee while watching the city stir to life.

I could see the skyline through my own reflection on the tinted windows. There were mornings when I wasn't sure I liked the man staring back at me. It was not the creases that ran away from the corners of my eyes, the flecks of gray or the softening of the jowls that

I found troubling. It was my eyes, and it was what I didn't see that troubled me.

They had lost their fire.

There had been a time in my not-too-distant past when, as a county prosecutor, I arrived at work every morning with an inferno in my eyes and my belly. Like a burning ember that fades from bright orange to gray ash, my fire slowly dissipated over the months I sat in the office of the Ohio attorney general. The Peter Principle states that we rise to our own level of incompetence. I don't believe I am incompetent. I believe I have risen to my own level of complete boredom and uselessness. Once, I was good at putting bad guys in jail. Now, I'm a bureaucrat and a politician, which is about one step above the scum I used to prosecute.

I campaigned hard and fought to be Ohio's attorney general, but once in office it didn't take long for me to realize how ill-suited I was for the job. I'd won the election because of my reputation as a no-nonsense prosecuting attorney. I once held press conferences to announce the arrest of suspected murderers and serial rapists. My last press conference as attorney general had been to announce a class-action suit against an out-of-state travel agency that had bilked Ohioans out of thousands of dollars with bogus vacation packages.

There were times when I fantasized about finishing my term and returning to Akron and again running for prosecutor. And those plans might have been set in place, were it not for Big Jim Wilinski.

Big Jim was the governor. He was in his second term and wildly popular. He was a former all-American tight end for the Ohio State Buckeyes and a four-time All-Pro with the Chicago Bears. Big Jim had chiseled good looks, hands the size of stop signs, and an Appalachian Ohio twang that he could summon on command when it played well with voters. He was a staunch conservative who had cut individual taxes, lowered regulations and corporate taxes, and attracted thousands of new, blue-collar jobs to his Rust Belt state. This had made him the darling of the national Republican Party and a favorite to win the nomination for president in 2008, if he decided to run. He acted noncommittal, but even a blind man could see he was prepping for a presidential campaign. He had the looks, the smarts, and most important, the ego.

A year earlier, I attended a fundraiser with Big Jim. After he had tossed back a few Wild Turkeys, he walked me off to a corner, draped an arm the girth of a sewer pipe around my shoulder, and said, "Padnah, when I get elected president of these here U-nited States, I'm going to need an attorney general, someone I know, someone I can trust." He winked and clicked his cheek a couple of times. "You know who that will be, don't you?" With his left arm he squeezed my shoulder with the grip of a python, and with the index finger of his right hand poked me three times on the breastbone. "That would be you, padnah."

Hutchinson Van Buren, Attorney General of the United States of America.

I do not like the bureaucracy and partisan politics that exist in Columbus, Ohio. God only knows what it would be like in Washington, DC. But I am not without ambition and vanity. While I would be happier putting away criminals in Akron, Ohio, I won't deny the allure of being the top law-enforcement officer in the nation. Thus, I decided that when Big Jim Wilinski won the presidency, I would firmly grab hold of his coattails and ride them all the way to Washington, DC.

After all, I was his padnah.

⋆ ⋆ ⋆

It was eight o'clock on a gray morning in Columbus.

That is to say, it was a typical day. It's almost always gray in Columbus, a city that ranks high when dermatologists come out with their annual ranking of best places to live, based on a gloom factor of how many days you fail to see the sun. Columbus usually ranks right behind Seattle and Portland. I'm guessing the number of people who don't die of skin cancer is offset by those with seasonal affective disorder who commit suicide, but at least they die with nice skin.

From my office, I could hear Margaret Benning in the lobby setting up for the day. At quarter after eight, she walked through my door. In her right hand was a printout of the day's schedule and in the left a stenographer's pad on which to write the various assignments that she would distribute to the staff at my behest.

Margaret had been with me since I was first elected prosecutor in Summit County in 1996 and was the only member of my former staff to follow me to Columbus. She is black, about five-foot-four-inches tall and just as wide (she refers to herself as "sturdy"), profoundly religious, and a heavy-handed single mother. She's also the most loyal human being on God's earth and protects my privacy and schedule with the ferocity of a pit bull. SEAL Team 6 couldn't get past her without an appointment. She's put up with me through at least four relationships, none of which ended well, including a torrid fling with my former campaign manager that ended in more flames than Mt. Vesuvius. Margaret serves as my moral compass and over the years has spent considerable time trying to protect me from my own bad judgment, particularly where women were concerned.

For example, a year earlier, an attorney in our crime victim services section requested a meeting to discuss funding issues. She was blonde, had legs that started just below her rib cage, and was as flirtatious as she was beautiful. She also was half my age. She was playing up to me because I was the attorney general, and I had the power to enhance her career. I knew this, but I still absorbed her flattery for a full thirty minutes. Not a minute after she left my office, Margaret came in and closed the door behind her. She beelined for my desk, her brows barreling down on her forehead like a hawk locked in on a bunny.

"What?" I asked.

"Don't you *what* me, Hutchinson Van Buren," she said, an index finger shaking in front of her face. "You keep your distance from Little Miss Sugar Britches."

"Little Miss Sugar Britches" was Margaret's catchall name for all of my exes and potential future exes.

"Margaret, I don't have any intention of snuggling up with one of my employees."

"Uh-huh. Let's hope not. Do I need to remind you what happens when men elected to powerful offices start messing around and can't keep their pants on?"

"Nothing good," I said.

"That's right. Nothing good. Don't forget that I moved here from Akron for you, and I'm not losing this job because you can't keep it in your shorts."

★ ★ ★

On this morning, Margaret was wearing a purple skirt and a floral blouse and smelled heavily of lilac, her favorite scent.

"Good morning, Margaret," I said.

"G' morning, Mr. V," she replied. She set her pad on the edge of my desk but didn't hand me the schedule, which was her usual routine. "You're not going to be happy about this."

I reached, and she slipped the paper between my thumb and index finger. She had blocked out nine o'clock to noon. Next to it, she had made the notation, *Leadership meeting with Governor Wilinski.*

I could feel my right eye start to twitch. "When did this happen?"

"There was a message from his assistant on my phone when I got in."

My voice climbed. "He calls and expects me to drop everything and come running?"

Margaret planted her fists on her ample hips and said, "Don't you raise your voice at me. I didn't schedule the meeting." She picked the receiver off my phone and held it out to me. "If you've got a beef, call the governor."

I took the receiver from her and set it back in the cradle. "I didn't raise my voice."

Her eyes widened. She was thrice divorced and had three teenage boys. Margaret Benning was used to the denials of men. "Oh, you raised your voice. Trust me."

I smiled and motioned for her to sit down. "My humble apologies, Margaret," I said.

"Accepted." She opened her pad. "So, what do we want to get done today?"

I rattled off a half-dozen assignments for Margaret. Before returning to her desk, Margaret would rattle off the list of people who wanted a piece of my time that day. The list was usually substantial.

I told her which ones to slot for that afternoon, which to slot later in the week, and which to hand off to one of my lieutenants. "Anything else?" I asked.

"One more thing. There's a gentleman in the lobby who wants to talk to you, too."

"Who is he?"

She looked at her notebook. "His name is Reno Moretti."

"Reno Moretti," I said out loud, feeling the creases building across my forehead. "Reno Moretti. Reno Moretti. I know that name. Who is he? What's he want?"

"He was waiting in the outer lobby when I got here. He said he's a prison guard at the Northeast Ohio Correctional Facility in Youngstown. He won't say what he wants to talk to you about, only that it's an extremely urgent matter."

"I've got this meeting with the governor." I looked at Margaret and frowned. "Reno Moretti. I should know that name." I shrugged. "See if there's someone else who can help him."

"Already suggested that, but he won't have any of it. He said he needs to talk to you. Says he'll wait as long as it takes."

I rubbed at my temples. "This isn't about a labor issue, is it?"

Margaret put two palms on my desk and leaned in toward me. "Since he won't talk to anyone but you, Mr. Van Buren, how would I know that?"

"Point taken, Margaret. Bring him back, please. Tell him he can have ten minutes—max."

A few moments later, Margaret opened the door and allowed Moretti into my office. I didn't know what a stereotypical prison guard looked like, but I had spent enough years as a prosecutor to spot a cop when I saw one. The moment he entered my office he began consuming his surroundings the way a cop surveys a crime scene, his eyes darting from wall to wall. He walked with the easy, fluid amble of an athlete, though he was carrying an extra twenty pounds around the waist and had dull yellow nicotine stains on his index and middle fingers. He looked uncomfortable in a navy suit that stretched tight across his shoulders. As I stood and walked out from behind my desk, he surveyed me as he had his environment, like a fighter measuring an opponent. He was a shade under six feet, had the flattened nose of a street brawler, and close-cropped black hair that was quickly losing dominance to the gray. His jaw was broad and a scar, stark white against his olive skin, ran from his lip to his nostril. Under his left arm were a pair of three-ring binders.

I extended my hand. "Hutchinson Van Buren, Mr. Moretti. Nice to meet you."

He shook my hand and said, "I apologize for showing up without an appointment, but it's a matter that I didn't want to become public knowledge. I appreciate you taking the time to meet with me." His hands were broad across the knuckles and his grip strong. I have long believed that a man's hands and wrists are indicators of physical strength. Reno Moretti possessed a raw-boned strength, not the kind you get in a gym, but the kind the good Lord bestows upon you at birth. He was a man you wanted on your side if things got rough. No doubt; he was a cop. And one I thought I should know. He looked familiar but gave no indication that we had ever met.

He sat down without being invited and set the black binders on the corner of my desk. "I know you're a busy man, Mr. Van Buren, so I'll try to make this quick. Are you familiar with Lester Yates?"

"Of course, the Egypt Valley Strangler."

"Or so they claim. Have you read much about the case?"

"I confess that I don't personally handle the death penalty cases at this level, but I am peripherally familiar with it, yes. What about it?"

"You're a proponent of the death penalty, right?"

"I think that's pretty well documented."

"Then you should be very concerned about putting Lester Yates to death, because he did not kill Danielle Quinn. And just so you know, I'm a death penalty guy, too. Lester's an innocent man."

"Okay, I'll bite. How do you know that?"

"About a year ago, I began working the night shift at the prison as a guard. There are a half dozen Death Row inmates on my block. Yates is one of them; he's an insomniac. He's up all night pacing around his cell; he's crazy scared to die. We talk a lot. He told me his story. I know how cons lie, and I was skeptical at first. But I listened. I've been around murderers and thugs my entire professional life, and

I'm telling you this guy doesn't fit the bill. They said he was guilty of killing eighteen women, and I have a hard time believing he's capable of squashing a bug, let alone be a serial killer."

"It takes more than a hunch to overturn a death penalty."

"I think what's in these binders is compelling, but I've got more information that might interest you. I've also got a snitch at the prison who works in our library, and we've worked out a little system where he leaves me notes hidden in a book. Obviously, that's information I would prefer you keep to yourself." I nodded. "There's a guy in general pop named Herman Fenicks, a nasty sort who got arrested for trying to strangle a prostitute somewhere in northeast Ohio. He likes to brag that he's killed women all over the Midwest. Apparently, he particularly likes offing prostitutes. He was a truck driver and told my snitch that he would sometimes dump bodies near a lake just off of Interstate 70."

"Do you think it's just talk, or do you think there's something to it?"

"Hard to tell with the cons. They'll lie when it's easier to tell the truth and brag if it gives them cred in the yard. Mostly, it's what my gut tells me about Yates. He just doesn't fit the mold, so I started looking into it on my own." He opened up the first binder to an index on the first page. The sections inside were tabbed and neat. It was an impressive piece of work. It contained arrest records, trial transcripts, newspaper clippings, transcripts of interviews, and photocopies of the victims' rap sheets and photos.

I flipped through the pages. "How long have you been working on this?"

"About eight months."

"It's impressive."

Moretti reached across the table and flipped open a section near the front of the binder. "Here are a couple of things I think are important." His index finger ran down a page of bulleted items.

- While Yates was supposedly involved in eighteen murders, no physical evidence linked him to any of the victims, including the woman he was convicted of strangling, Danielle Quinn.
- Yates had no known connection to Quinn or any of the other victims.

- Authorities originally said Yates was responsible for as many as twenty deaths attributed to the Egypt Valley Strangler. Yet, two other strangulation murders—Carla Antigo and Melody Ann Zwick—were eventually solved and two other men convicted.
- After Yates was arrested and incarcerated, there were as many as three other women strangled in the area.
- If he was the Egypt Valley Strangler, he would have killed his first victim when he was seventeen years old.
- Yates worked in a cement factory. On the day that Danielle Quinn was reported missing, he clocked in at 6 a.m. and spent most of the day making three separate runs to a pour for a church parking lot in Mount Pleasant, Ohio. He worked nearly five hours of overtime and clocked out at 6:43 p.m.

Moretti looked up and said, "Nothing matches up."

"Just because he was working the day she disappeared doesn't mean he didn't run into her later and kill her."

"If that's the case, it means she left work and was roaming the woods of the Egypt Valley all day waiting for him to show up and strangle her."

I flipped through a few pages. "How did Yates become a suspect?"

"About a month after her body was discovered, he got caught using her credit card trying to buy fishing gear in a sporting goods store. The card had been tagged, and the clerk called the cops."

"How in God's name did he think he could get away with using a woman's credit card?"

Moretti smiled; the scar at the corner of his mouth fish-hooked. "Lester's not the sharpest tool in the shop. He found the card and thought the name was Daniel. Her driver's license was in the purse, but he didn't make the connection. Prisons are generally not populated with members of Mensa."

I flipped through the pages of the binder and found the testimony of the county sheriff. I pointed to a passage where the sheriff, who I knew quite well, testified that after Yates was apprehended with the murdered woman's credit card, they found her purse during a search of his motorcycle gang's clubhouse.

"Lester said he found the purse in a thicket of reeds at Piedmont Lake when he was fishing. He had no idea it belonged to someone who had been murdered."

"Do you believe that?"

He reached across the table and tapped a photocopy of a newspaper story with an index finger. "First of all, the cops called it a gang clubhouse. You know what it was? It was an old chicken coop out behind his family's farmhouse where he and his buddies hung out. I drove down and checked it out. Think about this, Mr. Van Buren. Here's this supposed criminal mastermind, the Egypt Valley Strangler, the guy who evaded police for eight years without leaving a shred of evidence, and then suddenly he decides to use a victim's credit card to buy a fishing rod and casually leaves her purse on a table, in a chicken coop, on his family's property. No logical person could believe Lester Yates is the same guy who murdered those women."

"Didn't his defense attorney bring up any of this?"

Moretti waved at the air. "This poor schmuck had a public defender and got the worst representation in the history of the criminal justice system. Read the transcripts. It was pitiful. The guy didn't challenge anything. Lester might as well have defended himself."

I flipped through the pages. "Does Yates have any priors?"

"Yeah, one. For assault."

"Female?"

"Yep."

I squinted at Moretti. "That's not good."

"I asked him about it. He said it was a dustup in high school. He was charged with aggravated assault, but pled to simple assault and got probation."

"Still, he attacked a woman."

"Technically, yes. But he didn't kill one."

Margaret walked through the door and tapped her wristwatch. "Are you going to keep the governor waiting?" she asked.

I'd lost track of time. "Can I keep these binders?"

"I made them for you."

"Good, good. Thanks. I'll give them a good read." I reached down behind my desk and grabbed my portfolio. "Come on. Walk with me."

We took the elevator to the ground floor and began walking toward the governor's office on South High Street. "Help me out here, Mr. Moretti. What's your motivation?"

"I like Lester, and I feel sorry for him. He got set up and he's going to pay with his life. Nobody wants to see an innocent man get executed. If he rides the needle, eventually the truth is going to come out and that'll be the end of the death penalty in Ohio. The do-gooders will be dancing in the streets. I like the governor. He seems like a stand-up guy. I hear he's running for president."

"That's the rumor."

"Well, you tell him this. How's a man running for president going to explain to the American people that an innocent man, a sad sack like Lester Yates, was executed on his watch?"

I looked at Moretti. "Good point." We stopped in front of the Riffe Center. "Do you think the real killer is still out there?"

Moretti shrugged. "Who knows? From what I know about serial killers, they don't magically turn over a new leaf. Generally, they don't stop killing until they get caught or die. The last woman to be found strangled in the Egypt Valley was a woman named Nancy Lehman in 2004. That was more than three years after Yates was convicted. The murders didn't stop, but the cops don't have an explanation for that, and they don't want to talk about it. How can they claim to have captured and convicted the Egypt Valley Strangler when more women were killed? They want Lester to take the fall so they can pat themselves on the back and hand out the medals."

"Where does Yates stand in his appeals?"

"He doesn't. He's out of appeals. His case is headed to the parole board on a clemency request. If they deny it, his only chance is a reprieve by the governor."

"The governor has never blocked an execution."

"He better start. If not, they're going to execute an innocent man. If there's no interest on your part, you can tell the governor that I'm taking it to the media."

I reached out and shook Moretti's hand. "Let me ask you a question: Have we ever met?"

"Before today, no."

I shook my head. "You look like someone I ought to know."

"I get that sometimes."

"Thanks for bringing this to my attention, Mr. Moretti. You have my word that I'll look into it."

As I turned to walk into the Riffe Center, Moretti said, "By the way, Mr. Van Buren, you know who the sheriff was who arrested Yates, don't you?"

I nodded. "Oh, yes."

"I read the articles about him in the newspaper. He was pounding his chest and acting like this paragon of justice. I'll tell you what he did. He picked on a guy who couldn't fight back. He knew Yates wasn't the killer, but he wanted that notch on his gun belt. He wanted to be the guy who put away the Egypt Valley Strangler."

TWO

It was ten before nine when I got off the elevator on the thirtieth floor of the Riffe Center. I said good morning to the receptionist and nodded at the Ohio state trooper who was stationed outside the entrance to the governor's office. Sitting in his office at the far end of the suite was the governor's chief of staff, Alfonso Majestro.

I did not like Alfonso, though I feigned civility.

Alfonso didn't like me either, but was a less skilled actor.

He had arranged his desk so he could see everyone who entered the suite. On this day, he was sporting a white shirt starched to the rigidity of cardboard and a green and gold necktie, and his usual dour personality. He pretended to be busy when I entered the suite.

"Hey, Alfonso," I said, forcing him to lift his eyes and acknowledge my presence, which he did with the slightest of nods. This irritated him, which is exactly why I did it every time I walked past his office.

Alfonso Majestro had a compressed head with round cheeks and a pointed nose that gave his face the unfortunate resemblance to a ferret. He was small in stature, maybe five-seven and one hundred and thirty pounds, a moustache that a fourteen-year-old would have been ashamed of, and he had the tiniest feet I'd ever seen on a grown man. People who worked with Alfonso and didn't like him, and that number was substantial, joked that he bought his shoes at Stride Rite. That was one of the kinder things they said.

He was the least popular member of the governor's cabinet, which didn't bother Alfonso Majestro in the least. He was fond of saying, "I didn't come here to make friends."

If that was the case, he was succeeding magnificently.

He had grown up in Martins Ferry, in the heart of the Ohio River Valley. It was a place where strength and athletic ability were revered, and he had been blessed with the body of a clarinet player. It had grated on him his entire adult life. I have long believed the fields of law enforcement and politics are full of frustrated individuals seeking power in order to extract revenge on a world they perceive as unfair because they were born without athletic talent or with a little ferret face. That was Alfonso Majestro.

I continued past the state trooper and into the conference room. I was the first to arrive.

While I *technically* wasn't an underling of the governor, technically didn't apply when you were dealing with James D. "Big Jim" Wilinski. If you were involved in Ohio Republican politics, you had better understand the ground rules. In Wilinski's mind, everyone in state government was there to serve his needs. Period. The fact that I also was an elected official, and an important one, was of no significance to the governor. He was the alpha male. He expected undying loyalty, but there was no such thing as reciprocity where Wilinski was concerned. I was part of the club. However, if such a day came when I proved to be a liability or a deterrent to his political aspirations, he would toss me out like an undersized catch.

Wilinski was handsome, six-four, and you could land a small plane on his shoulders. He played professional football for ten years, then wisely retired while his body and brain were still intact. At age forty-nine, he still looked like he could suit up for the Bears. While in Chicago, he graduated from the Loyola University School of Law and married a local news anchor and former Miss Illinois. He returned to Ohio and practiced real estate law with a prestigious Columbus firm for five years, personally amassing the mineral rights to tens of thousands of acres in gas- and oil-rich Appalachian Ohio.

He ran for Congress as a Democrat in 1994, the same year he was inducted into the Pro Football Hall of Fame. In the middle of his second term, he switched parties, announcing that the Democratic Party and what he called its "environmental lunatic fringe" no longer served the best interests of a southeast Ohio district packed with steelworkers and coal miners. He won a third term in Congress before his successful run for governor in 2000.

He was extremely intelligent and street-smart, keenly aware of how God had blessed him. He took advantage of those gifts in his political career, which was to include a run for the nation's highest office.

I set my portfolio on the mahogany table and walked over to the end of the room where there hung a photograph of Wilinski in his Chicago Bears uniform. It had been taken from a low angle; he was crouched in a three-point stance, crystalline blue eyes beneath a furrowed brow, square chin, flattop haircut, and forearms that looked like a twisted rope. I was staring at the photo when the governor came into the room behind me.

"That's a young buck there, huh, padnah?"

"You don't look that much different today, Governor."

"Looks can be deceiving, my friend." He grinned, patting a stomach that from all appearances was still taut. "I'm spending too much time on the rubber-chicken circuit and not enough time in the gym."

The governor's bodyguard and members of his cabinet began to file in. The last to arrive was Majestro, who took a seat near the governor without speaking to anyone.

Majestro and four other cabinet members had been the first loyalists to jump on Interstate 70 and drive west from the hills and dales of eastern Ohio to Columbus after Wilinski won his first term as governor. This caravan of Wilinski devotees was derisively referred to as, "the Hillbilly Mafia." Wilinski, of course, was "the godfather," and Majestro was "the consigliere." Wilinski's bodyguard, "the enforcer," was a lifelong friend and mountain of a man named Danny Doyle, whose sport coats could be used as comforters on queen-size beds. Wilinski was a big man, but even he was dwarfed by Doyle, who was six foot nine and looked like an upended dirigible with a leather belt. He could always be found near the governor, his hands clasped, his eyes half shut and his mouth half open, with what seemed to be a perpetual scowl on his face.

It was said that there was nothing the members of his inner circle wouldn't do for the governor. Jess DiCanastraro, a Democrat state rep from Cleveland, once said, "They don't have the style of the Italian mob or the brazenness of the Irish Mafia, but those boys from the hills are twice as vicious."

When the rest of the cabinet was seated around the table, Majestro started the meeting. The governor, for his part, leaned back in his chair, swiveled, frowned, played with his phone, and jumped in when it appeared something wasn't to his satisfaction. The last hour of the meeting was less about policy and more about image, a pep rally of sorts, as he ramped up for his presidential campaign. He reminded us that he hadn't yet decided to run for president, but if he did, we could all expect to follow him to Washington. He winked at me.

When the meeting ended, I said, "Governor, do you have a minute?"

"Not much more than that," he said. "I've got an important lunch meeting."

"This won't take long," I said. "We're getting ready to start the final prep for the parole board on the Lester Yates case."

"The Egypt Valley Strangler."

"Exactly. We might have a fly in the ointment."

"How so?"

"I was approached by a prison guard this morning who wants me to look into the case. He's gotten to know Yates, and he thinks the guy is innocent."

"Every guy in prison is innocent."

"True, but this guy doesn't strike me as a bleeding heart. He says he's got some concrete proof and wants me to investigate."

"Yates is a white supremacist who is believed to have murdered, what, eighteen or nineteen women?"

"Eighteen. And yes, that's true."

"He got caught because he was trying to use one of the victims' credit cards, right?"

"Right again."

"What the hell is there to look at?"

"He says there are some things that don't add up. I haven't had a chance to give his information a good look, but I think we need to be careful about this. The guard is absolutely convinced that Yates is innocent, and he said he's prepared to go to the media with his information."

"The great equalizer of the liberals—their friends in the media."

"He's actually a fan of yours, and he makes a valid point. If you run for president, we can't be executing innocent men. It's not the kind of thing you want to see on a campaign commercial for your opponent."

"You're certainly not talking about a pardon?"

"No, of course not. However, the execution is less than two months away. I might need a stay to look this over. If it's shaky, you need to think about a commutation—life in prison with no chance of parole."

He frowned and shook his head. "You're kidding, right, Hutch? You want me to commute the sentence of one of the most notorious serial killers in US history, and a white supremacist, to boot? Wouldn't my opponents have a field day with that one? Remember, I'm supposed to be the law-and-order governor." He inched toward the door. "The Yates case was one of the highest-profile criminal cases in Ohio history, and you want me to stay the execution? The optics are terrible."

"Not as terrible as executing the wrong guy. Remember, he was only convicted of killing one woman. He was linked to all the other deaths by innuendo."

"Perception is reality, Hutchinson."

"I'm going to look into this and it's probably nothing we need to worry about, but I wanted you to be aware of it. I know you don't like surprises. If there's anything hinky about this case, we need to take a look."

"When is the execution scheduled?"

"August 24."

"That's plenty of time for you to do your due diligence, is it not?"

"Shouldn't be a problem, but . . ."

"Nope. Stop right there. It shouldn't be a problem. That's what I wanted to hear. Get it wrapped up. I can't have this hanging around out there while I'm . . ." He cut himself off.

"Planning your presidential campaign," I said, completing his sentence.

He winked and pointed. "Work your magic, padnah. But I don't want to stay this guy unless you can prove to me he didn't do it."

"Understood."

He was one step out of the conference room when he stopped, turned on a heel, and stuck his head back in the room. "The Egypt Valley Strangler—you know who arrested him, don't you?"

"Of course. He never lets you forget."

"That's a badge of honor for him."

"I know."

"If this is going to stir up a hornet's nest, make sure you talk to him."

I saluted with an index finger and he was gone. I gathered up my papers and headed for the elevator. I had just walked out onto High Street when I saw the governor's limousine with its tinted windows emerge from the underground parking garage and head east on State Street. His lunch meeting was likely being held at the Governor's Residence in the suburb of Bexley. The governor and his wife actually lived in a home in a gated community in Marble Cliff. The Residence, a mansion by another name, was used for social events and midday private meetings of which Mrs. Wilinski would certainly not approve, which I suspected was why he had been so anxious to get out the door.

That was the chink in Wilinski's armor that I believed would be his ultimate demise. Despite being married to one of the most stunning women I had ever seen, Big Jim had a libido that was as large as his ego. He was having affairs with any number of women, including one of his constituent aides, who was also the wife of a Columbus police officer. Big Jim certainly wasn't the first politician to have an affair, but he projected himself as a devout, conservative Christian family man, and those were the types of politicians who reporters like to put in their crosshairs, particularly in presidential campaigns.

I turned and headed north along High Street.

While the thought of being United States attorney general was enticing, I realized that I might be more of a liability than the governor realized. Most political pundits and consultants believed I won the race for Ohio attorney general in spite of myself.

When I was fifteen, I was on Chestnut Ridge behind my eastern Ohio hometown of Crystalton, hunting for arrowheads with three of my buddies—Deak Coultas and the Nash brothers, Adrian and Pepper. As we were coming down off the ridge, we were confronted by a local lunatic named Petey Sanchez, a kid who was a couple years older than us and completely unhinged from reality. He attacked Adrian with a tree limb, and in the ensuing confrontation, Adrian threw an Indian maul he had found into Petey's forehead, killing him instantly. We conspired to keep it a secret to protect Adrian, even when Deak's uncle, a ne'er-do-well and pedophile named Jack Vukovich, went to prison for the murder.

Thirty years later, I was the prosecuting attorney in Summit County. After securing a death sentence for one of God's mistakes, a psychopath who went by the street name of Ricky Blood, an Associated Press reporter asked me to comment on a defense appeal claiming the state of Ohio couldn't guarantee Ricky Blood a painless death. I said I was not concerned with the amount of pain he felt from an intravenous needle as it would be a fraction of the agony he had inflicted on the daughter of an Akron police officer who he had raped, tortured with lighters and razor blades, and burned alive. My comments were sent across the country, and the next day the chairman of the Ohio Republican Party was in my office recruiting me to run for attorney general.

In the midst of a campaign where polls had me ahead by as many as eighteen points, I was confronted by an old demon—Jack Vukovich, who had been released from prison and knew what really happened on Chestnut Ridge. He attempted to blackmail me and his nephew, Deak, a respected Steubenville minister who had remained one of my dearest friends.

In September of that year, less than two months before the election, I received a phone call from Deak, who was at his uncle's house. He said, "I need a little help here, buddy."

When I arrived, I found Jack Vukovich dead on the floor and my friend bleeding out from a belly wound. Deak had been shot in a tussle over a handgun, which he subsequently used to kill his uncle. He wouldn't let me call an ambulance. The blackmail payments he had been making to his uncle had been taken from the church coffers. He was under investigation for theft, and he said death was preferable to the humiliation that would follow.

I lied to protect the reputation of my friend, telling the police that Deak had been the victim in a murder-suicide. The deception we had carried out for three decades had resulted in the death of one of the most decent human beings I had ever known.

That is when I decided that the truth had to be told.

I called a reporter at the Akron *Beacon Journal* and confessed to my role in the cover-up of the death of Petey Sanchez. I told how we had conspired to keep it a secret to protect our friend Adrian. I knew that going to the newspaper with my story could end my political career. What it definitely ended was my relationship with my girlfriend and campaign manager, Shelly Dennison. She walked out of my life and my campaign.

Despite the chaos, I was still able to win the general election by nine points. However, that was Ohio. I was certain the Democrats would have a field day with the information if Wilinski won the presidency and wanted to tap me as his attorney general. If that happened, I would go from padnah to pariah for Big Jim Wilinski.

THREE

I had Margaret cancel my afternoon appointments, and I sat down at the conference table and began reading through the two binders Moretti had left with me. It was a thorough piece of work. When I had finished at a few minutes after six, I walked over to my desk and tapped out the number for Gretchen Verlander, the chief of my criminal division.

"You're here late," I said.

"I know where you park your car," she said. "I make sure I don't leave until I know the boss is gone."

"We need more people with that attitude. Do you have the case file on Lester Yates?"

"It's sitting right here on my desk."

"Can you bring it down, please?"

"Sure can."

Margaret was gone for the day, and Verlander was able to slip by the guardhouse and into my office. "The commandant's not at her post," she said. "That doesn't happen very often."

I said, "Margaret doesn't usually leave me unprotected."

Verlander slid two thick manila folders across the conference room table. "There's the Yates file. Why the interest?"

"His execution date is coming up. I want to make sure our ducks are in a row. Have you started looking into it?"

"I've given it a cursory read. It looks pretty cut and dried."

"I'll take a look." I held it up. "Thanks a lot. I'll get it back to you."

I didn't tell Verlander of my suspicions. I liked her, and she had done a credible job for me, but she was a holdover from the previous administration—a Democrat—and I had a nagging doubt about her loyalty. I felt like she was always looking for me to screw up, maybe spying for the next Democrat to take a run at the job. It could have been my paranoia, but it was no less a reality. I didn't want her in the loop on this one.

When she had disappeared through the lobby, I picked up my cell phone from the conference room table and tapped out the number of my chief investigator, Jerry Adameyer, who I knew had spent the day in Dayton investigating the chief financial officer of a charitable foundation chartered to buy backpacks and school supplies for children, but who was having problems explaining why he had credit card expenses for cases of expensive wine, airline tickets, and hotel rooms in Nassau.

"What's up, chief?" he said.

"What are you doing for dinner?" I asked.

"I'm waiting for a good invitation."

"I've got something here I need you to look at. How about meeting me at Minelli's?"

"Best offer I've had so far. I can be there in about an hour."

Adameyer had spent thirty-two years as a street cop and a detective with the Akron Police Department, where he went by the nickname Amana, because he was built like a refrigerator. He had a voice that sounded like a rasp being dragged over heavy-grit sandpaper, and a reputation for being profane, racist, and misogynistic. He also had a particular disdain for reporters, lawyers, and child molesters, which he lumped into the same subspecies. Whenever I had reason to visit the Akron PD detective bureau, he would take great delight in busting my chops, calling me "his goddamn eminence, the prosecuting attorney." He elevated cursing to an art form and always had a wad of chew wedged into his cheek, spitting into a foam cup he carried around. When they appointed a woman to head the detective bureau, it was more than Adameyer could swallow, and he retired from Akron PD and became chief of the Portage Township Police Department.

Despite his abhorrent character flaws, he was, hands down, the best investigator I ever worked with as the Summit County prosecutor.

When the position of chief investigator opened up in my office, Jerry applied; I interviewed him out of courtesy but had absolutely no intention of bringing that bag of controversy into my world. When he came to my office, we spent some time catching up, and I asked him a few perfunctory questions about the job. I think he sensed it wasn't a serious interview.

"I'd do a good job for you, sport," he said.

"There's no doubt in my mind, Jerry. There's not a better investigator in the state of Ohio. But here's my dilemma. This isn't the Portage Township Police Department. It's state government. It's inclusive. I have women heading up half of my service divisions; three of those women are black. I have four black men in leadership positions, one of whom is openly gay. There are probably a couple of other subcategories of people working for me that I'm not even aware of. I need someone who can work with all of them. Let me put this as kindly as I can: you have a reputation for operating like it's the 1860s."

A thin smile pursed Adameyer's lips. "Guilty as charged . . . once upon a time. I'm a changed man, sport."

I frowned. "Come on, Jerry, there are two things that don't change—gravity and old cops."

"Let me tell you a little story. Two years ago, I got a call from my daughter. She was crying so hard I could hardly understand anything she was saying. She was at Akron Children's Hospital with my grandson. He'd been diagnosed with bacterial meningitis, and it wasn't good. The doctors told us that his chances of surviving the night were about a thousand-to-one, and if he lived, it was likely that he would have severe brain damage. I went to the little chapel they have there at the hospital, got on my knees, and asked God to save his life. I told him that if he could see fit to do that, I'd be a changed man, and I'd try to right the wrongs of my past."

"And . . ."

"My grandson's on the high school golf and baseball teams. He writes for the school paper, plays the trumpet in the orchestra, and he's a good student. He'd probably be straight-As except he's got a lot of my genes in him. But I believe the Lord answered my prayers, so I made a list of everyone who I could remember offending or slighting, and I must admit it about filled a notebook. I knocked on every one of their doors, apologized, and asked for their forgiveness. Most of them accepted my apologies; some told me to go to hell. One woman was an elder at a black Baptist church, and she asked me to come talk to their congregation about my enlightenment. I did. I was so nervous I thought the skin was going to peel off my face, looking into the eyes of two hundred black men and women who I wanted to convince I was no longer the devil. There were some pretty offensive words that I used to spew with regularity that haven't crossed my lips since that boy walked out of the hospital. I haven't been able to completely cut out the swearing, but I try."

I nodded and pondered his comments. Before I could speak, he said, "Mr. Attorney General, everyone in this world makes mistakes. Sometimes they happen when we're adults, and sometimes they happen when we're fifteen years old." He let the words hang for a minute. "I think if someone shows proper contrition and tries to make amends, they deserve a second chance. Wouldn't you agree?"

The voters of Ohio had given me a second chance in spite of my involvement in the cover-up of Petey Sanchez's death. Shouldn't I extend the same consideration to Jerry Adameyer?

I did. I hired him on the spot. However, I made it clear that I would fire him just as quickly if he ever again referred to me as "sport."

* * *

I had just pushed myself away from the conference table and was ready to head out the door when a thought that had been orbiting my brain all afternoon again flashed on my mental radar. I went to my desktop and typed in *Reno Moretti*. I smiled at the search results and said, "Holy smoke. 'Reno Moretti—the Brier Hill Hammer.'" I was right on both counts—he was a cop, and I did know that face.

* * *

Minelli's Pizza is on Sullivant Avenue on the far west side of Columbus, and I knew it to be one of Jerry's favorite restaurants. It was nothing fancy—a small family operation where they made their own pasta and served one of the best pizzas in town.

"How'd it go in Dayton?" I asked.

"If that CFO has a nickel's worth of common sense, and I'm not sure he does, he'll go to the airport tonight and get on the first flight to a country where we don't have an extradition treaty."

"That bad, huh?"

"He's toast. They were going to fire him this afternoon. I'm no accountant, but I found north of thirty thousand dollars in bogus charges. He'd better just fly solo, too, because when he was out spending the foundation's money on hotels and airfare and meals, he was doing it with someone who is not Mrs. CFO. The girlfriend works at the same foundation. It's an unholy mess."

We ordered a large pepperoni, sausage, and mushroom pizza and a pitcher of beer. While we waited, I briefed him on my meeting with Moretti and the contents of the binders, which were on the table, along with the case file in the manila folders that Gretchen Verlander had given me. He started flipping through the binder with his left hand while shoveling squares of pizza into his mouth with his right. Jerry had been a competitive powerlifter in his younger days and continued to compete in the senior division, for which he justified an appetite that rivaled a Komodo dragon's. For the most part, if it was dead and he could lift it to his mouth, he'd eat it. I kept my hands away from the pizza for fear of losing a finger. By the time he had finished most of the pizza and a second pitcher of beer, he closed the folders holding the case file.

He wiped pepperoni grease from his mouth with a paper napkin and asked, "So this Moretti guy shows up unannounced and wants you to do what, get Yates off Death Row?"

"I think he'd prefer that I get him out of prison," I said. "He doesn't think he did it."

"What do you think?"

"It's too early in the game to make a decision, but I think we ought to be looking at it before we strap this guy to the gurney. Does anything you just read stand out?"

He flipped through the case file and retrieved two articles from the Martins Ferry *Times Leader.* "Read these."

The first article was dated March 23, 2001.

Area Man Charged With Using Missing Woman's CC

Lester Yates, 22, of Rayland, was charged with identity fraud yesterday after he attempted to use a credit card belonging to a missing Bethesda woman.

The credit card belonged to Danielle Quinn, who disappeared in September. Her body was found more than a month later swirling in an eddy in Stillwater Creek, just south of Piedmont Lake. Her death was attributed to the so-called Egypt Valley Strangler.

Yates attempted to purchase fishing equipment at Vanik's Sporting Goods at the St. Clairsville Mall. The card had been flagged as stolen and store owner Jeff Vanik contacted authorities.

Belmont County Sheriff Del Brown, who is heading up the investigation into Quinn's disappearance, said Yates is being held in the Belmont County Jail and is being questioned in connection with Quinn's disappearance.

Quinn, 32, was a waitress at the Shenandoah Truck Stop in Old Washington. She was last seen talking to an unidentified man in the truck stop parking lot after getting off her shift at 6 a.m. on Sept. 8.

Quinn's body was found Oct. 17. It was in such a deteriorated state that it had to be identified by dental records. The sheriff said there are still no suspects.

The second article was dated April 30, 2001.

Yates Pleads Guilty to Using Credit Card of Missing Woman

Lester Yates, 22, of Rayland, pleaded guilty to identity fraud in Belmont County Common Pleas Court yesterday for the attempted use of a credit card owned by Danielle Quinn, the Bethesda woman whose body was found swirling in an eddy in Stillwater Creek in October.

Yates was fined $1,000, ordered to perform 80 hours of community service, and given three-years probation.

Yates told authorities he found Quinn's purse while fishing in the lower section of Piedmont Lake near the Egypt Valley Wildlife Area. He later attempted to use her credit card to purchase fishing equipment at Vanik's Sporting Goods in the St. Clairsville Mall.

Quinn, 32, disappeared on the morning of Sept. 8 after finishing her shift as a waitress at the Shenandoah Truck Stop. She was last seen talking to an unidentified man in the parking lot. Her body was discovered more than a month later.

Belmont County Sheriff Del Brown said Yates was not a suspect in Quinn's disappearance or her death.

"Mr. Yates made a very serious error in judgment after finding Mrs. Quinn's purse," Brown said. "We questioned him extensively and have determined he had no involvement in her disappearance or her murder."

After his arrest, Brown said Yates was cooperative, showing sheriff's deputies where he had been fishing when he discovered the purse, and directing them to a shed behind his parents' home where he had hidden it.

When Common Pleas Judge Michelle Miller asked Yates how he thought he could get away with using the missing woman's credit card, Yates said he didn't read newspapers and was unaware of Quinn's murder.

He also said he thought the name on the credit card was "Daniel," and not "Danielle."

"I didn't know anything about her being gone or dead," Yates told the judge. "I thought maybe the card belonged to the husband of whoever's purse it was. I know that don't make it right, and I'm sorry about it."

Jerry said, "When they finally arrest Yates for Quinn's murder, it's nearly six months after Brown said he had nothing to do with it."

He flipped through the binder and found an October 16, 2001, story from the Cambridge *Daily Jeffersonian* under the headline:

Authorities Arrest Suspect in Egypt Valley Strangler Case

"Look at the lead in this story," Adameyer said, pointing at the first two paragraphs.

The leader of a white supremacist gang was arrested yesterday and charged with aggravated murder in connection with the strangulation death of Danielle Quinn and is suspected in as many as 17 other deaths linked to the so-called Egypt Valley Strangler, who has terrorized eastern Ohio for nine years.

"When in hell did he become a white supremacist?" Jerry asked.

Lester Yates, who goes by the nickname "Battle Axe," is the reputed leader of a white supremacist gang known as the "Soldiers of the Stars and Bars." Authorities also noted that Yates had a previous conviction for assault on a woman.

"What changed?" Jerry asked. "One minute he's this sad sack trying to buy a fishing pole with a dead woman's credit card, and the next he's a murdering white supremacist known as Battle Axe?"

"It doesn't add up," I said.

"Exactly. That body was in the water for five weeks and exposed to the heat, fish, and animals. I don't know how much of her was left, but given my experience with decomposition it couldn't have been much. So the likelihood of any physical evidence linking the dead woman to Yates is virtually nil. I'd like to know how they determined she was strangled. You know they ran this guy through the mill when he got caught trying to use her credit card. They probably checked him out six ways to Sunday trying to link him to the murders, but couldn't, and he got off with a slap on the wrist and a public admission from the sheriff that he had no involvement with her disappearance. In fact, they described him as cooperative." He pointed to another paragraph deeper in the story.

Quinn's purse was found in the headquarters of the Soldiers of the Stars and Bars during a raid by Belmont County deputies in June.

"So when Yates was just this poor schmo who couldn't tell the difference between 'Daniel' and 'Danielle,' he tells the sheriff where the purse is and most likely a deputy drove out and got it out of the shed. But later, the shed becomes the headquarters for a white supremacist group and the purse is found in a raid. I wonder who was responsible for that bit of creative writing."

"None of that means he didn't do it," I said.

Jerry pulled a list of Egypt Valley Strangler victims from the case file, sopped up the condensation from my beer glass on the table top with a napkin, and set the list in front of me.

"Here's another thing. Look at the dates of the murders. For the most part, they're all spread out—about six months apart. Whoever was doing this was spacing things out to avoid detection. Right after a murder, the cops and the public are on their toes. But like everything else, after a while they let down their guard. It's not in the newspapers every day and people get on with their lives. Then he strikes again. The exception is right here." His finger ran down the page to the bottom of the list. "There were two murders right after he pleaded guilty for using the stolen credit card, and they occurred within a month of each other."

"If it was him, wouldn't he want to stay low for a while?"

"Exactly. If he's this criminal mastermind, would he have taken the chance of hitting again after he had been busted using the credit card? Doesn't seem likely."

This was why Jerry Adameyer was the best investigator I had ever known. He had fully digested the case file and Moretti's binder while simultaneously digesting a large pepperoni, sausage, and mushroom pizza and most of two pitchers of beer.

"What is your gut telling you?" I asked.

"My gut is telling me somebody wanted this guy off the board."

"Why him?"

"There's the million-dollar question, chief." He touched his nose. "I've got a pretty good sniffer, and I can tell you when it smells, but I can't tell you what's going on just by looking at all this paper.

All I can tell you for sure is that somebody wanted him gone. They had to have taken this to the grand jury. What kind of evidence did they have?"

"I haven't gotten that far yet."

"We need to look at that, and we need to see if there's anything in the trial transcripts to determine what evidence or witnesses they used to convict him. If I had to bet, I'd wager that the sheriff or the prosecutor was tired of having this whole Egypt Valley Strangler thing hanging over his head and wanted to clear the decks. Here comes this guy Yates, who can't get out of his own way. He was convenient, stupid, and they drilled him. Or it could have been as simple as an overzealous sheriff looking to make a name for himself."

I couldn't conceal my grin.

"What?" Jerry asked.

"When you were reading through those papers, did you recognize the name of the sheriff?"

"No."

"Look again."

Jerry turned to the article announcing the arrest of Lester Yates. "Del Brown." His brows arched like twin peaks. "No way." He looked back at the article, then back at me. "Del Brown? That's not . . ."

"It is. That's our boy—D. Kendrick Brown. Apparently when you come to work for the state you need a name with a little more polish."

"That's too wonderful to be true. All those articles he has hanging on the wall of his office, that was this Yates guy?"

"Yep."

Jerry leaned against the back of the booth, and then it was he who could not conceal the grin. "My, my, my, but isn't that interesting."

"Jerry, we can't let personal feelings get involved here."

"I'd never dream of it, chief. However, if I could shove it up his tailpipe sideways, it would certainly make my decade."

FOUR

Seven weeks and four days before the scheduled execution of Lester Paul Yates.

My escape was nearly complete.

I had scrawled a note and put it on Margaret's desk, asking her to reschedule all my appointments that day. *I'll call you later* were the words written at the bottom of the page. Margaret hated when I did this, as she liked to start her day with a conversation and a clear set of directives. I was ready to head out the door, one hand cradling a cup of coffee and car keys, the other steadying a black leather backpack that wanted to slip off my shoulder, when I heard the unmistakable click of the dead bolt in the lobby door sliding from its strike.

The commandant had arrived ten minutes early and foiled my escape. I leaned against my desk and waited. A moment later Margaret walked into my office. She had already read the note, but she was pretending to be reading it for the first time for my benefit. It was her way of making me squirm. "Mmm-mmm-mmm-mmm-mmm, Hutchinson Wilson Van Buren. You were going to sneak out of here and leave me to clean up all your mess," she said.

That is exactly what I had intended to do, and I now had a case of cold sweats to prove it. Despite a string of failed relationships that would stretch from the shores of Lake Erie to the banks of the Ohio River, I had only feared two women in my life, and they were both no-nonsense single mothers—Margaret and my mother. My mom lived in Florida and had mellowed with age. Margaret was showing no signs of softening. "I have to run over to eastern Ohio to do some interviews, and they need to take precedence," I said.

"Today? You have to go today? Your calendar is full."

"There's nothing so pressing that it can't be rescheduled."

She squinted. "What about your lunch meeting with Mr. Carmine?"

"It can wait."

Stan Carmine was the chairman of the Ohio Republican Party; the meeting had been set for a month.

"Isn't that meeting about your campaign for next year?" she asked.

"It is, but we still have plenty of time to start on the campaign, and I need to do some research on a death penalty case, and Mr. Carmine has more time than the condemned."

She nodded once, her lips puckering into a tiny circle. "I see."

Margaret knew I wasn't as happy being the attorney general as I had been being the prosecutor in Summit County, and she feared I was putting off my meeting with Carmine because I was not going to run for reelection, which would leave her with the burden of finding another job in Columbus or moving back to Akron, neither of which were high on her wish list. I wanted to make a break for the door, but she had blocked the escape route and continued to glower at me. "Margaret, as God is my witness, I'm committed to running for reelection," I said. "I swear."

"Who is going to run your campaign?"

"I don't know. That's one of the things I need to talk to Stan about."

She planted both fists on her hips, the note crinkling in one hand, her head moving back and forth along her shoulders, and she said in a tone normally reserved for a son who had inadequately explained his actions, "Oh, you don't know. Is that your answer?"

"I really don't know."

"Mmm-mmm-mmm-mmm-mmm," she said before pivoting and marching out of the office.

Mmm-mmm-mmm-mmm-mmm was Margaret's all-encompassing expression for joy, sadness, anger, and disbelief, into which the last *mmm-mmm-mmm-mmm-mmm* had fallen.

There were only a handful of consultants in Ohio capable of running a statewide campaign, but there was one in particular that Margaret did not want to see back in my office—Shelly Dennison, my former lover and campaign manager. She was smart, beautiful, and an absolute predator on the campaign trail. She wasn't satisfied to simply defeat her opponents. Rather, she wanted to see them rocking in a corner with their thumbs in their mouths. As my campaign manager for Ohio attorney general, Shelly had expected unfettered access to me and that Margaret would take orders from her, as well.

Given what I have already told you about Margaret Benning, you can probably draw a pretty clear picture of how that worked out.

Margaret would have no part of Shelly trying to boss her around or barging past her to get to me. I was constantly refereeing their disputes. It got even more complicated when Shelly and I became romantically involved. Margaret refused to call Shelly by name and simply referred to her as "the girl." Shelly, the consummate counterpuncher, called Margaret "that large black woman who sits outside your office."

Since winning the election, I had seen Shelly at a few Republican fundraisers, but we had avoided any extended conversations. She attended the fundraisers with a northern Ohio congressman, with whom she'd had a years-long relationship. The last I knew, she had broken up with the congressman and was in the midst of a torrid affair with none other than Governor James D. Wilinski. Shelly had a thing for powerful men and was perpetually climbing the political food chain. I hated to admit that despite the rough treatment she had heaped upon me, I had never quite gotten over the breakup. I feared that if she again became my campaign manager, old and painful feelings that I had successfully stifled would erupt like a bad rash.

As I walked through the lobby, Margaret was pecking out numbers and rescheduling meetings. When she saw me, she turned the phone receiver into her breast and tilted her head, awaiting any last-second instruction. "You better clear the docket for tomorrow, too," I said. She nodded once and shooed me away with the back of her fingers.

Jerry Adameyer was in Dayton prepping the Montgomery County prosecuting attorney on the renegade CFO of the backpack foundation. He wanted to finish up that investigation before jumping in to help on the Yates case. We planned to meet that night at a hotel near Youngstown, then tag-team an interview with Lester Yates at the Northeast Ohio Correctional Facility the following day. I was certainly no stranger to conducting investigations, but I was no Jerry Adameyer, either. This is where he excelled. Before we had left Minelli's Pizza, he suggested that we start at the beginning of the case file and work our way forward.

"If you jump into the middle of a swamp, you're going to sink," he said.

"We don't have the luxury of time, Jerry," I said. "The execution date is only about two months out."

"I know. We'll have to work fast, but we can get through it. Let's start with the family of the first victim."

I looked at the list of victims believed to have been murdered by the Egypt Valley Strangler. The first name on the list was that of Donna Herrick.

FIVE

After interviewing Ed Herrick and Nick Dresbach, I had a late lunch of a sausage sandwich and an iced tea at The Roosevelt in Bellaire, then headed upriver on Ohio Route 7, the north-south corridor wedged hard between the Ohio River and the Appalachian foothills of eastern Ohio. I had grown up in this valley and at times missed it dearly. But my trips back were always bittersweet as "the valley," as we called it, was far from the one in which I had spent my first eighteen years.

Once, it had been the epicenter of the American steel industry, the region that had powered the industrial revolution. That might had been on full display along the river where sixty thousand men worked in the mills between Steubenville and Wheeling. The stacks belched smoke and caused streetlights to burn at noon. Exhaust pipes burned off gases that flamed into the night sky, and the air was heavy with the smell of sulfur. It had been a region full of first-generation immigrants with heavy Eastern European accents. I missed all those dialects and the babushkas and the old men at the Italian Club in Steubenville who smoked twisted little cigars, drank red wine, and played bocce on the courts across the Pennsylvania Railroad tracks from the A&P.

The Ohio Valley was a mere shadow of the one that I had known. There were a pitiful few steel mill jobs left in 2007, and the once-smoking behemoths that lined the banks of the Ohio River were mostly cold and silent. The air was clean now, but good jobs were few.

I drove past the old Wheeling-Pittsburgh Steel plants in Martins Ferry and Yorkville and got off Route 7 at the Tiltonsville exit. I passed the old skating rink and cement plant and drove into the parking lot of Warren Consolidated High School. As I had suspected I would, I found a car parked in a spot with a sign that read RESERVED FOR SCHOOL PRINCIPAL.

Scott Banaski was one of the hardest-working men I knew, and I figured he would still be at the school at four o'clock on a summer afternoon. The door by the parking lot was unlocked and I walked down the darkened hall to the principal's office, the clack of my shoes echoing in the empty corridor. When I opened the outer door, I heard the familiar voice from a back office. "Can I help you?"

"I hope so," I said, continuing to walk toward the voice.

He was at his desk, wearing a green golf shirt, a pair of readers perched on the end of his nose, the hair around his temples flaring gray against the black. He recognized me immediately and smiled, leaning back in his chair and peeling the readers off his face. He said, "Babe!" That had been his nickname for me years earlier. "I can't believe it—the best catcher I ever coached."

"That's because you didn't coach very long," I said.

He got up from behind the desk, shook my hand, and gave me a hug. Scott had been my baseball coach at Crystalton High School. Not long after I graduated, he earned his principal's certificate and was hired away by Warren Consolidated, where he had been ever since. He invited me to sit down at the small table in the corner. "You're about the last person I expected to see walking through that door, now that you're a big-shot politician," he said.

"I'd rather be remembered as a good catcher."

"I'm sure you would. What brings you back to these parts?"

"I wanted to see if you could help me with an investigation I'm working on."

"I don't know how that's possible, but I will if I can."

"I have a meeting at the Northeast Ohio Correctional Facility in the morning with one of your former students."

Scott nodded. "Oh, my. Lester."

"His execution date is coming up, and I'm doing some background research."

"You're the attorney general. Don't you have people who do that sort of thing for you?"

"Yes, but sometimes it's good to get out of Columbus and do a little honest work. What can you tell me about him?"

"What do you want to know?"

"I'm just getting started, so anything you remember will help. I read in the newspaper that he was the leader of a white supremacist gang—the Soldiers of the Stars and Bars."

Scott snorted. "The leader of a gang? Let me tell you something. Lester Yates couldn't lead someone out of the boys' restroom. I read all that nonsense in the paper when he was on trial. It was a bunch of baloney. Lester Yates was one of those sad-sack kids who just didn't fit in anywhere. He wasn't an athlete, didn't play in the band, didn't have any particular talent to speak of, like art or singing. He only had a few friends—fellow misfits. Do you want to know what his supposed white supremacist gang consisted of? Lester and a couple of his buddies from out on Turkey Point liked that television show where the guys had a Confederate flag painted on the roof of their car. Remember that?"

"*The Dukes of Hazzard*."

He snapped his fingers. "That's it. That's how it all got started. Lester had this old, beat-up Chrysler K-car. The wheel wells were all rusted out, there was a crack that ran all the way across his windshield, and you could hear him coming a mile away. The engine sounded like a washing machine full of nickels. Instead of spending money on a ring job, he bought paint and painted a rebel flag on the top of that K-car . . ." Scott started laughing. "It looked like the devil—it was this lopsided Confederate flag up there. But I'll tell you, he thought it was about the greatest thing in the world. As I recall, that's when he and his buddies got together and decided to form a club. I don't know that they ever called it a gang, but they were just these five or six lost kids who had T-shirts printed with a rebel flag and 'Soldiers of the Stars and Bars' on the front, and their club nicknames on the back. I can't remember what Yates's nickname was."

"Battle Axe?"

He laughed again. "That was it. Battle Axe Yates—all squirrelly hundred and five pounds of him."

"They were allowed to wear those shirts in school?"

Scott swatted at the air. "First of all, I'd bet a dollar that Lester Yates couldn't even tell you who fought in the Civil War. It was not a political statement. Secondly, I had a lot better things to worry about than those guys and their T-shirts. It gave them some sense of belonging. When I read those stories in the paper where they were making him out to be a public enemy number one, I would have laughed if it wasn't so sad."

"Do you know anything about the assault charge? I heard it was something that happened when he was in high school."

He shook his head and rolled his eyes. "You know, every class has a bully. In Lester's class, her name was Marsha Wollek. I swear to God, she was the meanest human being I have ever known, and my first teaching job was at a reformatory school for boys. I had to suspend her twice." He looked at me to make sure I was listening. "*Twice!* About every month or so she would pick out a new target and start in on them. Boys or girls, it didn't matter. She was an equal opportunity harasser. She would make up little rhymes about them, tease them, get up in their face. The spring of Lester's senior year was his turn in the chute. I remember her calling him Lester the molester. One day after school the kids were getting on the bus and walking to the parking lot and she started in on him. She got up in his face and he slapped her. Now, I'm going to tell you this, if Lester Yates slapped her, she had gotten on his very last nerve, because the kid was never a problem. If I remember right, I think he slapped her hard enough to leave finger marks on the side of her face. He told me that she head-butted him in the nose. I don't doubt that, but there was a Tiltonsville cop doing traffic duty to let the buses out and he didn't see the head butt. All he saw was Lester slap her. I wanted to take care of it at the school, but her dad filed a complaint, and Lester got charged with aggravated assault. They let him plead out to a lesser charge and gave him probation. I thought that was a travesty of justice. Then he got charged with that woman's murder, and I saw what a travesty of justice really looks like." He leaned back in his chair, took a deep breath, and looked out the window toward the athletic fields. "Have you met Lester?"

"Not yet."

"He's just a scrawny little guy with bad acne. I never believed for a minute that he was the Egypt Valley Strangler."

"How did they convict him?"

"Danged if I know. One of his other comrades in the . . ." He made air quotes with his fingers, "'white supremacist gang,' was the Marino kid. He testified against Lester. As I recall, he said he heard Lester say he killed the girl. And let me tell you this: Lester Yates is no genius, but he was a rocket scientist compared to Joey Marino. On top of that, Marino was completely untethered from reality—absolutely delusional. About a year after he graduated, I see him walking around wearing an Ohio University T-shirt and he tells me they gave him a football scholarship. Now mind you, this kid never got any closer to the football field in high school than the concession stand, but he swore up and down that the Ohio University coach saw him running down the road one day and gave him a full scholarship to return kicks because he was so fast. He was this pudgy kid who I never saw move any faster than a slow walk, but he put his right hand to God that he was playing football for Ohio University. He said down on campus they called him 'Flash' because he was so fast. He kept this going for years. Every Saturday when OU was playing, he would hide in the house all day, then come out Sunday and tell everyone how many kickoffs he returned. You know how people around here are. They started playing along, calling him 'Flash' and congratulating him on his great kick returns, and after a while I think the goofy bastard actually started believing it. The last time I talked to him he said he had graduated from Ohio University and was getting ready to go to astronaut school."

"Astronaut school? Is that really a thing?"

"It was in his world. That was the guy whose testimony helped send Lester Yates to Death Row, so if you're interested in knowing if I have a lot of faith in our judicial system these days, the answer would be no."

"Where can I find this Marino guy?"

"At Upland Heights Cemetery. He's dead."

"Dead? What happened to him?"

"He got killed in a motorcycle accident. It was a few years back, not long after the trial, as I recall." A wry smile pursed his lips. "It was a tragedy for the future of our space program."

SIX

Moretti's Restaurant was in Brier Hill, a section of Youngstown also known as Little Italy. The interior had knotty pine paneling, black-and-white photos of celebrities who had visited, and color prints of the pope. Each table was set with silver wrapped in linen napkins, a wicker-wrapped bottle of Chianti, and a candle burning inside a red hurricane holder with plastic fishnet wrapping. It smelled of tomato sauce, basil, garlic, and old wood.

I sat in a booth with Reno Moretti. It was his family's restaurant.

"How come you're not involved with the restaurant?" I asked.

"There's only one thing worse than working in the restaurant business," he said.

"I'll bite. What's that?"

"Working in the restaurant business with your family."

We laughed and toasted with glasses of Chianti.

A large color photograph wrapped in a gold leaf frame dominated the wall behind the bar. It was Moretti—the Brier Hill Hammer. He was young and taut and wearing a pair of boxing trunks that were red, green, and white—the colors of the Italian flag. He was holding up two massive fists that had been wrapped in tape. Around his waist was a heavy belt on which was printed LIGHT HEAVYWEIGHT CHAMPION OF THE WORLD. There were other photographs of Moretti in action around the restaurant.

I stared at them for several minutes. When I looked back at Moretti, he said, "Go ahead. Ask the question."

"Okay, how did the former light heavyweight champion of the world end up working as a prison guard?"

He winked. "That's the question, isn't it?" He took a hard swallow of his wine. "The answer is, because sometimes in life people don't make good decisions."

I nodded, waited for a moment, then said, "I'm interested if you want to tell me."

"I was a good football player at Cardinal Mooney High School, linebacker and fullback, and I got a scholarship to Youngstown State. I had a great four years playing football, and after my last game I packed up my bags, my 1.8 grade point average, and went home. I didn't see any advantage in a college degree. My dad went crazy, but you couldn't tell me anything. I knew it all. I'd always been interested in boxing, so I started working out with a trainer. I was pretty good, but I was behind most of the guys my age because they'd been boxing since they were ten or twelve. I've got nothing else going on in my life, so I'm in the gym all day. I'm training hard trying to make up for lost time. By the time I went pro, I was beating the living hell out of everyone they put in the ring with me. My manager made sure they were all bums, but I was winning. I fought in this undercard match in Atlantic City, and some promoter sees me and likes me. I beat up on a bunch of other bums, and the next thing I know, I'm getting a title shot at the light heavyweight champion, Alistair Moore. I fought the fight of my life. He knocked me down three times, but I got back up every time and kept going at him. He didn't take me seriously and hadn't trained. He thought I was just some dago out of Youngstown that they had set up for the TV money. He thought wrong. Halfway through the fourteenth he ran out of gas and dropped his gloves. That was it. I hit him with a right cross and he was out before he hit the canvas. Youngstown went berserk. Ray "Boom Boom" Mancini had just retired, and I gave them another world champion. They had a parade for me that stretched for miles. I fought Moore in a rematch and knocked him out in the first round." Moretti leaned in over the table and waved me in close. He whispered, "I think he took a dive. He knew he was done, but he wanted one last purse."

He leaned back as the waitress set two salads on the table. "Over the next three years I defended my title seven more times. All bums, but the light heavyweight division was full of bums in those days. My next match was against this Ukrainian—Oleg Zelenko. Mother of Christ, let me tell you this, and it's a stone fact: Ukrainians have the hardest heads in the world. I hit that son of a bitch with everything I had all night, and he never flinched. We finish eleven rounds and he's killing me. When I get to my corner, I asked my trainer, 'What quarter is it?' He yells at me, 'What quarter? Jesus H. Christ, you're not playing football. You're boxing. Well, he's boxing. You're just getting your ass kicked.' I head out for the twelfth round, and with what little brain function I had left, I know he's going to lead with his right. He does, and I duck it, and come with an uppercut with everything I have. I hit him under the jaw and I swear I heard his teeth crack. I start unloading on his right temple, and finally he went down. That was it for me. I knew he'd want a rematch, and I wanted nothing to do with him. I retired the next day as the undefeated light heavyweight world champion."

He poured us each more wine and ordered another bottle of Chianti.

"It all sounds pretty good up to this point," I said.

"Up to this point, it was all good. This is about the start of the bad decision-making. I came home with a wad of cash and I bought a Corvette, which I promptly totaled. No problem. I've got a lot of money, so I bought another Corvette. I spent money on women, vacations, more women, booze, jewelry. And pretty soon . . ."

"You're broke."

"Yep. It didn't take long to blow through that money. I had to sell the 'vette. Broke my heart. I wasn't in the sports section of the newspaper every day, so all of a sudden I'm having to buy my own beers, you know what I'm saying?"

I nodded. "I do."

"Anyway, the old man calls in a marker with the mayor and tells him that I'm on the ropes financially, and asks what he can do for me. He tells the old man he can get me on the police department. That didn't go over so well. You know, I grew up in the Little Italy section of Youngstown. My people were not exactly friendly with the authorities, if you know what I mean."

"Yeah, I think I understand your dilemma."

"The mayor says the police want me to run the Police Athletic League and be this ambassador of goodwill in the community. It sounds like a pretty good gig, so I take it. I hated it from day one. I felt like a sideshow freak. I'm going to elementary schools with my championship belt and telling kids not to take drugs, study hard, don't get in trouble. After about two years of that, I'd had it, but I liked being a cop. I did some street work and wanted a chance to get on the detective bureau. Eventually, I got assigned to help start up our crime scene search unit. We had always contracted with the sheriff for those services, and the chief wanted our own unit. I went to school and got my certification. I loved it, and we helped solve a lot of crimes—burglaries, assaults, murders, rapes. Then . . ."

Again, his voice trailed off and, again, I finished his sentence. "You punched your supervisor."

He frowned. "You knew about that?"

"There's a lot of information on the Internet. One of the stories I read said you had a blatant disregard for authority."

"What I had was a blatant disregard for dumbasses."

"The story said the attack was unprovoked."

"That part isn't true. He provoked me plenty. He was the captain of the detective bureau and he was always giving me the business, calling me a second-rate boxer and third-rate detective, crap like that. One day he said that Alistair Moore had obviously taken a dive in the rematch because that punch I threw couldn't have broken an egg shell. I could have just walked away, but I decided that whatever punishment was coming was worth it. I proved to him that the punch definitely would have broken an egg shell. I drilled him in the middle of his face; he went down faster than Alistair Moore." He finished the wine in his glass and refilled. "The captain didn't want to file charges, but it was still enough to get me booted off the force, which is what he wanted. The newspaper had a field day with it. There was a long editorial about how I could have been an inspiration to the youth of the city, but I turned out to be just another guy who couldn't control his temper. Given the circumstances, it's hard to argue with that one." He saluted with his wine. "I still had bills to pay, so . . ."

"You're a prison guard."

"Oh, how the mighty have fallen, huh?"

"I'm not judging. I've had plenty of coworkers that I wanted to punch."

He held up a single finger. "But you didn't. Therein lies the difference."

I stopped talking while the waitress slid an enormous serving of chicken parmesan in front of me. Moretti had the osso buco with gremolata. The waitress uncorked the second bottle of Chianti and topped off our glasses. "So, with all that said, what is your motivation with Yates?" I asked.

"Maybe I just don't want to see the wrong guy get the death penalty."

I twirled the pasta around my fork. "That certainly could be part of it, but I'll bet it's not the only reason. Those binders are impressive. That tells me that you're trying to prove something."

"I'm not sure I'm following you."

"It tells me you never got to prove your worth to the police department as a detective and that this is a little redemption, perhaps."

"You're an astute observer, Mr. Van Buren. I believe Lester Yates is an innocent man, but I also would love to prove to everyone that I could have been a good detective. But more importantly than that, I want to prove to myself that I'm not just some hothead who could never accomplish anything outside of a boxing ring."

SEVEN

Seven weeks and three days before the scheduled execution of Lester Paul Yates.

Jerry Adameyer was to meet me at a hotel in North Lima that night. By the time I got back from my dinner with Moretti, he had yet to check in. I was whipped. I left a message for him at the desk to meet me in the lobby restaurant at seven-thirty the next morning.

When I arrived, he was already in a booth with a newspaper and a cup of coffee. He was wearing a maroon necktie and a white shirt that was straining the buttons across his chest and squeezing his neck, turning his face the same shade as his neckwear. His head looked like a water balloon some kid was squeezing. "You better undo that collar button or you're going to have an aneurysm," I said.

"The starch makes the collar stiff," he said, wedging two fingers between the fabric and his neck. "It'll loosen up in a few minutes."

"I hope you last that long."

We talked about my meetings the previous day and what we wanted to accomplish during our time with Lester Yates. We agreed that the canvas was blank. We would let Lester tell us his story before we came up with a plan of attack . . . if one was even necessary. As we talked, Jerry polished off a platter of sausage, scrambled eggs, and fried potatoes and onions that would have been three meals for me. I watched in amazement. "How are you not four hundred pounds?"

"Discipline. I've cut way back on my calorie intake since I'm not powerlifting all the time."

"Really, you've cut back, huh?"

He grinned and dropped his napkin on the plate. "All right, chief, time to rock 'n' roll."

I got into Jerry's car and we rolled north on Route 7 toward the Northeast Ohio Correctional Facility. Before he'd put the car in gear, Jerry peeled off a stick of chewing gum and jammed it in his mouth. When he did, he shot me a look of mock disdain. One of the stipulations I made for working for me was that he could not chew tobacco on the job. "I'm not having my chief investigator walking around the state office tower spitting into a foam cup," I said. Rather than stop only while he was at work, Jerry had given up chewing tobacco altogether, though nearly three years after his last chaw he still had mighty cravings. Of course, that was my fault.

As we neared the prison, the Youngstown sky was a wide stretch of slate gray clouds, heavy rolls of steel wool that blotted out the sun. "Looks like the end of times," Jerry said. "A perfect day for interviewing someone headed to the gallows."

The correctional facility was a campus of beige brick buildings surrounded by a chain-link fence and razor wire. A humorless guard with a repaired cleft palate met us in the lobby and escorted Jerry and me to the maximum security section of the prison where Lester Yates was already in a glass-walled meeting room.

I saw immediately what my former baseball coach had meant. Lester Yates looked like every kid who ever had gotten lost in the shuffle of life. He was tiny—maybe five-six, one hundred and twenty pounds, at most—with a little round head and bristles of hair the color of a dirty penny that stood out a quarter inch all over his scalp, and crescent moons of acne rimming the corners of his mouth. The orange jumpsuit he was wearing looked comically large, the opening for his head stretching to the edges of his thin shoulders. The chains of his handcuffs were wrapped around his waist chain and laced through loops in a leather belt. Ankle cuffs were connected to a single chain that was locked to the same belt. In prison slang, it was known as a four-piece suit. The little room smelled of nervous sweat.

His brown eyes weren't sad, but simply resigned to a world that had dictated terms from the day he was born. I doubted anyone had ever taken the time to teach him how to throw a baseball or put on deodorant, or had helped him with his math homework. What he knew about life he had absorbed from the sidelines, never quite sure how to get in the game. His entire life had been spent taking orders from teachers and bosses and prison guards. This produced a quiet acceptance of his situation and the role he was to play in the world. He was the convicted, but no less the victim.

He looked up at us when we walked into the meeting room, but he said nothing and made no effort to stand.

We took seats across the table from him. He blinked and his head jerked from side to side, like a nervous little bird on the lookout for a cat.

"Lester, do you know who we are?" I asked.

"Not really," he said. "Mr. Moretti said somebody wanted to talk to me."

"My name is Hutchinson Van Buren; I'm the attorney general of the state of Ohio. This is my chief investigator, Jerry Adameyer. We're doing an investigation of your case prior to your execution date."

"Are you trying to get me off? That's what Mr. Moretti said."

"Not exactly, Lester. Our job isn't to try to get you off. Our job is to conduct an unbiased investigation and make sure justice has been served. In other words, we want to make sure we're not executing the wrong man."

Ridges ran across his brow as he considered this. "What's the difference? I didn't do it."

"Mr. Moretti believes you didn't do it. Unfortunately, a jury of your peers believed beyond a reasonable doubt that you did."

"But I didn't. I tried to use her credit card, but I never killed anyone."

"Okay, Lester, we've got some questions we want to ask you. Let's walk through this."

Lester Paul Yates was born on Halloween night, 1976, the youngest of four children born to Kirkland and Eunice Yates. His father had an eighth-grade education; he worked at the chemical plant in Martins Ferry and collected scrap metal to feed his family. His mother cleaned houses and took in wash and mending to help with the bills. Lester grew up poor in an area known as Turkey Point, which he described as being "Up there behind Rush Run a ways." He graduated from Warren Consolidated High School in 1994, though he said he was "not very good at school," and conceded that the diploma had been a gift, probably just to get rid of him. He got hired at the cement factory after high school and worked there until his arrest.

He was not close to his family, and he had not had a single visitor since his incarceration. His mother had died of breast cancer a year earlier. His father, he said, "don't know no one no more."

"Does he have Alzheimer's disease?" Jerry asked.

"I don't know what he's got. He just don't know no one. I think it was from working around those chemicals all the time. It messed up his brain. My sister put him in some kind of home a few years back."

"Is he still alive?" I asked.

Lester shrugged. "Beats me."

His sister lived near the family home and had "seven or eight kids. I can't keep track of 'em all." The eldest brother lived in one of the Carolinas, "or maybe Montana, I ain't for sure." Another brother hadn't been seen in more than ten years. Lester thought he might be in prison, too.

Lester said he was close to an uncle on his mother's side, Elmer Ellis, who he called "Uncle E." His uncle taught him to fish, and they frequently went bass fishing together.

"It was the only thing I was pretty good at," Lester said. "We'd go out to the lakes and strip ponds, and he taught me where all the honey holes was and how to hook them big ones. I wanted to get in some of them bass tournaments like you see on TV. They give out some big-money prizes, and I thought that would really be something if I got on the TV and got famous and rich for fishin'."

"That would be something," I said. "Lester, let me ask you a few things. I haven't read the trial transcript yet, but according to the newspaper articles, you told the Marino boy, 'I killed the bitch.' Is that accurate?"

"You mean did I tell him that?"

"Yes."

"Uh-huh, I said it."

"Did you kill her?"

"No. I already told you I didn't."

"Then why did you tell him you did?"

"I don't know. It was after I'd been arrested for trying to use that girl's credit card, and it was in the paper and everything. The guys in our club thought it is was pretty badass that I got arrested. I was the first guy in the club to ever get pinched. Francis, he asked me how I got a hold of her purse, and I told him I killed the bitch. I was just showing off, trying to talk tough. No one believed it."

"The jury believed it," Jerry said.

"I know, but I was just talking. I didn't know it was gonna come back and bite me like that. I never thought Francis would rat me out. If I'd done what Uncle E said and just put the purse back, none of this would have happened."

Jerry and I looked at each other. "Back up, Lester," I said. "What's this about your Uncle E telling you to put the purse back?"

"He told me to put the purse back 'cause there was no advantage to sticking your nose in other people's business."

I held up both palms. "Lester, are you telling me that your uncle was at Piedmont Lake the day you found Danielle Quinn's purse?"

"Uh-huh. We was fishing in the inlet not far from Holloway. It was one of our favorite spots. It was lunchtime and we had brought some headcheese sandwiches, so I ran back to the truck to get 'em. When I was walking back to the inlet, I saw the purse in the reeds. I didn't see it when we got there that morning, because it was still dark. But in the daylight, it was easy to see. It was yellow. I got a stick and fished it out and showed it to my uncle. He asked if there was any money in the wallet. I looked, and there wasn't. He said I should put it back. I said maybe we should turn it in because there might be a reward. He said there wouldn't be no reward because no one loses a purse out in the middle of a swamp. One way or another, it got there the wrong way and turning it in wouldn't lead to anything good. He said if it had been stolen, the cops might think that we were the thieves. That's when he said it wasn't any of our business how it got there. I saw there was credit cards in there, so I took it back to the truck and hid it in a bag I'd brought with me. It was a couple of days later, after work, that I went to that store and got busted. I wanted to buy me a good rod and reel in case I got in one of them bass tournaments on TV."

"Did your uncle testify on your behalf at the trial?" Jerry asked.

"You mean did he get up and talk for me?"

"Yes, that's what I mean."

"No."

"Did your attorney know that your uncle was with you when you found the purse?" I asked.

"I think so. I don't remember for sure, but I think I told him. He might not have paid any attention. He wasn't a very good lawyer."

"How can we get in touch with your Uncle E?" I asked.

"You can't. He's dead."

I slouched in the chair just as the air expelled from Jerry's mouth. "Of course he is," I said. "When did he die?"

"I don't know, couple of years ago, maybe. My mom sent me a letter and said he got the lung cancer and died." He snapped his fingers. "She said it killed him just like that. Then she got cancer, and it killed her just like that."

Jerry said, "Lester, this is important. Did your lawyer or the prosecutor tell the jury that your uncle was with you when you found the purse?"

"Maybe. I don't remember much about the trial. It was like there was a chain saw running inside my head the whole time we were in that courtroom. I couldn't follow half of what was going on."

"Let's go back to your legal counsel for a minute," I said. "Did I understand you correctly that you feel you didn't have adequate representation?"

"I didn't say nothing about representation. I said my lawyer wasn't no good."

I choked back a smile. "You don't think your lawyer was very good?"

"No, he weren't no good at all. He was like about my age or so, and right before the trial started we were in this little room right beside the courtroom, and he started puking in the wastebasket. I asked him, 'Are you sick?' He said no, that his stomach was just all jacked up because he was going to have to get up in front of all those people and talk. I said, 'Jesus H. Christ, didn't they teach you how to get over that in lawyering school? I'm the one who ought to be puking in the trash can. You get to go home and eat supper. They want me to ride the needle.' He just stared at me like he thought I was stupid. He said, 'You don't understand. There's a lot of pressure on me. I've never defended anyone in a murder trial before.'

"I said, 'Well, this is a hell of a time to start.' He was nervous as a cat. He had his handkerchief out mopping sweat off his forehead all through the trial. He just kept saying how I didn't understand. When we would talk in the mornings or during one of the breaks, all he did was moan and groan about how tough things were for him. I don't think we ever talked about how he was going to get me off. All through the trial, whenever we were talking, he kept saying how his uncle was a son of a bitch and sayin' how pissed he was at his uncle for doing this to him."

Again, Jerry and I stared at each other. Another uncle had entered the drama. I asked, "What's that mean, Lester? What did he mean when he said he was upset with his uncle for doing that to him?"

"Just what I said. He was pissed at him."

"What did his uncle have to do with your trial?" Jerry asked.

"I don't know. I never asked him that. I didn't give a flying whip about his uncle; I wanted him to save my sorry ass."

Despite the seriousness of the situation, I had to choke back laughter. "Lester, do you remember Marsha Wollek?" I asked.

"Uh-huh."

I waited minute. He didn't offer any additional information.

"Did you hit her?"

"I didn't hit her. I slapped her a good one, yeah, but only after she coco-butted me right in the nose. I don't like to be hitting girls, but Marsha was giving me the devil all the time. That day in the parking lot she rammed her forehead right into my face."

"Did they bring this up at trial?"

"You mean did they talk about it?"

"Yes, did they talk about it?"

"Uh-huh. The guy who was against me, he told the jury that I probably killed that lady because I already had a history of beatin' on women. He had the police report from when I did it and they gave it to the judge. I think he had to read it, or something."

"They entered it into evidence?"

"I don't know. I guess. They gave it to the judge."

"Do you think that hurt you in the trial."

"They gave me the death sentence, so it probably didn't do me no good."

* * *

Jerry and I did not speak about our meeting while we were being escorted out of the prison. We climbed into his car parked on the free side of a fifteen-foot tall steel fence capped with a spiral razor wire that glinted in the late-morning sun, then we headed back to the hotel to pick up my car. I rubbed my face with both hands, not sure where to start the conversation. "That little guy is about as sad a case as I've ever seen," I said.

"Makes me want to rethink my support of the death penalty," Jerry said. "I'm going to give the trial transcript a thorough reading. We also need to track down his defense attorney. Maybe he can give us some insight."

"I agree that we need to talk to him, but it isn't going to do us any good to try to relitigate the case. That train is too far down the tracks. If we believe Yates isn't responsible, then who is? Did his arrest really end the murders? We need to figure out who is doing this, or raise some serious doubt about Yates's guilt."

"I'm with you, chief. What are our next steps?"

"I need to have a talk with D. Kendrick Brown."

Jerry smiled. "Please say I can go with you."

"Let me handle this one on my own. In the meantime, I want you to clear the decks and focus exclusively on Yates."

"Got it."

He dropped me off in the parking lot of the hotel next to my car. As I was unlocking my door, I heard the whir of an electric motor as the passenger-side window of his sedan lowered. "Just a thought, chief. You don't think Yates made up that story about his uncle, do you? Could he have concocted that because he knows his uncle's not around to refute it?"

"Over the years, I've learned to never underestimate the creativity of an incarcerated man. They have a lot of time to let their imaginations run. But my gut tells me he didn't make it up."

"Why's that?"

"Because I don't think he's smart enough to have an original thought."

EIGHT

Seven weeks and one day before the scheduled execution of Lester Paul Yates.

Jerry Adameyer once called D. Kendrick Brown a snake.

I argued that the characterization was unfair to animals that slither around on their bellies and eat rodents. "When you're dealing with a rattlesnake, for example, you know what you're up against," I said. "It's no secret. A rattlesnake is single-minded in his mission. He wants to bite you. And, if you're small enough, he wants to eat you. Plain and simple. A rattlesnake will not wrap an arm around your shoulder, ask about your kids, and tell you an off-color joke while he is slipping a shank between your sixth and seventh vertebrae."

Suffice it to say that D. Kendrick Brown would not have been my first choice to be superintendent of the Ohio Bureau of Criminal Investigation.

Nor would he have been my second choice.

Or my twelfth.

However, back in the day when D. Kendrick Brown was just Del Brown and a folksy political hack stomping around Belmont County, he had the good judgment to attach his political fortunes to the man who would eventually become governor. When Jim Wilinski was a member of the United States House of Representatives for eastern Ohio, Brown hosted fundraisers and twisted arms throughout the hills and hollows for donations on behalf of Big Jim. He was loyal, and if there was one thing that Jim Wilinski appreciated—and demanded—it was unquestioned loyalty. As Jerry so eloquently put it, "D. Kendrick has his nose so far up the governor's ass you couldn't dislodge it with a crowbar and a Marine."

Del Brown had grown up in the coal mining community of Neffs and attended Bellaire St. John Central High School, where he was the manager for the basketball team and a member of the rocketry club. He commuted to West Liberty State College, for his undergraduate degree in law enforcement. He got a job as a dispatcher with the Bellaire Police Department and, when a position opened up, became a patrolman. He felt like a big deal patrolling the streets of Bellaire and working the festivals and the high school basketball games where he could be seen, a man of great authority, rocking back and forth on his buffed boots, his thumbs hooked into his gun belt.

He had risen to the rank of assistant chief of police when he was elected sheriff. On the night of his election, Belmont County's top law-enforcement officer was still single, still living in his parents' home, and still sleeping in his childhood bedroom with cowboys-and-Indians wallpaper.

His time as the Belmont County sheriff was largely unremarkable, other than the fact he had moved out of his parents' home and bought a house in Lansing. There were a few homicides that a fourth grader could have solved. He would speak to the St. Clairsville Rotarians or the Martins Ferry Kiwanis about the importance of law and order, and he loved to call press conferences whenever he got an indictment for domestic violence as he knew that was a hot button for female voters. It was a pretty cozy gig until the Egypt Valley Strangler started dumping bodies all over his jurisdiction. He put together a task force and held seminars for women on self-defense, but he didn't have a suspect or an inkling of how to stop the murders. But when clueless little Lester Yates dropped into his lap, Del Brown gained national fame as a first-rate lawman who had put away a serial killer.

Thus, shortly after Lester Yates was convicted, it was not difficult for Wilinski to get his old friend appointed superintendent of the Ohio Bureau of Criminal Investigation. Brown lined the walls of his new office with framed newspaper articles of the Yates conviction, adopted the more erudite name of D. Kendrick, and set about performing his duties as superintendent with the same indolent approach that had marked his tenure as Belmont County sheriff.

Wilinski, however, saw the advantage of having D. Kendrick Brown around. Wilinski would take him on campaign stops and use him as a political shill, bringing him out on stage and announcing, "Ladies and gentlemen, please say hello to my good friend, the man who single-handedly put the Egypt Valley Strangler on Death Row, D. Kendrick Brown!" The crowds would roar and Brown would take the microphone and say, "This here is a good man. Cast your vote for Big Jim Wilinski." He would then wave and walk off the stage. You could have trained a chimp to do it.

Brown was already ensconced in the superintendent's job when I took office, and I was instructed in no uncertain terms by the governor, who was again meddling in the affairs of the office of attorney general, that Brown would retain that position. Wilinski's order to retain Brown scorched my ass. I cursed, complained, vented to Margaret, and went to the gym and hit the heavy bag until my arms were numb and hanging limp at my sides. Then, I left him in the position without argument because I wanted to be United States attorney general.

Yes, we all have our price.

With all that said, I must admit that Brown had been moderately competent in his job. To the best of my knowledge, he had yet to totally screw up anything. In other words, for a bureaucrat in state government, he was exceeding expectations.

⋆ ⋆ ⋆

The Ohio Bureau of Criminal Investigation is located in London, Ohio, about thirty miles west of Columbus, near the grounds of the London Correctional Institution. It was one-thirty in the afternoon when I pulled into the parking lot. I had no sooner passed through security and into the inner hall than I saw D. Kendrick Brown walking toward his office.

He had terribly rounded and hunched shoulders that caused his suit jackets to arc across the small of his back. His head extended more forward than up, and his straining neck muscles gave him the appearance of a turtle. By his own admission, he drank a twelve-pack of diet cola every day; he had one in his right hand as he came down the hall. Because of the way his head thrusted forward, he had to cock his elbow, tilt the can above his nose, and catch its rim in a pocket created by his protruding lower lip. And he could do this while walking. While talking, he had an annoying habit of sucking back saliva between his molars and cheeks when he paused to take a breath. Jerry Adameyer had described this as, "like having a conversation with a shop vac around a puddle of water." His subordinates had nicknamed him "Slurpee."

"Mister Attorney General," Brown said when he saw me. "To what do I owe this honor?"

What he was really asking was, *Why the hell are you here? This is my turf. You remember that I'm friends with the governor, right?*

"We need to have a little talk, Del."

"Sounds serious."

"It could be."

"Well, I've got a few minutes. Come on in," he said, leading me into his office. He went behind his desk but didn't sit; neither did I. "I don't know what could possibly be so important that you had to drive all the way out here to Madison County. Why didn't you just pick up the phone?"

The tone of his voice made my jaw clench, and the grinding of my teeth sounded like a straining cable in my head. There is a certain dismissive attitude that people develop when they know they are untouchable, that short of shooting someone they cannot be fired. That was the attitude of D. Kendrick Brown. He was never outright disrespectful, and he always fulfilled any request I made, but he took the orders with a smirk, the slightest hint of condescension in the nodding of his head, a tacit message that he was the governor's boy and that I should not let that fact slip from my memory. The big dog was protecting D. Kendrick, and there was nothing I was going to do about it.

"We need to talk about Lester Yates," I said.

"We better make it quick, because that boy doesn't have much time." He snorted and laughed at his own attempt at humor.

I didn't.

"How sure are you this guy killed Danielle Quinn?"

His face looked as though he had bitten down on a piece of aluminum foil, and his demeanor changed in an instant. He had been lifting the diet soda to his lips; the can paused in midair and I could see the muscles in his hands tense as a darkness the shade of an eggplant enveloped his ears. Slowly, he set the can on his desk and said, "Whatever is more than one hundred percent; that's how sure I am. Why would you ask me a question like that?"

We glared at each other for moment. I said, "Because I'd like very much not to execute an innocent man."

"You won't be."

He nervously ran his fingers over his face and took a seat at his desk, behind which hung a framed front page of the Cambridge *Daily Jeffersonian* from January 18, 2002. The banner headline read:

YATES GUILTY; SENTENCED TO DEATH

I walked across the room and took a seat at the head of his conference table. He was playing a little power game, and I was having none of it. When he saw that I wasn't going to sit in one of the chairs with the stained cloth seats in front of his desk, he grabbed a pen and legal pad and walked over to the conference table.

"So you think Yates was the Egypt Valley Strangler and he killed all those women?" I asked.

"I can't prove that he killed every last one of them; there might have been a copycat or two in the mix, but I'd feel safe in saying he killed the majority of them."

"If there was a copycat or two, as you say, that means two families didn't get justice, and there are still one or two murderers roaming the streets."

"I was only concerning myself with the murder of Danielle Quinn."

"That's a convenient argument to make now, Del. But I read the newspaper articles. You said many times he was the Egypt Valley Strangler, end of story. You know that would've made him seventeen years old when Donna Herrick was killed."

"You've done your homework. Congratulations."

"It's easy math."

"I don't care how old he was when Donna Herrick was

murdered. He wasn't on trial for killing Donna Herrick. He wasn't on trial for killing any of the other unfortunate victims of the Egypt Valley Strangler. He was on trial for killing Danielle Quinn. And just to remind you, he was convicted."

"How about the women who were found murdered in the Egypt Valley after Yates was arrested?"

"Not . . . my . . . problem. Here's what I know for sure: a bad guy is always a bad guy. Lester Yates is a white supremacist and a gang leader. And, in case you didn't know, he also was previously convicted of assaulting another woman. In my book, that's one bad guy, and he was perfectly capable of killing someone when he was seventeen. What's your point?"

"I'll give you a couple of points. One, the previous conviction was horseshit, and you know it. The second and most important point is, I need to investigate this before we go strapping him down on the gurney. I want to make absolutely sure we've got the right guy. And, just so you know, I'm getting a lot of information that makes me suspect that he isn't."

"I don't know who you're talking to, but that boy is a stone-cold killer."

"You know, Del, we all have something to gain if Big Jim becomes president of the United States. He can still get to the White House if he commutes Yates's sentence to life in prison with no chance of parole. But he can't get there if he's governor when we execute an innocent man."

D. Kendrick was on the ropes, looking like he was trying to swallow a tennis ball. "Yates was caught trying to use the dead woman's credit card. He still had possession of the purse. I had a guy testify that Yates said he killed her. He said, 'I killed the bitch.' What more do you want?"

"Using someone's credit card is a far cry from strangling someone to death, and the guy you had testify against Yates thought he was going to win the Heisman Trophy and walk on the moon."

"What the hell does that mean?"

"Look, I'm not going to debate this with you. I wanted to give you the courtesy of telling you that I have some concerns with this conviction, and I'm looking into it. I didn't want you to be blindsided."

"He's still a degenerate."

It was my ears that were burning now. Between clenched teeth I said, "You see, Del, that's where we have a disconnect. Here in the great state of Ohio, we don't execute people for being degenerates."

"Lester Yates is guilty as hell and he can go tell his sob story to the devil, because that's where he's going to end up. If your goal was to keep me informed, thank you very much, you've completed your mission. But just so you know, if you're thinking of getting the governor to commute his sentence to life in prison, don't expect my blessing."

I stood to leave. "I don't need your blessing, Del."

He looked up, and I'm not sure I had ever seen such hatred in another man's eyes, and that included the ones I'd had sentenced to death. At that instant, I knew in my gut that I was onto something. D. Kendrick Brown's indignant, how-dare-you response was identical to that of every white-collar criminal I had ever questioned. It was feigned outrage. He was worried that he would be exposed for exactly what he was—an opportunist, a man more interested in grabbing headlines than administering justice.

I wanted to tell him just that, that he was a bully who had picked on the weakest kid in the class, that he knew Lester Yates could not have defended himself in an argument against a second grader. That's what I wanted to say, but I kept my mouth shut. I'd tossed a match in the woodpile and didn't see any need to add gasoline to the mix.

I would be lying if I didn't say this had become very personal. I wanted to prove Yates's innocence so that I could come back to D. Kendrick's office and watch him take the framed newspaper clippings off the wall.

NINE

Six weeks and three days before the scheduled execution of Lester Paul Yates.

The following Tuesday, I had a large whiteboard set on an easel in the front of the conference room off the lobby and ordered Margaret to have four phone lines set up in the room and a lock placed on that door. The conference room was being transformed into the Lester Yates war room. Jerry Adameyer selected his four best investigators and four interns he trusted to work hard and keep their mouths shut.

I was happy with his choices.

The investigator I had the most confidence in was Clarence Davidson, a strapping, six-four black man who looked like he had stepped out of a Marine Corps recruiting poster. He was in his midthirties, had close-cropped hair, a square head, and a square jaw. He was a perfect collection of right angles. Davidson had worked as a patrolman for Jerry in Portage Township and was the first person hired after he was named my chief investigator. He was analytical and methodic in his approach.

Jack McGowan was a former deputy sheriff in Perry County. He joined Jerry's staff after making an unsuccessful run for sheriff. If I had to guess, I would say he had a little trouble staying away from the bottle, evidenced by the rivers of purple veins that were beginning to snake across his nose. He was in his early fifties, quiet, and sported a dishwater moustache that gave him the unfortunate look of a walrus. He was observant and the best interviewer on Jerry's staff.

Mercedes Gonzalez was in her early forties, had a spray of salt-and-pepper hair that she wrapped tight in a bun, and had a master's degree in clinical psychology. She was off-the-charts intelligent. I had long wondered why someone with her pedigree wanted to be an investigator, but I hadn't asked because I avoided unnecessary conversations with Mercedes. I did this because I could never shake the uncomfortable feeling that I was being constantly analyzed. When she interviewed people, she always appeared to be confused and unable to grasp their responses to her questions. This was a tactic she deployed, lulling people into a false sense of security, all the while reading their body language and looking for hints of deception.

Charlie Akers was a holdover from the previous administration and, like Verlander in the criminal division, was one I didn't completely trust. Jerry, however, had great confidence in Akers, who he said was, "incredibly thorough." He was in his early thirties and went by the nickname of Tig. He never had a hair out of place and when he came to meetings, he always—*always*—had one ink pen in his hand and three others lined up in precise order to the right of his notebook.

I didn't know the interns very well. I had met them at a reception at the beginning of the summer, but they were pretty far down the food chain, and I had little interaction with them. Most of the background I had was from Jerry.

Chip Donahoe was the son of a state senator. He had thus far been able to remain in law school at Ohio State because he was the son of a state senator. And, yes, he had gotten the internship in my office because he was the son of a state senator. I didn't care for that kind of nepotism in my department, but welcome to the world of state politics. With that said, he had done good work in the criminal division, and he had been Jerry's first pick.

Austin Battenberg looked like he was about eleven years old. He was always smiling, had a pink face, and probably shaved once a month. He was a hard worker and eager to impress. His shoes were always polished and he wore tailored suits and Brooks Brothers neckties. He was not quite five foot six and shared a cubicle with Donahoe, who was six-five, always looked like he'd slept in his clothes, wore scuffed earth shoes, and had usually missed a belt loop on his khakis.

Addelyn "Addie" Nakamura was the only intern with whom I'd had any substantial contact. She had compiled a report on our consumer protection division's efforts to stem health insurance scams that preyed on the elderly. Her report had been quite thorough and actually showed a gaping weakness in our investigative techniques. She was incredibly bright, but universally disliked by her fellow interns, who behind her back referred to her as "Miss Addie-tuddie," for her smug disposition. That bothered me not a bit. This wasn't a popularity contest.

The last intern was Liberatore. I think I had met her at the reception, but I couldn't remember her first name, if I ever knew it. She was near the top of her class at Ohio Northern University, had been a two-time Ohio State high school gymnastics champion in the balance beam, and according to Jerry, was "about eighty pounds of nitro." She had done some research for Jerry in the charitable division; he described her work ethic as "tenacious."

There they were. The team I was going to send out to save the life of Lester Yates.

We assembled at one o'clock that afternoon with Margaret taking notes. Only Jerry and I knew the reason for the meeting.

When the team had assembled, I closed the door and said, "Absolutely nothing that is said in this room is to be repeated outside of this room—not to your spouse, not to your kids, your mother, or your dog. If you pray, don't even mention it to God. Is that clearly understood?" Everyone nodded. "I'd like to hear you say that you understand."

Several said, *yes*; several others said, *I understand*.

"Very good. You'll see that we had phone lines installed in this room. If you need to make phone calls concerning this project, they are to be made from this room, with the door closed." I nodded to Margaret, and she began passing out copies of the binders that Reno Moretti had prepared. In addition, I had added a cover sheet that listed the names of the eighteen known victims of the Egypt Valley

Strangler, their ages, the dates on which they were last reported seen, and the dates their bodies were found.

"In January of 2002, a twenty-two-year-old man named Lester Yates was convicted and sentenced to die for the strangulation death of Danielle Quinn, who is victim number fifteen in your materials. Mr. Yates has been identified as the Egypt Valley Strangler and is allegedly responsible for the deaths of all eighteen women. He is going to be executed by the state of Ohio in less than two months. That is why you are here today. Your mission is both simple and complex. You are to do everything in your power to make sure we have the right man on Death Row. If you cannot prove his guilt, I want you to present compelling evidence that prevents us from executing an innocent man. It's not good enough to go out there and prove this guy is a sad piece of humanity. I already know that, and that's not going to keep the state from putting a needle in his arm. We need to prove he did it, or he didn't. Black or white. If you come back here and tell me that he didn't kill Danielle Quinn or any of these other women, I expect you to tell me who did."

I gave them a historical overview of the Egypt Valley Strangler in general and Lester Yates in particular. Since I had already talked to the father of Donna Herrick, there was no need to revisit him. That left seventeen other victims. Each investigator would be assigned four victims. I kept Danielle Quinn for myself.

"I want you to approach this as though you are the lead investigator in the murder investigation. Track down relatives, interview witnesses, look for public documents. Since these were ostensibly investigated by the sheriff's departments in Belmont and Guernsey Counties, talk to investigators and ask to see their reports. I want to know who the victim's relatives believe was responsible for the murder; they always have an opinion. This is not going to be easy, and you can expect to be working sixteen-hour days for the next two months. Whatever else you have on your plate, I want you to clean it off and focus on this investigation. Are we clear?"

Yes, they said.

* * *

Davidson raised a hand. It was his military background. He wouldn't speak until given permission. I nodded at him. "Do you think Yates is innocent?" Davidson asked.

"I don't want to see the wrong man get put to death," I said.

"But you think the state is heading in that direction, don't you?"

"I think it's a pretty safe bet that I wouldn't be putting this team together if I was confident the right guy had been convicted. I want you going into this with an open mind, but I want you attacking it as if your father was the condemned."

He nodded. "Understood."

I divvied up the names, one of which was an unidentified victim, and assigned them to the investigators.

I turned to the interns. "Three newspapers covered the Egypt Valley Strangler extensively—the Cambridge *Daily Jeffersonian*, the Martins Ferry *Times Leader*, and the *Ohio Valley Journal* in Wheeling, West Virginia. I want you to begin with the disappearance of Donna Herrick and work your way up through the list. I want every newspaper article you can find related to the victims and the Egypt Valley Strangler." I pointed at Nakamura. "Addie, you are responsible for assembling the clips in notebooks. I want a separate notebook for each victim, and I want the clips arranged by date—oldest to newest. Got it?"

"Yes, sir," she said.

"These articles will have been in local papers and are unlikely to be archived online." I said.

"Where do you suggest we find them?" Liberatore asked.

It was the kind of question that sent flares of heat up my spine. I folded my arms and said, "You are a third-year law student and you have to ask me where to find newspaper articles?" Her eyes widened, and she looked as though I had slapped her in the face. "You're not going to be able to sit behind a computer and do this. The first murder was in 1993. I suggest you comb through the microfilm at the library. You'll be able to spot it. It's a big building with a lot of books."

Out of the corner of my eye I saw one of Margaret's brows arch like a pair of caterpillars. There was a chance I needed to work on my sensitivity. Even Margaret, who had zero tolerance for indolence and ineptitude, had accused me of sometimes having the management skills of a Viking warlord. Maybe Liberatore didn't deserve that, but Lester Yates and I were on a tight deadline.

I had Margaret pass out keys to the war room to everyone on the team.

I sat down in a chair at the head of the table. "Many years ago, we had a detective come to my high school for a career day. I still remember two things he said. One was that if you don't have a solid lead in a crime after the first twenty-four hours, the odds of solving it drop exponentially. The other was that when a case grows cold, it is rarely solved by science or good detective work. It gets solved because people can't keep their mouths shut. I happen to believe both of those points are true. I realize I may be asking you to perform the impossible. However, a man's life is at stake, and that man could be innocent. So, get out there and perform the impossible. Keep Jerry posted, and we'll reconvene soon." I tapped the glass crystal of my wristwatch. "Tick-tock, ladies and gentlemen."

Tick-tock, indeed.

TEN

I left them reading the materials I'd handed out; Jerry and I walked back into my office. When I had closed the door, Jerry asked, "What's my assignment, chief?"

"I need you to ride herd on that bunch and make sure they understand the seriousness of the situation," I said.

"Oh, I think you made that abundantly clear." He hoisted a thick thigh onto the corner of my desk. "You've got to leave a little meat on the bone for me."

I opened a notebook onto which I had scribbled some notes during my interview with Reno Moretti. "How about getting in touch with Moretti, the prison guard who compiled the binders? When I was talking to him, he mentioned that he had a snitch who told him that a guy named Herman Fenicks was bragging in the yard that he had killed more prostitutes than he could remember. He supposedly said he dumped them near a lake along Interstate 70."

"Piedmont Lake?"

I shrugged. "He didn't say. This Fenicks guy was supposedly a truck driver."

"Interesting connection."

"It might be a milk run, but it's worth checking out. Get in touch with Moretti and see if the guy will talk. I'm sure Moretti will set it up for us."

"I'm on it." He slipped off the desk. "How about you? What are you going to be doing? I know you're not just supervising on this one. This kind of thing is right in your groove swing."

"To be honest with you, Jerry, it's the first thing that's got me excited about my job in almost three years. I'm going to track down Yates's defense attorney; maybe he knows something beyond what's in the trial transcript. And I'm going to look into the murder of the Quinn girl."

"I'm off to the races," he said, passing Margaret on his way out of the office.

Without looking up, I said, "Margaret, I need some help. There's a lawyer, somewhere in the Martins Ferry–Bellaire area, that I need to talk to. His name is Jim Smith. He was Lester Yates's public defender. Would you please track him down and see if you can get me ninety minutes on his calendar, as early as tomorrow, if possible?"

She didn't respond, and when I looked up Margaret was standing in front of my desk, her lips puckered down to the size of a nickel, her eyelids fluttering with the rapidity of hummingbird wings. I had seen the look dozens of times, and I was sure Mount Margaret was ready to blow, but in a calm voice that belied the rage boiling below, she said, "Why sure, Mr. Van Buren. I'd be happy to do that for you."

"What's wrong, Margaret?"

"Wrong? Oh, nothing is wrong. In fact, it's all sunshine and kittens from where I'm standing."

"I know. I was a little rough on the intern. I'll apologize to her."

"I think that would be lovely if you did that, Mr. Van Buren."

She kept staring.

I set the notebook on the desk and folded my hands on my blotter. As a man with a stunning number of failed relationships to my credit, I had been accused on numerous instances of a particular kind of male blindness, an insensitivity to the nonverbal signals that are apparently so important in a relationship. This must have been one of those times.

I said, "Okay, I give. Why are you acting like this?"

"Acting like what?"

"Like it's all you can do to keep the top of your head from coming off."

"I certainly don't know what you're talking about. By the way, you have another unannounced visitor in the lobby."

"Is it Mr. Moretti again?"

"No."

The eyelids continued to flutter, and I was mildly surprised that papers weren't blowing off my desk. The balled-up fists that were digging into her hips had a palsy that twitched up into her forearms. "Don't keep me in suspense, Margaret. Who is it?"

Between clenched teeth, she uttered, "It's *the girl*."

"The girl" was Shelly Dennison, my former campaign manager and Margaret's archnemesis. I unsuccessfully tried to fight off a grin. "At the risk of having you take a giant bite out of the middle of my forehead, let me ask you this: Did she say what she wants?"

"Oh, no. She didn't say what she wanted because she was far too busy smilin' and actin' happy to see me, like we were old sorority sisters."

"Well, by all means, Margaret, please show her in."

"Is she going to be your campaign manager again?"

"I honestly don't know. I haven't discussed it with anyone. I assumed that we were going to cover that at the lunch meeting with Stan Carmine that I had to cancel."

Margaret looked at me as if every word that had come out of my mouth was a titanic lie. She shook her head as she turned and headed for the door, punching heel prints in my rug with each step, and in a barely audible tone that emanated from deep in her throat, I heard her say, "Mmm-mmm-mmm-mmm-mmm."

I quickly hoisted my feet to the corner of my desk and crossed them at the ankles, then grabbed that day's *Wall Street Journal* and pretended to be reading, hoping to give the impression that I was both surprised and disinterested in her visit.

When from the corner of my eye I saw a figure with a mane of ash blonde hair come through the door, I looked up, arched my brows, and said, "Well, well, well, as I live and breathe, Shelly Dennison."

She walked across the room in a way that could make a man forgive a thousand of her sins. In my eyes, there was not a woman alive as beautiful as Shelly Dennison, and not one as calculating, strong-willed, and dangerous. Mostly dangerous. I knew the moment I started sleeping with her during my first campaign that I was on borrowed time. She would slip between the sheets with the leading candidate for Ohio attorney general until someone more powerful and influential became available. When she found him, I became disposable as a lover, though as a candidate she still wanted the notch on her belt. I was fortunate that she dumped me when she did. I was wildly in love with her. If she had really set the hook deep before walking out of my life, I might never have left my house again.

"I don't get a hug?" she asked.

I folded the newspaper and flipped it on my desk. "The last time I gave you a hug was in the lobby of the Tangier restaurant. You came running through the door, your face all flushed, and you apologized for being late. You looked like twelve million dollars, and the head of every man in the place turned to watch you wrap your arms around *me.* You were wearing a cute red dress and the congressman's aftershave. That was the moment I realized the bloom was off the rose."

"Thank you for such a tender memory, Hutchinson. I'm so glad this is getting off on the right foot."

I dropped my feet from the desk and reached over to shake her hand. There was no warmth in the gesture. "It's good to see you, Shelly. Have a seat."

She looked at the chairs in front of my desk, then back at me. I was playing the same game D. Kendrick Brown had attempted with me. "Would you rather go out and get a cup of coffee?" she asked.

"Not really. I'm very busy." I extended a hand toward a chair. "This is good."

"I see." She sat down. "You're making me sit in front of your desk like I'm interviewing for a job?"

"I assume that you're here to talk about being my reelection campaign manager."

"I am."

"In that case, you *are* interviewing for a job."

The muscles in her jaw tightened; she set her purse on the chair next to her and crossed her legs at the knees. This was purely for my benefit. "If you hadn't blown off the meeting with Stan Carmine and me last week, we could have had this wrapped up by now."

"I didn't realize you were going to be part of that meeting."

"I had spoken to Stan several weeks ago and, given our past relationship, he believes it would be a fine idea for us to work together on the campaign."

"I see. Just for the record, when you say 'past relationship,' which one are you talking about? The one where you pledged your undying love to me before running out the door, or the one in which you were my campaign manager before running out the door?"

"First of all, I don't recall ever pledging my undying love to you or anyone else. And besides, the relationship was destined to fail. We were simply two different people. And I walked out of the campaign because you tried to self-destruct by going to that reporter and unburdening yourself of your involvement in the cover-up of that kid's death. And for the record, I had already built you such a substantial lead that you still cruised to a win in spite of yourself. I notice that at this very minute you happen to be sitting behind the desk of the Ohio attorney general."

"At least that much is true. Okay, Ms. Dennison, you have the floor. Tell me why you should be my campaign manager."

"It's very simple. You need me. You can't win without a strong campaign manager, and I'm your best shot."

"I won the last election pretty handily, and now I'm the incumbent. What makes this one so different?"

"The last one was a walk in the park compared to this. The Democrats are going to run Hal Thomas against you. He's the prosecutor of Franklin County, black, charismatic, and a former sheriff's deputy who worked his way through law school at night. He has a beautiful wife and an adorable family."

"I can't help it that I'm not black and married with an adorable family."

"True, but you could work on that dearth of charisma. They are going to present Thomas as a man of the people and a law-enforcement professional."

"I'm a law-enforcement professional."

"Yes, you are. And one who helped cover up the murder for which an innocent man spent thirty years in the penitentiary."

"He was a pedophile. I did society a favor."

"Here's my first bit of advice as your prospective campaign manager. Never let those words comes out of your mouth in the same sentence again. He didn't go to prison because he was a pedophile.

He went to prison because you helped cover up a murder for which he was wrongfully accused and convicted."

"That's old news."

"Oh, Hutchinson, you are so naïve. Every four years, what's old is new again. They are going to reopen that wound, pour salt in it, and bleed you dry. I can guarantee that it will be the centerpiece of their campaign against you."

"You don't know that."

"I know that for a fact, because if I was on the other side of the aisle, that is exactly what I would do." She sat back in her chair, raised her brows, and smiled. "You need me, Hutch. There's a lot at stake here. If Jim Wilinski wins the presidency, and I have every faith that he will, you will be the next attorney general."

"I've heard that, too. But things can change. A lot of favors will have to be repaid."

"No, he thinks very highly of you. He told me so."

"Really? A little pillow talk?"

I had crossed the line. Her nostrils flared, and for a minute I thought she might come over the desk after me. "I swear to Jesus, one more wiseass remark and I'll walk out of here. I'll let you sit there for the next year and watch Hal Thomas eat your lunch."

"Sorry, sorry, sorry. Really, I'm sorry. That was completely out of bounds."

"You can't become US attorney general if you don't win reelection."

"Agreed. My cards are on the table. I want to win reelection and I want to be US attorney general. How much time are you willing to contribute to make sure that happens?"

"Whatever it takes," she said.

"What other campaigns are you going to be working on?"

"Some local stuff. This will be the only statewide campaign."

"Are you going to be working on Wilinski's presidential campaign?"

"I don't know. At one point he said I would be his campaign manager, but . . ."

The most confident woman I had ever known dropped her head as her words trailed off. I would have bet my last dollar that Big

Jim Wilinski made that promise around lunchtime somewhere on the second floor of the Governor's Residence while they were both in an acute state of undress.

She said, "Let's just say he's been much less committal lately. I will probably do some work in Ohio, but my bet is he will hire one of the high-powered Republican firms in DC to take the lead. I certainly like the idea of being a national campaign chairman, and I think I could do it, but he probably has a lot of people in his ear telling him I don't have the chops for a national campaign."

If I was running a national campaign, the first person I would hire would be Shelly Dennison. By Election Day there wouldn't be enough left of my opponent to scrape into a matchbox. To Shelly, running a campaign is a blood sport. To my knowledge she had never lost a statewide race. Perhaps that was why she was so angry with me when I went to the reporter with the story of my participation in the cover-up of Petey Sanchez's death. She was worried that a loss would be a blemish on her record.

"So, we are good?" she asked.

"To be my campaign manager?"

She rolled her eyes. "What have we been talking about for the last twenty minutes?"

"I'll need some time to think about it."

"What is there to think about?"

"It's a big decision. I need a little time to think."

"Oh, for God's sake, Hutchinson. For how long?"

"I don't know. A while."

"We don't have time. Hal Thomas has already announced his candidacy. He's out there raising money and getting endorsements. We need to get rolling."

"Shelly, it's sixteen months until the election, and I'm the incumbent. It's not something that I need to decide this minute."

"There are other statewide candidates who are interested in my services. I can't wait forever."

"I can appreciate that, and I didn't say it would take forever. I will talk to Stan and let you know."

I couldn't tell if she was hurt, angry, or a combination of both. Perhaps she just found me exasperating. She wouldn't be the first. She stood, and as though with great effort, extended a limp hand across my desk. "I appreciate you stopping by," I said. "I'll be in touch."

She walked out without another word. I had to admit it was fun being in control of the situation with Shelly, which rarely happened. If I allowed her to become my campaign manager, and that was certainly the way I was leaning, it would be the last time I'd be in control for the next sixteen months.

After Shelly cleared the building, Margaret came back into my office. "Well?" she asked.

"Well, what?"

"Mmm-mmm-mmm-mmm-mmm. Mr. Van Buren, we have been working together a long time, so don't you dare play those games with me. Did you hire the girl to be your campaign manager?"

"You mean Shelly?"

"The girl," she repeated.

I started laughing. "I did not."

"Are you going to?"

"Maybe, and if I do, you need to negotiate a treaty with her." Her eyes started to squint. "I know she's a handful, and I know she got on your nerves during the last campaign, but she really is the best in the game. Now, I'm going to let you in on a little secret, and it has to stay between us."

"Nothing you tell me ever gets repeated."

"If Jim Wilinski is elected president of the United States, it is very likely that he is going to ask me to be his attorney general." Her eyes went from slits to saucers. "Margaret, how would you like to live in Washington, DC, and be the commandant for United States Attorney General Hutchinson Van Buren?"

"Why, I think I would like that just fine," she said.

"Okay, but in order for that to happen, I have to win reelection. If I can't win Ohio, he is not going to appoint me attorney general of the country. In order for me to win my state . . ."

"You need the girl," she said, completing the thought.

"That's exactly right. I need the girl."

She thought about this for a moment. "What's her name again?"

I smiled. "Shelly."

ELEVEN

Five weeks and six days before the scheduled execution of Lester Paul Yates.

It was a perfect morning for fishing. The sun had crested the willows that lined the eastern edge of the pond, and a slight breeze was blowing in from the west, sending tiny lines of waves into the muddy shoals.

I was glad to be out of the office to clear my head a bit, though Lester Yates was always dancing on the fringes of my subconscious. The duties of my job were considerable. However, in the days since the task force was formed, I had started pushing off more of those responsibilities to my subordinates so I could focus on Lester. I had spent hours poring over Moretti's binders.

I needed a break.

We were standing in Jerry's bass boat, tossing skirted jigs into the remains of a giant elm that had fallen into the shallows. A red-tailed hawk sat on the root ball of the elm and watched us cast. Jerry often threw carp or bluegill he caught onto the shore for the raptor. "I shouldn't do it; it makes him lazy," Jerry said. "Look at him, waiting for a free breakfast."

The largemouth were hitting hard. I had lost track of how many I had caught, but it was more than Jerry, which made him a little salty. When I landed a twenty-two-inch bass, Jerry said, "I think you're just catching the same damn fish over and over."

"That doesn't count?" I asked.

"Not if the fish is so stupid that it keeps biting on the same jig."

The nine-acre pond was northeast of Columbus on Jerry's property in Licking County. The spread was twenty-one acres, the most prominent feature being a log house with a towering peak and floor-to-ceiling windows that sat on a hillside and overlooked the pond and Bowl Run, a clear-running stream that rimmed the property to the west and fed the pond. I sent the jig back into the scrub and said, "Jerry, this is a hell of a nice spread. Just how much money did you make as a cop?"

"A lot," he said. "And I wasn't on the take. I worked every special-duty gig I could get. I was usually between one wife and the next, and I had a lot of time on my hands, so I had to keep busy. You know what cops normally do when they have a lot of extra time on their hands, don't you?"

"I'm not sure I do."

"They drink to excess and find other women to marry them. It's a vicious cycle. You end up with a bad liver and a host of women living in houses that you bought. Women marry cops because they think it will be exciting . . . until they're married to us for a week and a half. That's when they figure out that we can't leave our jobs at work, and we're soured on life because every day we have to deal with pedophiles, rapists, murderers, and every other degenerate that society pukes into our laps. Oh, and we drink too much. Did I mention that? Beyond that, we're absolute gems to be around."

I landed another bass.

He shook his head and turned away. After I released my captive, Jerry asked, "So how did D. Kendrick take the news that you have some doubts about his handiwork?"

"He lost his mind," I said.

"What's your heart telling you about all this?"

"My heart has faith in humankind and doesn't want to think that you'd put a man on Death Row to enhance your political career. Unfortunately, my gut tells me that D. Kendrick was looking for a ticket to Columbus."

"Lester Yates was the perfect foil—a disposable member of society." Jerry reeled in his jig, sat down, and began digging through his tackle box for a different lure. "Do you think we're going to get this done, chief?"

"It's a long shot, at best. I remember when I was a kid, I was watching this science fiction show, and this guy was living in the normal world, but everything around him was moving in super slow motion. He can see impending disasters, but he can't stop them. He sees this kid on a tricycle is going to get hit by a car, but he is powerless to stop it. It's as if he does not exist in that world. I thought about that show the other day. The clock is ticking toward Lester's execution; I am the most powerful law-enforcement agent in the state, and yet I feel powerless to stop it. To get him off, we're going to have to prove that someone else killed Danielle Quinn. Anything short of that and the governor won't even consider commuting the sentence. He doesn't want to appear weak on crime with a presidential bid looming. And I think he wants to protect D. Kendrick. He's a loyal member of the Hillbilly Mafia."

Jerry held up the line with the new jig. "I'm going to start reeling them in one after the other." He sent his line out. "Let me ask you this: You don't think there's anything special about Danielle Quinn, do you, other than Yates had the credit card?"

"I'm not following you."

"What is it about Quinn that made D. Kendrick so desperate to get a conviction? What do we know about her? Was there any connection with her and D. Kendrick? Was she having an affair with him or someone important? Maybe she knew things that could be damning to someone with political aspirations. Tell me what makes sense. They chased the Egypt Valley Strangler for years and all of a sudden they slap charges on little Lester Yates and pin all of the murders on him? According to those newspaper articles, after Yates was charged with trying to use the credit card, Brown said he had been cleared of any involvement in her disappearance. Then, bang, he's back in the crosshairs and arrested." Jerry turned and stopped talking until I made eye contact. "Was Lester arrested for political reasons that we don't yet understand? Or, was he arrested because they needed a conviction on the books to eliminate any suspicion of someone else in Danielle Quinn's murder? I think there's a lot about her that we still don't know."

TWELVE

Five weeks and four days before the scheduled execution of Lester Paul Yates.

Margaret had been unable to locate Lester Yates's defense attorney. She had checked the telephone and business directories for all of eastern Ohio, but she could not find a single Jim Smith with a law practice. She called the Ohio State Bar Association and learned that he had allowed his license to lapse in 2003, not more than a year after defending Lester. She had walked into my office late Friday and said, "He'd be a lot easier to find if his name wasn't Jim Smith. What do you want me to do, start calling every Jim Smith in Ohio?"

"Yes," I said. "And West Virginia, too."

"You are a very funny man, Mr. Van Buren."

"Let's start with the Jim Smiths in the Martins Ferry and Bellaire area. If he doesn't turn up, call some of the law firms in the area and see if anyone knows where he is and what he's doing."

"Monday?" she asked.

"Monday is fine."

That worked out well, as it freed me up to go with Jerry back to the Northeast Ohio Correctional Facility to question the inmate who had reportedly been bragging about killing prostitutes and dumping their bodies along the interstate. Jerry had gotten in touch with Reno Moretti on Friday afternoon to make the request. Moretti called back in ten minutes and told Jerry, "Fenicks said he would enjoy the company—ten a.m. Monday."

We arrived at the correctional facility at twenty before the hour and met Moretti in the lobby of the administration building. He handed me a typed sheet of information on the inmate.

"His name is Herman Fenicks, but he goes by the prison name of 'The Rap,'" Moretti said.

"Rap?" Jerry asked.

"No," Moretti said. "*The* Rap."

"What the hell does that mean?"

Moretti shrugged. "I try not to spend a lot of time trying to understand inmate culture."

As Moretti led us to the visitation room, I began reading the information he had provided on Fenicks. He was forty-two, black, and behind his back the inmates referred to him as "Skitzo," for his erratic behavior and inability to focus on a conversation. Reportedly had a high IQ. Junior college dropout. Two years in the Army, unremarkable. Tells people he is a black belt in karate. No confirmation. Had been self-employed as a truck driver and had no arrest record before August 1, 2001. At 1:15 a.m. on that day, a Cuyahoga County sheriff's deputy on regular patrol pulled into a parking lot in a secluded section of Cuyahoga Valley National Park near the village of Walton Hills. His cruiser headlights shined on Fenicks, who had a leather belt around the neck of a prostitute he had picked up at a nearby truck stop. Fenicks attempted to run, but he stopped upon the deputy's order. The prostitute was Darcy Morrison. She said Fenicks had beaten her in the cab of his tractor, forced her to perform oral sex, and then dragged her into the woods where he again beat her and attempted to strangle her. Only the deputy's happenstance turn into the parking lot saved her life. Fenicks was charged with attempted murder, kidnapping, and assault. He was subsequently convicted and sentenced to thirty years in prison.

"This guy sounds like a real charmer," I said.

"He's a tough nut," Moretti said. "Of course, this place is full of tough nuts."

"And this, from the former light heavyweight champion of the world," I said.

"Boxing was tough, but it was a walk in the park compared to life inside these walls."

We were led into the prison's visitation room. Tables were spaced throughout the room, like a small dining hall. I would have preferred something more private, but I wasn't going to make that request at that point.

Tick-tock.

Moretti led us to a corner of the room where a man with the most perfectly shaped shaved head I'd ever seen was slouched in a chair, a cigarette wedged between two fingers, looking amused. He continued to smirk as we pulled out chairs on the other side of the rectangular table and sat down.

"Thanks for meeting with us, Mr. Fenicks," I said.

"You got lucky. My social calendar was a little light this morning, so I could work you all into the schedule. Besides, I thought this might be entertaining."

He leaned forward and rested his forearms on the edge of the table. The muscular outline of his chest and arms was evident through the loose-fitting, prison-issue shirt. His eyes were so dark you could barely see the pupils. He took a draw on his cigarette and blew a plume of smoke above our heads.

"No restraints?" Jerry said. "We were in here last week interviewing an inmate and they had him wrapped up in chains like Harry Houdini."

"He must've been a very dangerous man," Fenicks said. "There are a lot of bad actors around this joint, but I'm not one of 'em. I'm just a gentle soul. They don't worry about people like me."

"Good to know," Jerry said.

"We want to ask you a few questions," I said.

"Let's back up a little bit," Fenicks said. "I haven't heard you tell me the most important part of this."

"And that is . . . ?" I asked, though I had dealt with enough convicts in my life to know exactly what was coming.

"What's in this for me?"

"You don't even know what we want."

He laughed. "Two peckerwoods in suits come to the joint to see me, it doesn't take a genius to figure out what you want. In-for-mation. That's what you're here for, right? You need some information, and you think I have it. I'm game, but let me ask you again. What's in it for me?"

"What do you want?"

"What do you think? I want to get the fuck out of here."

"I'm pretty sure we can't accommodate that request."

"Well, you all better put something on the table."

There is one thing I have learned over the years about dealing with convicts. They'll make ridiculous demands and say they're not going to talk until those demands are met. But most of the time they keep talking. Convicts are con men, and they'll keep running their mouths in hopes of being able to extract something of value from you. If you walk away, they know they'll miss that opportunity. Sometimes they would ask me to look at their appeals, or put in a good word to the parole board, while other times it's as simple as a carton of cigarettes or a Big Mac. To some of them, it's a game. They like trying to outsmart the cops. I never cared what their motivation was, as long as they kept running their mouths. That was the case with Herman Fenicks. He rambled on for a few minutes, complaining about the justice system and what he claimed was his wrongful conviction, complaining about the prison food, complaining about the disproportionate number of black men in prison, but mostly he complained about the Cleveland Browns, their coach, and their lack of offense. "Our prison team could beat those sorry sonsabitches."

Moretti's fact sheet had been on the money. Fenicks was all over the place. We let him talk himself out. By the time he took a breather to light another cigarette, Jerry had had enough. "What do you know about women being strangled and dumped in an area around Piedmont Lake known as the Egypt Valley?" he asked.

"Nothing. Why should I?"

"Before you went to prison, it was a dumping grounds for women who had been sexually assaulted and strangled. We have some credible information that you knew about those deaths, that maybe you were responsible for some of them."

His facial expression never changed. He looked at me; he looked at Jerry; he took another drag off his smoke. "Completely untrue," Fenicks said. "I don't know who would make such a harmful accusation."

"So, you never bragged out in the yard that you had strangled women and dumped their bodies around Piedmont Lake?"

"I can't imagine what kind of animal would do such a thing. Where is this Piedmont Lake that you're talking about? I'll tell my mom and sisters to stay away from there."

I said, "Herman . . ."

He cut me off. "If you're not going to call me Mr. Fenicks, I'd prefer that you call me The Rap."

I nodded. "Okay, *The Rap*, let's not bullshit each other. There's a reason why we're talking to you. We are investigating a series of strangulation deaths where the bodies were dumped in the woods. More often than not, the victim was a prostitute. You were convicted of attempting to strangle a prostitute in the woods." I paused for dramatic effect. "I'm sure you can appreciate the similarities." I lifted the background sheet Moretti had given me and pretended to read it. "Fenicks was a truck driver. He was bragging in the yard that he had dumped bodies all along Interstate 70."

He ground out the stub of a cigarette. "I was a trucker—king of the road—but I don't know who'd be spreading lies like that. I already told you. I'm a gentle soul."

"When you were a trucker, did you ever drive through the Piedmont Lake area?"

"Probably. I was an over-the-road trucker. I drove everywhere."

"Are you familiar with that area?"

"Not particularly."

"Does the name Danielle Quinn ring a bell?"

"Nope. But just so you know, when I was outside these walls, I was quite the ladies' man." He grabbed his crotch and squeezed. "It's hard to keep track of all my conquests." He chuckled.

Jerry went for the jugular. "If you're such a ladies' man, what are you doing picking up hookers in truck stops?" The smirk melted off Fenicks' face. "Was Darcy Morrison going to be one of your conquests or just another one of your victims?"

"That was just a business transaction gone south," Fenicks said. "She had agreed to certain parameters and was failing to live up to her end of the bargain."

"I'm not sure you're the kind of man I'd want to do business with if you try to choke someone to death to settle a disagreement," I said.

"We were just two consenting adults doing what consenting adults do."

"Sure," Jerry said. "Because consenting women everywhere want to be choked to death with a belt."

"Danielle Quinn?" I repeated.

"Never heard of her," The Rap said.

"In about five weeks, the state of Ohio is going to execute a guy for the murder of Danielle Quinn," Jerry said. "It'd be a terrible thing to get up every morning for the rest of your life knowing that a man was executed for a crime you committed."

"Let me see if I've got this straight. You come in here trying to get Lester Yates off the hook. Yeah, I know who you're talking about. Little Lester. The *strangler!* And to do that, you want me to confess to a murder that I didn't commit, is that it?" He laughed loud and hard. "You mafuckers must be grasping at straws. If you had something on me, you would have hit me over the head with it. I know how you cops work. You wouldn't even know my name if someone hadn't made up a story about me talkin' in the yard. You got nothin' to offer, but in your wet dreams I confess, and your little white boy goes free and the nigger goes to Death Row. You're the attorney general of the state of Ohio, and that is the best you can do?" He crossed his arms and shook his head. "I am starting to have serious concerns about the quality of individuals that we are electing to our state government."

I reached into my suit jacket pocket and removed a color photo of Danielle Quinn that I had printed from a newspaper website. I set it on the table and pushed it toward Fenicks. "Danielle Quinn," I said.

"Means nothing to me," he said, shoving it back with two fingers. "I appreciate you boys stopping by. I was right. It's been highly entertaining, but we're done here."

THIRTEEN

The irony of the situation was not lost on me.

Most of my life had been spent protecting a secret. That secret had allowed a man wrongfully convicted of a murder to spend more than thirty years in a state penitentiary. He was a disreputable human being of the first degree, but that didn't negate the fact that my silence allowed him to sit in prison for a crime he did not commit.

Although I had eventually come clean and taken my story to the newspaper in the midst of my campaign for attorney general, that would carry no weight to my political enemies. On one hand, I would always be branded for my years of silence. Campaign managers would look for opportunities to expose that transgression as a character flaw, the sign of a man who could not be trusted. People at cocktail parties whispered of it. It was certain to be more than a casual mention in my obituary. Despite the enormity of my transgression, it did not haunt my days or my nights. Jack Vukovich went to prison, I remained silent, grew from an adolescent with a varsity jacket and class ring into adulthood and a position of authority. For years and years, I did not break the pledge of silence I made to my friends, and the memory of that day grew ever fainter in my memory.

Now, however, I was desperate to prove another man's innocence of a crime I believed he did not commit. I'd had no problem allowing a reprobate like Jack Vukovich to sit in prison, but yet I found the victimization of Lester Yates appalling. Lester's situation was consuming my nearly every waking hour. He was like a bad song that gets stuck in your head, refusing to relent. Why? Why did Jack Vukovich dissolve away while Lester Yates droned on in my ear? Did I push Vukovich to the deep recesses of my brain as a defense mechanism? Maybe.

But that doesn't explain why Lester dominated my thoughts.

There were obvious reasons. I wanted to protect both an innocent man and my own political future. But there was a beehive of adrenaline surging in my chest, a renewed excitement for my job, and it was because little Lester Yates had put me back in the hunt. I wasn't sitting at my desk pushing papers. I was doing the work I was born to do, and it had become very personal. D. Kendrick Brown was out there doing everything he could behind my back to protect his reputation and make sure Lester was executed, and the mere thought of that was like a summer rash running up my back. I hate to lose. I did not like it on a ball field, and I certainly did not want to end up on the short end of a battle to save a man's life. I didn't know if I was going to be successful, but I was willing to run to complete exhaustion.

⋆ ⋆ ⋆

I knew approaching Herman Fenicks had been a long shot, but it was one we needed to take. Jerry sensed my disappointment. We were barely out of Mahoning County when he said, "You didn't really expect him to kick in to anything, did you?"

"No, but you know how cons are. I was hoping he'd start talking, figuring he was smarter than us, and drop something we could use."

"That would have been nice, but we had nothing to offer him, and he knew that. What if we asked Moretti to hook us up with the snitch?"

"That might work as an eleventh-hour bailout, but having a snitch repeat something he supposedly heard in the prison yard is certainly not enough to get a conviction, and I doubt it would be enough to convince the governor to delay the execution. We need something solid. Let's cross-check fingerprints and DNA and see if anything they lifted at the murder scenes can be connected to Fenicks."

We grabbed burgers at a fast-food drive-through and were back in the office by three o'clock. "How'd it go?" Margaret asked.

"Not great," I said. "Did you have any luck tracking down Yates's defense attorney?"

"That wasn't great, either. None of the Jim Smiths in the phone book are our boy. I called about twelve lawyers in the area. Some of them remembered him, but no one knows what happened to him. They said he just dropped off the radar. One of the secretaries I talked to said Smith was a friend of her cousin, and she heard he had moved out of the area. I asked her if she would check with the cousin and find out where he went, and she said she would."

"It's a start," I said.

Margaret's phone began ringing as I stepped into my office. I heard her answer the phone, followed by the sound of her chair rolling backward over the plastic floor pad. I hadn't yet taken off my jacket when she was in front of my desk. "It's Alfonso Majestro from the governor's office."

"Send it through." I let it ring three times before picking it up. "How's it going, Alfonso?"

Without preamble or niceties, he said, "The governor wants to know how the Yates investigation is going."

"Really? Then why doesn't the governor call me?"

There was a slight hesitation on the other end of the line, as if he couldn't quite process the question. When he did, I could hear the air rushing through flared nostrils. "Because he's the goddamn governor and he doesn't have to call. He's got people like me to do it for him. Now try not to be a smart-ass for five seconds and give me an answer. What's going on with Yates?"

"Nothing."

"What's that supposed to mean?"

"Exactly what I said, Alfonso. Nothing. We haven't had long enough to look at it. I've got serious doubts about Yates's guilt, but I can't prove he didn't commit the murder. By the way, I told the governor that I would keep him posted, and when I have something to report, I will. So why are you breathing down my neck?"

I knew the answer to that question. Three seconds after I had left the office of D. Kendrick Brown, he was most likely on the phone to the governor in a wild panic. He had a lot riding on Lester Yates's execution. Commuting Yates's sentence would not damage Wilinski's chances of getting to the White House. It could, however, destroy D. Kendrick's legacy, severely damaging his chances of being marched out for display during a presidential campaign or sucking down diet colas in a comfy office in Washington.

"You need to understand something, Van Buren," Majestro said. "The days of running the state of Ohio are about over. The politics around here are Mickey Mouse compared to running a presidential campaign. We're about ready to step onto the big stage, and I'm not leaving anything unchecked and that includes your little investigation. If there's anything new, I want to know about it."

"I told you there was nothing to report."

"I see. So what do you want me to tell the governor, that you've been sitting on your thumbs for the past week?"

For the record, I do not anger easily. You've got to poke the bear quite a few times to get me riled. But that was never the case when I was dealing with Alfonso Majestro. He could get under my skin like no one else. Every syllable that came out of his mouth dripped of condescension. Every time I had to deal with Alfonso, it was as though someone was blowing salt in my eyes.

The rage that was boiling up from my gut shot darts into my lungs and cannonades of flames into the base of my skull. My right hand strangled the receiver, and had Majestro been in the room it would have taken all my willpower not to rake it across the side of his little ferret face. I took one calming breath and said, "I gave you the answer you wanted. I'm hanging up now."

Ever so gently, I set the receiver back in the cradle; he was still talking when it clicked in his ear and the line went dead.

It wasn't ten seconds before the phone rang in Margaret's office. A few seconds later, my phone rang. "It's Mr. Majestro," she said.

"Of course it is. Please tell him I'm in a meeting and can't be disturbed."

At four-thirty, Margaret went upstairs for a baby shower for one of the secretaries in the environmental enforcement division. She had been surprised—and a little touched, I think—to have received the invitation, and I encouraged her to go. I gave her a hundred dollars to buy a gift from the two of us, and she happily went to the shower.

At five-fifteen, I locked my door and headed to the parking garage. I could hear voices coming from within the Lester Yates war room as I passed by it. I hoped they were having a more productive day than me. I took the elevator down to the parking garage and was lost in my thoughts; I was at the tailgate of my pickup truck before I saw Wilinski's bodyguard, the behemoth Danny Doyle, standing in front of my door, his arms folded and the seams of his sport coat stretching over his massive shoulders. I would be lying if I told you this wasn't a terrifying sight.

When I was growing up in Crystalton, I thought I was one of the toughest kids in town. But once you leave that cocoon and become a prosecutor, you realize there are people in the world who could hurt you very badly and take great pleasure in doing so, and you would be defenseless to stop them. Danny Doyle was one of those men. When you have to look up another man's nostrils to get to his eyes, and he has hands the size of catcher's mitts and arms as big as sewer pipes, no rational human being would claim not to be scared.

He glared down at me but didn't say a word. I said, "Do you want to move so I can get in my truck?"

He made one sideways motion of his head; I looked and saw the black sedan with tinted windows parked on the other side of the garage. I walked over and got into the back seat with Governor Jim Wilinski. He was smiling. "I understand we're having a little communications problem," he said.

"I guess it depends on your idea of communications. I don't have a problem communicating with anyone until they start talking to me like I'm the neighbor's dog taking a dump on their front yard."

"I understand that. Alfonso's a good guy. He's just wound a little tight, is all. That's a kind way of saying that he can be abrasive at times, but he has my best interests at heart. Moving forward, I would appreciate it if you would take that into consideration so that he doesn't have another complete meltdown in my office."

"I'll do my best. Perhaps you should sign him up for an etiquette class."

"I'll talk to him. In the meantime, where are we with Mr. Yates?"

"Exactly what I told Majestro. I have my suspicions, but I have nothing solid to prove he didn't do it. My gut tells me we've got the wrong guy in prison."

"I've got to have more than your gut, Hutch."

"I understand that, but you need to be very careful with this, Governor. If we execute him, that doesn't mean evidence stops coming in. We interviewed a guy in prison this morning who might be connected to some of the murders. If we find out he's connected after Yates is executed, we can't bring him back to life and the damage to your political future would be significant, and probably permanent."

He nodded, measuring my words. "You know, of course, that Mr. Brown is highly upset about all this."

"In all candor, Governor, he should be. His star witness was a total flake, and outside of the credit card there's nothing to link Yates to the corpse."

He nodded and wiped at his nose. "I'm the last guy who wants to see the wrong man executed, but you understand my dilemma. I'm also the last man who wants to see a serial killer walk."

"We're in the same boat, Governor."

He reached out and shook my hand. "Keep me in the loop. I've got confidence in you."

I reached for the door handle, then pulled back. I pointed at Doyle, who was now standing by the front fender of the limousine. "Why the muscle? You could have just picked up the phone."

"That's true, but I wanted to make sure you understood the importance of keeping the lines of communications open. Danny is a man of few words, but he's a very effective communicator in his own way, don't you think?"

FOURTEEN

Five weeks and three days before the scheduled execution of Lester Paul Yates.

Margaret beat me to the office the next morning and had the coffee going by the time I arrived. She brought in the pot and filled my cup. "Thank you, Margaret. What's on the agenda today?" I asked.

"I thought you were going back out of town."

"I am. Is there anything I need to take care of while I'm on the road?"

"Definitely. If I have to talk to Stan Carmine's assistant one more time and make an excuse for why you're not returning the calls of the chairman of the Ohio Republican Party, I'm going to scream."

"Okay, I don't want that. I'll call him from the car as soon as I'm on the road."

"You do that, please."

She stood at my desk. I knew the look. There was another question coming. "I've got a busy morning; out with it, Margaret."

"What was going on out there last night?"

I truly didn't know what she was talking about. "Last night?"

Her brows arched. "Last night, in the parking garage, with Goliath and the most powerful man in Ohio."

"Oh, that." I paused. "How did you see that?"

"I was getting in my car after the baby shower, and I saw you getting into the governor's limousine."

"It was nothing."

"It sure looked like something."

"That conversation I had with Alfonso Majestro yesterday afternoon went a little south, and the governor thought he needed to intervene."

"You're telling me that the governor of the state of Ohio needed to settle an argument between you and Mr. Majestro?" She set the coffee pot on my desk and folded her arms. "Why? Did Mr. Majestro scurry into his office like a little rat?"

I laughed out loud. Margaret had a way of breaking down situations to their most fundamental elements. "Probably. But things are a little tense over at the governor's office these days. He's getting ready to announce his presidential run, and they're stressed. They don't want anything blowing up in their face."

"I can see that." She sat down in the chair next to my desk. "Do you think Governor Wilinski has a real chance to be president of the United States?"

"Absolutely. He's the darling of the national Republican Party. He's the complete package—smart, handsome, former professional athlete, personable, good track record running the state. But he knows things are going to get a lot hotter after he announces his candidacy. The national media will be all over him looking for dirt. That's what happens when you declare a run for president."

"Does he have anything to worry about?"

"It depends. As long as all his lady friends keep quiet, he should be okay."

My profoundly religious assistant's eyes looked as though they were ready to launch from their sockets. "Lady friends?"

"The governor has a teeny little problem keeping his manhood holstered."

"Mmm-mmm-mmm-mmm-mmm, that boy had better get right with Jesus. He has a beautiful wife and he's out running around?"

I took a drink of my coffee and said, "Yes, he does and yes, he is."

She waited for my elaboration. I knew she was waiting and purposefully remained silent.

Her eyes turned from saucers to slits. "Do you think it's okay for him to cheat on his wife?"

"I didn't say anything of the sort. He's sleeping with two of the most gorgeous women I've ever personally known. And one of them is his wife. I think he's just greedy."

"That is not funny, Mr. Van Buren."

"It's sort of funny."

"Not even a little bit. Your attempt at humor speaks volumes."

"That is totally unfair, Margaret. I simply make it a point not to involve myself in other people's marriages, or their affairs, or anything else. Given the disaster that was my only marriage, I'm the least qualified person around when it comes to relationships. Besides, unless you're in that bedroom, you don't know what's going on . . . or what isn't going on."

"Oh, oh, is that how it is? If it's *not* going on, it's okay to cheat?"

With the thumb and middle finger of my right hand, I pinched my temples and said, "I've got a long day ahead of me, and you're giving me a headache, Margaret. I'm not saying that it's okay to step out on your wife. What I'm saying is, men are very simple creatures—we're like cats."

"Cats?"

"Yes. Cats. When a cat doesn't get fed at home, sometimes he wanders down the street."

"Mmm-mmm-mmm-mmm-mmm, Hutchinson Wilson Van Buren, I cannot believe what you're saying." Her head was sliding back and forth on her shoulders, a sign that I had angered her greatly. "Let me tell you something, Mr. I-Got-All-the-Answers. I was married three times, and I'm here to tell you those cats ate well—*very* well. In fact, every time they were hungry, they got fed. And every one of those kitties meowed their way down the street looking for a takeout menu."

"Sounds like the next time you get married you need to find a better kind of cat."

"There ain't gonna be no next time. I'm all done with those kind of kitties."

* * *

As I was heading out, I rapped twice on the door of the war room and walked inside. The four interns were at one end of the table with scissors and glue, putting together their notebooks of newspaper clippings.

"It doesn't take all four of you to do that, does it?" I asked. I didn't wait for an answer. "Liberatore, get your things and come with me. You'll need a pen and a notebook. I'm going to need you to take some notes at an interview."

She grabbed an oversized purse off the table and said, "I'm ready."

* * *

We took my state car, a nondescript, gray Ford Taurus that vibrated like a space capsule on reentry if you went over sixty-five miles an hour. I was a mile past the eastern outerbelt on Interstate 70 when I pulled my cell phone from my jacket pocket and punched in the number for the headquarters of the Ohio Republican Party. "It's Hutch Van Buren," I said when Stan Carmine's administrative assistant answered the phone.

"Well, praise the Lord," she said. "We thought you might be dead."

"No, that's just wishful thinking on the part of a lot of people. Is Stan available?"

"Hold on. He's in a meeting, but I know he wants to talk to you."

He picked up a few seconds later. "You're a hard man to get a hold of," he said.

"I know. I've been pretty busy lately—got a lot on my plate."

"Okay, then let's get right to the point—Shelly Dennison. She said she met with you."

"She did."

"Good. So, we're a go? She'll be your campaign manager?"

"I didn't say that, Stan. I still need to decide."

"Hutch, seriously, what's to decide? She is the absolute best in the game, and we need to get started."

"I know, but I've already done the dance with Shelly. You weren't around when I ran the first time, but she was my campaign manager and things didn't end too well."

"Yeah, yeah, yeah, I heard all about it; she walked out on you at the end of your campaign. I got it. But you were the one who went to the newspaper reporter with that story about the kid getting killed. Come on, Hutch, who does that? No wonder she walked out."

"Are you kidding, Stan? You think that walking out in the middle of my campaign was justified? You realize I was the client, right? I was the one writing the checks."

"Okay, I'll grant you that. She could have handled that a little better, but maybe there also was some particular animus there because of your personal relationship."

"You know about that, too, huh?"

"It's a pretty small pool we swim in. There really aren't many secrets. How about we let bygones be bygones and give Shelly the ball?"

I looked over at Liberatore, who was pretending not to listen. When she looked at me, I rolled my eyes. She used a cupped hand over her mouth to keep from laughing out loud.

I had known all along I was going to hire Shelly, but I was hoping to let her sweat it out for a few more weeks. I wanted Shelly to know I was over her. At least I think I was, but I could never be certain. "Okay, Stan, that's fine. Tell her she's hired."

"Great, great, great. That's really great. Do you want to call her?"

"No, you do it. She's too exhausting, and I don't have two hours to talk on the phone right now. Tell her we can get started whenever she's ready."

"You're going to be glad you did this, Hutch."

"I hope so, Stan. Gotta fly."

I hung up and said to Liberatore, "Do you want to be my campaign manager?"

"I don't think so," she said.

"Smart girl. Listen, Liberatore, I was a little rough on you the other day in the meeting. I just wanted to say that I'm sorry about that."

"That's okay. Don't worry about it. I'd been warned in advance about your temper."

I looked at her with what was no doubt an expression of absolute incredulity. "You had been warned about my temper?"

"Uh-huh."

"Really?"

"Yes."

"But I don't have a bad temper."

"That's not the way a lot of people who work for you see it."

"But I wasn't even angry with you. I just thought it was something an intern in my office should be able to figure out."

"I understand, and I appreciate your apology."

"But you still think I have a temper?"

She made the slightest of shoulder shrugs.

"Well I don't," I said.

"Whatever you say, Mr. Van Buren. You're the attorney general and you obviously have strong feelings about it, and I don't want to argue with you."

I did not like being played by a twenty-five-year-old, but I was pretty sure that was what just happened. I wanted to continue the argument, but she had already won. So I just shut up.

FIFTEEN

We exited Interstate 70 in St. Clairsville and drove down Route 40—the old National Road—toward Blaine. My cell rang; I didn't answer. When we turned on Barton-Blaine Road, I pointed out Ed Herrick's home to Liberatore and reminded her that his daughter had been the first victim of the Egypt Valley Strangler. She looked around and said, "This is a depressing area."

As we passed the baseball field, I said, "During the summers when I was in college, I played semipro ball there for the Blaine Bombers of the United Mine Workers Baseball League."

She didn't seem particularly impressed.

"I was a catcher. Played a little third base, too."

"Uh-huh."

"That was during better times. This valley used to jump like you can't imagine."

"You're right. I can't imagine it." Her brows pinched down. "You used to live around here?"

"Born and raised—just up the road a little ways in Crystalton."

She absorbed the information without comment.

I had explained our mission to Liberatore during the drive. There were a lot of factors that didn't add up in this case, and Danielle Quinn was one of them. She didn't fit the mold of most of the victims of the Egypt Valley Strangler. From the newspaper articles I had read about her, she seemed to be trying to do everything right. Quinn was a single mother of a two-year-old daughter who was described in one newspaper article as "the light of her life." She was working as a waitress at the Shenandoah Truck Stop at night while attending the local community college in pursuit of a nursing degree. A passage in one article quoted a coworker who said that in the weeks before her death, Quinn had bought a car—used, but new to her—and she was so proud of herself for saving the money and paying cash for the vehicle.

"The other victims were all . . . let's say, from the wrong side of the tracks—prostitutes, drug users, runaways," I said. "Most of them had a jacket."

"A jacket?" she said.

"It's law-enforcement jargon for the file in which a convict's information is kept."

"Interesting."

My phone rang again; it was from the same number as a few minutes earlier. Again, I didn't answer.

We were going to interview the brother of Danielle Quinn. His name was Wayne Tomczak. He lived in an area they called Cougar Ridge; he was two years younger than Danielle and worked the evening shift as a kennel attendant at Wheeling Downs, the greyhound track on Wheeling Island. I was banking on him being home.

"We don't have an appointment?" Liberatore asked.

"You don't make appointments with people like this, and before you ask me why, it's because they don't usually keep their appointments. More importantly, you want to catch them off guard. You have a better chance of getting an honest answer out of them if it's a surprise attack."

"What do you mean by 'people like this'?"

"A drunk who works cleaning crap out of dog cages."

"Have you ever met him?"

"No."

"Then how do you know he's a drunk?"

There was an accusatory tone to her voice.

"Because I did a background check, and he's had three drunk driving arrests in the last two years."

She nodded.

"It's not my first rodeo, Liberatore."

"Rodeo?"

The phone rang, and the same number came up again.

"Never mind," I said.

We drove through Barton and onto Hell's Kitchen Road, crossing over Town Run to where a mailbox was strapped to a steel post with duct tape. The gravel and mud drive that ran into the hills of Cougar Ridge had spilled its contents onto the asphalt during the last storm. The wheels of the state car dropped into muddy puddles and we climbed a grade, honey locust trees crowding the drive from one side, the rusting hulks of a dozen spent cars and pickups lining the other.

Liberatore's head spun back and forth, her mouth hanging open. I couldn't tell if the expression on her face was one of amazement, confusion, or fear. Or maybe a combination of all three.

"Where'd you grow up, Liberatore?"

"Upper Arlington."

It was one of Columbus's most affluent suburbs. "You probably don't see a lot of cars up on blocks in Upper Arlington, huh?"

"Not really."

"Welcome to the Ohio Valley."

We followed the drive around a hillside to where a house trailer that leaned hard to port was perched precipitously on the top of the hill.

Another call. I turned off my cell phone.

I parked the car behind a Dodge Neon that looked like it had been through a war—dings and dents everywhere, the driver's-side rearview mirror was hanging by its cables, plastic covered the front passenger window, a metal clothes hanger was wedged into the socket as a makeshift antenna, and it bore the bright yellow and red license plates issued by the state of Ohio to individuals with restricted driving privileges. "He's sporting his party plates," I said, using the street slang for the plates that are given for repeated drunken driving convictions. We stepped out of the car and headed up a muddy grade toward the trailer. Within a hundred-foot circumference of the trailer, I counted an additional four cars and two pickup trucks in various stages of rot and being consumed by the hillside—foxtail growing through the wheel wells and poison ivy snaking out the grills and hoods. The hillside was littered with an assortment of other trash, including a half-dozen lawn mowers, two go-karts, an ATV with a broken front axle, and a pleasure boat with its wooden hull rotted to the ribs. At the back corner of the trailer, a female German shepherd with a raw spot on her hip the size of a pie plate was standing on a bare patch of muddy earth; she was shaking, looked undernourished, and was tied with a jack chain to the underside of the trailer. She looked at Liberatore and me with sad eyes, and if she could have talked I'm certain she would have asked us to put her out of her misery.

The doorbell didn't work; I rapped twice on the door. It was opened by a woman who I imagined had been quite attractive at one time. Her brown hair was streaked with heavy strands of gray, and a spider web of wrinkles ran away from eyes the color of wet slate. A cream-colored blouse was tucked neatly into her blue jeans; she was holding a cup of coffee. She blinked, looked at me for a moment, then Liberatore, my car, then back at me. She didn't speak.

"Is this the Tomczak residence?" I asked.

She looked back at the car, staring at its state of Ohio license plates. "What do you want?" she asked.

"I'll take that for a yes." I handed her my business card. "My name is Hutchinson Van Buren. I'm the attorney general for the state of Ohio. This is my associate, Ms. Liberatore. We're investigating the death of Danielle Quinn. I understand that Mr. Tomczak was Mrs. Quinn's brother. We'd like to speak to him, please."

A yellow tabby appeared and wrapped itself around her legs. It was in remarkably good shape compared to the German shepherd. The woman stared at the card; it did not seem to register with her that the chief law-enforcement officer of the state was standing on the metal stoop of her house trailer. After a moment, she pushed the cat out of the way with her heel, released her grip on the doorknob, and said, "Yeah, he was her brother. Come on in."

The interior of the trailer was dark; a television flickering in the corner was tuned to a courtroom reality show. It was stuffy and smelled faintly of cigarette smoke, marijuana, and mold. The woman said, "I was on the phone with my mother. Let me hang up."

When she stepped away, I asked, "What's your first name, Liberatore?"

"What? You don't know my first name?" She sounded hurt.

"I'm sorry. I have a lot of balls in the air, and I don't make it a point to learn the names of the interns."

"It's Denise."

"Okay. Denise. Good to know."

In a gentle tone, the woman said, "I don't know, Mama. They want to talk to him about Danielle. I will. I will. I promise, I will. I'll call you later." No sooner had she hung up the phone than she turned her head toward the back of the trailer and yelled like she was trying to be heard over a jet engine, "Wayne, there's a man out here to see you."

"Who is it?" he yelled back.

She patted her pockets as though looking for her car keys. She was searching for the business card she had set on the counter by the phone. "What's your name again?"

Out of the corner of my eye I could see Liberatore stifle a laugh. "Van Buren. Hutch Van Buren."

"Mr. Van Buren," she yelled. "He's from the state."

"What's he want?"

"He wants to talk to you about your sister."

"Which one?"

She looked at me and shook her head. "Which one do you think? Danielle."

"I don't know nothing."

"Get out here and talk to the man."

The toilet flushed and pipes rattled before Wayne Tomczak came out of the bathroom and started walking toward the front of the trailer. He was pinching a longneck bottle of Iron City beer between his fingers while trying to zip and button his fly as he walked. Like his wife, I suspect there had been a time when he had been good-looking. There was moon-shaped decay on his teeth just below the gum lines, and his cheeks had the hollowed-out look of addiction. His hair was gray and greasy, and appeared to have been combed with his fingers. Before he had finished zipping his pants, he stuck out his hand and said, "How ya doin'? I'm Wayne."

I was hesitant to shake that hand, but did so anyway, making a mental note to slather it with hand sanitizer when I got back to the car. "I'm Hutchinson Van Buren, Mr. Tomczak. I'm the attorney general for the state of Ohio." I saved Liberatore the pain of introduction.

His wife, whose name I would later learn was Shirley, handed Wayne my business card. He looked at me, squinted, and asked, "*The* attorney general?"

"Yes, sir."

"The attorney general for the goddamn state of Ohio is in my living room. Well, I'll be a son of a bitch. And you're here to talk about Danielle?"

He liked to get close when he spoke, and his breath stank of beer and an acute disregard of dental hygiene, and I held my breath. "I am," I said.

"Well, hell's bells, sit down, sit down."

He sat down on the couch. I took a seat in the chair next to him; Liberatore moved cautiously toward a cloth chair that was stained with every major food group. The cat, of course, came over to rub against my leg. I tried to move him aside with my foot, but he wouldn't take the hint. I'm allergic to cats.

"Ah, Princess Sophie likes you," Shirley said.

"They always do," I said.

Wayne took a hit from his Iron City and said, "Why do you want to talk to me about Danielle?"

"We're taking another look at her murder, trying to do a little deeper dive."

"Why now?" Shirley asked. "She's been gone almost seven years."

The muscles around Wayne's jaw tightened, and I sensed he did not care for his wife's participation in the conversation.

"We're doing the investigation because the man who was convicted of her murder is scheduled to be executed next month."

Frown lines stretched across Wayne's forehead and his face contorted into a look of puzzlement, like an elementary school student standing at the chalkboard trying to solve a long division problem. I suspected this was news to him. "They ain't already killed him?" he asked.

"He just said they were going to execute him next month," Shirley said.

"I didn't ask you, did I? Shut the fuck up."

If the verbal assault upset Shirley, she didn't show it, and I assumed it was not an uncommon exchange. However, Liberatore's eyes widened. It probably wasn't the kind of language she heard around the living room in Upper Arlington.

"Were you close to your sister?" I asked.

"Not far," he said. "She just lived out around Bethesda."

"No, I mean were you a close family? Did you see her frequently?"

"Not real often."

"When was the last time you saw your sister before she disappeared?"

"I can't say exactly when. I seen her here and there, at the mall or Kroger, stuff like that. Shirley had a job waitressing at the restaurant in the Hampton Inn, and I went to pick her up one night, and I saw Danielle in there with some guy. I walked over to their table to say hello, and she acted like I had some kind of stink on me."

"Had you been cleaning cages at the dog track?"

"Yeah. I was on my way home from work."

"Maybe you did have some stink on you."

He frowned. "You don't pull no punches, do you?"

"No offense. Let me ask it this way: When was the last time you and Danielle spent time together with your family?"

He frowned and turned to his wife, looking for help. "It was at your mother's funeral," Shirley said.

"Yeah, I guess that was it—when my momma died," he said.

"When was that?" I asked.

Again, Wayne looked to Shirley, who said, "We hadn't seen Danielle in more than two years. She was pregnant at the funeral, and the baby had just had her second birthday when Danielle went missing."

"She was kind of high and mighty and didn't have much time for us," Wayne said.

"What's that mean?" I asked.

"Danielle forgot where she came from. She growed up just down the road in Barton with the rest of us, but as soon as she was out of high school . . ." He jerked a thumb over his shoulder. "Bam! She left and got her own apartment. She didn't want much to do with us after that."

"Is it fair to say you weren't particularly close?"

"I guess we wasn't."

"What happened to her daughter?"

"Her dad took her."

"The dad was in the picture?"

"They had a nasty breakup and the dad wanted . . . uh, what's the word, where he would get the kid?"

"Custody?" I asked.

"Yeah, when they got divorced, I heard it got real nasty. One of Shirley's sisters works at the courthouse and she said the dad wanted the kid really bad, but the judge gave her to Danielle."

I looked at Liberatore, who understood the importance of the statement.

"They had a contentious relationship?"

Wayne blinked.

"They hated each other's guts," Shirley said. "I don't know why they ever got married."

"When did they get divorced?" I asked.

"I don't know," she said. "Sometime between the funeral and when she got herself killed. Word was that she caught him fooling around, but I don't know that for sure. Like I said, we never saw her."

"What was the ex-husband's first name?"

"Cliff, but everyone called him Boots."

"Last name Quinn?"

"Yes, sir."

"Where does he live?"

"Hell if I know," Wayne said. "I ain't seen him in years. I heard after they got divorced that he moved down to downstate West Virginia somewheres."

We talked for a while longer. The conversation produced little else that would benefit the investigation. I was sure that Wayne Tomczak had the brains to clean out dog cages, but not much else. If he was an example of the rest of the family, I understood perfectly why Danielle Quinn had sprinted from the house after graduating.

I stood and looked out the window as the wind began to gust. The plastic sheeting had blown out of the window of the car and was flapping in the wind. I said, "The wind's blowing away your passenger-side window, Wayne."

"Yeah, that thing's a piece of shit, but it runs," he said. "That's the only thing I got left from my sister."

"Danielle?" I asked.

"My older sister got her television and jewelry, but that was only because she got to the apartment before the court sealed it up. Danielle had a couple thousand dollars in the bank, but the judge ruled that the money had to go to her kid, which was bullshit because why the hell does a two-year-old need money? I got the car."

"That's your sister's car—the one she was driving the day she disappeared?"

"Uh-huh. It's the only one she had."

"Mr. Tomczak, I'm afraid I'm going to need to search that car."

"Go ahead. There ain't nothin' in it but dirt and hamburger wrappers and beer bottles."

"No, I need to have it shipped to our laboratory near Columbus to be forensically searched."

"What? Oh, hell no. I don't care if you are the attorney general, that ain't your car and you ain't takin' it nowheres."

"I'm very sorry for the inconvenience, Mr. Tomczak, but I'm trying to make sure we don't execute an innocent man, and there may be latent evidence in that car that will help me do that."

"Yeah, well I'm sorry that sumbitch is rowing upstream, but I've got to get my ass to work tonight."

There was a key ring hanging on a hook by the door. "Are the car keys on that ring?"

Wayne dropped the beer bottle and foam spilled onto the carpet; he took two steps across the room as I reached for the key ring. "Keep your fucking hands off those keys" he said.

I pivoted on my right heel and snapped off a punch, driving my fist into his solar plexus. He was unprepared, and it stopped him like he'd hit a wall. Air rushed from his lungs; he wrapped his arms around his ribs and dropped to his knees, his face reddening as he struggled to pull in air, the nerves around his spine arcing like bare electric wires. He tried to speak; while his lips moved, all that came out was a noise that sounded like a scratching record, the saliva gurgling deep in his throat. Wayne's hands dropped to the carpet and he threw up his breakfast, which appeared to consist of about thirty-six ounces of beer.

Liberatore jumped up on her chair.

I looked over to Shirley to make sure she wasn't grabbing a paring knife to defend her man, but she had taken a couple of steps back into the kitchen, her eyes darting between me and her husband. And, unless I totally misread her face, there appeared to be a faint grin pursing her lips.

I squatted on my haunches next to him and said, "Wayne, we can make this as easy or as difficult as you want, but one way or another, that car is going to our lab. Understand?" He wretched and nodded his head a couple of times. "Good. I don't want to go through the aggravation of securing a search warrant. I need you to give me permission to take the vehicle. Do I have it?"

He nodded.

"I need to near you say, 'yes.'"

He eked out a barely audible, "Yeah."

"Very good. When you catch your breath and can talk, come outside."

"Where are the keys to that car?" I asked Shirley.

"They're right on that ring," she said, pointing.

"Get down off the chair and get them, Liberatore."

"That's the only car we've got," Shirley said.

"I counted at least a dozen cars out there in the yard."

"It's the only car we've got that *runs*."

"We'll work it out. Do you have a phone book—Yellow Pages?"

She opened a kitchen drawer and handed the book to Liberatore.

We stepped outside and walked across the gravel drive toward the car.

Liberatore said, "Uh-uh. Nope. Not at all. No temper whatsoever; not even a little hint of one."

I glared at her. "You and Margaret must get along famously."

"What's that mean?"

I ignored her question. "That was not a display of anger, Liberatore. That punch was simply self-defense."

"If you say so."

"Maybe you could learn a little lesson from that. A guy named Ricky Blood, who was probably the meanest human being to ever walk the streets of Akron, once told me if I knew a fight was coming that I should hit the guy right in the solar plexus."

"Why?"

"He said if a guy is high on mescaline, you can beat him in the face with a ball bat all day and he won't even know you're there, but if he can't breathe, he can't fight."

"How often do you get into a fight with someone like that?"

"My point is this, Liberatore: you're not very big, and if you stay in this business there'll come a time when you'll need to protect yourself. When that day comes, aim for the solar plexus and remember to drive your fist through the target."

"Are you friends with this Ricky Blood?"

"What? No. I try not to befriend psychopaths. Are you listening to anything I'm telling you?"

"Where is he?"

"If there's a God in heaven, he's burning in hell."

"He died?"

"I convicted him of murder, and he was executed."

"I don't believe in the death penalty."

"Is that a fact? Then how'd you manage to get an internship in my office?"

"I think it's unjustly administered."

"Really? Well, let me tell you about Ricky Blood. He kidnapped a beautiful young college student, the daughter of an Akron police officer, and tied her up in his basement where he tortured her for days, cutting her up with a razor and burning her with a cigarette lighter. He cut off her ears and repeatedly bit her, and do I need to tell you where?" I let the question hang unanswered for a moment. "He raped her repeatedly before taking her to a park where he set her on fire while she was still alive. Now, you tell me, Liberatore, does that sound like a guy we ought to be fighting to keep alive? Would you like him living next door to you?"

She swallowed hard and looked away. "That's horrible, but I don't understand why life in prison isn't a fit punishment."

"I never took any particular delight in seeing a man executed, but the punishment has to fit the crime."

"But now you're working to get Lester Yates off Death Row."

"That's because I don't think he killed Danielle Quinn. Jesus Christ, Liberatore, you're wearing me out." I pointed toward the Yellow Pages she was holding. "Find me a towing company with a flatbed truck. Tell them you work for me, and I need the car towed to the Bureau of Criminal Investigation in London, Ohio."

She looked at the phone book and grinned. "Who still uses a phone book?" she asked. "I can find one on my cell in ten seconds."

"However you would like to do it, Liberatore."

"That's going to cost a lot of money."

"Tell them the state of Ohio is good for it."

She began flipping through screens on her cell phone. "Oh, and for future reference, a throat strike is more effective at stopping someone than a punch to the solar plexus."

"Is that a fact?"

"Yes, it is a fact."

"Okay, first of all, I wanted to stop him; I didn't want to kill him. And you would know that how?"

"I'm a fourth-degree black belt in jujitsu." I looked her over. She was barely five feet tall and maybe a hundred pounds with her purse. Before I could say anything, she made a small, imaginary box with her hands. "I know what you're thinking, but you can pack a lot of dynamite in a little box, Mr. Van Buren."

Liberatore was growing on me. But I definitely needed to keep her away from Margaret.

SIXTEEN

While Liberatore was tracking down a tow truck, I walked toward the back of the property and the chained German shepherd. As I neared, she crawled beneath the trailer.

"Come here, girl," I said. She looked around, as though plotting an escape route. I knelt down. "It's okay. Come here." Her entire body quaked as she edged closer. When I reached out to pet her, she again moved away. "Come on, girl, I'm not going to hurt you. Come on. Come here." I held out my hand and let her have a sniff, then rolled it under her snout and scratched her chin. The rancid smell of rotting flesh filled my nostrils. Gently, I lifted her chin to see a leather collar embedded in the neck of the dog. It reminded me of the way a tree will ultimately consume a length of barbwire that has been nailed to it. She shuddered as I moved my hand closer to the collar; my fingertips were moist from the infection. "You poor rascal," I said, fishing my handkerchief from a hip pocket and trying to wipe the stench from my fingers. A steel bowl held a bit of rusty rainwater; there was no food. I continued to pet her while I turned on my cell phone. Six more calls from the same number, but no messages. I pecked out the phone number for Beth Kremer, who was the laboratory director at the Bureau of Criminal Investigation.

Beth was a holdover from the previous administration, but one I was happy to have on my team. My original intention had been to fire Beth and replace her with one of my own people. However, I gave her the courtesy of an interview and decided to keep her. I have always had a strict rule of never dating a subordinate, but I would probably make an exception for Beth if the opportunity ever presented itself. I had sensed the feeling might be mutual, but I hadn't tested those waters.

She was one of the smartest people I'd ever met. She was a scientist, ran a first-rate laboratory, and dealt in the black and the white. She also had a wicked sense of humor.

She picked up on the first ring.

"Beth, it's Hutch Van Buren."

"Mr. Attorney General. What can I do for you on this fine morning?"

"Quite a bit, actually. With any luck, in about four hours you're going to be receiving a Dodge Neon. It previously belonged to a woman named Danielle Quinn, who was murdered in 2000. I need you to go over the inside of this car and see if you can find any DNA samples that match up with anyone in the felony database."

"She was killed in 2000?"

"Yes."

"Please tell me the car has been sitting untouched in a garage."

"I would love to tell you that, but no. The victim's dunderhead brother has been driving it ever since."

"You're kidding me, right?"

"Nope."

"That will be like combing through a landfill. I can't make any promises; degradation of any samples will make it a longshot, at best. It's going to take a while."

"Unfortunately, we don't have a while for this one, Beth. I need you to put it into overdrive and make it priority one. There is a man on Death Row named Lester Yates who was convicted for the murder of the woman who owned this car. If there's any DNA evidence linking this car to a known criminal, I need to know about it yesterday."

"So I'm looking for a hair follicle, or a splatter of blood, or saliva that was dropped in the car seven years ago?"

"If it was in the car seven years ago, I can about guarantee that it's still there. I don't think this guy knows how to operate a vacuum cleaner."

"Sounds like some of the guys I date."

"Do the guys you date know how to operate a toothbrush?"

"Most of them."

"Well, the ones who do would be way ahead of this guy."

"Sounds positively charming."

"The car isn't any cleaner than its owner. I'm sending you a challenge. See what you can do for me."

"Got it. I'll get started as soon as it gets here."

"One more thing, Beth. D. Kendrick Brown doesn't need to know about this. He was the sheriff who arrested Yates and helped put him on Death Row."

"That certainly makes things a little more interesting. Okay, I'm on it. I'll . . . wait a minute. Lester Yates? Isn't he the strangler, the one in the newspapers that Mr. Brown has framed and hanging all over his office?"

"That's him."

There was a long silence on the phone as she processed the information. "You think this Yates didn't do it?"

"I'm having serious doubts. We can talk about that later. I've got some more work to do over here. If any issues come up involving Brown, you tell him this was a direct order from me."

"He doesn't usually get involved with things out here in the lab."

"If he knew it was related to the Yates case, he'd be perched on your shoulder."

As I walked back to the car, she said, "I'm on it, boss."

Liberatore was finishing up her phone call. "Big Valley Towing is on the way. They said they would haul it out."

"Good work," I said.

Another call. Again, I turned off the phone.

It was another five minutes before Wayne Tomczak staggered out of the house, one arm wrapped around his rib cage.

"You understand that you're one phone call away from going to jail for assault on a law officer, right?" I asked.

"If that's the case, how come I'm the one with the busted gut?"

I ignored the question, but the answer was obvious. *Because you're a dumbass.*

"Does your wife have a valid driver's license?"

"Yeah."

"Good. Here's what I'm going to do for you, Mr. Tomczak. Liberatore here is going to take your wife over to Wheeling and rent you a car so you don't miss work. I don't want to be responsible for someone losing their job." I pulled my money clip out of my pocket and gave my credit card to Liberatore. I pointed toward the door and said to Tomczak, "Go get your wife."

When he had disappeared into the trailer, I turned to Liberatore and said, "Make sure that vehicle is rented in her name, and load it up with as much insurance as you can."

Shirley bounded out the door and down the steps of the stoop, her hair pulled back in a ponytail, smiling—happy, I assumed, to be getting away from Wayne and the beer vomit. She and Liberatore left in the state car a few minutes later.

I was leaning against the hood of the Neon waiting for the tow truck to arrive when Wayne walked back outside. He stopped on the collage of gravel and weeds that were pounded into the ground around the stoop, pulled a pack of off-brand cigarettes from his shirt pocket, and fished out one with a pinkie and thumb. He cupped one hand around a disposable lighter and touched the cigarette to the flame. After he had taken a hit and exhaled the exhaust, he held out the pack and asked, "Want one?"

"No, thanks," I said. "I have enough bad habits."

He wandered a little closer, hesitantly, not unlike the cautious approach of the scared German shepherd. "That was a pretty good shot you gave me," he said.

"I needed to get your attention."

"You could have just asked."

"You didn't act like you were in any mood to listen to reason."

Over my years as a prosecutor, I had interviewed hundreds of criminals. I often found that once they had been bested and accepted defeat, they were generally more amenable to honesty. Or at least their version of honesty. I sensed I had a window of opportunity with Wayne. "Now that your wife's gone and it's just me and you, why don't you tell me a little bit about your sister."

"What else do you want to know?"

"Just tell me what kind of person she was."

"She was a pretty good girl, really. I read a lot of articles in the newspaper about the girls who were getting themselves killed by that strangler. All the articles made them sound like lowlifes and whores. That wasn't Danielle. In high school the boys liked her plenty. You know, when you're a girl comin' out in these hollows, every boy thinks you're easy pickin's. She wasn't like that. She married a guy who was a couple years ahead of us in high school. I don't know what happened for sure, but like I said, I heard Danielle caught him stepping out, and she wasn't the type for giving someone a second chance. They divorced when the baby was just teeny. After the divorce, she started back to school at the community college. She was studying to be a nurse. She was always smart—wicked smart. She was working nights at the truck stop because that scumbag ex-husband of hers wouldn't give her a dime to help raise that baby."

"Do you know that for sure? You said you didn't have much contact with her."

"I'd hear things. Gossip flies up and down these hollows like the wind."

"You mentioned that you saw your sister at a restaurant with a guy. Was that her boyfriend?"

"I ain't for sure. Maybe. She didn't say. I walked up to their table and said hi, and all she said was, 'Albert, this is my brother, Wayne.' He didn't shake my hand or nothin'. He just kinda nodded, like I shouldn't be breathing his air. He was a skinny little shit with a little rat face and a wimpy moustache. They went back to their conversation like I wasn't even there."

"A rat face?"

"Yeah—squished head and pointy nose."

A wave of ice rolled down my shoulders. "Could it have been a ferret?"

"Huh?"

"Nothing. You recall that his name was Albert?"

"It's been a long time and I ain't for sure, but it was something like that."

"Could it have been Alfonso?"

"Maybe. Could have been. I don't know. Alfred, Albert, Alphonso, something like that. What I do remember was that he was all pressed and neat, like one of those prissy boys who don't never get their hands dirty. We were on our way home later that night and the old lady was going on and on about how neat he was, and what nice clothes he had, what good manners he had, and did I see that his shoes were all polished? Shit like that. I remember that because I know Shirley doesn't think I'm much of a prize, and it was a chance for her to remind me of it."

"When was this?"

He shrugged. "I don't remember. Sometime before she died."

"Really? Sometime before she died?" I fought to conceal the grin. "You're sure about that?"

If he caught the sarcasm, it wasn't evident. "I don't remember when it was, exactly."

"This boyfriend, did he come to her funeral?"

"I don't recollect. I don't know if she was still seeing him when she got killed or not. He could have been there, but it was kind of a mess. When they caught that dude trying to use her credit card, we figured for sure he was the one who did it, but the police said he didn't have nothing to do with her murder. Then they turned around and arrested him."

"What did you think about that?"

"What was I supposed to think? The cops said he did it, so I figured he must've done it. I saw his picture in the paper and went to the trial. I can tell you this much, that weaselly little dude didn't look like anyone my sister would've been interested in. How he ended up out there at that lake with her . . ." Tomczak shrugged and flicked the nub of his cigarette into the weeds. "I guess we'll never know for sure. I didn't have the greatest relationship with my sister, but she deserved a lot better than this, I can tell you that much."

We were still standing in the yard when the groan of a diesel engine filled the hollow. Black smoke snaked into the trees along the gravel drive as the tow truck came into view. A lean man without a tooth in his head and a stump where his left hand should have been loaded up the car on the flatbed. I gave him a business card with the address of the lab and Beth's name and phone number.

He looked at the card and said, "You're sure those state boys are going to pay for this, right?"

"I'm one of those state boys, and you have my word that you'll get paid," I said. I peeled two twenty-dollar bills off my money clip and pressed them into his hand. "It's very important that this car gets to that lab in one piece."

He winked and stuffed the twenties in his shirt pocket. "I'll get 'er there, cap'n."

As the tow truck disappeared down the drive, Wayne asked, "You got any more questions for me?"

"Maybe. Do you have a computer with Internet access?"

"Yeah, we live in the hills, but it ain't Bedrock, for God's sake."

I followed him into the trailer. The computer was set up in a spare bedroom. Wayne pulled up a web browser, and I sat down on an old kitchen chair in front of the keyboard. He left the room; a moment later I heard bottles rattling in the refrigerator. I typed in some information and navigated to a photo. I pulled it up so the photo filled the screen, then held a magazine over the image. "Wayne, come here a minute." He walked back down the hall and turned into the room, a beer bottle in his hand. "When I move this magazine, I want you to look at the photo and tell me if you recognize this person."

He took a hit off the beer and said, "Okay."

I slid the magazine away from the screen. "Look familiar?"

"Oh, yeah. That's him, Mr. Prissy Pants, the guy who was in the restaurant with my sister."

"You're sure?"

"A hundred proof." He took another drink of beer. "Who is he?"

I closed the web browser without answering.

His name was Alfonso Majestro.

* * *

As we walked outside, my head was a maelstrom, a cyclonic whirl of brain matter trying to connect the dots—D. Kendrick Brown to Danielle Quinn to Lester Yates to Alfonso Majestro. That quickly, I felt like I possessed many of the puzzle pieces, but how did they fit together? I needed to get back to Columbus and run this one past Jerry Adameyer. He was a master at weaving through such mazes. "Did you know Lester Yates before he was charged with your sister's murder?" I asked.

"No."

"The man who was at the restaurant with your sister, did you ever meet him before that night in the restaurant?"

"I'm pretty sure no."

"Does the name Del Brown or D. Kendrick Brown mean anything to you?"

"There used to be a Del Brown who was the sheriff."

"Did you ever meet him?"

"Not really. I spent a few nights at the crowbar hotel when he was the sheriff, but I don't recollect ever meeting him."

"I appreciate the honesty and you talking to me, Wayne. You were helpful, and I want us to stay on good terms, but I want to tell you one more thing, and I'm deadly serious. You and your wife can live however you please. That's your business. But I'm making that dog my business. The next time I'm in the area, I'm going to stop by and check on her, and if she's still chained up like that and you haven't taken her to the vet to get that collar out of her neck and treat that raw spot on her hip, I'm going to give you more hell than you can imagine."

"If that's the case I might have to shoot her, because I don't have no money to take her to the vet," Wayne said.

"You're telling me you can drink beer for breakfast and have money for cigarettes, but you can't take care of your animal?" He looked away. The verbal shot looked like it hurt more than the one I'd given him to the solar plexus. "I'll tell you what, Wayne. I'll make you a deal. You give me the dog, and we'll call everything square."

"Square for what?"

"I'll completely forget that you tried to assault an officer of the law."

"How many times are you going to try to use that against me?"

"Just one more time. If that dog leaves with me, you'll never hear about it again."

"Fine. Take her."

"Good choice, Wayne. What's her name?"

"Adolf."

I stared at him for a long moment, not sure if he was kidding. "You named your female German shepherd Adolf?"

"It was the only German name I could think of."

* * *

By the time Liberatore and Shirley returned in separate cars, the Dodge Neon that Danielle Quinn was driving the morning she disappeared was on a flatbed tow truck a half hour west of Cougar Ridge. I was sitting on the top step of the stoop, holding Adolf's chain; she was lying next to me, her chin resting on my lap, her big eyes locked on my face, as though fearful that her reprieve might be temporary.

"This looks like an interesting story," Liberatore said.

"They always are," I said.

Liberatore opened the back door to the car. I unhooked the chain, looked down at Adolf and said, "Go on."

That was all it took. Adolf bolted for the car like a soldier running from a prisoner of war camp, which she probably would have considered an apt comparison. In a few seconds, Adolf and her muddy paws were snug in the back seat of my state car. The odor from the infection was overwhelming, and we rolled down the windows trying to air it out. We stopped at the Kroger in St. Clairsville, where a guy with a name tag that said Bernie pointed me toward the pet care section. I bought two plastic bowls, a small bag of dog food, a six-pack of bottled water, and a can of air freshener. There was a grassy area beyond the parking lot where we let Adolf out to eat and drink. As I suspected, she gulped down her food like she hadn't eaten in a week. I gave her a second helping. Before she got back in the car, I soaked down the interior with the air freshener.

"Help me come up with another name before I take her to the vet," I told Liberatore.

"How about Lucky? She's lucky you came by," she said.

"She's a German shepherd. Let's come up with something a little more dignified."

We went through a fast food drive-through before heading back. As we merged onto Interstate 70, Liberatore said, "I must say, Mr. Van Buren, this has been an interesting day. You apologized for being mean to me. You claimed you didn't have a temper an hour before you punched the brother of a murder victim—a guy with rotten teeth who drinks beer for breakfast and who named his female German shepherd Adolf. You paid for a rental car with your own money so he doesn't get fired from his job cleaning dog cages. Then, you stole his dog."

"I didn't steal his dog, Liberatore. I rescued it."

The dog who was soon to no longer be named Adolf had wedged her head between the seats, resting her snout on the console. She smelled ghastly, and I couldn't finish my burger.

"You're not as mean as everyone thinks," Liberatore said.

"Who are you talking to, me or Adolf?"

"You."

"Let's just keep that our little secret, okay? There's no need for that kind of information to be getting around the office."

Liberatore turned in her seat so she could massage the top of the dog's head and hand-feed her pieces of hamburger. "Yes, sir," she said. "This has been an interesting day."

SEVENTEEN

On the drive back to Columbus, Liberatore called her family's veterinarian and explained my unplanned adoption of a full-grown German shepherd with a sweet disposition and a terrible skin condition. The vet agreed to examine the dog as soon as we got to town. I still had her leashed with the length of jack chain attached to a leather collar when we walked into a nondescript cement block building in the suburb of Grandview Heights.

"Is this our girl?" the veterinarian asked.

"This is she," I said.

"What's her name?" she asked.

I stammered for a minute before saying, "Lucky."

Liberatore made no attempt to conceal her smile.

The vet took the leash and led Lucky over to an examination table. She stroked her head a few times, called her by name, and slowly slipped a muzzle over her snout before lifting her to the table. "Do you have any records from her previous vet?" she asked.

"No," I said. "If I had to guess, she hasn't seen a vet in years, if ever."

She ran his hand over her ribs, and I noticed for the first time how truly thin the dog was. She checked her eyes and ears, lifted her chin, and carefully probed the area with a gloved hand where the collar was embedded in her neck. Lucky jumped at the touch. "It's okay, girl, it's okay," she said. "What I'd like to do is wrap a leather collar around the necks of people who treat animals like this."

I liked this vet.

She examined Lucky's neck for another few minutes, then said, "Let me get a couple of X-rays and see if there's anything else going on."

It took about fifteen minutes. When she returned, she said, "It isn't good. She has an advanced infection. I'm surprised she can even swallow. If you decide to treat this, it's going to require extensive work. Her flesh is growing around that collar, so I'm going to have to put her under to remove it, which is going to require removing the overlying tissue and treating the open wound. Once that's done, she's going to require wound care and antibiotic treatments. I'm not going to lie to you, it's a long shot at best, and it's not going to be cheap. It's your call."

"Are you recommending that she be put down?" I asked.

"I'm not making any recommendations. I'm just telling you that her odds of surviving this are not good. There's no guarantee the antibiotics are going to work at this advanced stage of infection. I know you're trying to rescue the dog, but those are the realities."

"What about the spot on her hip?"

"It's dermatitis. She's loaded with fleas, so most likely that's the cause. We can treat that with steroids. Compared to the infection, it's a minor concern."

Since I'd never had children, I'd never understood when another man would tell me it was impossible to say no to a daughter when she looked at you with pleading eyes. That is, I never understood it until that minute, because I'm guessing that was the look Liberatore was giving me as I contemplated Lucky's fate. She didn't have to say a word. The message was crystalline.

I exhaled and said, "I can't very well give her the name Lucky and then give up on her that quickly," I said. "Let's see if we can save her."

Liberatore grabbed my forearm with both her hands and shook it.

"If she makes it, she'll be here for a while," the vet said. "I'll do the surgery right now and get an antibiotic IV started while she's under. Let's touch base tomorrow, and I'll give you an update."

As we walked to the car, Liberatore said, "Wow, you're such a softy. This day just gets more and more interesting."

★ ★ ★

The parking garage was nearly empty when I parked the paw-printed state vehicle. I doused it with more air freshener before walking Liberatore to her car. I hopped into my pickup truck and followed her onto Third Street. She turned right on Broad Street; I turned left on Broad and left on Fourth, heading north through town toward the entrance ramp for Interstate 71 North.

As soon as I got on the interstate, I punched up Beth Kremer's cell phone number. "You're working late," she said.

"Sounds like you are, too."

"The car got here this afternoon. Did you tell that guy with one hand that I'd give him a check?"

"No."

"He was all upset because he didn't get paid. He said he was going to be in trouble with his boss."

"I'll call them tomorrow and take care of it. How's it going?"

"We're just about done with the collection process. The fun will begin tomorrow when we start sorting through everything in hopes of finding some DNA for you."

"What's the timeline?"

"In all honesty, the easy part is behind us. Sorting through that heap of garbage and hoping we can find six-year-old DNA is going to be time-consuming."

"Sorry to lean on you, Beth, but I need it as soon as humanly possible."

"I understand."

"Thanks, Beth. I owe you."

"Yes, you do. When this all settles down, I'll let you make it up to me." The comment took me off my pins. There was a long pause while I considered her statement and wondered if there was a hidden message behind it. And I hoped there was. "You still there?"

"I'm here," I said.

"We're good?"

"Absolutely."

"All right, I'm going to get back to work."

EIGHTEEN

I stopped by the Water's Edge, a little sports bar near Alum Creek Reservoir, and ordered a pizza to take home. I lived on seven acres on the outskirts of Galena, a speck of a town about ten miles north of the Columbus outerbelt, in an old brick farmhouse that I was restoring because I am an absolute glutton for punishment. I had restored an old Victorian house in the Akron suburb of Fairlawn Heights and vowed I would never again do something that idiotic. But my memory was apparently short, and I fell in love with the brick Federal home that had been built decades before my great-grandparents ever walked this earth. I had replumbed and rewired the entire house, put on a new metal roof, replaced the eaves and gutters, hung new cabinets, and put down ceramic tile. There wasn't any part of the house that I hadn't touched. While the heavy lifting had been done, there was never any shortage of projects. The renovations never stop on a house that is more than a hundred and fifty years old. At that time, I was replacing the windows, a project I was anxious to complete.

By the time I turned onto the gravel drive and snaked through the tunnel of old-growth oak, walnut, and maples, it was nearly ten o'clock. I had the truck windows down so I could listen to the chirping of the tree frogs along the drive. It was one of my simple pleasures.

When I came into the clearing near the house, the headlights shined on a dark brown SUV that was tucked into the shadows beside the garage. There was someone behind the wheel, but I couldn't make out the figure through the darkness. I lifted the console and reached into a lower compartment where I kept my 9mm Luger. I chambered a round and brought it up near my hip.

In my lifetime, I had put hundreds of men behind bars and sent more than a handful to Death Row. My nickname in the Summit County Jail had been "the button man," because the prisoners believed I enjoyed seeing the button pushed to release the lethal dose of chemicals used to execute prisoners in Ohio. This wasn't true, but that was my reputation, nevertheless. Thus, I had always been on my guard for ex-cons or family members looking to extract some revenge for what they inevitably believed had been a miscarriage of justice.

I got out and stood behind the open driver's-side door, the weapon in my hand at my side. A heartbeat thumped in my ears; my mouth had gone dry. The door of the SUV opened, and Shelly Denison stepped out from behind the steering wheel. "Where have you been?" she said. "I've been waiting here for more than two hours."

"Good God," I said, bending over and resting both hands on my knees, waiting for my heart to return to a normal beat. I could hear the gravel crunching under her shoes as she walked across the drive. "Do you know how to use a telephone?" I asked.

"Actually, I'm quite proficient with a phone. Do you know how to answer one? I must have called you twenty times today."

We had been in each other's company about twelve seconds and already we were back to the caustic exchanges that were the hallmark of my last campaign.

"I'm assuming that was you blowing up my phone all day."

"You didn't know it was me?"

"How would I know it was you? Unless, of course, you're implying that I should have saved you as a contact on my phone after our relationship ended, which I didn't."

I stood and pushed the safety on the pistol before slipping it into my belt.

"You pulled your gun on me?" she asked, her jaw dropping to her collarbone.

It was a rhetorical question and didn't warrant a response. "What was so important that you had to sit in my driveway for two hours?"

"More than two hours."

"Okay, more than two hours."

"My God, Hutch, what do you think? We need to talk about the campaign."

I was somewhere south of exhausted, and my pizza was getting cold. There were still sixteen months until the election, but there was no use arguing with her. "Let me park my truck."

I pulled the pickup into the garage and got out holding the pizza. "I can offer you dinner," I said.

"Thanks, but I ate dinner at the normal time people eat dinner."

"It's been a long day, Shelly. Please don't make it any longer." She followed me through the mud room and into the kitchen.

"What is it with you and old houses?"

"They have character."

"They're a lot of work."

"So are you."

She set her leather briefcase on the kitchen island. "You can eat. I'll talk," she said.

"Of this, I have no doubt."

I set the pizza box on the kitchen island next to her briefcase and put the Luger in a cabinet before getting a bottle of beer from the refrigerator. "Beer?" I asked.

"Merlot would be nice."

There was an open bottle of cabernet on the counter. I poured her a glass and Shelly, who is a bit of a wine snob, didn't notice the difference. I flipped open the pizza box, pulled out a wedge, and leaned against the kitchen counter. Shelly sat on one of the high-top stools at the island and strategically began placing her spreadsheets and maps on the granite top. It had been nearly three years since the demise of our relationship, but things suddenly seemed very familiar. She used her little finger to push her hair off her forehead; her perfume wafted into my nostrils—the scent of orange blossoms, perhaps—and I was immediately thrown back to a time and place that I thought I had long been erased from my memory. While my brain had the capacity to think logically, my loins did not.

I wanted to chew off every piece of her clothing and take her on the island. I could not remember wanting anything as badly in my life as I wanted Shelly Denison in that moment, and that included the office of United States attorney general. I remembered how she would brush her fingernails across my shoulders, or stand close so I could smell her perfume or feel her breasts press against me. After our breakup, Shelly had taken up residence in my head and didn't leave for months and months. I hated to admit that one person, one woman, could hold such sway over me, but that is exactly what happened with Shelly. I thought I was over her, but I wasn't even close.

I picked up my beer and took a couple of hard swallows. I could not allow that to happen. She would get back inside my head and screw with me like no other. For the sake of my job, Lester Yates, and my sanity, I was not going to yield to my temptations.

She looked up, smiled, and asked, "Are you okay?"

"Fine, why?"

She shook her head. "Nothing. You just had a distracted look on your face."

Of course, Shelly knew exactly what she was doing to me and was probably enjoying every minute of it. In her mind, she was still owed payback for the stunt I had pulled during my first campaign.

She unfolded a map of the state of Ohio. Every county was labeled by name, along with the number of registered Republican and Democratic voters. She had used a green highlighter to mark the counties she believed I needed to win to secure reelection. She began talking and pointing to various counties with a pink lacquered fingernail. Political strategy was like cocaine to Shelly. She immersed herself in numbers and percentages and political logic. This also is when my eyes started to glaze over. I finished the rest of my beer and went to the refrigerator for another.

She started talking and jotting down numbers and notes on the map while I drank my beer, ate another wedge of pizza, and tried to pay attention, though I couldn't have been more uninterested. There were a lot of reasons why I hated politics, and the strategy sessions with Shelly were very close to the top of the list. I didn't care about the minutiae of a campaign; that was exactly why I wanted Shelly in charge. She would set up the rallies, the luncheons with the Rotarians and Kiwanians, and whatever else she wanted, then give me a list of places I needed to be. I would do it without complaint. I am actually a good campaigner. I'm comfortable in front of people and they respond to my blue-collar roots and support for victims, but I don't like doing any of the heavy lifting.

After about twenty minutes of talking and pointing, during which time she may have only taken three breaths, Shelly looked up, smiled, and said, "And if we can pull that off, you should have no problem getting reelected Ohio attorney general."

"Sounds great," I said, smiling back at her and realizing that if she pulled an exam out of her briefcase, I wouldn't be able to answer a single question. She held up her empty wine glass. I refilled it with the cab and pushed it across the island to her waiting hand.

"Tell me about this investigation you've got going," she said.

I squinted, "What investigation?"

"The one you're doing into that guy on Death Row."

"How did you hear about that?"

"What did Stan Carmine tell you this morning? Ohio Republican Party politics is a small pool."

"Stan called you and told you about it?"

"He didn't have to; I was sitting in his office while you were talking."

"Perfect."

"So tell me about it."

"There's not much to tell. The guy's name is Lester Yates, and he is scheduled to be executed in a little over a month. I have serious doubts about his guilt, and . . ." I could feel my brows knit down toward the bridge of my nose. I held up an index finger, the same way I did when I wanted a jury to remember a particular point. "Wait a minute. Back up. You may have been in his office, but that doesn't tell me how you know about the investigation. I didn't discuss the investigation with Stan. In fact, the only one I've discussed it with outside of my office is the governor. How did you find out about it?"

There had been rare times during my many interactions with Shelly when she was on the defensive, and this was one of them. She couldn't work up enough spit to swallow. She shrugged, sipped her wine, and said, "I don't remember."

"You're lying to me, Shelly. I'm starting to smell a rat. Please tell me the governor didn't ask you to probe me for information."

"He did nothing of the sort. He just happened to bring it up the other day at lunch."

"Lunch?" I set my beer bottle on the counter. "Shelly, tell me why in God's name you're still seeing the governor."

"I don't need a lecture, Hutchinson."

"I'm not going to give you one. I just don't understand why you'd jeopardize your career and his for a fling."

"It's actually not what you think. It's not a fling, at least on my part."

"You're in love with Jim Wilinski?"

"I know, it's terrible, but . . ."

"Shelly, really? You know, he's never going to leave his wife. That would destroy his political aspirations."

"He said he loves me and he wants to leave her."

"You can't possibly believe that."

"My heart does."

"Your brain will eventually trump your heart. You need to be careful."

"I know. I will. Can we get back to business?"

"Please."

"We were talking about his presidential campaign and he brought up the investigation because he's worried about it. I was just curious. Besides, I'm your campaign manager and you have a lot at stake here, too, you know?"

"Not as much as Lester Yates. If I lose the election, no one is going to pump lethal chemicals into my veins."

"Okay, fine, don't get all huffy. I was just asking. As you know from our previous relationship, I don't like surprises, and you have a habit of dropping H-bombs in the middle of a campaign."

"If you think an H-bomb can damage a campaign, wait and see what executing the wrong man will do. If he's the governor when we execute Lester Yates, instead of being president he'll end up hosting a sports talk show in Portsmouth."

I could feel a wave of fire rolling up my neck. I had a bad feeling about this. It was the politics of conspiracy—another reason why I hated this business. "I'm not sure I believe that you asking about Lester was simply a coincidence. And I'm starting to believe the governor would be happy to execute Lester if it brought him three more votes. He had Alfonso Majestro call me the other day on a fishing expedition to find out what was going on in the investigation, and the next thing I knew I had Sasquatch breathing down my neck."

"Sasquatch?"

"Danny Doyle."

She forced a burst of air between her lips. "You don't need to worry about Danny. He's a big teddy bear."

"Right. A six-foot-nine, three-hundred-and-twenty-pound teddy bear with more hair on his knuckles than I have on my head."

"He's actually a very nice guy. He's just not smart enough to think on his own. He wouldn't fart without first asking Alfonso."

"Or the governor."

"No, just Alfonso."

"Why is that? Doyle's the governor's bodyguard."

"Let me educate you a little bit, my dear. I have very strong feelings for the governor, as you have noted on several occasions. However, in my opinion he took a few too many shots to the head during his football-playing days. Alfonso is the brains. He runs the show—first, last, always. The governor is handsome and friendly and popular and slaps people on the back and calls them 'padnah.' He also does whatever Alfonso says."

"Really? Interesting. Alfonso is the great and powerful Oz behind the curtain?"

"Precisely. Big Jim Wilinski is just the front man, and that isn't going to change, even if his next address is 1600 Pennsylvania Avenue."

"That's a little scary."

"No, it's positively frightening. Majestro is devious, and he takes calculating to an entirely new level. He makes my skin crawl, and that comes from a woman who has spent her entire professional life working with some of the slimiest politicians on earth. He is wholly without conscience. Truth be told, I think Danny and the governor are both scared to death of him. Majestro looks like he couldn't beat a third-grade girl in an arm-wrestling contest, but he'd slit someone's throat for political advantage. And I mean that. Try not to cross him."

"I'm afraid that train's left the station."

"If there's a problem with Majestro, we'll patch that later. Let's concentrate on your reelection."

She scooped the road map to my reelection from the granite and slipped it into her leather briefcase. "We need to talk about fundraising," she said.

"Another time, Shelly. I'm gassed."

I turned on the garage lights and walked Shelly to her car. I stayed near the front fender so there would be no uncomfortable goodnight hug. She started the engine and rolled down the window while stopping beside me. "We're going to be all right working together, right?" she asked.

"Absolutely."

"We can be honest with each other?"

"Of course."

"Good. Buy some decent merlot, and don't try to fool me again with a cheap cabernet."

NINETEEN

Five weeks and two days before the scheduled execution of Lester Paul Yates.

At seven-forty-five the next morning, Denise Liberatore walked into the lobby of my office and, well aware of the protocol, stopped at Margaret's desk and asked to see me.

"He's busy getting ready for the meeting," Margaret said.

"Oh, I'm sure he'll want to see me," Liberatore said.

Margaret's brows arched. "What's it about?"

"I have news about our dog."

"Your *dog*?"

"Uh-huh."

"You and Mr. Van Buren have a dog together?"

"Yes, a German shepherd."

"A German shepherd?"

Liberatore smiled. "She's so beautiful. You'll have to meet her sometime. Her name is Lucky."

Margaret slowly nodded her head, puckered her lips, and said, "Let me see if Mr. Van Buren is available."

When she walked into my office, the muscles in Margaret's forehead were twitching. It was obvious that something had set her off, and I could only hope that I was not the subject of her ire. Unfortunately . . .

"There is someone in the lobby who would like a moment of your time," she said, her voice calm. "I told her you were busy, but she seems to think you'll still want to see her."

"Oh, God. Is it Shelly Dennison? She didn't leave my house last night until after midnight."

Her jaws snugged tight.

"It was all business, Margaret."

"What you do on your time is your concern. But it's not Miss Shelly. This woman wants to talk to you about your German shepherd."

"Denise?"

"Ms. Liberatore."

"Yeah, her first name is Denise. Great. Did she say if she stopped by the vet to see how Lucky is doing?"

"She didn't, but she did say that I would have to meet *Lucky* someday."

I chuckled and lifted my hands to shoulder height, palms out. "Don't blame me for that one," I said. "I wanted to name her something Germanic or regal, like Gretchen, but Denise wanted to name her Lucky, so Lucky she is, so to speak."

"Lucky!" Margaret reared back and hit me in the right shoulder with an open hand and nearly knocked me off the chair. "Have you taken leave of your senses? That girl is an intern and not even half your age."

"Half my age? What are . . . no, no, no. No, it's not like that."

"The two of you have a dog named Lucky, but oh no, there's nothing going on here? I was born at night, but it wasn't last night, Mr. Van Buren. You have apparently been hanging around the governor too much."

I was going to have a bruise on my shoulder. "Send her in here, and you stay."

I explained to Margaret how I came into possession of the German shepherd, and Liberatore confirmed my story. Yes, it was "our" dog to the point where Liberatore shared her hamburger with the dog and I was shelling out God-only-knew how much in veterinarian bills. She had stopped at the vet's office on her way into work. The surgery had been successful, and Lucky was still sedated for the pain. The vet said it would be several days before she knew if Lucky was responding to the antibiotics.

"Fingers crossed," I said.

"Yes, fingers crossed," Liberatore said.

Margaret's left eye squinted at me as though she was looking down the barrel of a rifle.

* * *

The meeting of the Lester Yates task force began at eight o'clock. By eight-thirty it was obvious that very little progress had been made in the investigations of the victims of the Egypt Valley Strangler. Each of the investigators had been told to focus on the first two names on their list. Their reports were ominously similar. The investigators were struck by the dearth of information in the investigative files.

Clarence Davidson, the investigator who had worked for Jerry Adameyer as a patrolman before joining my office, asked, "You know who the sheriff in Belmont County was when these murders were taking place, don't you?"

"D. Kendrick Brown," I said. "That's one reason why you're not to speak of this project outside the walls of this room."

"So everything we say is staying inside this room?"

I grinned. "Absolutely. Feel free to speak."

"How can someone who apparently bungled these investigations so badly end up running the Ohio Bureau of Criminal Investigation?"

"That's a good question, Davidson, but one for another day. Right now, we need to keep moving forward on these investigations. We're running out of time. Let me just give you a brief update on a few things that Jerry and I are working on in regard to this case. The car that belonged to Danielle Quinn is at the crime lab being searched for any DNA samples that we can connect to the felony database. That process just began yesterday. Given the years since the murder occurred and the condition of the car, it's going to be a long shot, but it's one we need to take. Jerry and I made a trip to the Northeast Ohio Correctional Facility to interview a convict named Herman Fenicks, who was an over-the-road trucker before he was arrested for attempted murder after he was found trying to strangle a prostitute. The MO matches that of the Egypt Valley Strangler. We had gotten a tip that Fenicks had been bragging that he strangled numerous women in eastern Ohio. We were hoping that he might give us a little scrap to work with, but he wasn't the least bit cooperative. He's a strange ranger; he demands that you either call him Mr. Fenicks or The Rap. Since we didn't have any evidence to use against him or anything we could offer him in terms of a reduced sentence, he blew us off."

"Is it worth following up on?" Davidson asked.

I looked at Jerry.

He said, "If we can find his DNA in the Quinn woman's car, yes. Beyond that, given the time constraints we're working under, it's not a good use of our time trying to link him to the murders without physical evidence."

Ridges popped up along Davidson's forehead. "Why's he call himself The Rap?"

"Beats me. Maybe he's a rap star in the joint," Jerry said.

"All right, let's get started on the next two names on your lists," I said. "Folks, we've got to dial up the intensity level." Liberatore started flipping through one of the notebooks that she and the other interns had put together. It was mildly annoying, but I didn't stop talking. "There have got to be friends and relatives of the victims who we can talk to. Don't rely solely on the sheriff's old files. Track down the family and . . ."

"It's him," Liberatore said, interrupting.

"It's who?" I asked.

"That's our guy." She was out of her chair and walking to my end of the conference table with the notebook.

"What are you talking about?"

"That guy, The Rap, he's the connection to the Egypt Valley Strangler."

She set the notebook on the corner of the conference table; it was open to a photocopied newspaper article. Ordinarily, I wouldn't have allowed an intern this much latitude in one of my meetings, but Liberatore had earned her chops the previous day.

She pointed to a passage in an article and said, "This is from the *Daily Jeffersonian* in Cambridge; the article ran two days after the body of Anne Touvell was found lashed to a tree with baling wire."

Hendrysburg resident Noah Gibson said he was driving south on Egypt North Road just before midnight on Tuesday when he spotted a tractor-trailer pulled off the west side of the two-lane road with its hood pulled forward, exposing the engine. Gibson told the sheriff's department that a man he assumed to be the truck driver was standing on the gravel berm, shining a flashlight into the engine compartment.

According to a report filed with the sheriff's office, Gibson said it was unusual to see a tractor-trailer on Egypt North Road. Gibson said he slowed down and asked the man if he needed help. The truck driver said "no," but never turned to face Gibson.

The man was described as black, muscular, and acting agitated.

Gibson said the trailer was white or possibly gray. The tractor was white and had what appeared to be an eagle or large bird painted to look like a fighter jet, with flames shooting out of its wings.

Gibson said he called the sheriff's department after reading a newspaper article about Touvell's murder and realized the body had been discovered in the area where the tractor-trailer had been parked.

Liberatore looked at me like she'd discovered a cure for cancer.

"Help me out, Liberatore. I don't see the connection," I said.

"It's his name," she said. "I'll bet it's not pronounced *fen-ex*, it's pronounced *fee-nix*. That wasn't an eagle made to look like a fighter jet painted on the door of the truck, it was the mythical bird, the phoenix. According to mythology, the phoenix was a giant bird that lived for something like five hundred years before combusting in air and falling to the ground in flames. It was then reborn from his own ashes. I'll bet the painting on the truck was the phoenix in its death fall. And his nickname, The Rap, isn't because he thinks he's a rap star. It's 'rap,' as in 'raptor.' A raptor is a bird of prey, and this guy fancies himself as a predator." She tapped her finger on the newspaper article. "This is our guy."

I looked at the newspaper article, then back at Liberatore, and over to Jerry, who nodded.

"That is excellent work, Liberatore," I said. "Really, really excellent work. You are onto something."

She beamed.

"We've got to find that truck," Jerry said.

"Yes, we do."

I looked at the interns. "Are the notebooks complete?"

"They're done," said Nakamura, pushing the remaining two notebooks toward the middle of the conference room table.

"Good work," I said. "Jerry, I need you working on finding that truck. Liberatore, you help Jerry. You investigators, put the other three interns to work. If we can't count on the sheriff's department files to help us, go through those notebooks for leads. Get after it, folks. Tick-tock."

TWENTY

Twenty minutes after the meeting, Margaret walked into my office and dropped an index card on my desk. On it she had written:

APPALACHIAN MINISTRIES CENTER
141 RIVER ROAD
CHESAPEAKE, OHIO

She was still giving me the stink eye. I picked up the card and examined it for a moment.

"Is this where you think I should go for my redemption?"

"If you're messing around with Miss Shelly or that little intern, or *both!,* you may be beyond redemption, but if you'd like to find Lester Yates's defense attorney, Jim Smith, that's where you'll go."

Ten minutes later, I was in a state car that did not smell like an infected German shepherd and heading toward Chesapeake, a southern Ohio River town of about seven hundred people. Margaret had gotten the information from the law firm in Martins Ferry. They didn't have a home address for Jim Smith but believed he was living across the river from Chesapeake in Huntington, West Virginia.

It was nearly a three-hour drive from Columbus to Chesapeake, mostly along Route 23, which winds through the hills of southern Ohio, one of the most lush and beautiful parts of the state. Sadly, like my native Upper Ohio River Valley, most of the river towns in southern Ohio had been decimated by the collapse of their blue-collar industries. The unemployment rate was beyond fifteen percent, opioids filled the valley like floodwaters, and many souls who had never known anything but a blue-collar life were left sitting on their porches, watching time and the muddy Ohio drift along beyond their reach.

The Appalachian Ministries Center was located on a brick street in an old Ford dealership, squeezed between Route 7 and the Ohio River. Jim Smith was the director of the center, which offered a Christian-based substance abuse program, a food pantry, a thrift store in the old service bays, and a soup kitchen in the old showroom that, when times were good, had sported gleaming Crown Vics and Edsels. I arrived at lunchtime. There were about forty people at the center for the free lunch. I walked up to a table where a man was eating by himself. His bearded face was down, inches from his food, a mottled hand wrapped around a spoon and his arm wrapped around a tray in a protective manner. If I had to guess, it was a tactic he had learned in prison to protect his food. "Hey, partner, is Mr. Smith here?"

He pulled his spoon from his mouth and looked up only with his eyes. "Pastor Smith?"

"His first name's Jim."

He used his spoon to point at a man in a white apron standing behind a stainless steel counter. He was putting sandwiches on plates and scooping soup from a steaming pot.

I walked between tables of the hungry and homeless to the back of the room where I met a plump woman with a missing eyetooth and beads of sweat on her upper lip. She smiled and said, "Is there something I can help you with, sir?"

"I was hoping to speak with Pastor Smith when he's not busy."

"I'll tell him. Things are slowing down a bit."

The woman spoke to Smith, who leaned forward and looked my way before untying his apron, folding it in half, and setting it on the counter. He appeared to offer some instructions to the woman before walking toward me, wiping his hands on a tea towel. I reached out to shake his hand; he took it without conviction. "Pastor Smith, my name is . . ."

"I know who you are, Mr. Van Buren. We have cable in Lawrence County."

He was direct. I liked that. "I'd like a few minutes of your time to talk to you about Lester Yates."

"I figured as much." He pointed toward the rear of the building. "Why don't we go back to my office? It's a little quieter."

We walked down a center hall; the thrift store and food pantry were on the left and small offices on the right. "This is an impressive operation you've got going here, Pastor Smith."

"Thank you. Unfortunately, it's badly needed. There's no shortage of issues that we're forced to deal with in southern Ohio. It's the perfect storm of unemployment, drugs, alcoholism, and depression. When you go up to Columbus and see how it's thriving, it's hard to believe we're part of the same state. This . . ." He made a circling motion with his arm. "We do it all with volunteer help and donations."

We sat down in his spartan office, which was outfitted with a battered metal desk, a couple of steel folding chairs, and a bookshelf full of pamphlets on alcoholism and addiction services. He moved some papers off one of the folding chairs and extended a hand, a tacit offer to sit.

There is a look I have seen on the faces of street cops and social workers and doctors. I always referred to it as the "lost soul" look, because it seemed that the spirit of life had been drained from their bodies, leaving their eyes vacuous, their shoulders slumped in defeat. It was a look of self-resignation, the realization of the futility of their efforts. Cops know that no matter how many gangbangers or jackrollers they take off the streets, there will be others to fill the void. The bad guys always keep coming. Social workers know there are still kids going to bed at night with empty bellies and women selling their bodies for the next hit on the pipe. Doctors know the instant a gut-shot victim comes through the emergency-room door that they have no chance of survival, but they must still go through the motions before talking to the family. That doesn't mean they will ever quit fighting the good fight. It just means for all their noble efforts, their successes are limited.

That was the face I saw on Jim Smith when we entered his office. His fingernails had been gnawed down to the quick. And for one so young, there were already deep lines running from eyes so dark it was hard to discern the pupils. Streaks of gray stained hair the color of charcoal. He was slight, with thin wrists and delicate hands.

"How did you get out of the law and into the ministry?" I asked.

Smith sat down behind his desk. "It wasn't a difficult decision. If I'd followed my heart, I would have gone into the seminary, but I succumbed to family pressure and went to law school."

"Family pressure will do that."

"I didn't hate practicing law, but the Lester Yates case . . ." He looked away and shook his head. "That is what permanently turned me against working in the legal system."

"How so?"

"Come on, Mr. Van Buren, if you've been looking into this case it should be no secret to you that little Lester Yates isn't a serial killer, he isn't a white supremacist, and he certainly did not murder Danielle Quinn. It also should be no secret, though you may be too kind to say so, that he received terribly inadequate legal representation. I am well aware of that. Given all those factors, it should be obvious why I decided to leave the bar."

"If you don't mind, why don't you back up and walk me through it?"

"After law school, I went back home and set up a little practice in Martins Ferry—mostly family law. I was doing wills, trusts, adoptions, domestic relations, custody battles, abuse cases, stuff like that. I was making okay money, and I liked what I was doing. My uncle called me one day and said I should get registered to be a public defender. He made it sound like the opportunity of a lifetime—great experience, I wouldn't have to chase after my money, and it would get my name out there and help establish my practice."

"How would your uncle know this?"

"He's a lawyer. He told me I would usually be representing guys on shoplifting beefs or drunk drivers. You know, Mickey Mouse stuff. He said most of the time they plead out and you don't even go to trial. 'Give it a shot,' he said. My dad died when I was a kid, and my uncle had always been my father figure. I wanted to please him, so I registered as a public defender. Two week later, *two weeks*, I'm defending Lester Yates in a capital murder case. I didn't know whether to wind my watch or go blind. I'd had a few basic criminal defense courses in law school, but I didn't know what I was doing. I was drowning, and this guy's life depended on me. I went to my uncle and told him I was in way over my head, and I needed help. He just shrugged it off and said, 'Do the best you can. That guy is guilty as sin, and no one expects him to get off, anyway.' My uncle was the reason I wanted to be a lawyer, and he tossed me right under the bus. And there sat Lester, that poor son of a gun. I'm not sure he ever realized how serious things were, and he ended up getting the death penalty."

"Don't be too hard on yourself, pastor. The Egypt Valley Strangler had been terrifying people in that area for years, and they wanted those murders solved. It didn't matter if it was Lester Yates or Mother Teresa, they wanted a conviction, and they got one."

"The bad part personally was that I think I got set up."

"How so?"

"My uncle was buddies with the sheriff—Del Brown. Do you know him?"

"I do. Del works for me."

Smith blinked a couple of times, as though he hadn't heard me right. "Del Brown, the former sheriff, works for you?"

"He now goes by D. Kendrick Brown, but it's him. He's the director of the Ohio Bureau of Criminal Investigation. It was a patronage job for being loyal to the governor."

"I think they wanted Yates to go down hard, and they knew if he had a green defense attorney it would make it a lot easier. Granted, I'm not the one sitting on Death Row, but Lester Yates wasn't the only victim. I couldn't sleep for months after that trial. My law practice started to fail, along with my marriage. My mother hardly speaks to me anymore because she can't believe I'd walk away from a law practice to minister to the poor. My uncle and I haven't spoken in years."

"When I interviewed Lester, he said you told him how angry you were with your uncle. Was it because you thought you were set up?"

"That's exactly why I was upset. I was angry with him for putting me and Lester in that position."

"Is your uncle still practicing law?"

"I don't think so. I assume he's still a member of the bar, but he hasn't practiced in years. I'm sure you know him."

"Why would you think that?"

"Because he's the governor's chief of staff."

I did my best not to look like I had been slapped. "The governor's chief of staff?"

"Yes."

"Alfonso Majestro?"

"Uncle Allie? That's what we called him growing up."

"Alfonso Majestro was the uncle who encouraged you to get registered to be a public defender just before they charged Lester Yates with murder?"

"Belmont County is a very politically incestuous swamp."

"What was he doing at the time?"

"The same thing he's doing now; he was chief of staff for Jim Wilinski."

"Why would the governor's chief of staff be interested in making sure Lester Yates was convicted of Danielle Quinn's murder?"

The pastor swallowed hard. "I can't answer that. I don't know."

"Were you aware that your uncle had been dating Danielle Quinn?"

"In all candor, Mr. Van Buren, I've tried not to give a lot of thought to that. The reasons I no longer speak to my uncle are manifold, but a lack of honesty on his part is certainly a factor. I've prayed for his soul, and that's the best I can offer him."

We walked back out through the dining room, where some of the same men who were eating when I came in were washing down tables and sweeping. "We give them a few dollars for cleaning up after meals," the pastor said. "I don't hire the meth addicts because they'll spend it on drugs. For these guys, it's beer and cigarette money." He looked at me and offered a faint smile. "It's the lesser of evils. I'm a realist about my flock."

As we walked onto an asphalt parking lot that was crisscrossed with cracks, the sun bright overhead, Pastor Smith put his hands in his pockets and looked out over the dark waters of the Ohio and the outline of downtown Huntington and Marshall University beyond. "What do you think is going to happen to Lester?" he asked.

"The odds are not in his favor," I said.

"They never were."

"You're exactly right. He never had a chance."

"They'll execute Lester, and then everyone involved will pat themselves on the back. They'll toast each other and proclaim that they've done society a great service by extracting this evil from the world. But they're just kidding themselves. The evil that took the lives of those women is still out there, because it wasn't Lester Yates."

TWENTY-ONE

I was just north of Portsmouth when my cell phone rang; it registered as the main number for my office.

"Van Buren here," I said.

"What's the good word, chief?" Jerry Adameyer asked.

"Heading north."

"How'd it go?"

"It was very educational. In fact, between my meeting yesterday with Danielle Quinn's brother and my chat today with the good reverend, I've got some news that you're going to find extremely interesting. It's probably best that we don't discuss it over the phone. We might have a suspect."

"You have my complete attention. What time are you getting back?"

"I should be pulling into town about five o'clock."

"I'll be waiting. Oh, one more thing before we hang up. We had an interesting visitor today."

"Who might that have been?"

"D. Kendrick Brown."

"What did he want?"

"I think it's killing him that he's out of the loop with the investigation. He dropped into the lobby about twelve-fifteen. My guess is he hoped everyone would be at lunch and he could go in and snoop around the war room. Fortunately, I just happened to be talking to Margaret when he walked in. He was all chummy and smiles, and he said he wanted to find out what was going on with the Yates case. I told him it was progressing. He pointed at the door and asked, 'Is that the war room I've heard about?'"

"I said, 'That's it,' like it was no big deal, and I'll be damned if he didn't start walking toward it like it was his living room. I stepped in front of him and said, 'Where do you think you're going, bubba?' He said, 'I just want to have a look and see what's going on. I have the right. I work for the attorney general, too.' I said, 'That's true, but that room is for task force members only, and your name's not on the guest list.' He got all huffy and reminded me that he was head of the Ohio Bureau of Criminal Investigation. I told him, 'That doesn't carry any weight here.' His face got so red I thought he was going to have an aneurysm. He put a finger in my chest and reminded me that he was higher on the attorney general totem pole than me."

"How'd that go over?"

"Not well. I told him I didn't give a rat's ass where he was on the totem pole; if you're not the top Indian, the view's all the same. I also told him if he put a finger in my chest one more time, he was going to lose it. He stormed off. I suspect he ran right to the governor to tell him how mean I was to him."

"If he did, it won't be the first time and certainly won't be the last. How do you think he knew about the war room? Someone has been running their mouth."

"Yeah, someone's jaws have been flapping. As soon as D. Kendrick left, I rounded up the team and read them the riot act. I don't think there was a major breach, but I wanted to head it off at the pass. I didn't say anything to Margaret."

"Good. Don't. You wouldn't like her reaction. Margaret would take a bullet before she would talk out of school."

"Okay, chief, I'll meet you in the war room when you get here."

"Meet me in my office. I don't want anyone else to hear this."

⋆ ⋆ ⋆

I got back to the office at five-twenty. Margaret had gone home. Jerry was sitting in my office at the conference table, a manila folder sitting on the lacquered mahogany. "You've been a road warrior the last couple of days," he said. "I asked Liberatore what happened when you two went down to the valley yesterday, but all she would tell me was that you stole the guy's dog."

"I didn't steal his dog," I said. "I rescued it."

"I guess it's all a matter of semantics."

"Did she tell you what we learned?"

"Nope. She said I needed to ask you. I reminded her that I was her superior, but she said you were more superior and you had told her to keep her mouth shut, and that she had seen you when you get angry and she didn't want any part of that."

"She's solid."

"She is, indeed. So, Mr. Superior, fill me in."

I draped my suit coat over the back of my chair, walked over to the conference table, and took a seat around the corner from Jerry. "Liberatore and I interviewed Quinn's brother. He cleans dog cages for a living at Wheeling Downs, gets a DUI about every other month, abuses animals, and lives in a dilapidated house trailer surrounded by twenty or thirty junk cars."

"Okay, I'm getting the visual."

"He told me of an encounter he had one night in a restaurant where his sister was eating with her date. He described the man as meticulously dressed and coifed—'prissy' was the actual word he used. He said this guy had a little rat face and to his recollection the man's name was Albert, or something like that."

I paused for a moment, but there was no hint that Jerry had put it together.

"I asked him if the guy could have looked more like a ferret than a rat and if his name could have been Alfonso, and he said it could have been."

Jerry's eyes widened and he said, "No way."

"I pulled up Majestro's photo from the state website, and Quinn's brother said there was no question that it was him."

"You're telling me that Alfonso Majestro, the governor's chief of staff, was dating the girl that Lester Yates was convicted of strangling? Jesus H. Christ."

"It gets a little better. Jim Smith, Yates's defense attorney, was so traumatized by this event that he quit practicing law and went into the ministry."

"Didn't they teach him in law school that most people charged with crimes are actually guilty?"

"He was never interested in being a defense attorney. His uncle was a lawyer and Smith's father figure; he convinced Smith to become a public defender. Two weeks later, he gets assigned to represent Lester Yates in a capital murder case and everything goes down in flames. Care to guess who his uncle is?"

"Not Majestro?"

"Yep, he called him Uncle Allie."

Deep frown lines created little mountain ranges that stretched hard across Jerry's forehead, and his brows pinched down on his nose as he processed the information. "Any chance this was a revenge play on Majestro's part? Maybe he was in love with this woman and wanted his nephew to represent Yates to assure they got a conviction."

"It doesn't add up, Jerry. First of all, Majestro is incapable of loving anyone more than he loves himself. I can't see him getting so involved with a woman that he would risk his reputation for her. Quinn's brother isn't even sure Majestro went to the funeral. There had to be another reason why they wanted to pin it on Yates."

"Like maybe Majestro wanted a conviction in her death so there would be no need for any further investigation?"

"That would be a good reason, wouldn't it? It also might answer some questions about D. Kendrick Brown, too. Maybe he didn't get the job as head of the crime bureau for being loyal to the governor. Maybe he got it for being loyal to Majestro. Given what I know about Majestro's control of the governor's office, it might make sense. It would also explain why D. Kendrick was over here snooping around today. Sending Yates to Death Row because of blind ambition is not a crime or even provable, but if it was part of a cover-up . . ."

Jerry winced. "I don't know, chief. I'm not sure that Majestro and D. Kendrick are smart enough to pull off a cover-up. Maybe it was just a bizarre coincidence."

"I don't believe in coincidences."

"Me neither."

I stood and walked over to the bank of windows that lined the south side of my office. Below, rush-hour traffic had the downtown in gridlock. I said, "In the meantime, let me muddy up the waters a little bit more. I went to those notebooks the interns put together. I have to give them credit, they did a pretty thorough job. So thorough, in fact, that they collected articles about four other women who were strangled in the area, but their deaths were not directly attributed to the Egypt Valley Strangler."

"How could that be?"

"Because when Lester Yates went to prison, so did the Egypt Valley Strangler. The articles don't mention the Egypt Valley Strangler because all four women were murdered after Yates was arrested."

"Did any of the intrepid reporters bother to question the authorities about any connection to the strangler?"

"Not a one. Reporters are like water. They follow the path of least resistance. Once they had an arrest and their headlines, they went back to writing about bake sales and Fourth of July parades. These women were all found out in the sticks. The big papers have enough murders in their circulation area to keep them busy; they're not going to go stomping around in the Egypt Valley."

"The fact that the murders continued after Lester went to prison is good circumstantial evidence that he isn't guilty, but it is not going to be enough to get a stay from the governor."

"There's another chapter to the mystery," I said. "Not only were those four women murdered after Lester went to prison, but the last of the four occurred a week before Harold Fenicks was taken off the board. With these four included, there were twenty-two women strangled and their bodies dumped in and around the Egypt Valley between July of 1993, when Donna Herrick was killed, and August 2003, when Fenicks was arrested. Since his arrest . . ." I made a zero out of my thumb and fingers. "Nada."

Jerry drummed his thick fingers across the mahogany. "We've got to find that rig."

"It's imperative. Danielle Quinn was last seen alive at the Shenandoah Truck Stop in Old Washington. Herman Fenicks was a truck driver. They have to keep logbooks of where they've been."

"How sweet would it be to find out that he was in the Old Washington area on the day she disappeared?" Jerry asked.

"Sweet, indeed," I said. I walked back across the room and sat down. "Let's get one of the interns to call the Cuyahoga County prosecutor's office in the morning and see if there are any logbooks in the evidence bin from the case up there."

"If she was last seen at the Shenandoah, what are the odds that they would still have security camera footage on file?"

"I'd say the chances are virtually nonexistent. Most of those systems are on a loop and get taped over every two weeks or so. Unless the prosecutor or the sheriff confiscated it?"

"If I was investigating a missing person who disappeared from a truck stop parking lot, the first thing I would do is look for a security video," Jerry said. "If I was the sheriff trying to cover up an abduction, the first thing I would do is destroy the video."

"I'll go down and check out the prosecutor's file for myself," I said. "In the meantime, get one of the interns to contact the Shenandoah and see if they had security cameras running the morning Danielle Quinn disappeared." I slouched in my seat, exhaled, and began loosening my tie. "Tell me, Jerry, what is the connection between Alfonso Majestro, a polished attorney and the governor's chief of staff, D. Kendrick Brown, and Herman Fenicks, a truck driver and convict?"

"How do you know there is one?" Jerry asked.

"Because I still don't believe in coincidences, remember? Alfonso Majestro was dating Danielle Quinn. She ends up murdered. Alfonso talks his nephew into registering to be a public defender to assure that Yates gets convicted. Fenicks goes to prison, and the murders stop. It can't all be coincidental."

⋆ ⋆ ⋆

Jerry went to the war room and asked Liberatore to come back to my office to update us on the progress in tracking down the tractor-trailer rig Fenicks had been driving when he was arrested.

She walked into the room and, without hesitation, said, "I checked on Lucky this afternoon. The vet said she's doing better than expected, but she's still really weak."

Jerry looked at me, one brow arched. "The dog you stole?"

I ignored him, pointed to a chair, and motioned with a finger for Liberatore to have a seat. Jerry smirked and took a seat across the table from her. "How goes the effort to find Fenicks's truck?" I asked.

"Not bad, but not great. I contacted the detective bureau at the Cuyahoga County Sheriff's Office and got lucky. The lead detective on the case, a guy named Thacker, happened to be working. He was a detective then; he's now the chief of detectives. He said the truck sat in a county impound lot for eight months. The prosecutor would not clear it to be repossessed until Fenicks had gone to trial. Once he was convicted, it was repossessed by the loan company that held the title. Thacker said that was the Oil City Lending Corporation in Tulsa, Oklahoma.

"I called Oil City and spoke to a woman in commercial lending—Helen McKee—who could not have been more uninterested in talking to me. She was trying to blow me off and said she couldn't look up anything unless I had the vehicle's VIN, which fortunately I had because Thacker was kind enough to share it with me. She said the trailer was owned by OCO Leasing of Oklahoma City and it went back to them. The tractor was sent to First Florida Auctions in Sarasota for resale. She said it was sold on July 13, 2004, but she has no record of who purchased it. She made a point to tell me that was not germane to her job and any additional information would need to come from First Florida Auctions."

"Did you call the auction company?"

"I did. That's where the 'not great' part comes in. The guy I talked to was only slightly more cooperative than the woman at the loan company. He said they auction off or sell sixty to seventy thousand cars and thirty thousand trucks a year—some to dealers, some to trucking companies, some to brokers who ship them overseas, and some to individuals. If the tractor went to them, the transaction records were there. He said if we have a VIN and a subpoena, we're welcome to go down there and look at their records."

"Good job," I said. "I'll have legal start drafting the subpoena. You get a flight to Sarasota."

"I'll book a flight in the morning."

"Book one for tonight."

TWENTY-TWO

Five weeks and one day before the scheduled execution of Lester Paul Yates.

After our meeting, I decided to send Jerry to Florida with Liberatore. She was a tough cookie, but there was nothing like having a powerlifter with an attitude and a subpoena for getting results. I checked my emails the next morning from home. Liberatore had sent me a message at 2:42 a.m. saying they had checked into their hotel and would update me after visiting First Florida Auctions, and would I please be sure to check in on Lucky. I left from the house and headed back to the Ohio Valley to do my own research on the Danielle Quinn case.

I called Margaret and asked her to get me thirty minutes on the governor's schedule the following week. I needed to have a serious talk with him about the fate of Lester Yates, but I still wasn't sure how to start that conversation.

While I believed I had enough compelling evidence to create reasonable doubt in the mind of a reasonable person, I was dealing with a man with a mammoth ego and even larger political aspirations. Reasonable was nothing more than an adjective in this case. Jim Wilinski trusted Alfonso Majestro. Even if he had taken too many shots to the head, Wilinski was smart enough to understand that Majestro was critical to his getting to the White House. Wilinski would never hesitate to put a head on a stake to protect his political career. But this created a particularly unique challenge. If Majestro was involved in this mess, as I suspected, he was certain to be a liability to the governor's ambitions. However, Majestro also was the mastermind of Wilinski's ascendancy to the presidency. Thus, Wilinski would likely protect Majestro at all costs.

The two men were close. The governor had to know about Majestro, that he had been dating Danielle Quinn. If that was true, did he realistically believe that his chief of staff's relationship with a murdered woman wouldn't come out in an FBI background check? He couldn't possibly be that naïve.

Sadly, I felt that if Yates was executed as a sacrificial lamb for the political future of Jim Wilinski, there were a handful of politically powerful people who would be just fine with that. It wasn't a human life; it was simply collateral damage. If a pimply little guy from the hills of eastern Ohio had to be sacrificed for the greater good, so be it.

My phone rang when I was on the far side of Cambridge. It was Jerry Adameyer; he was calling as he and Liberatore drove to First Florida Auctions. He said Austin Battenberg, the dapper intern, had talked to the manager of the Shenandoah Truck Stop without much success. "The manager said they have security cameras all over the lot, but he's only been there a year and he doesn't know if they were there when the Quinn woman was abducted. He said he'd check, but he knows the current system is on a seventy-two-hour loop, so there's nothing on the videos more than three days old. He'd never even heard of Danielle Quinn and doubts they have any footage."

"Tell Battenberg not to waste any more time on it," I said.

Swing and a miss.

The Belmont County Courthouse in Saint Clairsville was built in 1886 with sandstone quarried in northern Ohio. It was built in the Renaissance Revival style, which was popular in the day, and sits at the highest point in town. It was impressive by any standard. I arrived at the prosecutor's office at a few minutes past nine o'clock. Anchoring the front desk was a neatly coifed woman who smelled heavily of drugstore perfume and was looking over the top of a pair of blue reading glasses with a gold chain dangling from the temples. A plastic nameplate on her desk identified her as Shirley Bascom. "I was hoping to look over a file of a murder case," I said.

"Are you from the attorney general's office?" she asked.

"Yes, I am."

"Come on back. I'm going to start charging you boys rent."

Shirley led me down a hallway to a room that was lined with metal file cabinets and featured a battered wooden table in the middle. "There you go," Shirley said, and headed back to her desk. Sitting at the table were two of my investigators, Davidson and Gonzalez, legal pads and manila folders spread before them. "Hey, boss," Davidson said.

"How's it going, guys?" I said.

"Still trying to piece together the puzzle," said Gonzalez, who had two yellow pencils running through her hair bun like crossed arrows.

"Are you here doing research?" Davidson asked.

"The Danielle Quinn case."

Gonzalez pulled a pencil from her hair and pointed to four cardboard boxes at the far end of the table. "One of us has been here every day, so they put all the Egypt Valley Strangler files in those boxes," he said. "They were tired of fishing them out of the file cabinets every time we walked in."

"That's a compliment," I said. I walked over and began flipping through manila folders tabbed by name—Mason, Pavlik, Schmidlin, Sephardic, Touvell. I looked again, then searched the other two boxes, figuring the Quinn file was out of order. But it wasn't there.

I walked back out to the front desk. "Excuse me, Shirley, but I was looking for the Danielle Quinn file and it doesn't seem to be in any of those boxes."

"Really? That's odd," she said. She spun in her chair to face a woman who was seated behind her. A cup of coffee with pink lipstick smeared across the rim and a pastry she had purchased from a vending machine were on her desk. Shirley said, "Agnes, he said the Quinn file is not in there."

Agnes shook her head and said, "It isn't. I couldn't find it anywhere."

"It was there last week."

"It wasn't there yesterday. I looked."

Shirley turned her head away from her coworker and rolled her eyes. "I know it's back there," she said, putting both palms on her desk and with great effort pushing herself to her feet. "Come on; we'll find it." I followed her back down the hall. "I know for a fact that it was here last week because our former sheriff was here looking at it."

It was instantaneous. Again a wave of heat that felt like an acetylene torch pressed to my spine ran up my back and out across my shoulders. I took a moment to absorb her words and to make sure I didn't overreact to the information. The coworker had been right; the file wasn't going to be back there. After a cleansing breath, I said, "Your former sheriff, you say."

"Yes. Our former sheriff, Del Brown, he was in to look at the Quinn case file."

"Why was that?"

"He was the sheriff when the Quinn woman was murdered. It's very exciting. He said he is writing a book about the case." She turned her head back to me and said, "He said he's going to put all our names in it."

"Is that right?"

"I can't wait until it comes out. I've never had my name in a book. I've got my name in the *Times Leader* a couple of times, but never in a book. Sheriff Brown, he's the one who captured the Egypt Valley Strangler, you know?"

"I did know that."

"He has a big job with the government out in Columbus now. He works directly for Governor Wilinski."

"He does, huh?"

"That's what he said."

We entered the room. From behind Shirley I looked at Davidson and Gonzalez and pressed an index finger to my lips. I had not identified myself to Shirley as the attorney general and didn't intend to do so at this point. She opened a drawer to one of the metal cabinets.

"Yes, Mr. Brown has a big job out there."

"And he reports directly to the governor, you say?"

"Um-hum."

"There is a D. Kendrick Brown who works for the attorney general. Is that him?"

"That wouldn't be him. Mr. Brown works for the governor; he told me so. He said he talks to the governor all the time and he's like some kind of senior adviser or something. Everyone around here is pretty proud of him. He caught the Egypt Valley Strangler and he works for the governor, and he's going to put our names in that book." She opened another file drawer, peeked inside, then pushed it shut. Then another, and another, and another. "That is so strange. I know it was in here because I saw him looking at it."

"You said that was just last week?"

"Yes, we were all surprised to see him. He came walking in just about lunchtime. We were all getting ready to take Agnes out for her birthday. There's a little Mexican restaurant she likes in the strip mall down by the interstate. They have the most delicious fried ice cream. We asked Sheriff Brown, that's what we all still call him, Sheriff Brown, if he wanted to come along, but he said no because he had a lot of research to do for his book. I told him, 'Well, you know where the file is,' and he came right down here and got it. My car was out back and I peeked in as we were heading to lunch, and he was sitting right at this table looking at the file."

"Who put it back?"

"I assume he did. He was gone when we got back from lunch. Maybe he misfiled it." She continued her search through the file cabinets.

He didn't misfile it. It left the building with him, and I was consumed by both anger and curiosity, wondering what was in the file that D. Kendrick Brown did not want me to see.

★ ★ ★

I stopped by the office of Sheriff Douglas Hyde. He was an affable man with a belly hanging over his gun belt and the tiniest pink mouth I'd ever seen on a man his size. He had been the chief of detectives during the Yates case, but said he had been relegated to the bench as the former sheriff had controlled the entire investigation. "How'd that make you feel?" I asked.

"Suspicious," he said. "But I'd never admit that outside of this room."

"I don't think you're alone. I'm looking for the investigative work that led to Yates's arrest. I was hoping you might still have something on file."

"To the best of my knowledge, all our work product went to the prosecutor's office. All we have on file here is the original missing person report."

I thanked him for his time and left. When I got to my car, I called Margaret and asked her to see if she could find the address for the prosecuting attorney who handled the Yates case—Clarence Medville. She gave me an address on Cadiz Pike near Colerain. The house was a mid-century ranch that sat on a hillside that fell toward a stream that ran beside a winding, two-lane blacktop road. A woman with gray hair and a sharp, chiseled jawline was at the kitchen window when I pulled onto the concrete apron in front of the garage. I pretended not to see her and walked to the front door, where she was by then standing, holding open the aluminum storm door with one hand. "Mrs. Medville?"

"Yes, can I help you?"

"Yes, ma'am. I'm Hutchinson Van Buren; I'm the attorney general for the state of Ohio."

She pushed the door open further and said, as though she had been expecting me for tea, "Oh, of course, please come in, Mr. Van Buren."

I stepped into a slate foyer. "Won't you sit down?" she said, leading me into the living room. The windows were open and a light breeze pushed at the curtains; the house smelled of the blanket of zinnias that bloomed just outside. The couch and a love seat were modern and bright green; her cropped pants were an equally bright yellow. There was nothing about the room or its inhabitant that would indicate the staleness of age.

I sat down in the love seat. "I was hoping to speak to Mr. Medville," I said.

"I'm afraid that would be quite impossible, Mr. Van Buren. My husband passed away three years ago."

The red sting of embarrassment oozed into my ears and cheeks. "Oh, I am so very sorry. I had no idea."

She grinned and said, "Obviously."

"I looked him up on the Internet and saw that he didn't run for reelection a while back, but I didn't know he passed away. I'm very sorry."

"There's no apology necessary, Mr. Van Buren."

"I must admit, Mrs. Medville, I'm a little taken aback. You acted as though you knew I was coming."

"I've known it for a long time."

"Ma'am?"

"My Clarence always said there would come a day when someone would knock on that door and want to talk to him about Lester Yates. He said it would most likely be a reporter, or a defense attorney, or maybe an advocate from one of those anti death penalty groups, but he said eventually someone would knock and want to talk about Lester. I'm certain he never believed it would be the attorney general for the state of Ohio. The poor soul, he would have so enjoyed talking to you, but he didn't live long enough to answer the door." She smiled. "That is why you're here, isn't it, Mr. Van Buren, to talk about Lester?"

"It is, indeed."

"I'm not sure I can offer anything of substance, but what is it you're looking for?"

"As I'm sure you know, Lester has a date with the executioner next month. I'm conducting an investigation into his conviction. I was hoping to talk to Mr. Medville to get some perspective on the trial and the original charges, and I was hoping he might have some transcripts or documents that I could review."

"Those would all be on file at the courthouse, would they not?"

"In a perfect world, yes. But they seem to have disappeared."

"I see. I'm afraid I can't help you there."

"I'm curious, Mrs. Medville. Did he tell you why he believed that someone would knock at the door?"

"I suspect you already know the answer to that, Mr. Van Buren. If you've been looking into Lester's case, I'm sure you have the same doubts as my husband. He described it as like having a rat in his gut trying to eat its way out. I apologize for that visual, but that's the way Clarence described it."

"But he was the prosecutor. He was the one who brought the charges and prosecuted the case."

"That is correct. I can tell you that my husband did not want to prosecute Lester Yates. He said it was an abomination and a travesty of justice. He was under great pressure and, in the end, he relented."

"Who was applying the pressure?" For the first time, she didn't appear to want to answer. She looked out at the zinnias and nervously worked her hands, one over the other. "Was it former Sheriff Brown?"

"I don't think he was acting alone, but yes, that little worm was at the forefront."

Without comment, she stood and walked out of the room. She returned a few minutes later with two glasses of iced tea, each with a sprig of mint and a wedge of lemon perched on the rim. She set them on coasters on the glass-topped coffee table between us. She took her glass, sat back in the chair, and sipped at her tea.

"The worm," I said.

"Yes, dear Mr. Brown. He arrested that Yates boy for trying to use the dead woman's credit card. I'm guessing you know about that."

"I do."

"I can't remember exactly what Clarence told me about Lester, but essentially it was that he wasn't the most intelligent young man he'd ever met, but he didn't believe he had anything to do with the Quinn woman's death. Then, it wasn't much longer after that, the sheriff dropped a file on Clarence's desk and said he was going to arrest Lester for her murder. Clarence pushed it back across the table and said there wasn't enough evidence to substantiate a murder charge, and Sheriff Brown said, 'Are you going to be the one who lets the Egypt Valley Strangler walk? That boy is a stone killer.' Or something like that. Clarence started laughing and said, 'What the hell are you talking about?' Excuse my language, Mr. Van Buren, but that's the way Clarence talked when he got upset. He said, 'You know, Del, you're not much smarter than the people you arrest. That boy didn't kill her, and you know it.' They had some kind of transcript where they interviewed one of Lester's friends, who said that he was bragging about killing the girl. Clarence said that was all a bunch of baloney and he didn't know what Brown was up to, but he didn't want any part of it. And you can believe me, that under normal circumstances, where Belmont County jurisprudence was concerned, my late husband was the absolute final word. Then, the next thing I know, they had indicted Lester. I had never seen Clarence look so defeated in my entire life. He wasn't angry, just sad and defeated. When I questioned him about it, all he would tell me was that things would get really bad for him if he didn't get with the program."

"Did he say what that meant?"

"No, he never said, and I didn't press him on it. You know, Mr. Van Buren, we all have secrets. We all have parts of our past that we would like to keep hidden." She smiled. "Given your history, I'm sure you can appreciate that."

I nodded. "I can, indeed."

"Clarence was no different. I'm sure he had things that he wanted to remain secret, even from me. Perhaps it was infidelity; perhaps he fudged evidence somewhere along the line; maybe he misappropriated some campaign funds. I don't know what it could have been, but I can guarantee you that Del Brown, or somebody in his circle, had something on Clarence. And whatever it was, he caved to their pressure and prosecuted the case, and it tormented him until the day he died. He was a good man, my Clarence. Not perfect, maybe even less perfect that I realized, but a good man, nevertheless."

TWENTY-THREE

Maybe Liberatore was right.

Maybe I did have a bad temper and for years had simply tried to smother that reality.

For as long as I could remember, I was never one to rile too easily. When sufficiently incensed, my mother was known to lob both vindictive salvos and water tumblers, so I can only imagine that my easygoing temperament was something passed down from my absentee father, who I knew only from a shoebox of yellowing photos that I kept in an old trunk in my den.

I'm not sure when my disposition changed so dramatically. Perhaps it was the day I looked into the eyes of Akron Police Detective Nick Westmoreland after his beautiful daughter had been raped, tortured, and burned alive. Maybe it was after the helplessness I felt when I was called to the rough Firestone Park section of town to look upon the bodies of a young black mother and her nine-month-old daughter. Shanice Johnston had been pushing her baby in a stroller when they got caught between battling drug gangs; they were sprayed with so much automatic weapons fire that they were unrecognizable. Maybe it was prosecuting a serial rapist and sadist named Enrique Martinez, who smirked and mocked his victims throughout the trial. I had felt proud and satisfied, and I accepted the congratulations of my colleagues after I secured a conviction and sentence that assured Martinez would never again take a breath of free air. That night, we went out for drinks to celebrate our victory. Then, two months later, I cried at my desk when I learned that the victim and my star witness, a lovely woman named Penny Donley, who was an accountant with an MBA and a three-year-old son, had hanged herself in the basement of her parents' home.

Regardless of its genesis, I now had a hair-trigger switch that sent my internal engine from idle to redline in a single breath; fire would arc across my chest one instant and tentacles of ice would shoot down my arms in the next. I was too often consumed by a rage that I found difficult to control, even when I knew it was going to be a detriment to both my livelihood and my mental stability.

That was exactly where I was as I drove back from Belmont County early in the afternoon after visiting with Mrs. Medville. As I headed west on Interstate 70, the twisting in my bowels was sending geysers of acid into the back of my throat, and though I had a crocodilian grip on the wheel that had turned each knuckle to ivory, my hands visibly trembled.

Two-and-a-half hours later, I had not lost any of this intensity when I entered the office of D. Kendrick Brown at the Ohio Bureau of Criminal Investigation. He was sitting behind his desk, a pen in one hand, a can of diet cola in the other. If he sensed my presence, he didn't show it; he didn't look up until the door latch clicked into the plate, sending a metallic echo through the room. The phony smile he used to greet visitors melted from his face, and he nervously swallowed.

Between clenched teeth I said, "What's your game, Brown?"

He swallowed again. "What are you talking about," he said.

"Don't insult my intelligence. I was just down at the Belmont County prosecutor's office. The Danielle Quinn file is missing and, shockingly, they said the last person to look at it was their former sheriff, a guy named Del Brown."

He took a drink of his soda. "I was doing a little research for a book I'm writing."

"I doubt you could read a book, let alone write one. I'll ask you again, slowly this time, so you understand: Where is that file?"

"You'll excuse me, won't you, Mr. Van Buren? I have a meeting to get to." He grabbed a legal pad and started toward the door. The flames that had been roasting my gut erupted in a rush of adrenaline and anger. I grabbed him by the lapels of his jacket and slammed him with everything I had into the wall. The soda can fell from his hand and spewed foam across the carpet. One of the framed newspaper articles fell to the ground, breaking the frame and shattering the glass. I had him pinned, his lapels wrapped up inside my fists. My face was inches from his. Before I could speak, he said, "I assume you're going to pay for that frame." He sucked for air, the saliva rattling between his teeth and gums.

I shoved him harder against the wall. "You know, most three-year-olds learn to take a breath without sounding like a leaking air hose."

"You're very mature for mentioning it."

I pulled him off the wall six inches and slammed him again. "I have no time for your games, Del. Where are those files?"

"The last time I saw them they were on top of the file cabinet in the Belmont County prosecutor's office, right where I put them."

I threw him toward his desk. He stumbled. One foot kicked the soda can, the other crunched busted glass. His knee hit the side of the desk like a sledgehammer. "Are they in here?" I said, walking across the room and grabbing the top drawer in a file cabinet. I yanked it open and pulled it completely off its runners. Papers and manila file folders flew across the room, and the cabinet dropped to the floor like a felled pine. I threw the file drawer that remained in my hand against the wall, then took a moment to catch my breath and survey the damage.

"I think you need some anger-management classes," he said.

"Where are those goddamn files?"

"You know what always used to amuse me when I was the sheriff? There would be these idiots who knew they were under investigation, or at least under suspicion, and we would execute a search warrant and sure as shit, the weapon or the stolen merchandise we were looking for would still be in their house. See, that's what separates the idiots from people like you and me, Mr. Attorney General. If we were hiding something that we didn't want found, we would put it someplace where it could never be found. That's why smart guys like us never go to jail. You know what I mean?"

"I don't know what you and your buddy Majestro are trying to hide, but you can count on this: I'll figure it out."

"When my book comes out, I'll be sure to send you an autographed copy. Hell, I might even dedicate it to you: 'To my good pal, Hutchinson Van Buren, a beacon for justice.'" He patted his pockets and said, "You got any change on you? I'd like to get another diet cola."

I left before the urge to strangle him completely overwhelmed me. I was on the interstate heading back to Columbus when Margaret called me on my cell phone. "I thought you wanted me to set up a meeting with the governor for next week," Margaret said.

"I did."

"Well, apparently you set up one for yourself. The governor's secretary just called and said he wants to see you in his office immediately."

The call was certainly no surprise. I knew the minute I walked out of Brown's office that he would call the governor. When I walked into Jim Wilinski's office he was sitting at his desk in a pressed white shirt, red and blue striped tie, and gold cufflinks in the shape of the state of Ohio holding together his French cuffs. He raised one eyebrow and leaned back in his chair.

"Hutchinson, I'm assuming that you haven't completely lost your mind, but you're making that difficult to prove," he said. "It is going to be extremely difficult for me to nominate you as attorney general of the United States of America if you keep beating up your subordinates."

"I didn't beat up a subordinate." I said.

"That's not exactly the story I received."

"Mr. Brown and I needed to have a difficult conversation. It got a little heated and it's possible his lapels got wrinkled, but that was it."

"What in God's name is going on with you, son? You're unwinding clear down to the spool. Was this all about the Lester Yates case?"

"Mostly it was about Mr. Brown's penchant to lie every time he opens his mouth, but the Yates case was central to the discussion."

He shook his head. "What put this bee in your britches about this Yates fella? He's a serial killer. Why is this the dragon you think you have to slay?"

"Because I think we're going to execute an innocent man."

He squinted and pinched the bridge of his nose. "Hutch . . . What started all this, that file you showed me?"

"That's what made me aware of the situation, yes."

"Refresh my memory; who was it that put that together, some jailhouse lawyer?"

"No, it was a prison guard, a guy named Moretti. He befriended Yates on the block and started researching his story."

He frowned. "What's his name, the prison guard?"

"Reno Moretti."

"Not the boxer?"

"The very same—the Brier Hill Hammer."

"He was the light heavyweight world champion, for God's sake. What's he doing working as a prison guard?"

"Seeking redemption."

"What does that mean?"

"He's made some bad decisions along the line. He doesn't think Yates is guilty, and he started working on investigating the case."

"He's the one who did all the background on this, huh?"

"He did. He has a snitch inside the prison. The guy we've identified as a possible suspect in these murders is an inmate there. He's been bragging about strangling women in eastern Ohio. Moretti has the snitch working to get us more information. The inmate is a former truck driver who got caught trying to strangle a prostitute. We think we've made a connection that puts him in the area at the time of at least one of the murders."

Jim Wilinski took a deep breath, crossed his arms, and asked, "Can you make the connection, and I mean tie it up with a neat bow?"

"I hope. I think the possibility is strong enough that it warrants a stay of execution."

"How long of a stay?"

"I can't answer that yet."

"You're not helping me, Hutch. You know what it's going to take. You have to bring me something proof positive. Don't come back here talking to me about reasonable doubt. The jury already decided he was guilty beyond reasonable doubt."

"I can't tell you for sure who killed Danielle Quinn, but I can tell you who didn't—Lester Yates."

"Padnah, you are flat wearing me out. If you want a stay of execution, give me something tangible." He pointed to the door. "Get out of here, and quit beating up your people."

* * *

I closed the door to my office, loosened my necktie, and took a seat in one of the two padded chairs that sat opposite a round coffee table in the glass-walled corner of my office. Far below me, the four streets that encased the statehouse square were again jammed with rush-hour traffic. I watched the cars and buses creep past while I allowed my stomach to calm and my heart to return to a normal rhythm. It was almost there when Liberatore called me on my cell.

"Tell me something good, Liberatore," I said.

"We found it. The auction house sold Fenicks's truck to a broker in Missoula, Montana."

"Get on an airplane for Missoula."

"No need. Jerry called the broker, and the guy was really friendly. He was able to look it up. He sold it to a truck dealer in Kennewick, Washington. We tried to call the dealer, but the phone has been disconnected."

"Of course it has."

"Jerry wants to know if you want us to fly out there."

"Absolutely."

"Okay. I'll touch base when we get there."

"Please do."

"How's Lucky?"

"Lucky? Oh, great. She's doing great. Really great."

There was a moment of silence on the phone. "You didn't check on her, did you?" she asked.

"No. It's been a hell of a day, Liberatore. I'll do it in the morning. I promise."

TWENTY-FOUR

Four weeks before the scheduled execution of Lester Paul Yates.

I recognized Reno Moretti's phone number on my cell. "Good morning, champ," I said.

"I'm feeling more chump than champ this morning," he said. "I thought the politics in Youngstown were cutthroat, but at least they hit you above the belt, not like you boys down in Columbus."

"Excuse me?"

"There must be some important people down there who don't want to see Lester Yates walk out of prison."

"I'm not sure I understand where this conversation is going."

"Let me help you out. When I got into work this morning I was ordered to the warden's office, where I was promptly suspended pending an investigation for inappropriate contact with an inmate."

I sat up straight. "Why? What's that all about?"

"You tell me. The warden said he had solid information from a reliable source that I was conducting an inappropriate internal investigation and extracting information from an inmate that violated department of corrections regulations."

"Is this about your snitch?"

"He didn't say, but that's a pretty safe assumption."

"Does that really violate department of corrections regulations?"

"Guards use jailhouse snitches all the time. This only violates the rules because it has apparently upset someone much higher up the political ladder than where I'm standing, which is right now on the ground."

"Is that what the warden told you, that he got a call from someone?"

"He didn't have to. It doesn't take an Einstein to see what's going on." His voice was climbing. "The warden couldn't even look me in the eye, and I've always gotten along with him. Before Christmas every year he'd ask me to come to his office to autograph posters and photos he'd bought on the Internet so he could give them as gifts. He has a framed black-and-white on his wall that I signed: 'To my friend, Connor Adkins.' When I asked him what this was really about, he just said it was out of his control. When I asked who had lodged the complaint, all he would say is that it was not important for me to know."

"Do you think it came from down here?"

"You're the only person I've ever told about the snitch."

"The only one?"

"That's it. You can't spread stuff like that around or someone will get a shiv in their liver out in the yard."

"Reno, I don't know what to say. I've only told two people."

"You're batting five hundred, because one of them put the screws to me. Who did you tell?"

"My chief investigator, who I would stake my life is solid, and one other person."

"Who?"

"I'd rather not say right now. Give me a little time to see what I can find out."

"And I get to swing in the wind in the meantime, right?"

"Just give me a little time. I'll talk to some people, and we'll get things back to normal."

"I don't know what your version of 'normal' is, but it's never going to happen here. The warden told me the Youngstown *Vindicator* had already gotten wind of it and had called for a comment. That means whoever called the warden also called the newspaper. They're going to get another chance to crucify me in print. What are people going to think when the newspaper runs a story that says I had inappropriate contact with an inmate at a men's prison? This is awful. This was supposed to be my chance to show that I could do something besides throw a right hook. It's beyond embarrassing; it's going to ruin my life."

"Reno, I know you've got your own problems right now, but I have to ask this: Does anyone else know who the snitch is?"

"No. Just me, but it's going to be a mess. He's a real nervous type. Once he finds out I've been suspended, he'll be half out of his mind."

★ ★ ★

Margaret came into my office, dropped a stack of papers to be signed on my desk, and asked, "What happened to Mr. Brown?"

"I don't know what you mean."

"He was just here to drop off the second-quarter financial reports, and he was wearing a neck brace. I asked him what was wrong and he said, 'Ask your boss.'"

"I think he tripped over his ego."

She turned and started back to her desk. "Mmm-mmm-mmm-mmm-mmm."

★ ★ ★

I called Jerry Adameyer's cell phone at nine-thirty Eastern time. I wasn't sure where he and Liberatore's travels had taken them or what time it was on his end. He picked up the phone and mumbled, "'lo."

"Good morning, sunshine. Where are you on this fine day?"

He yawned and grunted before answering. "Some fleabag hotel outside of Pocatello, Idaho. We flew in last night through Tacoma and Salt Lake City. I think I've had about four hours of sleep in the last three days."

"What's the update?"

"We went to the address of the truck sales operation in Kennewick. It was closed up and no one knew anything about it except the guy who ran it had a terrible overbite, a nervous laugh, and a particular fondness for prostitutes. I got the impression that even if we had found him, he wasn't the type to keep accurate business records. We drove over to Olympia and got some help from the state department of motor vehicles. They had the title transfer. Mr. Giggles in Kennewick sold it to a guy in Pocatello—Terry Hollis. We're going to try to track him down today."

"Keep me posted."

"I'll do it."

"In the meantime, we're dealing with another mess here. I just got a call from Reno Moretti. He's been suspended."

"For what?"

"Technically, inappropriate contact with an inmate."

"What's that mean?"

"It means someone doesn't want Lester Yates to miss his date with the executioner. They knew Reno had a source on the inside and they got him suspended on a trumped-up charge. My guess is, they're afraid Moretti and his snitch are going to pin something on Fenicks that would spring Lester."

"How the hell did they find out he had a snitch? Who did he tell?"

"He said I was the only one he told."

"Who'd you tell?"

"You, for one."

"You know better than that, chief. I never told a soul."

"I know."

"So, who else did you tell?"

"Jim Wilinski."

There was a moment of silence as Jerry considered the comment. "You think the governor is involved in this?"

"I don't. I think I screwed up royally. I had what you might call a small confrontation with D. Kendrick Brown and the governor called me on the carpet. We were . . ."

"Wait, wait, wait. Back up. What's that mean, 'a small confrontation'?"

"I didn't punch him, but I might have roughed him up a little."

"You're my hero, you know that?"

"I'm my own worst enemy."

"What's that have to do with Yates?"

"The governor thinks the Yates case is making me crazy. He may be more right than I care to admit. We got to talking about Yates, and

I told him we were close to identifying another suspect at the prison. I told him Reno had a snitch on the inside and he was working him for more information."

"Why is that such a screw-up?"

"Because the governor tells Alfonso Majestro everything. The governor has bigger fish to fry, but Alfonso wants Yates executed so this all goes away. We know he was dating the murder victim. I think he knows that we are getting close to Fenicks, and this was one way of blowing up the investigation. Unless I miss my bet, he got on the horn with the warden and got Moretti suspended."

"Why don't you let me pay Mr. Majestro an after-hours visit?"

"Because I have enough problems, and I need to keep you employed."

"Oh, I see how it works. You're allowed to beat up D. Kendrick, but I have to keep my hands off Majestro."

"Call me when you find Terry Hollis."

"You got it, chief."

⋆ ⋆ ⋆

I had no problem with face-to-face confrontations. In fact, I rather enjoyed them when I knew I had the goods on someone. Early in my prosecutorial career, I would leap upon a suspect at the first hint of a lie. But over time, I found there was something oddly amusing about watching someone lie to save their skin. In fact, I got to the point where I would play along with the lie, allowing them to think that I was taking the bait. Then I'd drop the evidence in front of them.

Sometimes it took weeks or months to allow them to complete their book of lies. Unfortunately, Lester Yates didn't have months.

I kept this in mind when I dialed up Alfonso Majestro's phone number. The call rolled to his assistant, who patched me back through to Majestro, but only after a suitable wait on hold. When he picked up, the telltale condescension in his voice exposed the disdain he held for me. "What can I do for you, Mr. Attorney General?"

"Why don't you tell me what you know about Reno Moretti getting placed on administrative leave?"

"Not a thing. Who is he, anyway?"

"I don't know what kind of game you're playing, Majestro, but just so you know, I'm committed to figuring it out."

"Do you enjoy talking in riddles?"

"I mentioned to the governor that Moretti was the guy who could vindicate Lester Yates, and suddenly he's placed on administrative leave on a bogus charge. This has your fingerprints all over it."

"I don't know anything about it. Maybe the governor called."

"The governor couldn't be bothered. He told you about our conversation, and you took it upon yourself to put some pressure on the warden of the prison."

"You are failing to see the big picture here, Van Buren. This isn't just some schmo on Death Row. This is the Egypt Valley Strangler—Lester Yates. He's a white supremacist and a gang leader. He's a bad dude. History is going to remember him in the same breath as John Wayne Gacy and Ted Bundy. When we strap him on the gurney, the national media is going to be here—the networks, Fox News, CNN, every major newspaper."

"Well, if the national media is going to be there, then by all means, let's execute him. We wouldn't want to disappoint our friends in the media."

"See, you just don't get it. It's a tremendous opportunity for a potential presidential candidate to be seen as a law-and-order guy. He's going to be the one to rid the world of Lester Yates. The attention he will get will be invaluable when people go to the ballot box."

"Even if an innocent man dies in the process?"

"Knock it off with the sanctimonious bullshit, Van Buren. This guy didn't fall out of the sky. He had her credit card, and a jury found him guilty. In our judicial system, that's all we need."

I decided to show Majestro one of my hole cards. "I see. So, in your world, it makes no difference that the woman he was convicted of murdering had been dating the governor's chief of staff. Is that what you're telling me, Alfonso?" The silence on the phone stretched to five seconds, then ten. I could hear Majestro's stuttered breath in the receiver. "You know what I think, Alfonso? I think there's a lot more going on here than your interest in a presidential campaign. I just think that's your excuse."

"What's that supposed to mean?"

"Take it however you like. I'll be in touch."

He was starting to speak when I hung up the phone.

I picked up my keys from the desk and walked to the parking garage. I was tired of dealing with human trash. I drove over to Grandview Heights to visit Lucky.

TWENTY-FIVE

Three weeks and four days before the scheduled execution of Lester Paul Yates.

At 11 a.m. on Monday, July 30, students, alumni, well-wishers, and Republicans from every hollow between the Ohio River towns of Marietta and Hannibal packed the gymnasium of "The Fort," the local nickname for Fort Frye High School in tiny Beverly, Ohio.

The high school band played the school fight song and "Stars and Stripes Forever." The music reverberated off the walls and spilled out of the school and could be heard across the Muskingum River in Waterford. Television cables ran from the gymnasium to the remote vans in the parking lot, where signal towers protruded into the eastern Ohio sky. Every major news outlet in the state of Ohio—print and electronic—crowded into the gymnasium. Reporters filled time by telling how the real Fort Frye was built on the banks of the Muskingum River in the late 1700s to protect settlers during the ten-year Northwest Indian War. They took photos and video of the school's wall of fame, where a young Jim Wilinski posed with his number 81 jersey and game face. They spoke of his humble roots in a town of thirteen hundred. Gail Hogan, a television reporter from the NBC affiliate in Columbus, got the scoop of the morning when she secured an interview with Wilma Wilinski. She was eighty-one, had the shoulders of a bull, and a fresh hairdo from Macy Johnson at Castle Hill Coiffures, who had manicured her nails for free for the big day. Wilma dabbed away tears with a balled-up tissue and said how proud she was of her son, and that her only regret was that her husband, the original Big Jim Wilinski, wasn't alive to see this day.

When the gymnasium could hold no more people, school superintendent Ken Farmwald walked to the podium, which had been set up in the center jump circle. He cleared his throat and said, "A few weeks ago, Jim Wilinski called my office. The school secretary asked if I had time to talk to the governor." He paused and smiled. "I said yes, that I could probably carve out a couple of minutes for the governor of the state of Ohio." The crowd laughed. "The governor said he needed a place to make a big announcement and wondered if the high school gymnasium might be available. I said, 'It's the middle of the summer, Governor. I think we can work you in.'" More laughter. "Now I don't know what that important announcement might be . . ." He arched his brows. Still more laughter. "But let's hear it from the man himself. Ladies and gentlemen, it is a great honor to introduce Fort Frye High School's most distinguished alum. He starred on gridirons here in Beverly, at Ohio State University, and at Soldier Field in Chicago. He later served honorably and with great distinction in the halls of the United States House of Representatives and now as the governor of the great state of Ohio. Please welcome the boy who once proudly wore the uniform of the Fort Frye Cadets, our very own, Governor Jim Wilinski."

No last-second winning shot in that gymnasium had ever generated such applause. The band began playing the fight song, and the roar drowned out the band. Wilinski emerged from the home locker room and strode across the floor toward the lectern, pumping his fists at the crowd.

When the cheering finally died down, Wilinski leaned into the bank of microphones and yelled, "We are . . . ?"

The packed gymnasium responded, "Fort Frye!"

And the cheering began anew.

"I want to tell you something," Wilinski said. "When I hear that fight song, I still get goose flesh."

Again, they cheered.

Jim Wilinski was in his element; these were his people. He talked about bringing jobs back to eastern Ohio—good blue-collar jobs, like they had in the fifties and sixties. He spoke of the rugged individualism that had carved a state out of the wilderness. He talked about coal mines, steel mills, and glass and aluminum factories. Jobs were needed to end the cycle of drug abuse and depression. "Work," he yelled. "Our people need work."

He was interrupted by wild applause with nearly every sentence. When a woman in the crowd yelled, "We love you, Jim," he responded with, "I love you, too. I love Fort Frye, I love Beverly, I love Washington County, and I love being from right here in God's country."

He spoke for forty minutes before he said what everyone in the gymnasium had come to hear. "That is why, today, in my beloved hometown and at my beloved high school, I am announcing that I am a candidate for the presidency of the United States of America."

As the band began to play and the crowd cheered, I reached for the remote and turned off the television in my office. "There's not a better campaigner in the country," Jerry Adameyer said.

"You're right," I said. "The only thing standing in the way of him becoming the next president will be the corpse of Lester Yates."

TWENTY-SIX

Three weeks and one day before the scheduled execution of Lester Paul Yates.

Tick-tock.

We were creeping closer to the execution of Lester Yates without much progress by the task force.

The car belonging to Danielle Quinn had been returned to her brother while my crime lab director, Beth Kremer, continued to sort through the contents she had collected from the car, which looked like a sweeper bag of debris, hoping to locate a single DNA sample that matched someone in the criminal database. More specifically, Herman Fenicks.

To date, she'd had no luck.

I had thought of trying to connect Alfonso Majestro to the car, but I didn't have his DNA or his fingerprints and no realistic way to obtain them. Even if I did, what did that prove? They had previously dated. It wouldn't be unusual to find evidence that he had been in the car.

We had been equally unsuccessful in locating the tractor rig formerly owned by Fenicks, or its new owner, Terry Hollis of Pocatello, Idaho. Jerry Adameyer and Denise Liberatore had returned to Columbus after spending two days knocking on doors in Pocatello, but Terry Hollis was an enigma. We hired a private investigator to track him down through the Idaho Division of Commercial Vehicles.

The only positive aspect of the entire investigation was that Lucky the German shepherd was at my house and recovering nicely. Liberatore had been pleading with me to allow her to come visit the dog. Against my better judgment, I allowed it. She arrived with doggie treats, toys, and a new collar. "Are you sure you're in a position to take care of her?" Liberatore asked. The message was clear: the intern wanted to steal my dog.

The task force met in the war room for the second full meeting. Unfortunately, it went much as the first. I didn't blame the investigators. They were being diligent. Witnesses had moved or didn't want to talk. Parents had died or disappeared. And a large number of people they interviewed simply thought Lester Yates was the killer, case closed. Let's get him executed. Each investigator gave a report and we worked through the names—Brown, Kaminski, Wetzel, Gardner, Farmer, and Schmidlin. It was looking like Herman Fenicks had been our best shot, but it was going to be extremely difficult now that we didn't have Reno Moretti working for us on the inside.

Clarence Davidson began reading his report on the last named on the list—Louise E. Love.

"Louise E. Love was the last victim whose death had been attributed to the Egypt Valley Strangler. She was a twenty-one-year-old black female. At the time of her death, she was a senior at Capital University where she was majoring in political science. She was last seen on the afternoon of . . ."

"Wait a minute," intern Chip Donahoe interrupted, nearly launching himself out of his chair. "Louise E. Love? What's the E stand for?"

Davidson flipped through his papers. There was a look of agitation on his face. "Elizabeth."

"Oh, my God! That's Lizzy Love."

"I don't know that anyone called her Lizzy," he said.

"Everybody called her Lizzy. She was an undergrad at Capital when I was there. She was one of the victims of the Egypt Valley Strangler?"

"Donahoe, are you kidding me?" I said. "You helped put the notebooks together and you're telling me you didn't discover that you knew one of the victims until this minute?"

"I had the early years—ninety-three to ninety-six. She wasn't killed until 2001. I wasn't paying any attention to the names of the other victims. I was just looking for stories about the Egypt Valley Strangler. I may have seen her name on the list, but I didn't make the connection between Louise E. Love and Lizzy Love."

"How well did you know her?" I asked.

"Not real well. She was a senior, and I was a freshman. But I was on the basketball team and teammates with the guy they thought killed her. That was a big deal when she got killed. That's all anyone at Capital talked about for months. She was smokin' hot, about six foot one. She was a volleyball player and crazy good. Then one day she disappeared, and they found her murdered and floating in some lake. It didn't make any sense. Everyone figured the boyfriend did it."

"Why was that?"

"She told some friends she thought she was pregnant. She was supposedly worried that the boyfriend was going to be mad. He was really good and thought he had a chance to play professionally and this was going to screw things up."

"So they actually believed he killed her to save his basketball career?" Liberatore asked, incredulously.

"That does seem a little far-fetched," I said.

Jerry said, "I heard a story once about a bunch of kids who covered up a murder to protect the quarterback of their high school football team."

I squinted at Jerry.

"Did they have serious reason to believe that he killed her, or was it just wild speculation?" I asked.

"I don't know," Donahoe said. "Right after she was killed, he dropped out of school. To be really honest with you, that was all I was concerned about at the time. I was his backup, so when he left I moved into the starting lineup."

* * *

Twenty minutes later, Jerry and I were in his state car heading toward Capital University, a small, liberal arts school located in Bexley, an affluent suburb on the near east side of Columbus.

"What's wrong with this picture, Jerry? All the other victims were white and had a ton of baggage—prostitution arrests, drug addictions, running with the wrong crowd. The exceptions were Danielle Quinn, who we know was connected to Majestro, and Lizzy Love. How did a black political science major and athlete from a college in Columbus end up floating in a lake in Belmont County?"

"I've got no answer for you on that one, chief. Sounds like it could have been the boyfriend."

"Could have been, but they want us to believe that five-foot-five, one-hundred-and-twenty-pound Lester Yates was able to strangle a six-foot-one college athlete. Where did they meet? How?"

We parked in front of the campus security office, a squat building with glass block windows being consumed by Virginia creeper. The chief of security was Kent Shafer, a former Columbus police commander. He had only been at Capital a little more than a year, but he was familiar with the Love case and pulled a substantial file out of a metal cabinet. "People around here still talk about this like it happened yesterday," Shafer said. "I've read the entire file. She sounded like the ideal kid—won all kinds of awards, was a member of a sorority, Fellowship of Christian Athletes, Young Republicans, all-conference volleyball player. Everyone adored her. And I got the impression it was genuine, not just something they were saying because she'd been killed. She was genuinely a good kid. She was voted homecoming queen the week before she disappeared." He set the file on the edge of the desk and frowned. "If you don't mind me asking, what's your interest in this, Mr. Van Buren? Wasn't her murder solved?"

"No one was ever charged," I said. "They pinned her death on a guy who's scheduled to be executed for another woman's murder."

"I see. I don't know what you're looking for, but you're welcome to go through that file. I'm not sure there's anything in there that will help you out. It's a lot of speculation and hearsay."

"What do you know about her actual disappearance?" Jerry asked.

"Only what's in that file," Shafer said. "She disappeared on a Saturday. She was last seen walking across campus late in the morning. She was caught on a security camera outside her dorm."

"You have her on videotape?" I asked.

"I have the tape, but I'm not sure it would be much help. Fortunately, my predecessor had it digitized a couple years back." Shafer turned his computer monitor toward Jerry and me and started the video. The image was black-and-white, and grainy. The timer in the lower left corner of the screen featured a digital time stamp: 09-29-2001; 11:41 a.m. From behind, a woman with close-cropped black hair, a white long-sleeved shirt, pants, and what appeared to be a full backpack over one shoulder could be seen walking out from under a portico and heading across a small parking area and onto the campus green. The video lasted about fifteen seconds before she walked out of view of the camera.

"She was heading north, toward Broad Street," Shafer said, starting the video over. "The only person known to have talked to her that day was her boyfriend, a kid named Nathan . . ." He opened the files and searched through the papers. "Pryor. He was a basketball player. He said they'd been having problems and he was on his way to her dorm to talk to her when he saw her walking across campus. He said she had been ignoring him and he wanted to know why. He said he thought she was going to break up with him, thought maybe she was seeing someone else, and he was going to confront her about it. He said they talked for less than five minutes near Mees Hall. According to his statement, she started crying and said she didn't know how she felt about their relationship anymore. He said he got upset with her and told her he didn't care if she lived or died. Those were the last words he ever said to her." He slipped the report back in the file. "How would you like to have that on your conscience for the rest of your life?"

"We heard the scuttlebutt around campus was that he was the one who killed her," Jerry said.

Shafer shrugged. "Isn't the significant other always the first suspect? I didn't see anything in his background that would suggest he was capable of murdering her. I think he was seen at the football game later that afternoon. There was no indication that he ever saw her again."

"You've never talked to him?" I asked.

"He was long gone before I got here. I wouldn't know him if he walked through that door, except he was seven foot one." He checked his watch. "Gentlemen, I've got a meeting that starts in ten minutes. I need to scoot." He pointed to a conference room across the hall. "You're welcome to take the file in there and read it. There's a copy machine in the lobby if you find anything of significance."

"Just a couple more quick questions, if you don't mind," I said. "Did she tell anyone where she was going that day?"

"Not that I know of. I didn't see anything like that in the file."

"Did you hear any rumors that she was pregnant?"

"No, nothing like that." He pointed to the file. "Guys, everything I know is in that manila folder; I only know what I've read."

We sat at an old oak table in the conference room and began flipping through the pages of interviews and reports. Included was a page from the 2001–02 Capital basketball media guide. It was a profile on the player who was to be the school's starting center in the upcoming season—Nathan Pryor. He was a preseason all-American and, according to the write-up, "destined to become one of the greatest players ever to wear the uniform of the Capital Crusaders." There was a photo of Pryor next to the write-up, unsmiling, serious, his blond hair cropped close to the head.

"And he packed up his clothes and went home before the season even started," Jerry said. "I find that very interesting."

I read his bio. "Here's something even more interesting. He's from New Philadelphia. What's that, thirty miles from Piedmont Lake?"

"What are you thinking, that he saw her walking across campus, cajoled her to go somewhere and talk about their relationship, and she ended up dead?"

"He lives in the area where the Egypt Valley Strangler was working, so he had to know about the murders. Maybe it was a convenient way to get rid of her body so it would get blamed on the strangler."

"Maybe, but this guy couldn't be the Egypt Valley Strangler. He would have been a kid when the murders started. I can see some big-headed jock letting his ego and his testosterone getting the better of him and strangling his girlfriend, but no way was some seven-footer stomping around the Egypt Valley strangling prostitutes and going unnoticed."

"I agree with you, Jerry. But right now, we don't need to prove he killed all those women. All we need to do is solve one of the murders that was blamed on Lester Yates and create some doubt with the public. We do that, and the governor has to halt the execution."

TWENTY-SEVEN

Three weeks before the scheduled execution of Lester Paul Yates.

At 10:40 a.m. on Friday, August 3, the Columbus bureau of the Associated Press moved the following story, bylined by Andrew Welsh-Huggins.

The Ohio Parole Board today recommended against clemency for Lester Paul Yates, the man identified by authorities as the notorious Egypt Valley Strangler, who for years terrorized eastern Ohio.

The seven-member board was unanimous in its recommendation.

A lawyer for the Ohio Public Defender's office had argued in support of clemency, citing the dearth of physical evidence in the case and noted that other women had been found strangled in the same area after Yates was arrested and incarcerated.

The parole board, however, was not swayed. In a statement released shortly after the hearing, the board concluded that, "Yates acted alone and with great calculation" in the murder of Danielle Quinn, 28, a single mother from the tiny Belmont County village of Bethesda.

Yates' fate now rests in the hands of Governor James D. Wilinski, who just last week announced that he was a candidate for president. Wilinski can use his executive power to overrule the parole board and commute Yates' sentence to life without chance of parole.

Wilinski's chief of staff, Alfonso Majestro, said the governor would make a determination on Yates' fate in the coming weeks.

Yates is scheduled to die by lethal injection on Aug. 24 at the Southern Ohio Correctional Facility near Lucasville.

D. Kendrick Brown, who heads the Ohio Bureau of Criminal Investigation and was the Belmont County sheriff who gained national notoriety for the arrest of Yates and identifying him as the Egypt Valley Strangler, told the Associated Press that Yates' execution would end a sad chapter in Ohio history.

"There is only one fitting punishment for Mr. Yates, and that will come at the end of a needle," Brown said. "As far as I'm concerned, he is the face of evil. He asks for clemency from the state, but he offered no such charity to his victims. The world will be a better place one moment after Mr. Yates takes his last breath."

While Yates was convicted in Quinn's death, authorities believe he could be responsible for as many as 17 other murders attributed to the Egypt Valley Strangler.

The only way Lester Yates could now avoid execution was by gubernatorial pardon or a miracle finding by the task force.

Both seemed highly unlikely.

TWENTY-EIGHT

Two weeks and four days before the scheduled execution of Lester Paul Yates.

Dr. Jasper Love had been the first black man to be named chief of cardiology at the prominent Feldman Clinic in Philadelphia. His father had been a member of the Tuskegee Airmen, and he'd said he had not fought for the right to kill Germans and had not endured every discrimination imaginable to see his son work in an Alabama melon field. He pushed his son to get an education and lived to see him called "doctor."

The man who answered the door that morning in Philadelphia was a distinguished-looking man who appeared much older than his fifty-seven years. This, I assumed, was what life did to you when you learn that your only child was found floating in an eastern Ohio reservoir with a nylon cord around her neck. His hair was the color of pewter, his eyes sallow, and his shoulders had started to pitch toward the floor. When he welcomed me into his house on the north side of Philadelphia and shook my hand, I detected a slight palsy. He led me into a wood-paneled den that was adorned with many framed certificates and as many photographs of his late daughter.

We had been talking for a few minutes, exchanging pleasantries, when he picked a framed photo from the edge of his desk and said, "I will tell you this, Mr. Van Buren, losing my daughter drained my will to live. After Lizzy's murder I was mired in self-pity and living in a dark place from which I could not escape. I left my practice. There were days that I was so heartsick that I could hardly crawl out of bed, and those were the good days. It was no easier on my wife. She passed away two years after Lizzy. Beatrice had a lot of health issues, including diabetes, but that didn't kill her. You'll never find the words 'broken heart' on a death certificate, but that's exactly what she died from."

"How are you doing now?" I asked. It was a question I felt compelled to ask, but instinctively knew the answer before the words had finished leaving my mouth. He would never get over it. I thought of my friend, Akron Police Detective Nick Westmoreland. His daughter had been about the same age as Lizzy Love. Neither man would find peace in this world.

Dr. Love eased himself into a red leather chair. He extended an arm, a tacit invitation to sit on a matching couch. "I am doing okay. I volunteer a couple days a week at the Sykes Free Clinic near Temple University. I attend to a lot of children, and I like that. They call me the love doctor. They think that's funny. It's nice to again appreciate the smile of a child. With that said, you don't ever get over the death of a daughter, but working at the clinic helps. Do you have any children, Mr. Van Buren?"

"No, sir. I was married once, for a short time, but there were no children."

"Should you be so blessed someday, pray to Jesus or to whoever you want to pray to that you never lose them."

I looked at what I assumed was his daughter's high school senior photograph. It was large, twenty-four-by-thirty-six. Young Lizzy Love had flawless skin, a slight overbite, and a gap-toothed smile, "She was a beautiful girl," I said.

"She was naturally beautiful, inside and out. At least she was until someone stole it from her." He pointed. "She had that space between her front teeth from the time she was seven. I pleaded with her to get braces, but she said no, that was too vain. She said that gap gave her character. Sometimes, she would fill up her mouth with water, then strike a pose and squirt it out between that gap in her front teeth like she was a fountain. She thought that was the funniest thing ever. Lizzy never tried to put on airs; she never tried to be something she wasn't. She was just Lizzy Love, everybody's friend. The only place she wasn't a sweetheart was on the volleyball court. I used to call her 'the tigress.' She was as fierce a competitor as I have ever known. If we played dominoes or checkers and she lost, she would get so upset. She was a daisy, that girl. She loved to win."

"How did she end up at Capital University?"

"One of her high school teachers went to Capital. We took a visit, and she loved it. She said she didn't need to see another school. She had offers for volleyball scholarships at some big universities—Temple and Villanova, right here in town—but that's where she wanted to go. It's a strange world. I think of the things that occurred that put her on that campus that ultimately led to her murder. It rips me apart." He took a breath and looked me in the eye. "I suspect we've done enough chitchatting, Mr. Van Buren. What brings the attorney general of the state of Ohio to Philadelphia to talk to me about Lizzy?"

"As you know, they never charged anyone in your daughter's death."

"It wasn't a death; it was a murder. I would like for people to never forget that. Death connotes dying, and that makes it sound too peaceful for what Lizzy went through in her final hours."

"I couldn't agree more. We are looking into Lizzy's murder. Did you know her boyfriend—Nathan Pryor?"

"I can't say I knew him well; I met him once. I was not nearly as impressed with him as he was with himself. It was my understanding he was quite a good basketball player, but perhaps like many fathers, I didn't think he was good enough for Lizzy."

"There was a lot of talk on campus that he may have been the one responsible for your daughter's murder."

"I wouldn't know what to say to that. The authorities in Ohio did a very poor job of keeping me apprised. I got a call from someone at Capital who said she had disappeared. My wife and I flew out there, of course. The next call I received was after her body was found. We rented a car and drove to Cambridge to speak to the sheriff. We were told it was most likely the work of a man they called the Egypt Valley Strangler. That was the last time I spoke to anyone of authority from Ohio until you called."

"You said you didn't believe Nathan Pryor was good enough for your daughter. I'm guessing you knew him well enough to make that determination."

"As I said, I didn't know him well, and I may have been a little prejudicial in my opinion. Living through the civil rights movement and having liberal leanings, I can't say I was thrilled that she fell in love with an egotistical white boy who valued basketball more than education. But I remained quiet, figuring it would all pass in time. Unfortunately, I didn't realize how little time was left."

"You're a liberal, but I saw in one of the reports that your daughter was a member of the campus Young Republicans."

He chuckled. "That was part of the reason I loved my daughter; she could think for herself. She would pick arguments with me just so that we could debate. She was only about fourteen years old when she told me she was a Republican. I laughed because I didn't think she knew a Republican from a submarine. She told me that Abraham Lincoln was a Republican and that was good enough for her, and if she could, she would cast a vote for George Bush. It was like an arrow to my heart. I told her that every member of our family was a Democrat, and her response was, 'Not *every* member of the family, Daddy.'"

"You had to love that spirit."

He nodded and smiled. "Every day." He blinked away a tear. "She was about four years old when she announced that she no longer wanted to be called Louise. She said she preferred Elizabeth. I told her that Louise was a beautiful name and that she was named after my mother. She thought about that for a minute, then looked up at me and said, 'Uh-huh, I still want to be called Elizabeth.'" He could no longer hold back the tears. He pulled his handkerchief from his pocket and wiped his cheeks. "Sorry about that."

"No apology necessary. Dr. Love, the other victims were white, some were prostitutes or women with drug and legal problems, but that wasn't your daughter."

"No, it certainly was not Lizzy."

"It's more than a hundred miles from Capital University to where her body was found. Why would she have been out there?"

"I would love to know the answer to that if you ever find out."

"Did you ever see the autopsy report?"

"No. Being both a physician and a father, I could not look at an autopsy report of the clinically dissected body of my own daughter.

As I said, I was in a dark place to begin with and I didn't need any more chilling details."

"I understand. I will apologize for this in advance, but I need to ask a difficult question."

"Go ahead."

"Do you know if your daughter was pregnant?"

Dr. Love's head jerked backward, and his eyes widened. I don't think a punch to the gut could have delivered a bigger jolt. He blinked away tears and looked out the window for a long moment. I felt guilty for bringing such grief upon him. "Are you telling me that not only did I lose a daughter, but I lost a grandchild, as well?"

"I don't know that for anything remotely resembling a fact. It was a rumor, no more substantiated than Nathan Pryor's involvement in her murder. I brought it up because I wondered if she had shared it with you. The rumor of Pryor's involvement in her murder was tied to the rumor of her pregnancy. I was told that Pryor had hopes of playing professional basketball and knew he couldn't achieve that goal with the responsibility of a wife and child."

"And his solution was to strangle my daughter?"

"As I said, Dr. Love, right now it's nothing more than a rumor."

"We've covered quite a bit of territory, but I must admit that I'm still a little perplexed as to why you came all this way to talk to me about Lizzy."

"Even though no one was ever charged with her murder, it has been linked to a man who is on Death Row with an execution date in the very near future."

"He is this so-called Egypt Valley Strangler?"

"To be honest, Dr. Love, I have very serious doubts to his guilt."

"And you were hoping that I had some insight that would enable you to look in another direction for the real killer of my daughter."

"I was."

"I'm sorry that I can't help you with that."

TWENTY-NINE

Two weeks and two days before the scheduled execution of Lester Paul Yates.

Unlike the elusive Terry Hollis, the truck driver from Pocatello, Idaho, who continued to evade us, Nathan Pryor was not difficult to find. An Internet search located an assistant basketball coach at the University of Tennessee at Martin by that name. I found a team photo, and in the back row saw a somber-looking man with a mop of blond hair and who was every bit of seven feet tall.

"Where is Martin, Tennessee?" Jerry asked.

"No place that we can get a flight to," I said.

"How far's the drive?"

"Seven-and-a-half hours."

"Ouch. Can we afford to spend two days on the road?"

We couldn't. Tick-tock.

Carl Hopkins was a local pilot and the son of a man I had played baseball with in college. I called him up to check his availability and to see how much he'd charge to fly Jerry and me to Paducah, Kentucky, which was the closest airport where I could get a rental car.

"I'm not licensed for commercial flights, so I can't officially take money from you," Carl said. "But I can give you a lift to Paducah, and if I was to find eight hundred dollars in a paper bag in the cabin when we got back, that would be okay."

It seemed steep, but I didn't have the time to quibble. We landed in Paducah shortly before ten in the morning. I got a rental car and headed for Martin, which was about sixty miles south. I had called ahead and talked briefly to Nathan Pryor. Ordinarily, I favored surprising people who I wanted to interview, as I felt it gave them less time to craft their lies. However, I didn't want to hike all the way to western Tennessee only to find him out on vacation or gone on an extended recruiting trip. I contacted him at his office. He was not unfriendly and agreed to talk to me, but preferred that we meet away from the school. He suggested a restaurant in nearby South Fulton.

It was eleven-thirty when we arrived at Lenny's, an old feed store that had been converted into a barbecue joint on College Street. Jerry asked for a coffee; I ordered unsweetened iced tea. The waitress looked at me like I was from another planet. "Unsweetened?" she asked, just to make sure.

"Yes, ma'am," I said.

Her eyes rolled into the top of her head, and she turned on a heel.

"What was that all about?" Jerry asked.

"Everybody down here drinks sweet tea. It's practically heresy to drink unsweetened iced tea in a Southern barbecue joint."

He tucked away the information.

Precisely at noon, Nathan Pryor walked into Lenny's. There was no mistaking him. He had to duck to get through the door. I'm guessing there was no mistaking us for anyone but cops from Ohio, because he walked right over to our table. I stood to shake his hand; the top of my head didn't reach his shoulders. He had paws the size of a frying pan and his fingers could have encircled my hand twice. If he was concerned about the meeting, you wouldn't have known it by his appearance. He was wearing a pair of high-top tennis shoes, unlaced, a University of Tennessee at Martin golf shirt, untucked, and a pair of coach's shorts. His shaggy hair hung limp and unkempt. Jerry shook Pryor's hand and said, "Jesus H. Christ, son, what size shoes are those?"

"Twenty-ones," he said. "I have to get them special-order."

"No doubt."

We chatted for a few minutes and ordered lunch. Jerry and I had barbecue sandwiches and coleslaw; Pryor ordered a full rack of ribs and iced tea. I assumed that people who were seven feet tall needed a lot of fuel for the engine.

"We appreciate you taking the time to talk, Mr. Pryor," I said.

"Not a problem, but I don't know that I can be of any help," he said. "I don't really know very much." Frown lines stretched across his forehead. "Just curious. Why is this coming back up now?"

"Investigations into unsolved murders never really go away. There's no statute of limitations on murder. We periodically go back and review old cases just to see if anything got missed the first time around."

He nodded. "I thought that one guy killed her, that Egypt Valley guy."

"No one was ever charged in Lizzy Love's murder."

"If you have questions, I'll tell you what I know, but like I said, I don't know much."

"You were her boyfriend?"

"Yeah, I guess."

"You guess?" Jerry asked.

"We had started seeing each other that spring, like about six months before she disappeared. We both stayed at school over the summer and it was pretty hot and heavy for a while, but things had started to go south that fall."

"How come?" I asked.

He shrugged. "I honestly don't know. She just seemed to lose interest in the relationship."

"Was there someone else?"

"I don't know. Maybe. Not at Capital. It's a small school and I would have known about it. I've had a lot of time to think about it, and I probably just wasn't a good fit for Lizzy."

"Why do you say that?"

"I don't know what the right word is—rigid, structured—but Lizzy always had a really defined idea of how her future looked. She had a plan for everything. She wanted to go to law school, and it had to be an Ivy League school, and she wanted to be done in three years. After that, she said she would join a law firm, but it had to be in either Philadelphia or Washington or New York City. She used to say that her ultimate goal was to be the first African American and the first female to be elected president of the United States. She asked me about my ultimate goals and I told her I didn't even know what I was having for lunch, but if she was asking what I wanted to do after college, it was play pro basketball. That used to drive her crazy. She'd say, 'You can't play a little boy's game forever, Nathan.'"

"How did you respond to that?" Jerry asked.

"I told her I'd play a little boy's game for as long as I could." He grinned and shrugged. "It was an honest answer, but it really set her off. She wanted me to be as passionate about education and law and politics as she was, and that just wasn't going to happen. I was a jock, and I was okay with that."

"You said the relationship was going south. What did that mean?"

"I could just tell that something wasn't right with us. She got cold toward me, avoided me, and when we were together, she started picking fights. I'd ask her what was wrong and she'd fly off the handle. That was really unusual for her. I figured she wanted to break up but didn't know how to do it."

"We were told the two of you had a nasty confrontation the day she disappeared," I said.

"Not really. People blow everything out of proportion. I called her and she said she didn't have time to talk. I was walking over to her room to see her. I'd had enough. I was going to force her to make a decision. Either we were a couple, or we weren't. I ran into her walking across campus, and she had her backpack over her shoulder. It looked full. Maybe she was going to the library, maybe she was going to go spend the night with some dude. I didn't ask her. I said, 'I'll make this easy for you, Lizzy. We're done.'"

"You didn't tell her that you didn't care if she lived or died?" Jerry asked.

He shook his head. "That may have been implied, but I didn't say it."

"Isn't that what you told the investigators?"

"What investigators? I never talked to any investigators."

"You were never interviewed in connection with Lizzy's death?" I asked.

"No."

"Seriously?"

"I was never interviewed. I talked to the campus security guard when she was missing, but that was it. I was never questioned about her murder."

"But you were the boyfriend. You were the first one they should have interviewed."

"By that time, I was the ex-boyfriend. Look, I'm not sure how to say this without sounding callous, so I'll just say it. I was upset that she had died. That was terrible. But when I walked away from her that day on campus, I was over her, and I put the relationship behind me."

"That's getting over her pretty quickly, isn't it?" I asked.

"I was in college where there were girls everywhere, and I was an all-conference basketball player. That makes it a lot easier to get over someone."

"Do you know if she was pregnant?"

"I heard those rumors. No, she wasn't. Well, if she was, it wasn't mine."

"You were sexually active?"

"Very, but I always wore protection."

"Nothing is foolproof. Accidents happen."

"We were really careful. We were both athletes, and neither of us wanted to screw up our careers. That whole pregnancy thing was just a rumor that got started after she died."

"Supposedly, she had told a few of her friends she was pregnant."

Again, he shrugged. "Well, she didn't tell me."

"Why did you leave school?" Jerry asked.

"Why do you think?"

"I'm asking you."

"Look, I'm not stupid. I know why you're here. It's because people on campus suspected me of killing Lizzy."

"Your name did come up."

"Six years ago it came up, over and over and over again. Every time I walked across campus, I could feel the eyes on me. That's not unusual for a guy who is seven foot one, but it was different. All anyone on campus was talking about was Lizzy. They weren't asking each other if I was capable of murder, they were asking each other why I did it. I got tired of hearing it."

"You left school because everyone thought you killed her?" I asked.

"Yeah. Who wants to live with that? I went home and worked for my dad for a while. Word got out that I wasn't playing at Capital, and Malone College in Canton offered me a scholarship. I played my last two years up there."

"What kind of work does your dad do?"

"He has a delivery business back in New Philadelphia. Mostly he moves appliances and furniture for some of the box stores."

"Trucking?"

"I guess you could call it trucking. He has a fleet of panel trucks and vans."

"You didn't want to go into the family business?"

"He still wants me to come home and do it, but I like coaching." He took a long drink of his iced tea and set the empty glass on the table. "Look, I've told you guys everything I know. If you're investigating her murder, you're wasting your time talking to me. I had nothing to do with her disappearance or her murder. I'm sorry it happened, but that was a different life ago. I moved on. I'm married now; I've got a two-year-old daughter and another one on the way."

"Congratulations," I said.

"Thanks. I met my wife when I was playing pro basketball in Iceland. She knows about Lizzy; I told her that I'd been dating her before she was murdered, but she doesn't know that I transferred because everyone thought I was the killer."

"Seems like something you would share with your wife."

He shook his head. "Do you think she would have married me and moved from Iceland to Martin, Tennessee, if she suspected I was a murderer?"

"Probably not."

"Absolutely not. Look, I didn't do anything wrong. It's in the past, and I'd prefer to keep it that way."

"How did you end up down here?" Jerry asked.

"A guy I played with overseas, he's the nephew of the head coach here at UT Martin. That's how I got the job. I like it here.

I like where I am in my life, and I'd very much like not to see it disturbed."

Jerry and I gave Pryor our business cards and told him we would keep him posted on any developments in the case. He said, "I appreciate that, but you really don't need to bother." He got up, shook our hands, and left. When his car had left the parking lot, I asked for a plastic carryout bag. I put the glass, the paper napkin, and the fork Pryor had used in the bag and tied it shut.

I paid the bill and dropped an additional twenty dollars on the table to cover the items I took.

When we got to the car, Jerry said, "It would appear that you don't believe Mr. Pryor's story."

"Did you notice that he contradicted nearly everything we believed to be true about her disappearance and murder? The only thing he confirmed was that everyone on campus believed he killed her. And he had access to his father's panel trucks and vans in New Philadelphia, thirty-five miles, give or take, from where the body was found."

"I think you're grasping at straws, chief. He just doesn't strike me as the type."

"This guy I know, one hell of an investigator, once told me no one is immune to a moment of rage."

He grinned. "That's true. Even so, what good is a DNA sample on a six-year-old homicide case where the victim was found in the water and has been in the ground for six years?"

"I've got a guy on Death Row who shouldn't be there, Jerry. You're right, I'm grasping at straws, but that's all I've got to grasp at the moment."

We headed north on Route 51 toward Paducah. It was overcast; dark gray clouds closed down on the soybean and corn fields that lined the road. On the back seat was the carryout bag containing soiled dinnerware and Nathan Pryor's DNA. "Do you ever think about what we do?" I asked.

"Not too often; it'll give me a headache," Jerry said. "But, for the sake of conversation, what do you mean?"

"Pryor seems like a decent guy, living his life in Martin, Tennessee. He's doing well, coaching basketball, married with a second child on the way, and if we were honest, we'd admit that we'd love to find some way to jam him up and link him to the murder of Lizzy Love so that we could get Yates off the hook."

"That's the part of the job that gives me a headache. In the end, it's a one-for-one trade."

"True, but if you put Nathan Pryor and Lester Yates side by side, who is going to make the bigger contribution to society—the guy who's working with kids and coaching college basketball or the guy who tried to use a dead woman's credit card to buy a fishing pole?"

"None of that matters. If you're an Eagle Scout and you commit a murder, you go to prison. If you didn't murder someone, it doesn't matter that you painted a Confederate flag on the roof of your car; you get out of jail."

"I know," I said. "But sometimes it just seems like an odd way to make a living."

THIRTY

The plane set down at Bolton Field on the far west side of Columbus about dinnertime. Jerry went back to the office, and I headed to the crime lab in London. I had called Beth Kremer before we left Tennessee and asked her to wait for me at the lab. I pulled around back to the bay door, and she met me in the parking lot. I handed her the carryout bag and said, "I need you to run these for DNA."

"Will do. I assume you want me to compare them to the criminal database?"

"You don't need to do that. This guy has no priors."

"Okay, so what am I looking for?"

"In all honesty, Beth, I haven't a clue. It's probably a total water haul, but I'd like to have it available in case I need it down the road."

She smiled and scratched at her temple. "Do I move this ahead of the work on Danielle Quinn's car, or can it wait?"

"I need them both yesterday."

"I see." She pointed to her right eye. "Mr. Attorney General, sometimes you give me a headache right behind this eye."

"Uh-huh. You and Jerry Adameyer need to get together and compare notes."

* * *

It had been a long day. I wanted to stop by the office to check my emails, return any calls that couldn't wait until later, then go home and see Lucky. Unfortunately, that train went off the rails the instant I walked into my office. Margaret had gone home for the day, but there was Shelly Dennison, camped out at my conference table with pages of flow charts and polling data spread out in front of her.

In all the years I had known Shelly, I had never once seen her cry. One of her political clients once described her as being "tougher than a baked owl." I thought it was an appropriate description. But on this day, she had red-rimmed eyes and a tiny sniffle. I could see a little quiver in her lips, and she was trying to conceal a wadded-up tissue in her left hand.

"Having a bad day?" I asked.

She rolled her head in a circle, as though she could not quite decide. When she tried to speak, she pulled hard for air, causing a stuttering sound as it rolled over her lips while unsuccessfully warding off tears. I have never done well around crying women. I retrieved the box of tissues from my bottom desk drawer and brought it to the table. She plucked two in rapid succession. When she finally caught her breath, she dabbed at mascara-stained tears and said, "You were right. You were right all along."

"I love hearing that from you, Shelly, but I haven't the faintest idea what you're talking about."

"That son of a bitch never had any intention of leaving his wife, not now, or after the election."

"Oh, that," I said, pulling out a chair at the conference table and sitting down next to her. "When did you find this out?"

"Earlier this afternoon, about thirty seconds after he rolled off of me at the Governor's Residence."

It was more information than I needed . . . or wanted.

She blew her nose and dabbed at more tears. "He said he just couldn't do it to her right now because she was looking forward to becoming the first lady and she had developed some plan to help underprivileged kids in Appalachia learn to read; that was going to be her . . . ," Shelly made quotation marks with her fingers, "'cause,' when she became first lady. I told him it was a stupid fucking idea and if the little assholes would pay attention in school, they wouldn't need a special reading program. Admittedly, it wasn't my finest moment." She blew her nose again. "He knew all along that he wasn't going to leave her, just like you said. Go ahead and say it: 'I told you so, Shelly.' Rub it in; you've earned it."

"I'm not going to rub in anything. That's not my style. Look, I'm certainly not one to give advice on affairs of the heart, but why in God's name did you let this happen?"

"Because I love him. I know you don't believe that, but it's no less a reality."

Shelly Dennison could have had any man in the world, except the one she wanted.

She took a couple of breaths, then pounded her fist twice on her thigh. "I hate him. He used me. He used me, and I took the bait. I feel dirty and stupid."

Naïve was the term I would have used, but over the years I had developed a policy of restrictive honesty in certain situations, like this one.

"Then, to top off a perfect afternoon, on the way back that little shit Alfonso Majestro pulls over to the side of the road and says, 'Now that you and the governor aren't an item anymore, maybe you and I can discuss an arrangement.' The mere thought of it made me want to take a shower. I said, 'First of all, you don't know that the governor and I aren't an item anymore. Secondly, I have a can of pepper spray in my purse and if you don't get this car moving, I'm going to empty it in that fifty-five-gallon drum you call a nose.'"

"What'd he say to that?"

"Nothing. He just laughed and drove me back."

"Why was Majestro driving you back?"

"He would always pick me up and take me back from my . . . meetings with the governor. I was never allowed to have my car at the Governor's Residence. Jim was worried that someone would see it or it would get picked up on the security cameras."

"Seems like overkill. You're a consultant. You could justify the visits."

"He said the security videos are state property and have to be kept like a public record. He didn't want some newspaper reporter getting tipped off and looking into them."

"Or a good divorce lawyer."

"Or that." She blew her nose again. "That son of a bitch probably has no plans to use me in his presidential campaign, either. I was just another punch for him. I was so stupid to think I actually meant something to him."

"You're far from stupid. Maybe he has feelings for you but felt the political pressure was simply too great."

Of course, we both knew that wasn't true. Where sex was involved, Jim Wilinski had the moral compass of a hungry alligator. I was desperately searching for words that would make her stop crying; I had nothing. Eventually, she would realize it was a hard slap to the face, but one from which she would recover, and the old fighting spirit that had reduced political opponents to fodder would return. If Shelly Dennison was anything, she was resilient.

I walked over to the phone and called Liberatore. I asked her if she would mind running up to the house to feed and walk Lucky. She was thrilled. I told her where I'd hidden a key to the back door, and she hung up before I could tell her where to find the dog food. She'd figure it out.

"Let's go out," I said. "I'll buy you a couple of manhattans and dinner, and you can tell me how you're going to get me reelected attorney general."

"I explained all that to you the other night."

"I know, but I wasn't listening."

★ ★ ★

When I got home, it was after eleven o'clock. There was a note on the kitchen table.

Lucky wanted to have a sleepover at my place. I didn't think you would mind.

Liberatore

The intern stole my dog.

THIRTY-ONE

Two weeks and one day before the scheduled execution of Lester Paul Yates.

The next morning, I was at my desk by seven and rereading the newspaper articles on the Egypt Valley Strangler collected by the interns, paying particular attention to those about Lizzy Love. I called Jerry Adameyer in the war room at eight and asked him to come over to my office. By the time he arrived, I had several articles spread out on the conference table.

Jerry looked every bit the detective when he walked into my office with a foam cup of coffee, his sleeves rolled up, and his tie askew. He was ready for work. "What's up, chief?" he asked.

"I want you to look at these articles and tell me what you think." I slid one from the Martins Ferry *Times Leader* in front of him. "I highlighted the passages I need you to read. This one was published on Monday, October 1, 2001."

Belmont County Sheriff Del Brown responded to a call early Sunday after the body of a female was reported being dumped into Piedmont Lake beneath the boat docks on the eastern banks of the reservoir.

An unidentified male caller said he witnessed a large man dumping the body of a female in the shallows beneath the docks in an area known as the Hilltop.

The call came in just after 3 a.m. Brown was on patrol in the western part of the county and responded to the call. The Flushing Fire Department was called in to assist with the search.

However, rescue workers were unable to locate a body.

The area surrounding Piedmont Lake has been the dumping ground for the so-called Egypt Valley Strangler for eight years.

Jerry pushed the article back to the middle of the table.

"What strikes you as odd about that?" I asked.

"Why was the sheriff out on patrol at three o'clock on a Sunday morning?"

"Exactly. That's the graveyard shift, and it was just happenstance that he was in that area when the call came in? I don't think so. I think he was there because he knew that someone was going to report a body under that dock and he wanted to be the first on the scene." I pushed another article at him. "Now, read the highlighted graphs here. It's from the *Daily Jeffersonian* in Cambridge, dated October 5, 2001—four days later."

The body of a black female was discovered floating under the docks of the Piedmont Lake Boat & Yacht Club this morning.

Guernsey County Sheriff Nolan O. Haley said the body was discovered by the club's janitor while he was hosing off the docks.

Haley said a nylon cord was found wrapped around the woman's neck and the death is being investigated as a homicide.

The body was sent to the Franklin County Coroner's Office for an autopsy.

When he finished, I asked, "Why was a body that was reported under a boat dock on the eastern side of the lake in Belmont County found under a dock on the western side of the lake in Guernsey County three days later?"

"Maybe the caller was confused," Jerry said. "He could have panicked after he saw the guy dumping the body."

"Doesn't seem likely. The caller specifically said it was under the docks near the Hilltop area on the eastern side of the lake."

"Interesting. How far is it across the lake?"

"I looked on the map. I'm guessing it's three miles, maybe more."

"It certainly didn't float across the water."

"No, definitely not. Brown was supposed to find it in Belmont County. Someone screwed up."

I handed him another article. "Read this from the *Daily Jeffersonian*. It ran the following Tuesday, October 9."

A 21-year-old Capital University student whose body was found floating in Piedmont Lake on Thursday was seen in a local automobile repair shop and convenience store Saturday afternoon, the day authorities believe she disappeared.

Phil Stubblefield, who owns Stubblefield's Auto Repair and Quickie Mart near Londonderry, identified Louise E. Love as the woman who came into his business after seeing her photograph in yesterday's edition of the Daily Jeffersonian.

In an interview this morning, Stubblefield said he immediately contacted the Guernsey County Sheriff's Office after seeing the photograph.

"It was definitely her," Stubblefield said. "She bought a bottle of water and some cheese crackers. We chatted at the counter for a minute. She was very friendly."

Stubblefield's is about five miles from where Love's body was found.

Sheriff Nolan O. Haley said Love's sighting in Londonderry will be investigated for links to her death and to help create a timeline of her final hours. Haley said it is the last known time she was seen alive.

"Interesting, but I'm not sure that's going to be any help to us," Jerry said.

"Read this one," I said. "It ran in the same paper two days later."

The owner of a local automotive repair shop has recanted his story of seeing strangulation victim Louise E. Love in his business just hours before authorities believe she was murdered.

Phil Stubblefield, owner of Stubblefield's Auto Repair and Quickie Mart near Londonderry, contacted the Guernsey County Sheriff's Office yesterday and said he was mistaken about identifying Love. According to Sheriff Nolan O. Haley, Stubblefield offered no explanation for the mistake.

"It's a little perplexing, to say the least," Haley said. "An attractive, six-foot-one black woman walks into a convenience store in rural Guernsey County and buys cheese crackers, and he now says it wasn't her? I don't know what's going on, but it doesn't make sense to me."

The Jeffersonian contacted Stubblefield, who said he would have no further comment on the matter.

"What the hell?" Jerry asked.

"What the hell, indeed," I said.

"Someone got to him."

"Sure sounds like it. I think I'll take a drive out to Guernsey County and poke around. Want to come along?"

"I better stay. I'm working with that private investigator in Idaho trying to track down Terry Hollis."

"The Idaho truck driver?"

"I can't believe we can't find this guy. Plus, I have the interns working on a project for me. I'm sending them out to the auditors' offices in Belmont, Guernsey, and Harrison Counties to check property records."

"For who?"

"I want to see if Nathan Pryor's family owned a cabin anywhere around Piedmont Lake."

My brows arched. "That's a good idea."

"It's a long shot, but it might answer some questions."

"Okay, I'll fly solo."

"Take Liberatore. I assigned her Guernsey County."

* * *

I fetched Liberatore from the war room, and we headed toward the parking garage. "What's our mission today?" she asked as she slid into the passenger seat.

"We'll get to that in a little while. How's my dog?"

"You mean *our* dog? She's fine."

"No, I mean *my* dog. The one you stole last night."

"She was lonesome and wanted to come home with me. She told me so, and we had the best time last night."

I shook my head. "You're a handful, Liberatore."

I drove south on Third Street and jumped on the entrance ramp to the interstate. In a few minutes we were clear of the city and eastbound on I-70, heading toward Guernsey County. I was ready to explain our task to Liberatore when she said, "So now that we've gotten to be friends, what's your deal?"

"My deal?"

"Yeah, are you gay?"

"What? Gay! No! Why would you ask me that?"

"It's okay if you are. I'm just curious."

"Why would you even think that?"

"You're a nice-looking guy, no visible scars, cool job, you make six figures a year—it's public record; that's how I know—and yet you don't have a wife or a girlfriend to speak of. How come?"

"Liberatore, you're an intern in my office and that is not the kind of question you are supposed to be asking your boss, especially when he's old enough to be your father."

"Come on, I'm not seventeen. We're both adults. What's the story, morning glory?" She grinned wide, accurately assessing my discomfort.

"How do you know I don't have a girlfriend?"

"I looked around your place last night before I took Lucky for the sleepover. No woman would decorate a house like that."

"You snooped around my house?"

"I didn't have to snoop. You can tell it's a guy's house. You use the kitchen table for a desk and the living room walls have nothing but photos of you and your fishing buddies and you playing sports from like a hundred years ago, some certificates, and the stuffed head of that musk ox or water buffalo, or whatever it is."

"It's a bull elk. I shot it in Montana."

"Whatever. No woman would ever go for that. So, what's the deal?"

"It's a long story."

"We're going to be in the car all day."

I paused for a moment to ponder how much I wanted to share. "Let me explain it this way, Liberatore. Do you have any girlfriends who you think are mean, vindictive, and crazy?"

"Sure. I had a sorority sister or two that fit that bill."

"Did you ever go to a party and see one of these friends with a guy, and he seems really decent, no visible scars, as you like to say, but he's absolutely clueless about the fact that the woman he's with is stone crazy, and you think to yourself, what in God's name is he doing with her?"

"All the time."

"Well, I'm that guy. I have this incredible knack of attracting women who are not good for me. When I was younger, I thought it was just a string of bad luck. But when I got a little older, I realized it wasn't just bad luck, but a serious character flaw. After all these years, I still can't discern a good woman from one that's going to pull a voodoo doll of me out of her purse and start stabbing it with pins. *That*, Liberatore, is why I don't have a wife or girlfriend."

"What are you going to do? Be celibate the rest your life?"

"Liberatore!"

"What? It's a legitimate question."

"It's not a legitimate question that an intern should be asking the attorney general for the state of Ohio."

She waved at the air. "Wow, you really are wound up tight. No wonder you have such a bad temper."

* * *

Guernsey County Sheriff Nolan O. Haley greeted us in the foyer and, with a wave of his hand, invited us to follow him back to his office. He was scarecrow-thin, and his shirt and pants looked cartoonish on his bony frame; his gun belt hung around his hips like an anchor. It seemed with great effort that he made his way around the desk, holding hard to its edge as he eased himself into a chair, his arms quivering with the effort. He took several deep breaths and said, "I apologize for my lack of vigor. I'm five weeks into chemotherapy, and it's whippin' the blue Jesus out of me."

"Sorry to hear that," I said, taking a seat in front of his desk; Liberatore followed suit. "What kind of cancer?"

"Lung." My eyes immediately went to the half-empty package of cigarettes on his desk blotter and then to the nicotine-yellow stains on the fingernails and first knuckles of the index and middle fingers of his right hand.

"How's the treatment going?"

"I wouldn't recommend it. But they caught it early, and the doctor's confident I can beat it." He picked up the package of cigarettes. "Of course, he wants me to give up these."

"That would seem like a good idea."

"No doubt, but I'm too stubborn to change and too old to care. The damn things are hard to shake, even when the Grim Reaper is tapping on your shoulder. However, I'm sure you didn't come here to discuss my health. What can I do for you, Mr. Van Buren?"

I gave Haley the shortened version of our investigation into the Egypt Valley Strangler and my particular interest in the murder of Lizzy Love. He nodded and said, "You're welcome to everything we have. Unfortunately, it's not much." He leaned forward and pushed a button on his intercom. "Wanda, would you bring me the Love girl's file, please?" He turned to me. "We're a small department, so I oversaw the investigation, but there wasn't much to investigate."

Wanda came into the office a few minutes later with a manila folder. It had an incident report of a body being found under the dock of the Piedmont Lake Boat & Yacht Club. It contained some photos of the body, but not a whole lot more. The report noted that the body had been sent to the Franklin County coroner's office, but there was no copy of the autopsy. A separate report recorded both Phil Stubblefield's account of seeing Lizzy Love in his convenience store and the subsequent report of Stubblefield recanting his earlier claim. There were several more pages of typewritten notes.

"You're right," I said. "It's pretty thin."

Haley coughed into his fist. "You can't make a silk purse out of a sow's ear."

"What's that mean?"

"It means I've never seen a murder investigation with fewer clues or witnesses. This woman's body was found under the docks. We talked to the manager of the boat club, everyone who had a boat docked there, and everyone who lived in nearby cabins. No one said they heard or saw anything. Our black population in the county is about one percent. Yet, a young black woman shows up dead under a dock in Piedmont Lake, and no one saw or heard a damn thing. We don't even know how she got from Columbus to the lake. Makes no sense."

"She didn't have a car?"

"Nope."

"What's the story with Stubblefield? I read the newspaper stories. Any idea why he recanted?"

"None. One day he's telling us that he could positively identify her from the photo in the paper. No doubt in his mind, he said. Absolutely positive. The next day he calls back and says he doesn't think it was her, says he doesn't even know if the woman in his store was black or Mexican. Jesus H. Christ, when a six-foot-one black woman walks into a convenience store in backwater Guernsey County, you don't confuse her for a Mexican."

From the corner of my eye I could see Liberatore fighting off a grin.

"Did someone get to him?" I asked.

"Nah, I don't think so."

"Did you ask him?" Liberatore said.

This scalded Haley, and his jaw muscles tightened. "I've been doing this a long damn time, little lady. I know the people in Guernsey County. They want to be helpful, but they get hinky when they realize they're in the middle of a murder investigation. They see their name in the newspaper and get cold feet. That's all that happened."

"But you don't know if he was coerced or not because you didn't ask him," she said.

Haley started rolling his teeth over his lips. If he'd had more energy, he might have come up out of his chair. Unlike Liberatore's questions about my personal life, I agreed with this one. It was legitimate, but I didn't want to lose Haley's cooperation. I jumped in before the temperature around the desk could rise any further. "Was she with anyone?" I asked.

"Stubblefield said he didn't remember. He said she walked in by herself, bought the crackers and water, and left. I tried to get some other details, but he said there were other people in the store and he wasn't paying particular attention to anyone else."

"No security cameras?"

"No."

"So, the investigation just died?"

"More or less. I wasn't making much progress, then I got a call one day from Del Brown. He used to be the sheriff in Belmont County. He works for the government out in Columbus now. Do you know him?"

"I do. In fact, he works for me."

"Is that a fact? Well, sorry for your luck. That guy's a damn piece of work. Anyway, he calls me up and says they've made an arrest in the Egypt Valley Strangler case and that I didn't need to be wasting a lot of time working to solve the Love girl's murder because they were going to pin it on the guy they arrested. I can't remember his name."

"Lester Yates," I said.

He snapped his fingers. "That's it. Yates. Brown said they were going to squeeze Yates and he was sure he was going to talk. I was pretty grateful, actually. We're stretched pretty thin, and I didn't really have the resources for a big investigation like that. I thought, well, if they're sure they got the right guy, that's fine. I figured they'd be charging him with the Love girl's murder."

"And . . . ?"

"Never heard from him again." He leaned back and took a few hard breaths. "We did what we could. We interviewed her friends, her parents, and her boyfriend, some great big rascal. I think he was a basketball player."

"Nathan Pryor?"

"I don't remember his name right off, but he was one tall drink of water."

"But you talked to him?"

"Drove over to Columbus and interviewed him in the lobby of his dormitory. He couldn't tell us much."

"We talked to him yesterday, and he said he had never been interviewed by the authorities."

"Really? His memory must not be very good."

"Do you have a summary of your conversation?"

He shook his head. "Nah, I didn't bother. He didn't tell me anything worth writing down."

"I saw the body was sent to Franklin County for an autopsy."

"We don't have the capabilities to do those here. We contract out for those services."

"I don't see a copy of the autopsy report. Is it somewhere else?"

"To be real honest, I don't ever remember seeing it."

I thanked Haley for his time, and we left.

Liberatore and I had barely cleared the courthouse steps when she said, "What a dick. *I've been doing this a long damn time, little lady.* If he's such a great investigator, how come he didn't keep any notes from the interview with the victim's boyfriend, and why isn't there a copy of the autopsy report in the file?"

"The sheriff is an elected position," I said. "You don't have to be competent, just popular."

"He's fighting lung cancer, but he's still smoking? Is that the intelligence level we're dealing with? He doesn't belong within ten miles of a murder investigation. And he's a dick. Did I mention that?"

"Yes, I think you mentioned it."

When we got to the car, I tapped out Jerry Adameyer's number on my cell. "Jerry, when are the interns going out to look at property records?"

"They just left here about fifteen minutes ago."

"Together or separately?"

"Together. They were going to tag-team it."

"Call them and tell them I want one to go to Harrison County and one to Belmont County. I want the names of all the property owners and the dates they purchased the property, by tonight. Tell them to tell the auditor that the attorney general's office will pay any overtime expenses to keep the office open until they're done. I want those reports on my desk in the morning."

"Are you onto something?"

"Maybe. I just talked to the Guernsey County sheriff. He said he personally interviewed Nathan Pryor."

"The same Nathan Pryor who said he never even talked to a cop?"

"Yep. Oh, and one more thing. Do some research and see if you can find the maiden name of Pryor's mother. Sometimes those cottages stay in families for years. I don't want to miss anything because we don't know the family name."

"Good call."

"I'm going to leave Liberatore at the Guernsey County auditor's office. Make sure one of them gets in contact with her and brings her back to Columbus."

"I'm on it."

When I hung up, Liberatore said, "I've got it. Get the names of the property owners and the dates they purchased the property. If I have to stay after hours, tell them the attorney general's office will pay any overtime." She got out of the car, her face still the shade of an eggplant from her encounter with the sheriff, and slammed the door. As she walked away, the last words I heard were, "What a dick."

THIRTY-TWO

It was a half-hour drive along winding Route 22 to northeast Guernsey County and the speck on the map known as Londonderry. Stubblefield's Auto Repair and Quickie Mart sat on a bluff a quarter-mile beyond the tiny enclave. Both bays of the garage were busy, and there appeared to be other cars waiting for service. There was no one in the convenience store when I entered. A bell went off when I opened the door, and I could see a slight-built man with a ball cap perched on the back of his head making his way from the connected garage to the store, wiping his hands on a red rag as he approached. I got a bottle of water from the cooler, and we made it to the counter at the same time. He was all smiles; a patch on his left breast identified him as PHIL.

"How's it going?" he asked.

"Not bad," I said, putting a dollar on the counter. "You're Phil Stubblefield?"

"I am."

I pulled a business card out of my pocket and handed it to him. "I'm Hutch Van Buren, the attorney general for the state of Ohio. I was hoping I could talk to you for a few minutes about a woman you knew as Louise Love."

Over the course of my career as a prosecutor, I had seen smiles melt off the faces of dozens of people when I introduced myself. Very few smiles are reserved for prosecutors. I get it. But when Phil Stubblefield saw my business card and heard the words, "Louise Love," the smile left his face like a shotgun blast.

He swallowed hard, like he was trying to force down a dish towel. "I, uh, I don't know anything about that," he said.

"You might know a little more than you think. I understand you reported to the sheriff that you saw Ms. Love here in your store a few days before her body was found."

"That was what I originally told them, but I think I was mistaken."

"Really? Because I read the police report and saw the statement you made. You seemed pretty definitive."

Stubblefield licked his lips and looked back into the garage before speaking in a tone barely above a whisper, "Listen, Mr. Van Buren, that was a long time ago. I don't want any trouble."

"Why would you say that? There's not going to be any trouble."

"I'm pretty sure you would be wrong on that."

I unscrewed the plastic lid on my water and took a swallow. "Let me ask you this, Phil: Did you get nervous about seeing your name in the newspaper in connection with a murder investigation, or did somebody pay you a visit and, let's say, *encouraged* you to change your mind?"

He continued to wipe at the grease on his hands with his rag. "I'm a grandfather. I've got two grandsons and a granddaughter who thinks the sun comes up every morning just so it can shine on Papaw's face. This is the greatest time of my life. I can't wait to close the station at night just so I can get over to see her. I would like for that not to change."

"I understand that perfectly. And I have no desire to interfere with that. Do you have someone back there helping you today?"

"Yeah, my brother Floyd's back there."

"Why don't you tell Floyd to take over for a bit and let's take a little walk."

There was a clearing behind the business that was mowed and had a couple of picnic tables sitting perpendicular to the slope of the hill. "We can talk out here," he said.

Floyd stared at us as we walked past the open bay doors. We sat down on opposite sides of one of the picnic tables, and he continued to work at his hands with the rag. It wasn't about hygiene; his nerves were in overdrive. "Was it her, Phil?"

"If I was to say yes, what kind of trouble would I be in with the sheriff?"

"I'm guessing that you didn't intentionally lie to the sheriff. I think what happened was that over the years you had time to reconsider and simply came to a different conclusion."

He nodded and looked out over the rolling hills. Tiny beads of sweat dotted his upper lip; he swiped at them with the sleeve of his shirt. "Why is the attorney general interested in this? I thought homicides and such were local matters, and it's been years since it happened. Is this one of those cold-case investigations?"

"Sort of. There's a guy on Death Row, and his life may depend on whether I can solve this case in the next two weeks. This might be my last shot at saving the life of a man I don't believe is guilty." We sat for a full minute. I broke the silence. "What do you think?"

He took a deep breath. "It was her. As sure as I'm sitting here, it was her; she was in a car with a white guy. She got a bottle of water from the same cooler you did a few minutes ago. She grabbed the cheese crackers from the rack by the cash register. She had a dollar bill and some change in one hand, and she counted out the exact change for me. I remember that because she made a joke about saving her pennies."

"What about the guy?"

"He got gas, then came inside to pay. We were pretty busy and there were three or four guys who came in about the same time. I don't know which one she was with—God's truth—and I couldn't identify any of them anyway. The only reason I remembered her was because she was black and so tall."

"You're absolutely sure it was her?"

"No doubt in my mind."

"Why'd you recant?"

"That's where things got a little dicey. The story ran in the paper about me identifying her, and I was feeling pretty good about it. The sheriff said it was the first clue they'd had, so I felt like I might have helped out. The next day I was closing up the store and shop around ten p.m., and this guy who I'd never want to meet in a dark alley comes into the store and locks the deadbolt behind him. He was about the biggest human being I'd ever seen in my life. He didn't try any rough stuff or anything. He just walked over to the counter and in this real calm voice, he said, 'You need to rethink what you saw last Saturday afternoon, because I don't think there were any black girls in these parts that day.' I'll tell you something, Mr. Van Buren, I'd like to think I'm not a coward, but I was so scared I didn't know whether to run or wind my watch. He said, 'Are we in agreement? There was no black girl in your store last Saturday, was there?' I said no. He told me to call the sheriff's office in the morning and tell them I was mistaken and that it wasn't Louise Love I'd seen. I said I would, and he said, 'Good, 'cause I don't want to have to come back here.' I called the sheriff's office the next morning. I knew if that guy ever came back, he'd do more than talk."

"Have you ever seen him since?"

"No, but I'll never forget him."

"Was he tall?"

"I'm five foot seven, Mr. Van Buren. Everyone's tall. But this guy was a giant. He might have had to duck his head when he walked in the door. As soon as I got off the phone with the sheriff's office the next morning, my wife and I went up to Amish country for a couple days, just to get away. In all honesty, I was hiding. I wished I'd never said a word to the sheriff." He swallowed and looked down over the hills. "I wish I'd never said a word to you, either."

"Let's back up a little bit. You said the guy that Ms. Love was with came inside to pay for gas. Did he pay with cash or with a credit card?"

He shrugged. "I don't know because I'm not sure which one she was with."

"If he paid with a card, would you have processed it with a card reader?"

"No, I didn't have a reader in those days. Technology is slow to reach Guernsey County. I had an old manual slide machine."

"The kind that made carbon copies?"

"Yep."

"If he had paid with a credit card, would you still have the receipt?"

"I have every receipt of every credit card transaction I've ever made at this place. I always figured one of these days those IRS boys would come knockin', and I wanted to be prepared."

"Would you mind if I took a look at them?"

"I've got them separated by month, but I can't stop work to look for them; I've got cars backed up to Route 22 for service. I need to get back to work. They're up in the attic. I've got your card. I'll pull them out tonight or tomorrow and give you a call."

* * *

It took ninety minutes to drive from Stubblefield's Auto Repair and Quickie Mart back to Columbus and the Franklin County coroner's office on King Avenue. I gave my business card to the receptionist and she summoned Dr. Jeffrey Wu, the deputy coroner and chief forensic pathologist. We went to his office, and I explained my need for the autopsy of Louise E. Love.

"If we conducted the autopsy for another county, I cannot release it to you without a court order," Dr. Wu said.

"Autopsies are public record," I countered.

"They are, but they're not *our* public record. Since we work on a contract for Guernsey County, the autopsy is their property. I don't have the authority to release it."

I knew this, of course. "Dr. Wu, I understand that we all have protocols. But I've got a guy who I believe is going to be wrongfully executed very soon, and I don't have time to do this dance."

"I appreciate your predicament, Mr. Van Buren, but I can't legally give it to you. It could cost me my job. The autopsy was conducted before I came to the coroner's office. I'm not even sure if we have it on file." He grabbed his car keys from the top of the desk. "Let's see if we even have it."

A file room off the main hallway contained lateral file drawers with thousands of autopsy reports. "What was the name again?" he asked.

"Love. Louise E. Love."

He searched for a few minutes, then pulled out a file that was as crisp and neat as it had been six years earlier when it was filed away. He flipped through the first few pages as he walked back toward me. "We do have the original autopsy report," he said. "However, I'm sorry, I'm not going to be able to help you with this. I cannot give it to you without a court order." He set the file on the edge of a copy machine. "I really wish I could help you. My apologies for running off, but I have an appointment outside the building. I probably won't be back for a couple of hours."

* * *

Beth Kremer and I enjoyed a dinner of vending machine pretzels at my conference table that evening. "You sure know how to treat a lady," she said, flipping through the autopsy report of Lizzy Love. "What do you want to know?"

"Anything that might point me in the way of a suspect," I said.

"She died of strangulation."

"I know that."

Beth held up an index finger. "But . . . what you didn't know is that she was not strangled by the nylon cord that was wrapped around her neck."

"How do you know that?"

"Because her hyoid bone was crushed and there are acute cricoid cartilage fractures."

"Say it in English, Beth."

"Those are fractures you see in manual strangulations. Also, there are a series of bruises on the back of her neck, most likely the result of someone's fingers, and a large bruise on the front of her neck."

"The thumbs."

"Most likely. This was done by someone strong and most likely with large hands. There are lacerations from the nylon cord, but they are just under the jawbone and away from the hyoid. Plus, there is no subdural hematoma associated with these injuries. You get a subdural hematoma when there is moving blood. She was dead when someone wrapped the nylon cord around her neck."

"A diversion?"

"That would be my guess, but subterfuge is more your area of expertise. I can just tell you what the report indicates."

"How about the toxicology report?"

"Negative for alcohol and drugs, which makes sense."

"Why, because she was a college athlete?"

"No, because she was nine weeks pregnant."

THIRTY-THREE

One week and four days before the scheduled execution of Lester Paul Yates.

The morning started off badly and went downhill from there.

At eight o'clock, Jerry Adameyer walked into my office with a folder that contained the property records the interns had put together. "I went over them line by line," Jerry said. "No one by the name of Pryor or Sterling, his mother's maiden name, owns property along Piedmont Lake in any of the three counties."

"It was a long shot at best," I said.

"Seems like that's all we have these days."

At a few minutes before nine, my phone rang; I recognized Beth Kremer's number on the screen. "Tell me something good, Beth."

"Not this morning, I'm afraid," she said. "I've got all the DNA results from that landfill I collected in Danielle Quinn's car. I've got nothing for you. There wasn't a single hit matching anything from the car with the felony database, and that includes your boy Herman Fenicks."

Not an hour later, Phil Stubblefield called me from the little office in the back of his convenience store. "I have twenty-three credit card receipts from the Saturday that the Love girl was in my place," he said. "Is there a particular name you're looking for?"

"Pryor," I said. "P-R-Y-O-R. First name, Nathan."

I could hear him flipping through the receipts. After a minute, he said, "Nothing even remotely close. Do you want to look at these yourself?"

"Not right now, but if you'd keep them handy, I'd appreciate it."

All of the primary leads had dissipated in less than two hours. Lester Yates and I were running out of time and options.

At ten o'clock, Jerry walked back into my office. I filled him in on the DNA results and the credit card receipts. "Want me to cheer you up a bit?" he asked.

"I wish someone would."

"We found Herman Fenicks's old truck and Terry Hollis."

"You have my complete attention. Where'd you find him?"

"We didn't find him; we found her. Turns out Terry Hollis is a she. It didn't say male or female on the registration, or I wasn't paying attention. In all candor, it was a rookie mistake and sloppy police work on my part, and I apologize for that."

"Go on."

"She got married, so her last name is no longer Hollis; it's Mellon. And she no longer lives in Pocatello, Idaho. She moved to near Logan, Utah, with the new hubby. I just got off the phone with the private investigator. He said the rig is sitting in a gravel drive next to the house where she and her husband live. The husband has a commercial driver's license, too, and the investigator thinks they drive together."

"I don't want that rig to leave their property until we've gone through it. Find out who the sheriff is and tell them we need a search warrant for that truck."

"I've got Davidson working on it right now."

An hour later, Jerry was back in my office. "The Cache County sheriff said he can get a judge to issue the search warrant and impound the truck on-site for seventy-two hours—max. He is going to personally take the request to the judge, and he'll let us know what's going on. He said the judge is a reasonable sort and it should take about a half an hour. In the meantime, he said he'd post a deputy on the property until we can get there. Do you want me to fly out?"

"No. I don't want my best investigator out of the office for three days collecting evidence."

"Want me to send Davidson and another investigator?"

"No, I need someone with experience in this. I might have to send Beth Kremer." I picked up the receiver on my desk phone, then set it back in the cradle and held up a finger. "Reno Moretti."

"What about him?"

"He was on the Youngstown Police Department's crime scene search unit for years. He could do this."

"He's probably not registered as a vendor with the state of Ohio."

"I'm sure he's not, and I don't care. Get him on the phone and see if he'd like to do some contract work for us. It'll do him good, and it'll get us out of a jam. Tell him he needs to be on an airplane for Utah today."

⋆ ⋆ ⋆

I walked two doors down Broad Street to a diner and bought a hamburger and an unsweetened iced tea for lunch. The waitress did not roll her eyes at my request.

As I got off the elevator and started toward my office, Liberatore and the other interns were coming out of the war room and heading for lunch. "Liberatore, where's my dog?" I asked.

"I don't know where your dog is, but *our* dog is at my mom's today," she said. "She's puppy-sitting for us."

"I want my dog back."

As the foursome stepped into the still-open elevator, she hit the down button on the panel. "We can talk about it later, okay? But I must tell you, she's really bonding with me."

"Of course she is. I still want her back."

As the door closed, I overheard Nakamura say, "You and Mr. Van Buren own a dog together?"

THIRTY-FOUR

I would be lying if I said that my main motivation as the Summit County prosecuting attorney and as the Ohio attorney general was born out of purity and a lifelong pursuit of justice. The truth is, sometimes it got very personal. I like to win. I liked winning on the ball field when I was a kid, and I liked winning in the courtroom as an adult. Losing was like a mouthful of curdled milk; the aftertaste stayed with me for days and weeks. It was that competitive nature that made me a good prosecutor.

That was how I was starting to feel about the Lester Yates case. I certainly did not want to see an innocent man go to the death chamber. But it had grown very personal; I did not want to see Alfonso Majestro or D. Kendrick Brown win. In their little, black hearts, they had to know that Lester Yates was innocent, but it didn't bother them in the least to see him die if it enhanced their political fortunes.

What kind of man does that?

I did not want to believe the governor was a bad man, but simply one who was easily influenced. If Shelly Dennison was right, the governor would not make a move without Majestro's blessing. Unless I could put a viable suspect in front of Jim Wilinski, it would be Majestro who would decide if Lester lived or died. Leaving that decision in his hands was the equivalent of filling up the syringe for Lester Yates.

This was on my mind when I unwrapped my hamburger and pushed a plastic straw through the lid of my iced tea. On my desk was the folder Jerry Adameyer had dropped off earlier that morning containing the names of the individuals who owned property around Piedmont Lake. Mindlessly, while I ate, I began leafing through the pages, giving each no more attention than I would a battered magazine in a doctor's lobby.

I had flipped through six or seven pages when I had a déjà vu moment. In that instant, I was transported back to an antique mall in Baton Rouge, Louisiana. It had been eight years earlier, and I had gone down to attend a conference for prosecuting attorneys. It was miserably hot and humid, and I was killing time between sessions in the air-conditioned mall. I was scanning glass cases full of what some people call antique treasures and what others call junk, when my brain absorbed an image that had failed to immediately register with my consciousness. I stood for a minute while I waited for the image to resurface in my mind's eyes. When it did, the name "Van Buren" flashed across my cerebrum like a photograph. Somewhere amid the bric-a-brac I had seen my name. I retraced my path through the glass case and found it on a metal tin wedged between a catcher's mitt and a stack of old railroad stock certificates.

VAN BUREN BROTHERS CIGARS

ROANOKE, VIRGINIA

EST. 1870

EXCEPTIONAL QUALITY

At that moment, the property records in my hand, I was having a similar experience. Just as Van Buren had appeared like a snapshot that sultry day in Baton Rouge, another name was flashing across my brain. Yet it didn't seem possible. Rather, it appeared to be remote and distant, like something that flies by your side window as you're speeding down the highway, and I thought perhaps my brain was playing tricks on me. I flipped back one page, then two. My eyes scanned down the list until they stopped four lines from the bottom.

It certainly had not been my imagination.

For thirty seconds I could not discern fire from ice. Perhaps my guts crystallized and frozen tentacles spread through my intestines and into my loins like frost on a glass pane. Or perhaps my heart had turned into a blast furnace that was sending arcing, orange flares throughout my chest.

Or maybe it was both.

At that point in my life I had won hundreds of ball games, championships, dozens of court battles, and a statewide race for attorney general. Yet those victories and their associated adrenaline charges seemed insignificant to the exhilaration I felt at that moment. I had, indeed, seen a name, and for several long moments I stared at the line on the page. How, I wondered, had it slipped past Jerry Adameyer.

But there it was.

Alfonso A. Majestro.

When my hands had quit shaking, I went online to the Harrison County auditor's office. The property—a two-story, three-bedroom, two-bath house—was located on the western banks of the lake and had a Morrison Road address. Majestro had purchased the property in 1991 from Ray and Virginia Eberts for seventy-eight thousand dollars. There were no liens on the property. He had paid cash. The tax bill was sent to an address in the Columbus suburb of Marble Cliff. I didn't need to check any further to know, without question, it was our boy.

I called Phil Stubblefield. "Phil, it's Hutch Van Buren. I need you to look for another name on those credit card receipts."

"I'd like to help you, but right now I'm up to my elbows in Jeanne Lodge's transmission. I can check it after work or . . ."

"Phil, stop talking. This is important; I need you to check on a name and I need it right now."

He took a breath and said, "Give me a minute." When he picked up the phone in his office, he asked, "What are you looking for?"

"Last name, Majestro. First name, Alfonso or initial A."

Again, I could hear him flipping through the cards. "No card was used with that name."

"Damn. Okay, thanks for checking. I appreciate it."

I hung up and slouched back in my chair, pondering my next move. How was I going to link Alfonso Majestro to the disappearance of Lizzy Love? Could I link him?

Barely a minute had passed when Margaret appeared at my door. She said, "There's a Phil Stubblefield on line one. He said it's important."

I picked up the receiver and pressed the flashing button. "What's up, Phil?"

"I didn't notice this at first, but I think I've got something here. One of the cards I ran that afternoon was issued to State of Ohio, Office of the Governor."

The fire and ice returned. "Go on."

"I can't be one hundred percent sure, because the signature looks like chicken scratch, but if I had to guess it looks like it was signed by A. A. Majestro."

"Hold on to it. I'm on my way."

I walked over to the war room. Jerry Adameyer was working on a laptop. When he looked up, I said, "Let's go for a ride."

* * *

As I drove back from Stubblefield's, the credit card receipt signed by Alfonso Majestro in my suit jacket pocket, I could see Jerry's jaw muscles roll; his thick hands were clenched into fists, his fingernails digging into his palms. We had just reached the interstate when he said, "That son of a bitch killed that girl."

"I think maybe you're right, Jerry."

"You think *maybe* I'm right? Jesus Christ, he signed a credit card receipt at the gas station where she was last seen. He's got a cabin on the lake where her body was found. Maybe it's time we hit Wilinski over the head with the evidence we have on his chief of staff. Or better yet, let's take it to a grand jury."

"If it was Majestro, why would he have used a credit card and signed a receipt in his name if he planned to kill her?"

"Maybe he didn't plan to kill her? Maybe it was supposed to be a fun weekend at the lake and for some reason things got out of hand?"

"Right now, all we know for sure is that Majestro owns a house at the lake where the body was found, and he bought some gasoline in the area. Beyond that, we can't connect him to Lizzy Love. If

Stubblefield hadn't recanted his story, that would help. But he publicly stated it wasn't Love, that he'd made a mistake. Stubblefield's a nervous little guy to begin with. A defense attorney would destroy him on the stand. Don't get me wrong, I know Majestro is dirty, but we've zero evidence that he knew or was with Lizzy Love the day she disappeared."

"He's in this up to his eyeballs. Don't forget that he conned his nephew into becoming a public defender and somehow stuck Lester Yates with a crappy defense to cover for the murder of Danielle Quinn."

"He did. And that has absolutely no bearing on Lizzy Love's murder."

"I know."

"Makes you wonder, though. If he killed Danielle Quinn and dodged that bullet, why did he get back in the game so soon?"

Jerry looked like he wanted to slap me. "Do you really have to ask that question? Because he's a goddamn serial killer and that's what they do—they kill people. They may change their hunting grounds, but they never stop hunting."

THIRTY-FIVE

The case was like a continual swirl in my head. I fought sleep at night because I couldn't get my brain to shut down. Lester Yates. Alfonso Majestro. Danielle Quinn. Herman Fenicks. Lizzy Love. Jasper Love. They had all taken up residence in my brain and would give me no peace. On the nightstand beside my bed I kept a notepad so that I could jot down ideas and to-dos that awoke me from a fitful sleep.

That evening, after Jerry and I had returned from Stubblefield's, Margaret had come into my office and said, "You look like six miles of bad road."

"You need to quit sugarcoating everything, Margaret."

"When's the last time you had a good night's sleep?"

"My junior year in high school."

"That is not funny. Your eyes are bloodshot, you've got dark circles under 'em, and your skin is gray. You look like one of those dead people that eats live people's brains."

"A zombie?"

"Maybe. You white people watch those scary movies; I don't. You get yourself home, right now, and get some rest."

"Margaret, I've got . . ."

Her eyes turned to slits and her fists went to her hips. "Mmm-mmm-mmm-mmm-mmm, you are not going to even think about arguing with me." She pointed to the door. "Out. Now. I'll see you in the morning."

I had a bowl of raisin bran and a beer for dinner. Shelly Dennison called and asked if she could stop by and go over a list of appearances that she wanted me to make for the reelection campaign. I said, "Please, no. Just schedule them and tell me where and when you want me to be." She seemed fine with that. In fact, I think she preferred it.

I went to bed that night thinking about a baseball game. It was played between the Crystalton Merchants and the Smithfield Jets the summer I was fifteen. I was catching for the Merchants and led off the game with a shot that short-hopped the chain-link fence in left-center field for a triple. Deak Coultas was up next; he hit a line drive back up the box that the pitcher caught by accident; one out. Pepper Nash followed with a screaming shot that the shortstop caught in the top of his webbing; two outs. Pepper's brother, Adrian, then hit a towering drive to straightaway center field, which their center fielder snagged with his back leaning against the fence; three outs, no runs.

That was the way the game went. We pounded the ball every inning but couldn't squeeze across a single run. Adrian, our ace, was on the mound and throwing a no-hitter. With two outs in the bottom of the ninth, Adrian walked a batter. The next kid hit a lazy fly ball to short right field that Deak lost in the sun for a second before it skipped off the heel of his glove. The runner on first had started moving at the crack of the bat and was heading to third. Deak uncorked a throw that went over the third baseman's head by ten feet and into the bleachers.

The runner was awarded home plate, and the Jets won without getting a single hit.

That's the way I was feeling about the Lester Yates case. We were hitting the ball all over the park, but we had not a single run to show for our efforts. Like Jerry, I knew Alfonso Majestro was a creep, and I suspected his involvement in the disappearance and murders of both Danielle Quinn and Lizzy Love. But I had no concrete evidence to connect him to either. For a career prosecutor, it was beyond maddening.

I stared at the ceiling of my bedroom. In my mind's eye I saw Lester Yates sitting in his prison cell, rocking back and forth on his bunk. I watched Deak's peg from right field sail into the bleachers and Adrian Nash's shoulders slouch as his head and spirit fell. The swirl continued. It was an hour, maybe longer, before I fell into a tormented sleep. An old demon of the night was the first to visit. It was Petey Sanchez, the boy whose death I had helped to cover up the same summer we lost to the Jets. He always arrived clean and articulate, two words that could never have been used to describe Petey when he walked the earth. His forehead was smooth and without the bloody divot that had been left when Adrian struck him with the Indian maul we had found on the ridge. When Petey invaded my dreams, they always ended the same way, with him screaming that he would haunt my sleep for as long as I had breath. He left, and the screen went dark.

I was in a room, but I sensed I was not alone. There was the click of a pull chain turning on a bare light bulb hanging from a cord. The light shone down on a wooden chair, where sat my old friend Deak Coultas, his hand covering the bloody bullet wound that had killed him four years earlier. "You're going to do what's right, aren't you, Hutch?" he asked.

"I'm not sure what you mean, Deak."

He smiled and blood ran down over his fingers, like water running over the ribs of a washboard. "I wouldn't be dead if we had done what was right. If we'd told the authorities that Adrian had killed Petey, we could still talk on the phone and not just in your dreams."

"I know."

"Do what's right, Hutch."

He reached up and pulled the chain, and the room again was dark.

I may have awakened for a moment, maybe not. It could have been part of a larger dream. When the light returned, it filtered through the canopy of an oak forest of my youth. Shelly Dennison was walking through the undergrowth in a tiara of daisies and a flowing nightgown with cockleburs clinging to the hem. Jim Wilinski followed in her footsteps, wearing the uniform of the Chicago Bears, closing in for the tackle. I wanted to yell, but Alfonso Majestro suddenly appeared and forced a hand over my mouth. I tried to push it away but lacked the strength. The governor was close to Shelly, and Majestro used his other hand to cover my eyes.

When Wilinski's shoulder pads slammed into her back and I heard the air rush from her lungs, Majestro removed his hands and I was looking down a tree-lined street. Far in the distance, a solitary figure walked my way. It was a hazy image, but I could tell it was a woman, a tall, graceful, athletic woman. I squinted, trying to bring her into focus. I reached for her, urging her closer. I wanted the confirmation, but I knew who it was and I called her name.

"Elizabeth," I said.

Then I jerked awake.

For several long moments I sat in my bed, sweat matting my T-shirt to my back, the sounds of my panting filling the room. I have long believed in the power of dreams. It is not something I talk about in public, as people will stare at you as if you have confessed belief in vampires or tooth fairies. But I believe they are avenues for messages from another realm or pathways for imprisoned thoughts to escape the subconscious. I dream every night, and I've learned to pay attention.

The jolt I received that night was like an Adrian Nash fastball to the ribs.

I unplugged my cell phone from the recharging cord on the nightstand and tapped out Jerry Adameyer's number. The time was 4:01 a.m. The call rolled to voice mail. I called again. He answered on the third ring and said, "When I get a phone call at four a.m., it's usually because someone has died."

"I just learned something a few days ago. Did you know the state keeps all security video recordings in the archives like public records?"

"You're going to have to help me on this one, chief. Why would I care?"

"Lizzy Love was last seen walking north on the Capital University campus, right?"

"Right."

"Capital University is in Bexley. What else is in Bexley within walking distance of the school?"

"My brain doesn't work too well at four in the morn ..." He paused while the fastball tailed into his ribs. "The Governor's Residence."

"Exactly."

THIRTY-SIX

One week and three days before the scheduled execution of Lester Paul Yates.

There was no going back to sleep. The adrenaline surge that sent needle pricks of ice into the base of my skull had me in overdrive. I went to the kitchen, started a pot of coffee, and waited for it to brew so I could take a cup into the shower. I had been at the office for an hour when Jerry walked in at seven o'clock. He was carrying a box of doughnuts and a rough schematic of the Governor's Residence and the surrounding streets.

"The governor's chief of security is a former detective with Lorain PD," Jerry said. "I've known him for years. I called him an hour ago and talked to him about the security cameras at the Governor's Residence. He said there are eight external cameras that cover every inch of the property and the streets and sidewalks coming from every angle. These are the locations." He pointed to eight numbered locations along the edge of the mansion and its grounds.

"Didn't he want to know why you wanted that information?" I asked.

"Of course, he did; he's a cop." Jerry pushed the box of doughnuts across the desk. "Relax and have a doughnut. I told him I was helping a local department do some research on a cold case that might have gone down in the area, and we wanted to look at some archival tapes to see if we can find anything. It's mostly true, but nothing that would raise any suspicions."

"How do we get the tapes?"

"They're on file with administrative services. At some point they went all digital, and it would be a simple download. But, since nothing is easy about this case, the videos we want are all on VHS tape and we'll have to get copies; they won't let you remove them from the archives. It's the usual governmental rigmarole."

The Ohio Department of Administrative Services was in the Rhodes State Office Tower, just a few floors down from my offices. Jerry went down to get copies of the tapes and was back in my office in twenty minutes. "They're stored in an off-site warehouse," he said. "It will take them at least twenty-four hours to retrieve the tapes and another twenty-four hours to make the copies."

Nothing moves quickly in government, even when you are trying to save someone's life.

"That's unacceptable," I said.

"That's what I told the supervisor," he said. "I might as well have been talking to that box of doughnuts."

I called the director of administrative services, explained that I needed those tapes immediately. He said to send one of my people out to the warehouse near the Ohio State Fairgrounds and he would have someone there to hand over the tapes. He would trust me to make the copies and return the originals. Jerry left immediately and called me an hour and a half later, saying he was still waiting on someone from administrative services to let him into the warehouse. I made another call and received another promise. It was quarter to three in the afternoon when Jerry returned, carrying a cardboard box of tapes and spewing venom. I'd already had Margaret search the building for a VHS tape player. She'd found one, and it was sitting on my conference table and hooked up to a monitor by the time he returned.

"The tapes were rotated out every eight hours," he said. "There are twenty-four tapes in the box. I took everything that was recorded on September 29, the Saturday she disappeared."

"The security camera from Capital shows her leaving the dorm at eleven-forty-one in the morning," I said. "She talked to Pryor on campus for what, five minutes?"

"That's what he told us," Jerry said. "Of course, he also said he'd never been interviewed by the authorities."

I looked at the schematic Jerry had drawn and decided the camera located near the corner of N. Parkview Avenue and Maryland Avenue might have the best angle. I sorted through the box until I found a tape labeled in Magic Marker: GOV. RESIDENCE, CAMERA 3, 8 A.M. – 4 P.M., SEPT. 29, 2001. I started the tape, and the digital image in the lower left corner read 8:01 a.m. I hit fast-forward. "Let's start watching at noon and see what we find."

"You realize she might not have gone to the mansion," Jerry said. "Someone could have picked her up on campus."

"She went to the mansion."

"How do you know for sure?"

I looked at Jerry, swallowed hard, and said, "I saw her walking down the street in a dream."

"You don't say."

"I woke up and had this weird sense that Parkview was the street."

Jerry shrugged and fought back a grin. "I've had hunches that worked out based on less than that."

"Just the same, I'd appreciate it if you didn't share that with anyone outside this room."

I stopped the fast-forward button and ran it at normal speed. The digital readout was at 12:10 p.m. I backed it up to noon. The view was the one I'd hoped for; the camera was pointing south on Parkview. In the foreground, a black sedan was parked in front of the mansion. There was a figure behind the wheel, but the view was obscured by the glare on the hood and windshield. Far in the background, a figure could be seen walking north on Parkview. I leaned in closer to the screen. It was her, the woman in my dream. It was Lizzy Love. I pointed at the small figure. Jerry said, "I see her."

It was another five minutes before she crossed Boston Avenue and came into focus. She was tall and lean, and she had an athletic bounce to her step. She was wearing a long-sleeved white shirt and carried a full backpack over one shoulder, just as we had seen in the dormitory security video. It was six minutes after noon.

As she neared, the driver's-side door opened and out stepped Alfonso Majestro.

"Home run, chief," Jerry said.

"Indeed," I said.

"We've got him. We've got the son of a bitch."

Majestro was wearing sunglasses and a golf shirt. He walked around the front of the car and opened the passenger-side door. The woman was, without question, Lizzy Love. She was brown, beautiful, and smiling. Majestro said something. She displayed a certain comfort level when she placed a hand on his shoulder and laughed. They chatted for a few seconds before she unshouldered her backpack and got into the car. Majestro closed the door, returned to the wheel, and pulled out.

"Now, can we at least go to the governor?" Jerry asked. "This should be all he needs to at least grant us a stay of execution."

I continued to stare at the screen. "Let me back that up a little bit," I said. "Did you see someone in the back seat?"

"I didn't."

He backed it up and slowed down the tape. Lizzy got back into the car. "Stop it there," I said. "Look right behind the driver. Can you see him?"

"You're right. He's in the shadows."

"Zoom in."

"Is it the governor?"

"No. It's not the governor. Look at the size of the melon on that guy. That's the governor's muscle—Danny Doyle."

THIRTY-SEVEN

One week and two days before the scheduled execution of Lester Paul Yates.

By the time we had finished reviewing the tapes, it was after four o'clock. As we were wrapping up, I asked Margaret to call Wilinski's office and check his availability. His secretary said the governor and Majestro had already left town for a fundraising dinner near Cincinnati, but he had fifteen minutes open at one o'clock the next day. I told her to book it.

When I walked into his office he was leaning back in his chair, his feet propped on the corner of his desk and crossed at the ankles. He was sporting a pair of dark brown ostrich cowboy boots that had yet to be scuffed on the soles. There was a string tie around his neck with a bolo in the shape of the state of Ohio cinched up under his chin. The whitest Stetson I'd ever seen in my life was pulled low on his brow.

"This is a new look for you, isn't it?" I asked.

He grinned and peeled the hat off his head and dropped it on the desk. "Good guys wear white," he said.

"And you're one of the good guys?"

"Always."

"What's the occasion?"

"I'm going to the sale of champions out at the state fair. My job is to run around the ring and jack up the bidding. It's good publicity for a presidential candidate. It shows I'm a man of the people."

"Well you certainly look the part."

"Thank ya, padnah." He clicked his cheeks and winked. "The auction starts at two. What's on your mind, Hutch?"

"Lester Yates."

The governor slowly shook his head and said, "Boy, you can flat wear me out. You are like a broken record with this Lester Yates stuff." His feet dropped from the corner of his desk with a thud; he sat up straight and folded his hands on his blotter. "Hutch, how many times do we have to have this conversation? Unless you can show me compelling evidence that someone else is responsible for those murders, I am not going to overturn the will of the people."

"I'm not asking you to overturn anything. I just need more time."

"Why? What is so compelling that the execution needs to be delayed?"

I knew that question was coming. How could I tell him the reason I needed more time was because I believed his chief of staff may have murdered a college volleyball player and dumped her body in Piedmont Lake? And the fact was, I couldn't tell him. Not yet, anyway.

"Governor, you're asking me to prove a negative. I can't do that, but I can raise some very serious doubts about his guilt. That should be enough to at least give me a stay of execution."

"A jury of his peers found him guilty beyond a reasonable doubt. He's a convicted serial killer and a known white supremacist, so if you want me to delay the execution or commute his sentence, I need some solid proof that he didn't do it."

"What you're saying is, the only way you'll grant an extension is if I find the person responsible for the murders of all those women. Come on, Governor, be reasonable."

He slowly shook his head. "Sorry, Hutch. It's the will of the people."

"There were at least four other women strangled after Yates went to jail. They stopped completely after a guy named Herman Fenicks went to prison. I'm working like crazy to see if Fenicks is connected, but I can guarantee you that Lester Yates is not your man."

"Got to see some proof."

"You've got to see the political minefield you're walking through with this. Yates is not guilty, and if your cronies in Belmont County hadn't been so excited to see their names in the paper, he would never even have been charged."

He squeezed his eyes tight. "Hutch, you are starting to grind away at my good nature. You and I need a little quality time together." He got up from his desk, grabbed his Stetson, and started toward the door. "Come with me to the sale of champions."

"I can't. I've got a bunch of work to do."

He stopped at the door and looked back. "It wasn't a request; let's go."

I followed him into the lobby, where his driver, his bodyguard, the behemoth Danny Doyle, and his wife were waiting.

Kathryn Wilinski was looking as spectacular as ever. She had long, chestnut hair and a smile as broad as her husband's shoulders. She was wearing straight-leg jeans with rhinestones on the pockets, low-cut boots, and a white blouse that hugged her tight and revealed a hint of cleavage. I did my best not to stare.

We took the express elevator to the parking garage and got into the governor's limousine. Danny Doyle got up front. Kathryn Wilinski sat between the governor and me in the back seat; she smelled like the cherry blossoms on Chestnut Ridge from my youth.

The limousine pulled out of the garage onto State Street. Before we had traveled a half-block to Front Street, Jim Wilinski asked, "Did you ever play any ball, Hutch?"

I had. I was a three-sport athlete in high school and had played both football and baseball at the University of the Laurel Highlands in Pennsylvania. We'd had this conversation no fewer than a half-dozen times over the past three years. The reason he continued to ask the question was because he never once listened to my answer. He didn't give a hoot if I had played ball; he just wanted a segue to tell me a story about his playing days. But I played my role and repeated my answer in order to provide him with his platform.

"Yes, I played in both high school and college," I said.

"There is nothing like sports to build a young man's character, huh?"

And so it began.

"When I was playing at Ohio State for Woody Hayes . . ."

"We played in the Rose Bowl that year against . . ."

"I was just a rookie with the Bears, but no way was I sitting on the bench . . ."

"We were playing the Eagles at Soldier Field, cold as all get out . . ."

It took him about three minutes of preamble before he got to the passages he really wanted to deliver. I'd heard the story so many times I could recite it myself.

Papa Bear George Halas came out to practice one day and says, "Jim, I believe you are the greatest tight end in the history of professional football."

Big Jim Wilinski leaned up in his seat, looked around his wife at me, and said, "This one day, George Halas, ol' Papa Bear himself, he wasn't the coach then but he was still the owner of the Bears, he pulls me aside at practice and says, 'Jimmy Wilinski, I believe you are the greatest tight end I have ever seen in all my days in professional football.'"

I hope I live to see you get into the Pro Football Hall of Fame.

"He said, 'I hope I live long enough to see you inducted into the Pro Football Hall of Fame.'"

I didn't get it exactly right, but I was in the neighborhood.

When he leaned back in his seat and continued, noting that Halas had died in 1983, three years before his hall of fame induction, Kathryn Wilinski's head turned slightly toward me and her right eyebrow arched. I looked away and stared out the window.

Our limousine was the middle vehicle in a five-car caravan. We were slotted between four Ohio State Highway Patrol cars, which entered the fairgrounds from Seventeenth Avenue with lights flashing. An announcement had been made that the governor would soon arrive, and a throng of people had crowded up to the orange and white barriers leading into the Celeste Center exposition hall. As decorum dictated, the governor and presidential candidate exited alone to garner the love of the people and media attention. His wife would follow a few moments later so they could be photographed together. The governor was very popular, and when he stepped out and waved to the crowd, the applause drowned out the carnival barkers and the canned music from the rides. A uniformed state trooper moved in front of the open back door and blocked it.

When the applause began to wane, Kathryn Wilinski said, "Time for my entrance." Instead of putting her hand on the seat to push off, she grabbed my leg and dug her lacquered nails into my inner thigh, like a predator clutching prey. I jumped. The strike had been sharp and quick, and she released the grip in an instant. "Excuse me, trooper," she said. He moved to allow her to exit. When she did, she turned her head, pushed back the hair that had dropped over one eye, and winked.

I sat motionless, not because it was protocol, but because I was so taken aback that I couldn't move. They waved to the crowd and answered some questions from the local television reporters. After several minutes, the governor leaned his head back down into the open door and said, "Come on, padnah, you're part of the team." We walked between the barriers toward the Celeste Center, the Wilinskis shaking hands and giving out high-fives. In his cowboy boots and Stetson, the governor looked eight feet tall, which I'm sure was the goal. I tagged along behind, wedged between a couple of humorless state troopers. No one even noticed me, which was just fine.

We were ushered into the exposition hall and to a reserved area that had been cordoned off with velvet rope. The governor and the auctioneer immediately walked to the middle of the show ring. As they did, Kathryn drummed her fingers on the empty chair next to her and said, "Sit next to me, Hutch. I want to talk to you."

I wanted to run like my hair was on fire. This wasn't five minutes after she had sunk her claws an inch from my package, and I couldn't imagine anything good was going to follow. Still, she was the future first lady of the United States, so I obediently sat down.

The grand champion market turkey had been walked to the middle of the show ring, and the auctioneer began soliciting bids. Governor Jim Wilinski paced along the edge of the ring, his cowboy boots kicking up sawdust as he pointed into the stands at bidders and urged them higher. Talking under the din of the crowd, Kathryn leaned closer, her breath like a cutting torch in my ear, and said, "Jim tells me that if he gets elected president you have a particularly bright future in his administration, and he expects you to be on the campaign trail with us. That is so exciting. I have always wanted to get to know you a little bit better."

I nodded. "That would be great," I said, immediately regretting the comment.

She smiled. "I don't know if you know this or not, but George Halas, Papa Bear, once told my husband that he was the greatest tight end in the history of pro football. Have you ever heard that before?"

"Once or twice."

"Really? Only once or twice? Do you know how many times I've heard it?"

"Probably more than once or twice."

She slapped me on the arm just above the elbow with the back of her hand and laughed. "I've heard it so many goddamn times it makes me throw up in my mouth." She smiled at her husband and waved with her fingers, looking every bit the adoring wife.

As we watched the sale of champions, her knee would imperceptibly touch mine, then move away, again and again. I tried to ignore it, but, for the record, even when you know her husband is a former pro football lineman who holds your political future in his fickle hands, it is virtually impossible not to get aroused when a former Miss Illinois who smells like cherry blossoms is whispering moist heat in your ear and bumping your knee. It is simultaneously arousing and terrifying.

It was stifling hot in the exposition center. The governor was running back and forth in front of the crowd, pointing and gesturing for the bids to keep climbing. Sweat rolled down his face and seeped through his dress shirt.

"He's certainly in his element, isn't he?" I said.

"He certainly is." She smiled and gave her husband a smile and a thumbs up. "Don't you find it amazing that he can still run around like that considering how much energy he expends during his lunch hours at the Governor's Residence?"

I was looking for a hole into which I could crawl. "I wouldn't know anything about that," I said.

"Really? Then you, Mr. Van Buren, are either a terrible liar or the only person in Ohio's state government who doesn't know about his lunchtime trysts. I'm betting you're just a terrible liar."

"If you don't mind me saying so, Mrs. Wilinski, this is really an uncomfortable conversation to be having in an arena with five thousand other people, one of whom is your husband."

"I agree. When would you like to talk about it? I'd love to look for a place that is a little more private."

"I see. So, what you are saying is that I should just go ahead and slit my political wrists anytime I'm ready."

"My, my, Mr. Van Buren. I didn't take you for such a worrier."

"It may be what I do best."

After the grand champion market goat had gone off the block, the governor walked back over to the reserved section where we were sitting. He rested his forearms on the steel railing that rimmed the show ring; beads of sweat dripped off his nose in rapid succession, staining the concrete. An usher handed him a bottle of water. He pulled out a handkerchief and mopped his face before wiping at the sweatband of his Stetson. His shirt clung to his skin. He said, "I haven't worked this hard since my days with the Bears." He took a drink of his water. "Are you having a good time, Hutch?"

"Loving every minute," I said.

"You should be. You're sitting with the most beautiful woman in the arena."

"No doubt."

He loosened his string tie and lifted it off around his head before undoing his top shirt button. His neck flared red with heat. He then took off a pair of turquoise cufflinks and handed them to his wife. It was the most casual I had ever seen him. He asked for a second bottle of water and began rolling up his sleeves, revealing the forearms that for years were feared by defensive linemen throughout the National Football League. They were scarred from thousands of attacks at the line of scrimmage and equally vicious battles under heaps of players where fingernails and cleats and teeth often became weapons.

I stared for a long moment at those forearms and the man who possessed them. The cherry blossom perfume filled my nostrils, and images invaded my brain that I could not control. Nor did I want to. Where was this all going to end? I saw Reno Moretti walking into my office with those black binders on Lester Yates. That was the morning the first domino fell, and everything had led up to this point. The governor went back to the show ring. His wife's knee again touched mine. Her hot breath was back in my ear, but I could not discern the words. Lester Yates rocked on his bunk in a tiny cell near Youngstown. Alfonso Majestro and D. Kendrick Brown huddled together and conspired and plotted their ascension to Washington, DC. The dominos continued to fall, and my brain was a maelstrom. I didn't know how it would all end, but I knew what my next move had to be.

THIRTY-EIGHT

As the auctioneer at the sale of champions prepared to start bidding on the grand champion Holstein, I excused myself under the pretense of going to the restroom. Kathryn Wilinski said, "Hurry back."

I called Margaret from an outer hall. "Where are you?" she asked.

"I'm at the state fair."

"The what?"

"It's a long story."

"You had a three o'clock meeting scheduled with Clarence Duffy."

I had completely forgotten that I had scheduled a meeting to fire the deputy director of my charitable division and a perpetual thorn in my side. He would live another day.

"I need you to book two tickets to Philadelphia first thing tomorrow," I said. "Call Beth Kremer and tell her she's going with me. I don't care what she has on her schedule, she needs to clear the decks. I'll call her later to explain. In the meantime, is Denise Liberatore around?"

"I think she's in the war room."

"Tell her to go to my office and shut the door. I don't want to tell her this around the other interns or even the investigators." Margaret put me on hold. Liberatore picked up several minutes later.

"Are you alone in my office?"

"Yes."

"Is the door shut?"

"Yes."

"Okay. I want you to share this with Jerry Adameyer but no one else, understand?"

"Yes."

"This takes priority to whatever you're doing. I want you to put a photo lineup together. We don't have time to track down actual photos, so you'll need to print them from websites. Try to make them look as uniform as possible. I want you to print the photos of Nathan Pryor; he's a basketball coach at the University of Tennessee at Martin. The governor's chief of staff, Alfonso Majestro, and the governor's bodyguard, a guy named Danny Doyle. You might have to go through security for Doyle's photo. Mix those in with five other white men. Tomorrow morning, I want you to drive to Stubblefield's Auto Repair and Quickie Mart near Londonderry in Guernsey County. The owner is Phil Stubblefield. I want you to hand him the photos and ask him this question: 'Is there anyone in here that looks familiar to you?' If he says yes, ask him when and where he saw him, and get him to sign the back of the photo. Got it?"

"Got it."

* * *

I was held captive while the governor posed with prize Herefords and their 4-H owners: he turned on his Appalachian twang while he talked to reporters; he pretended to enjoy a dinner of corn dogs and French fries with vinegar at a midway booth operated by a woman with tattooed forearms and four teeth, which was nothing more than a photo op; he then talked to reporters again and signed some autographs. By the time he finished campaigning, my day was shot. It was seven o'clock when they dropped me off in front of the Rhodes Tower. The governor said, "That was fun, padnah. Let's do it again." He reached across his wife to shake my hand. She glanced my way, the thinnest of smiles pursing her lips, but said nothing. I walked to the parking garage with sawdust in my eyes and the smell of animal manure and cherry blossom perfume still heavy in my nostrils. I called Jerry Adameyer from the car.

"Did you buy a goat or a cow or something?" he asked.

"How did you know where I was?"

"I saw you at the sale of champions on the six o'clock news—sitting next to the governor's wife. I didn't know you were going out there."

"Neither did I. It was an impulse decision by the governor. I feel like I'm in the fourth grade when I'm around that guy. I'm not allowed to make a decision for myself." Jerry laughed. "Do you have time for a beer?"

"I always have time for a beer," Jerry said. "Where?"

"How about the Water's Edge in Galena?"

"Give me thirty minutes."

I ordered a pitcher of Yuengling and a meat lover's calzone, which arrived at the booth just as Jerry Adameyer walked through the door. He slid onto the bench as I was pulling a slice of the calzone onto my plate. "Help yourself," I said. He did.

"Don't keep me in suspense, chief," he said. "How'd it go?"

"The governor is still inclined not to intervene in the Yates case."

"What? Even after you told him what we know about Majestro?"

I took a breath, not wanting to give him the answer. "I didn't tell him about Majestro."

The calzone that was heading toward his mouth went back to the plate. "Why the hell not?"

"It just wasn't the right time."

"Really? Lester Yates is going to be executed in what, nine days? When exactly is the right time?" His eyes were boring in on me. "What's going on with you, chief?"

"Nothing. Why?"

He stared at me for a long minute, silent, slowly rolling his beer glass between his palms. It was an old detective and reporter trick. Most people start blathering to fill the uncomfortable void. I had used this same tactic myself. I knew better and didn't bite. "I'm really surprised you're such a good politician, because you're a terrible liar," he said, breaking the silence. "You've got enough circumstantial evidence on Alfonso Majestro to flay him wide open, but you didn't tell the governor? Is someone squeezing you?"

"No. No one is squeezing me. We're dealing with a sensitive issue here. Majestro is the key to Wilinski's success. He's the brain trust.

I think Majestro's a weasel, but the governor trusts him and believes he's key to his presidential aspirations. I think he would do anything in his power to protect Majestro."

"Maybe he would protect Majestro, but you don't seriously think Wilinski would sacrifice Yates for political purposes?"

"I think he would do whatever Majestro tells him to do, and Majestro would gladly put the needle in Yates's arm if it resulted in political points. We've been over this ground before."

"Let's take it to the media."

"What if it's not Majestro? What if it's Danny Doyle, or Nathan Pryor, or Herman Fenicks, or someone else?"

"If we take it to the media, it will force Wilinski to give us a stay. We need that while we try to put the pieces together. I don't care if Alfonso Majestro becomes collateral damage. Screw him. He's dirty. You know that. It will give us time. We still don't know what Reno Moretti found in Fenicks' truck. That could be the key to this entire case."

"No media. Not yet."

His right brow arched. "Why, because it might torpedo Wilinski's run for president and if that happened you would never be United States attorney general?"

A flush of heat went up my neck. "Do you think you could be any more insulting?"

"Then tell me what the hell is going on. You've been like a pit bull on this case since day one. Now that we've got Majestro in our crosshairs, you get skittish on me. Why?"

"We're not back in Summit County dealing with the commissioners, Jerry. These are powerful people. Right now, everything we have in this entire case is circumstantial. I want this bottled up tight. I'm taking Beth Kremer to Philadelphia in the morning. I think the key to this case is hiding in Lizzy Love's casket."

THIRTY-NINE

One week and one day before the scheduled execution of Lester Paul Yates.

Beth and I were on the 5:55 a.m. flight from Columbus to Philadelphia the next morning. She was a lab geek and didn't understand—or particularly care—about the nuances of our various investigations. However, when I gave her a particular assignment that required her scientific expertise, she was on it. She told me this assignment was particularly fascinating, and she had her nose buried in a technical manual the entire flight. A professional wrestler returning home from a show in Columbus the previous night was seated on the other side of me, and he regaled me with tales of the ring for the entire hour-and-forty-minute flight. He roared at his own jokes. I laughed, too. Everyone in our section turned to look except Beth, who remained consumed with her research.

I found him a refreshing, if only temporary, distraction from Lester Yates.

We rented a car and drove to the home of Dr. Jasper Love, but he wasn't there. I searched on my phone and found the Althea O. Sykes Free Clinic on North Percy Street, where he told me he volunteered. It appeared to be a converted grocery store; metal chairs lined stark walls and children played on a rubber mat in the middle of the room. We were the only white people in the building, and it seemed that every eye was upon us. I approached a woman who sat at a steel desk near the front door. Before I could introduce myself, however, a door to an examination room opened and Jasper Love emerged wearing a knee-length lab coat and a look of compassion. He had a stethoscope around his neck and an arm on the shoulder of a young woman whose toddler was balanced on her hip. He glanced my way, looked down at his clipboard, then back at me when my face registered.

He walked slowly toward us. The look of compassion had been replaced with one of trepidation, or perhaps weariness. "This is a little surprising, Mr. Van Buren," he said. He clutched the clipboard with both hands and offered no further greeting. "What brings you back to Philadelphia?"

"I was hoping for a couple minutes of your time," I said.

"As you can see, I have quite a few people waiting."

"I understand, but it's extremely important, and it will only take a few minutes."

His nod was barely perceptible. "Come on in," he said, walking back into the examination room.

I introduced Beth. He barely looked at her. There was no reason to attempt to exchange pleasantries. "I have made what I believe is a significant discovery that may lead us to your daughter's killer. The chief of my legal staff is at this minute working with a local law firm. We are petitioning the court for an order to exhume the body of your daughter so that we can conduct additional tests."

He crossed his arms, squeezing the clipboard to his chest; his head was tilted back and his eyes closed. "Why? They conducted an autopsy on her."

"Yes, sir. But I am looking for information that is not in the autopsy."

"I would prefer that you allow my child to rest in peace, Mr. Van Buren."

"She can't rest until there's justice."

"Please don't tire me with your trite words. There can be no legitimate reason for this."

"You need to trust me. There is."

"I will call my lawyer and have him block any attempt at exhumation."

"Dr. Love, I have been running into roadblocks everywhere. A man is going to be executed very soon. He is not guilty. The key to stopping that execution may very well be lying beneath your daughter's headstone. Please don't try to block this. Every minute counts."

FORTY

One week before the scheduled execution of Lester Paul Yates.

At seven o'clock the following morning, the engine of a backhoe backfired and then groaned to life, breaking the silence at Laurel Hill Cemetery on the banks of the Schuylkill River. A few minutes later, it began peeling away earth and sod at the grave of Louise Elizabeth Love. Buckets of dirt dropped onto a blue tarp spread next to the gravesite. The morning dew held grass clippings to the sides of my shoes. Diesel exhaust hung thick in the air.

Beth and I stood around the grave with the Philadelphia County medical examiner, a sheriff's deputy, and three workers from the cemetery, one of whom leaned on a spade and stared at Beth while he spat tobacco juice into the grass. I looked around to see if Dr. Love had shown up; he had not. A local judge had granted an order for the exhumation and agreed to seal it for thirty days. That would give us the time we needed without the attention of the media.

It was only a few minutes before the bucket scraped the top of the vault. A winch was pushed into place over the grave, and inside of an hour the cherrywood casket carrying the body of Lizzy Love and her unborn fetus were placed into a hearse.

The sheriff's cruiser led the hearse out of the cemetery. We dropped in behind and followed them to the office of the county medical examiner on University Avenue. The hearse went behind a gated chain-link fence and backed into a bay door at the rear of the building. Beth and I went inside and waited in the lobby. While we waited, the body was removed from the casket, undressed, and placed on a stainless steel examining table. The process was cold, sterile, and supremely necessary. A lab assistant came into the lobby. "Are you both coming back?" she asked.

I had witnessed numerous autopsies during my days as the Summit County prosecuting attorney, but I had no desire to witness what was about to occur. "I'll stay here," I said. "Beth can handle it. Good luck. No pressure. Nothing at stake here but a man's life."

"Thanks for that."

"Beth, I've got one more thing I want you to do for me."

* * *

The receptionist offered me a coffee, which I accepted. I took it to a chair in the corner of the lobby. After finishing my coffee, despite the infusion of caffeine, I napped a bit. Then I perused a copy of the *Philadelphia Inquirer* from the receptionist's desk. It was two hours before Beth emerged with two plastic specimen containers in a clear, plastic bag.

"Did you get what you need?" I asked.

"There are aspects of my job that I find fascinating from a scientific perspective that are absolutely heartbreaking," she said. "That was one of them." She sat down next to me. "That little fetus was only about two inches long." She held up her thumb and index finger to illustrate the size. She took a few deep breaths and slouched in her chair. "I would like very much never to have to do that again."

"You're a trouper, Kremer."

"I'm not feeling so tough."

I waited a few seconds. "You didn't answer my question."

She lifted the plastic containers off her lap. "I made the mold and, yes, I should be able to provide you with DNA from the fetus."

FORTY-ONE

Our plane touched down at Port Columbus International Airport at 5:40 p.m.

As we were taxiing to the gate, I said, "Can I buy you dinner, Beth?"

"I'll take a rain check," she said. "I'm going to run out to the lab and get these started. I know we're on a tight deadline."

I was grateful for her dedication, but personally disappointed.

As I pulled out of the airport and onto Interstate 270, I tapped out Jerry Adameyer's phone number. "How's it going, chief?" he asked.

"I'm not sure. I just saw a giant bull elephant run across the outerbelt. I'm not sure if I'm hallucinating because this case is getting the best of me or because I'm running on about four hours of sleep over the past seventy-two hours."

"Don't discount the possibility that it was real. Are you back in local orbit?"

"Just landed. What are you up to?"

"I'm home. Come on out. I've got something for you."

I was at Jerry's house inside thirty minutes. When I exited the car, I could hear gunfire coming from the back of the property. It sounded like the pop of a .22-caliber. I yelled before turning the corner at the edge of the house.

"I'm on the deck," he said. "Come on up."

Jerry was reclining on his deck in a lounge chair, barefoot, in gym shorts and a T-shirt. There was a .22-caliber rifle between his legs, a bourbon and ice on the deck beside the chair, and a cigar in the corner of his mouth. "If I took a picture of that, it would sum up your entire existence," I said. "What are you shooting at?"

"Squirrels. I've already got two laying out there I need to pick up."

"Is it squirrel season?"

"It's my property, goddammit. It's always squirrel season. Have you ever had fried squirrel and onions?"

"Can't say that I have."

"You don't know what you're missing."

"Jerry, you are a dandy."

"You want something to drink—beer, bourbon?"

"Nothing. I'm already exhausted. I don't need to add alcohol to the mix."

He put his cigar in an ashtray and reached under the recliner for an envelope that I had not noticed. He flicked it at me like a Frisbee. "I thought you might find this interesting."

I pulled out the photocopied headshots that Liberatore had taken to Phil Stubblefield. Examining the backs of the pages, I flipped through them until I found Stubblefield's signature, then turned it over.

"Danny Doyle," I said.

Jerry nodded. "Stubblefield told Liberatore that Doyle was the one who came to his store that night and told him he never saw a black woman in his convenience store. She said as soon as Stubblefield saw the picture, he turned it over and signed it. No hesitation."

"Interesting. Majestro, Doyle, and Lizzy Love were in the car together when they left the Governor's Residence. Doyle must have stayed in the back seat while Lizzy bought her water and crackers, and Majestro pumped and paid for the gas. Most likely, Doyle went back to intimidate Stubblefield on Majestro's orders. It also means that one of them was following the story in the Cambridge paper, or they wouldn't have known about Stubblefield's comments."

"Had to be Majestro. I don't think Doyle can read," Jerry said. He took a sip of his bourbon, then set it down and sighted his rifle on a squirrel that had come out on the limb of a giant oak directly behind the deck. Number three dropped to the ground.

"So what happened in the twelve days between the time Majestro gassed up and Doyle walked into the convenience store?" I asked.

"That's the million-dollar question, isn't it? Let's not forget one other important fact. Sheriff D. Kendrick Brown was patrolling the boondocks of western Belmont County at three a.m. on Sunday morning. He and Majestro are thick as thieves. Whatever happened, that rat bastard was part of the equation." He picked up his cigar. "What happened in Philly?"

"We had the body of Lizzy Love exhumed. We got a judge to seal our request and the results of the search for thirty days. Beth is working on processing the DNA as we speak. With a little luck, we'll get samples that will confirm paternity. Of course, now comes the real challenge. I need his DNA to test against the fetus, and Beth says it's best if we have blood or semen."

"Unless you slit his throat, that only leaves one option."

"It certainly does."

"What's your plan? And please don't say it involves me."

"It doesn't. I'm going to ask Shelly Dennison to take one for the team."

* * *

I was two minutes down the road from Jerry's house when my cell phone rang. I answered without looking at the number.

"Don't you return your phone calls?" the voice demanded.

It was Alfonso Majestro, but just to be annoying, I asked, "Who's this?"

"You know who it is, goddammit. Why didn't you return my call?"

"It's been a long day, Alfonso, and I don't know what you're talking about."

"I called your office this afternoon. Didn't you get the message?"

"Get to the point."

"This will be quick, but extremely enjoyable for me. The governor asked me to call you because he will not be granting any kind of reduction in sentence or a delay in the execution of your friend the white supremacist. Unless you indict someone else and put a signed confession on the governor's desk, little Lester Yates is going bye-bye. Don't ask again. That's his final word."

Now the silence was on my end. Majestro was delighting in my frustration.

"Not surprising," I said.

"Here's one other thing you should know, Van Buren. This is probably not a secret, but let me say it anyway. I don't like you, not even a little bit, and I trust you even less. I'm just telling you that so there's no misunderstanding about your wet dream of becoming United States attorney general after Jim gets elected president. If you think that's ever happening, you're delusional. I'll never let you anywhere near his administration."

"You might want to have a conversation with the governor. He's thinking otherwise."

"That's funny. You actually think he's calling the shots, huh? He listens to everything I say like it's the Gospel, every goddamned word, and when I tell him that you are a liability of the first degree, he'll drop you yesterday."

"You know, Alfonso, sometimes things don't always turn out the way you plan them."

"Whatever the hell that's supposed to mean. Good luck, Van Buren. You're chasing purple elephants."

"He wasn't purple."

"What?"

"Good night, Alfonso."

FORTY-TWO

Six days and one hour before the scheduled execution of Lester Paul Yates.

"Have you lost your mind?"

It was the exact response I had expected. I had left her a message the previous evening and asked her to meet me Saturday morning at my office. She assumed I wanted to discuss my campaign. This was a broadside she hadn't expected.

"Shelly, I wouldn't ask if I wasn't desperate."

"Desperate may be your word. The one I'm thinking of is repulsive."

"More repulsive than letting an innocent man go to the death chamber?"

"Hutchinson Van Buren, that is not fair."

"Let me put it to you on a more personal level. The governor used you. You fell in love and thought you were going to be the first lady of the United States. You believed he felt the same way, but by your own admission he was just using you for sex. I know you think this is reprehensible . . ."

"Repulsive is the word I used."

"Yes, sorry, repulsive. However, I'm presenting you with an opportunity to do something that could very possibly destroy his path to the White House."

She didn't grin, but I sensed she wanted to. She grabbed her purse and headed for the door of my office. "Fine."

FORTY-THREE

Four days and one hour before the scheduled execution of Lester Paul Yates.

Reno Moretti sat in on our meeting of the Lester Yates task force. With him were sealed plastic lunch bags containing the material he had collected in the semi rig formerly owned by Herman Fenicks. He had the bags in a metal briefcase-like container. Each was labeled. A typed report accompanied the evidence. Like the binders he had presented me, his work collecting the evidence had been very thorough.

"What's your gut telling you about this, Reno?" I asked.

"I'm not feeling very positive," he said. "If Anne Touvell was ever in that rig, it was thirteen years ago. I went over every square inch of that cab and the sleeper cabin. If her DNA was in there, I got it, but the odds are not in our favor."

"We'll need a DNA sample from Anne Touvell's corpse for comparison. Do we have it?"

"No," said Jerry Adameyer.

"Please tell me she wasn't cremated."

"She wasn't. I checked that before I sent Reno to Utah. She's buried near Byesville in Guernsey County."

"Contact legal and tell them to start the paperwork for an exhumation. I want it done before noon. Let's get the samples Reno collected to Beth Kremer at the lab."

* * *

Shortly after two in the afternoon, Shelly Dennison walked into my office and set a brown envelope on my desk. "I'm going home. I'm going to get in the shower and stay there until I run out of hot water. I don't want to ever hear another word about me walking out on you in the middle of that campaign. After this, we're even. In fact, the scales are now tipping in my favor."

She scratched at her arms as though bugs were crawling all over her, then left.

I put the envelope in my briefcase and drove out to the Bureau of Criminal Investigation offices. I walked past D. Kendrick Brown's empty office to the laboratory. Beth Kremer was doing paperwork at her desk. She had successfully extracted DNA from the tissues of the fetus in Lizzy Love's womb and was waiting for something to compare it to. I set the envelope on her desk. "What's that?" she asked.

"Semen."

"Oh." She folded her hands under her chin. "How did you get it?"

"All I can tell you is that I had absolutely no involvement in the collection of that specimen."

"That's good. If you had, I have to admit I'd be disappointed." She raised her brows and tilted her head. "Know what I mean?"

I did. And, when this investigation was over, I was definitely going to make this up to her.

She opened a desk drawer and pulled out a latex glove that she worked onto her hand. As she straightened the metal clasps on the flap and opened the envelope, she peeked inside as though it might contain a live animal. She slid her hand inside and removed a sealed baggie with the tips of her index finger and thumb. She looked at the contents and said, "Well, that's certainly the real deal." She dropped it back in the envelope. "I'll get back to you on this as soon as I know something."

FORTY-FOUR

Three days and sixteen hours before the scheduled execution of Lester Paul Yates.

At 5:00 a.m. on Tuesday, August 21, 2007, four prison guards entered the cell of Lester Yates at the Northeast Ohio Correctional Facility. One of the guards, a rough-hewn man with a crew cut, a wide jaw, and a tattoo of a teardrop outside his left eye, woke Lester up by twice banging on the edge of his bunk with a nightstick. Lester was permitted to urinate before being wrapped in a leather belt and shackled at the wrists and ankles. The connecting chains ran through loops in the belt. He was wearing a blue prison shirt and pants and flip-flops as he was led down the catwalk toward the front of the cellblock, the ankle chains dragging on the concrete and jangling with each step.

From the darkness across the common area that separated the cells, a prisoner said what everyone was thinking: *dead man walking.*

Lester was flanked on both sides by the prison guards as he was marched out of Building 3 and into a white Ohio Department of Rehabilitation and Correction van that had been brought into the yard. The door to the van was open, and two guards put their arms under his pits and helped him in. The same crew-cut guard ran a chain through a loop in an ankle shackle, preventing movement beyond six inches, then strapped a safety belt across Lester's waist. Lester's stomach was percolating to where he was ready to vomit, but he thought it funny that they would take the time to strap him in with a safety belt while transporting him to his execution.

None of the guards spoke to Lester. One sat on a bench seat behind him. Lester was separated by a steel mesh screen from the driver and a second guard in the passenger seat, who was carrying a 12-gauge pump shotgun. As the prison van exited the compound, an Ohio State Highway Patrol car with two armed troopers dropped in behind the van as added security and they began the four-hour drive to the Southern Ohio Correctional Facility near Lucasville in Scioto County.

For the next three nights, Lester Paul Yates would be held in a cell just a few steps from the room where they planned to put him to death.

⋆ ⋆ ⋆

Before Lester reached the prison, I answered the phone at my desk.

"You have your match," Beth Kremer said.

"You're sure."

"It's not my opinion, Mr. Attorney General. It's good science, and good science doesn't lie. It's a definite match. Your boy fathered that fetus."

"He impregnated Lizzy Love."

"However you'd like to stack those blocks is fine with me."

FORTY-FIVE

I sat in a padded chair in the corner of my office, two fingers of bourbon in a paper coffee cup on the table within reach, the Columbus skyline and the state office tower in the background. From where I was sitting, I could count the floors and look into the office of Ohio Governor James D. Wilinski, the man who would be president.

There, he was planning his ascension to the Oval Office.

Around central Ohio, the majority of the population had other concerns; they were consumed with Ohio State University's season-opener against Youngstown State.

The attorney general was drinking booze from a paper cup.

And a two-hour drive down the road, Lester Yates was waiting in a cell to die for a crime he didn't commit.

Tick-tock.

Jerry Adameyer came in and sat down in a matching chair directly across the little table from me. "What's your plan, boss?" he asked.

"I was hoping you had one," I said.

He pointed at my cup. "Got any more of that?"

I pointed over my shoulder with a thumb. "Middle drawer on the right, toward the back."

He poured his bourbon into a clear tumbler, making no attempt to hide it, and walked back to his seat.

"They're celebrating over at the governor's office," I said.

"You've got good eyes," Jerry said.

"I don't need good eyes. Wilinski got an early endorsement today—Kyle Ferguson, the Republican senator from Pennsylvania. Wilinski is lining up his support, and Republicans all over the country are falling into line because they believe he's the man. A couple of prospective candidates backed off as soon as Wilinski announced his candidacy." I took a sip of my bourbon. "Meanwhile, I'm trying to find a way to drop a snake right in the middle of their party."

"I'd say you have ample evidence to blow things up right now."

"Maybe. You know, there were times in Summit County when I absolutely knew that Slimeball A killed Slimeball B. There was no doubt in my mind of Slimeball A's guilt. But I couldn't prove it beyond a reasonable doubt, so Slimeball B got buried and Slimeball A got to walk. It happened a bunch of times. There was this drug dealer in Akron, a nasty bit of a human being named Elmer Glick. Remember him?"

"I do. Elmer and I tangoed on several occasions."

"The police charged him with first-degree murder for allegedly bashing in the brains of a competitor with a shock absorber. The cops knew he did it. I knew he did it. Elmer knew he did it. But I had no physical evidence on him, and the only witness was a jailhouse snitch trying to cut a deal. I dropped the charges before it went to the grand jury."

"Why are you telling me this?"

"The other day you accused me of not being aggressive enough because I was trying to protect my political skin."

"That was a comment made in the heat of the moment."

"I know, but the fact remains, up to this point, all we've had is circumstantial evidence."

"Back up a bit. What's that mean, 'up to this point'?"

I pulled a small cassette recorder out of my pants pocket and set it on the table next to my coffee cup. "I've always been bothered by the fact that D. Kendrick Brown was patrolling western Belmont County at three o'clock on a Sunday morning when the 911 call came in that someone, a guy, was dumping a body under the docks on the eastern banks of Piedmont Lake. I knew that smelled, but how do you prove it all was a setup? I had a hunch, so yesterday I sent Liberatore on a little mission."

"A hunch. Is that like one of your dreams?"

I sipped bourbon, grinned, and shook my head. "No. A hunch is just something my gut was telling me. I had her go over to Belmont County and review the 911 call logs for that night. Remember, the caller said it was a guy, and he just saw someone dumping a body under the dock."

"I remember."

"According to the log, the call was made from a pay phone outside of Clay's Drive In, an ice cream and burger joint in the little town of Piedmont in Harrison County. That's three miles away."

Jerry shrugged. "If they didn't have a cell phone and were anxious to get out of the area, maybe that was the first place they stopped."

"Maybe, but I don't think so. Most of the time, 911 tapes are recorded over after thirty days, unless they pertain to a potential felony. Miraculously, this was still on file in the prosecutor's office. When our boy D. Kendrick went down and stole the Quinn file, he forgot to snag this little gem. Liberatore convinced the prosecutor to let her borrow it." I leaned over and hit the play button.

"911, what's your emergency?"

"Yeah, I just saw a big guy in a boat . . ." Static fuzzed the voice. *"Dumping a body under a dock . . ."* More static. *"In Piedmont Lake."*

"Whereabouts in Piedmont Lake?"

"By the docks . . ." Static bloomed, faded. *"Down in front of the Hilltop area. Near . . ." Static. "Lake Ridge Road."*

"Can you identify the man in the boat?"

The call suddenly cut off. I clicked the stop button.

"Sounds pretty cut-and-dried," Jerry said.

"Did you think the voice was muffled?"

"Maybe. That's not unusual for 911 calls. People don't want to get involved. It's pretty clear except for that static."

"That wasn't static." Jerry frowned; I smiled. "It was muffled because it was someone trying to disguise his voice, and unless I miss my guess, what you mistook for static was D. Kendrick Brown sucking saliva between his teeth and cheeks, the way he does every time he takes a breath while talking."

Jerry pointed at the recorder and said, "Play that again." I did. "D. Kendrick was in the area because he made the call."

"He didn't make it from Belmont County. He was up in Harrison County. If you were at Majestro's house on the lake, you have to drive north to get around the lake. That road takes you into Harrison County."

"You think he left Majestro's place and made the call because he knew a body was being dumped in the lake?"

"He wanted to be the one to find it so he could control the investigation."

"But the body wasn't there. It was found a few days later on the other side of the lake."

"Exactly. The body wasn't where it was supposed to be, which screwed up their plan. That's why they had to arrest Lester Yates. They wanted people to think the Egypt Valley Strangler had been captured. That way, the sheriff in Guernsey County would back off the investigation of Lizzy Love."

Jerry took a hard hit from his bourbon. "What the hell happened in Majestro's house?"

"Whatever it was, they all have to know. The evidence we have is still circumstantial. We need to get someone to talk."

"Are we going to squeeze D. Kendrick?"

"That wouldn't work. He's not the sharpest knife in the drawer, but he was a cop. He knows to keep his mouth shut, and he'll call the governor for cover."

"Majestro?"

"He's too smart, and we couldn't intimidate him. He would never cop to anything."

"Then it's Danny Doyle."

I nodded. "Yes, it is. The behemoth is the weak link. We're running out of time. How do we get to him? If Majestro finds out we want to question him, he'll never let it happen."

"You're thinking like a lawyer, or worse, a politician," Jerry said. "For this job, you need to have a street cop in charge." He grinned and saluted. "Gerald P. Adameyer, reporting for duty, sir."

FORTY-SIX

In the opulent dining room of his mansion in the Columbus suburb of New Albany, billionaire businessman Benson T. Buckmaster hosted a ten-thousand-dollar-a-plate fundraising dinner for Republican presidential candidate James "Big Jim" Wilinski. I had not been invited, which was a relief because I could not have afforded the appetizers. Rather, while Buckmaster's guests dined on Kobe beef, lobster, and crab ravioli, Jerry Adameyer and I were having iced teas and hamburgers in the parking lot of a fast-food restaurant on North High Street in the Old Beechwold neighborhood.

Across the street was a strip mall with a secondhand clothing store, Chinese carryout, nail salon, and a fifties-motif diner where the multicolored lights of a reproduction jukebox were reflecting off the windows. Backing up to the north side of the strip mall was an enclave of World War II–era duplex homes of brown brick that had been converted into condominiums. Across an asphalt parking lot from the diner was the back door of the home of Danny Doyle. A faint light burned in the kitchen and spilled onto the wooden stoop.

At 9:46 p.m., Jerry's phone rang. It was his investigator, Clarence Davidson, who was sitting in a car not far from the entrance to the Buckmaster estate. The governor's limousine had just left the compound. The driver would take Wilinski and his wife home to Marble Cliff, then drop off Doyle at the state office parking garage downtown. When the limousine had disappeared onto Reynoldsburg–New Albany Road, Davidson waited two minutes, then drove downtown. He parked on State Street and called again at 10:21. Doyle had just left the parking garage in his black Cadillac.

Jerry drove across North High Street and pulled behind the diner, parking alongside a chain-link fence and nosing up to a garbage dumpster. We got out and walked into a row of overgrown arborvitaes, waiting in the shadows until the Cadillac pulled into the one-car garage at the side of Doyle's property.

"Ready?" Jerry asked.

"Ready," I said.

This was Jerry's plan. I was simply a foot solider.

I walked around the house; Jerry remained at the rear of the property in order to come up behind Doyle. I crouched behind a row of yews in front of the connected condominium. Doyle emerged from the garage balancing a large pizza box and a six-pack of beer on his open left palm. He punched in a code on a keypad attached to the jamb and started toward the condo as the garage door dropped. By the glow of the streetlight, I could see Doyle's face. It was the first time I remembered seeing him when he wasn't scowling. He was off the clock; there was no one to intimidate. His face looked soft, like that of a pudgy ten-year-old boy, and the short walk to the recessed porch that hid his door appeared to be a struggle; he wheezed lightly as he pulled air into his lungs.

As he stepped onto the porch and fumbled for his keys, I stood and said, "A lovely evening, don't you think, Danny?"

He looked as though he had grabbed a hot electric cord. The pizza, beer, and keys flew from his hands. One beer can exploded and shot foam across the concrete porch and into the flower bed. He stooped over to grab the pistol he kept in an ankle holster, but before he could get his hand on the hem of his pants, he felt the barrel of a .357 snub nose press into the base of his skull and heard the hammer lock into place. He froze. "In case you're wondering, Danny, that's a .357 Magnum I'm pressing into the crease where your spine and that peanut-sized brain meet. There's a hollow-point round in that chamber. I'm telling you that because if you reach for that pistol, I'm going to put a slug in the back of your skull that will blow your face all over this porch and that pizza box. Are we clear?"

"You don't know who you're messing with," Danny said.

"That's the wrong answer, Jumbo." He pressed the revolver harder into one of the fleshy rolls mounded on the back of Doyle's neck. "Try again."

"I understand."

"Very good. Now, stand up real slow and put your hands on your hips." He did as he was told. Jerry looked at me and said, "Get the pistol out of the holster on his right ankle." I came out of the shadows and took the weapon. "What's he carrying?"

"A 9mm Beretta," I said.

"What the hell kind of bodyguard are you, anyway, Doyle? Two guys are lurking in the shadows of your own yard, and you don't even see them."

He finally saw my face. "Van Buren?" he said. "What the hell's this all about?"

"Hey, Jumbo, we'll ask the questions," Jerry said.

"What do you want?"

"I want you to shut up, pick up your keys, and unlock the door. We're going inside to have a little chat." Doyle bent down and picked up the key ring. He nervously fumbled with it for a minute before unlocking the door. It skidded on the jamb. Before it was a foot open, Doyle spun and threw a sloppy elbow at Jerry.

The fight, if that is what you would call it, lasted all of about four seconds. Jerry ducked the elbow and, in a single motion, threw a leg behind Danny as he fired the heel of his left hand under the big man's chin. Danny Doyle probably outweighed Jerry by an easy hundred pounds, but Jerry had a powerlifter's strength and a street-fighter's mentality. When his palm struck the chin, Doyle's teeth crunched like an ice cube under heel, and he went into free fall, landing in a rose of Sharon just off the edge of his porch. I swear the ground shook when he hit. Air rushed out of his lungs and he lay sprawled in the yard, his shirt untucked, his clip-on tie lost in the dark, his gelatinous gut spreading out like a giant water balloon.

"He looks like something that washed up on the beach," Jerry said, stepping into the mulch. He grabbed Doyle by the collar of his sport coat and started pulling him up. "What's wrong with you,

Doyle? Are you ugly and stupid? I've got a .357 and you're trying to take me down with an elbow?"

Doyle got on all fours, took a moment to catch his breath, then grabbed the corner post of the porch and slowly pulled himself up. I looked down the street. Someone walking a dog was heading our way. "Get him inside," I said.

Jerry nudged Doyle through the door. I picked up the beer and pizza and followed. We walked to the small kitchen in the rear of the condo. "Sit down and mind your manners," I said. I turned on the overhead light and closed the curtains before setting the pizza box and beer on the kitchen table. Jerry stood off Doyle's right shoulder, arms folded, the .357 hanging from his right hand.

There were no fewer than fifteen pizza boxes stacked up on the counter and table. The trash can was full, mostly with empty beer cans and more pizza boxes. "Christ almighty, Danny," I said. "Do you consume anything besides pizza and beer?"

"It's easy," he said, taking a few hard breaths. "What do you want?"

I pulled out a chair across from Doyle and sat down. He was still trying to catch his breath; pieces of mulch were embedded in his hair. His cheeks were red and moist. I opened up the pizza box and slid it in front of Doyle; it was a sausage and mushroom pizza, and in remarkably good shape for the abuse it had gone through. I snapped open a beer and let the foam run onto the floor. When it had settled, I set it next to the pizza box.

"Eat up, Danny," I said. "Enjoy your pizza and beer. It'll be the last you have for a long, long time. Maybe ever." I looked up at Jerry. "Do they serve pizza and beer in prison, Jerry?"

"I'm pretty sure not."

Doyle worked his lips between his teeth, and his eyes shot back and forth between Jerry and me. "What are you talking about?"

"Danny, come on, we know you're not as stupid as you look. You know that we've been working the Egypt Valley Strangler murders. I know you listen in when the governor and Majestro talk about it, right?"

He was silent.

"I want you to tell us what you know about Louise Elizabeth Love—Lizzy Love."

"I don't know what you're talking about. I didn't have nothing to do with that girl's death."

"Oh, but you know who she is, right?"

"I've heard her name before."

"But you don't know anything, huh?" Jerry asked. "Nothing at all?"

"No. Nothing."

"That's funny, because Mr. Van Buren and I just saw a security tape of her getting into a car in front of the Governor's Residence the day she disappeared. Do you know who else was in that car, Danny?" Doyle swallowed but said nothing. "Need a hint? His initials are Danny Doyle."

Beads of perspiration began to appear on Doyle's upper lip. I stared hard at him. He swallowed with great effort and said, "I want to call the governor."

"I'm sure you do," I said. "If I was as screwed as you, I would want some help, too." I leaned in toward Doyle, my hands folded on the table. "Tell us how you did it, Danny. Tell us how you murdered Lizzy Love."

He took the beer, gulped three hard swallows, and wiped foam and sweat from his lip with the sleeve of his suit jacket. "You're crazy," he said. "I didn't murder anybody. Not ever."

"I saw the autopsy report. It said she had been strangled by someone strong, someone with big hands." From my folded hands I extended an index finger. "Look at the size of those paws of yours. I can guarantee you this, Danny, when the prosecutor tells the jury that Lizzy Love was strangled by someone with big hands, you better be sitting on yours, because every member of that jury is going to look at the defense table to see your hands. They're going to say to themselves, 'Yep, that son of a bitch murdered her.'"

"I told you, I didn't . . ."

"I'll bet they went around her neck pretty easily, didn't they? You put your thumbs on the center of her neck and squeezed the life right out of her, didn't you? How long did it take, Danny? Huh? How long did it take you to choke that girl to death?"

"No, no. I . . . I would never."

"Did you do it for Majestro? Was he the one who ordered you to kill her?"

He looked like he might start to cry. He was weak and afraid.

I reached into my shirt pocket and pulled out a twice-folded sheet of paper and set it on the table in front of Doyle. "We figured out a few things, Danny. This is a transcription of the 911 call from the Saturday night that Lizzy Love disappeared. We know where the call came from and who made it. It was your buddy, D. Kendrick Brown. He made it from an ice cream place near Majestro's house on Piedmont Lake, so we know he was there. You were seen in a car with Majestro and Lizzy Love that went to Piedmont Lake that very day. Majestro is just a little guy. He couldn't have strangled someone like Lizzy Love. But you, Danny, someone your size, you could have done it very easily. That's what happened, wasn't it? You killed her, then you and Majestro hatched this plan with Brown to cover up the murder, didn't you? Look at this transcription . . ." I tapped at the paper. "A big guy dumping a body."

"No, uh-uh," he said.

"We know it was you," Jerry said. "Maybe Brown screwed up and got a little too descriptive when he said 'a big guy.'" Jerry leaned in close to Doyle's ear. "Or maybe he meant to say that. Maybe he wanted to catch you in the act of dumping the body so he could arrest you. You know, do the old double-cross. That way he could help protect Majestro and the governor."

"No. This is crazy. I don't know what you're talking about."

"Oh, I think you do," I said. "We know you did it, and you're going to prison for a long, long time. Jim Wilinski is going to be president of the United States of America, and you're going to watch the inauguration from your prison cell. Your buddy Alfonso Majestro is going to be chief of staff, eating those great steaks they serve in Washington, DC, women hanging all over him. Even a dumbass like D. Kendrick Brown will probably get himself a nice position in the administration. But not you, Danny. No, sir. You'll be sitting in a prison cell with some bubba who thinks you've got nice lips."

"I'm calling the governor." He started to reach for his cell phone in the inside pocket of his sport coat. Jerry gave him a chop to the side of his neck. A chunk of mulch fell out of his hair and onto his pizza.

"You are going to sit right there until you tell us how you killed her," Jerry said. "And I want the truth. And if you didn't kill her, you better start talking. Remember this, Danny: the first one to the door gets the deal."

And Danny Doyle, the mountain of a man, began sobbing like a baby.

FORTY-SEVEN

Twenty-two hours before the scheduled execution of Lester Paul Yates.

The Red Brick Tavern stands along the old National Road in the tiny Madison County community of Lafayette. The building is Ohio's second-oldest stagecoach stop, built in 1836 from bricks fired just down the road. In 2007, it was a fine restaurant with a full bar and where D. Kendrick Brown spent his lunch hour every working day. We sat in Jerry's state car along Third Avenue and watched until Brown's car pulled into the parking lot and he disappeared around the front of the building.

"It's showtime," Jerry said.

I called the cell phone number of the chief deputy of the Guernsey County Sheriff's Office, who was parked a mile from the Red Brick in a patrol car. "I'm heading in," I said.

Jerry remained in the foyer while I walked into the bar area. D. Kendrick Brown was seated on a stool, his hunched shoulders arcing toward the bar. As a waitress set a glass of diet cola in front of him, he looked into the mirror behind the bar and saw me standing behind him. Our reflections locked eyes for a moment, then he pulled his soda closer and sipped it from a plastic straw. "To what do I owe this pleasure?" he asked, sucking saliva between his teeth and cheeks. "Did you stop by to rough me up some more?"

I sat down on the stool next to D. Kendrick and waved off the waitress. Without saying a word, I set my digital recorder on the bar and hit play.

"911, what's your emergency?"

"Yeah, I just saw a big guy in a boat . . ." Static. *"Dumping a body under a dock . . ."* Static. *"In Piedmont Lake."*

"Whereabouts in Piedmont Lake?"

"By the docks . . ." Static. *"Down in front of the Hilltop area. Near . . ."* Static. *"Lake Ridge Road."*

"Can you identify the man in the boat?"

I turned it off. "Want to hear it again?"

"Why would I?"

"Let's not play games. It's you, D. Kendrick, and you know it. It's the call you made from Clay's Drive In on the night you were trying to get control of the Lizzy Love investigation so that you could protect your Hillbilly Mafia buddies."

He sipped his diet cola. "You're delusional. That doesn't even sound like me."

I looked at him and sucked saliva back through my mouth. "Sound familiar?" I asked. The color began to drain from his face. I reached into my suit-coat pocket and produced a copy of a Guernsey County grand jury indictment that had been handed up early that morning. I said, "This indictment out of Guernsey County, Ohio, charges one Delbert Kendrick Brown with obstruction of justice, tampering with evidence, and conspiracy to cover up a crime in connection with the strangulation death of one Louise Elizabeth Love, twenty-one, of Philadelphia, Pennsylvania."

He turned on his stool, his eyes wide, a look of utter panic on his face. He patted his jacket and reached for his cell phone. I grabbed his wrist and said, "The governor can't help you on this one, D. Kendrick."

"Whoa, whoa, whoa," he said. "No, no, I didn't kill her."

"I didn't say you did. You tried to cover it up."

He grabbed my arm. "I'll talk. Cut me a deal, and I'll tell you everything you want to know. Everything."

"I don't need your help, D. Kendrick. Danny Doyle has already been very, very helpful."

He looked as though he might vomit. I waved in Jerry and the three Guernsey County deputies and one from Madison County, who I had contacted as a courtesy. "Don't make this any more difficult than it needs to be," I said. "We're going to cuff you and walk you outside. We'll read you your rights there."

"I know my rights," he said.

A deputy grabbed D. Kendrick Brown by the shoulder and backed him off the stool. He was pulling hard for air as they cuffed his hands and walked him to the waiting cruiser. The waitress came out with an order of meatloaf and mashed potatoes. I dropped a twenty-dollar bill on the bar and said, "He's not hungry."

FORTY-EIGHT

There is a simple reason why some prosecutors don't pursue the powerful.

They're afraid.

The powerful have the political clout and the bank accounts to punch back. It is easy to prosecute the Lester Yateses of the world, for they lack the strength or finances to fight. Many times, they have been so beaten down by life that they simply play their role and succumb to the system. They are easy targets, the low-hanging fruit. A prosecutor who picks on the weak is not unlike the class bully who looks for the kid he knows will not fight back.

I had learned at an early age to take a punch. I had grown up in the Ohio River Valley, where fights regularly broke out for good reason or no reason at all, and I was raised under the roof of the hard-handed Miriam Van Buren, a humorless woman who carried mail eight hours a day to keep me fed and who had no time for negotiating or such niceties as timeouts. She meted out punishment with the flat of her hand or whatever implement of discipline was within arm's reach, though her favorites were leather belts and kitchen utensils. I once had a bruise on my thigh in the shape of her steel spatula. These two factors had hardened me to both defeat and bloody noses, neither of which, I had learned, were fatal. Thus, when I became the Summit County prosecuting attorney, I attacked both the powerful and the weak with the same vigor.

Still, my guts were on fire as I rode up the elevator in the Rhodes

State Office Tower with six law officers and Jerry Adameyer on my flanks.

We came out of the elevator and through the glass door to the governor's suite. The receptionist's eyes widened; I was no stranger to his office and her look appeared to be more perplexity than fear. The door to the governor's office was closed, but the one I was walking toward—that of Alfonso Majestro—was open and right in front of me. Since he had positioned his desk so that he could see anyone who walked into the suite, he had a clear view of me at the tip of a wedge of gray shirts and badges heading his way. This time, he could not ignore my presence, and the Adam's apple in his skinny neck bobbed like a skittering yo-yo. As I passed her desk, the receptionist reached for her phone. "No calls," I said. A deputy placed his hand on the receiver.

Two campaign consultants—a man and woman—were sitting in front of Majestro's desk. They turned their heads in unison when they saw his eyes lock in on me as I walked in. Without comment, I yanked the cord coming out of the back of his desk phone. The plastic clip that held it in place snapped off and landed in the woman's lap.

"What the hell do you think you're doing?" he asked.

"Don't go anywhere, Alf. I'll be over to see you next." I turned to the deputy who had followed me in and pointed at the consultants. "Get them out of here. I then pointed at Majestro. "He doesn't go anywhere. If he tries to leave, break his legs; if he tries to make a call with his cell phone, break his fingers."

I walked back into the foyer and entered the governor's office alone. He was sitting at the conference table with Stan Carmine, the chairman of the Ohio Republican Party. A thin smile crossed Jim Wilinski's lips, and he seemed amused by my unannounced entrance. He leaned back in his chair, rolled an ink pen between his fingers, and said, "Something on your mind, Hutch?"

I pointed to Carmine and said, "You need to leave, Stan."

"Whoa, padnah, since when do you come into my office and start barking orders?"

I stared down at Wilinski but said nothing. He looked at Carmine and said, "Sorry about this, Stan. Can you give me a minute?"

Carmine got up and left without comment. The governor didn't speak until the door to the foyer clicked shut. "You are getting on my last nerve, boy. Let me guess. This has something to do with Lester Yates."

"Maybe peripherally, but it has everything to do with Lizzy Love."

He frowned. "I'm afraid I don't know who that is."

He was cool under pressure; I would give him that.

"I'm in no mood for games, Governor. You know who she was, because you impregnated her and then strangled her."

His brows arched in feigned shock. "I don't know what kind of game you're playing, but . . ."

"About an hour ago I put D. Kendrick Brown under arrest for conspiracy after the fact in connection with the murder of Louise Elizabeth Love. In case that name doesn't ring a bell with you, her name was Louise Elizabeth, but everyone called her Lizzy. Brown was indicted by a Guernsey County grand jury this morning." Wilinski's jaw muscles began to flex and a red tide crept up his neck, but his facial expression never changed. "You were indicted, too, Governor—murder one. I'm putting you under arrest."

He grinned. "What is this, some kind of joke or a political hit job? I have no idea what you're talking about, and I don't know who this Love girl was."

"No?"

"Nope. Never met her in my life."

"Let me refresh your memory." I reached into my inside jacket pocket and produced several folded sheets of paper. I peeled off the top sheet and dropped it on the conference table. "That girl you said you'd never met—here's a copy of an article and photo from the *Columbus Dispatch*. That's you and Lizzy Love in a photo taken at the state Young Republicans conference in June of 2001."

He looked and shrugged. "I meet a lot of people."

I picked it up and read a passage I had highlighted. "Here's what you said: 'The future of the Republican Party is in good hands with young, bright people like Lizzy Love joining our ranks.'"

"Perhaps I'm guilty of making a gratuitous remark about a college student I don't remember. I beg your forgiveness. That doesn't mean I knew her."

"You're correct. That doesn't, but this certainly does." I took the next sheet of paper and slid it across the table. "Miss Love was pregnant when she was murdered and, according to a DNA test we conducted, you were the father."

He looked briefly at the document, then shoved it back at me. "That's bullshit. I've never in my life submitted a sample for a DNA test."

"You submitted a sample; you just didn't realize it at the time." He frowned. I grinned. "Hell hath no fury like a woman scorned, Governor."

He swallowed. "Shelly Dennison." I nodded. His rage was now nearly uncontrollable. "That will never hold up in court."

"It doesn't have to. I have the samples I need from the fetus. I'll get a judge to force you to submit a court-sanctioned test. It'll all be very official, and I assure you that the results will be the same. You fathered that child."

"You're on a fishing expedition."

"I researched all those murders of the Egypt Valley Strangler, but Lizzy Love's death had me perplexed. How did a young black woman from Philadelphia, an athlete and an honor student, get to the bottom of a lake in Guernsey County? I even went to Philadelphia to talk to her father. He's a tragic figure, overwhelmed with grief. You should see his office. It's a shrine to the daughter he lost, his only child, a beautiful girl with a gap-toothed smile. I just couldn't figure out how she ended up strangled and in that lake. What was she doing out there? But I caught a break. You forced me to go to the sale of champions at the state fair. Remember how hot it was in the Celeste Center? You were working the crowd and sweating like crazy. You came over for some water, and you took off your cuff links and handed them to your wife. And then you rolled up your shirt sleeves. That's when I saw the scar on the inside of your right forearm—the bite mark." I pointed across the room at the photo of the young Jim Wilinski when he had been with the Chicago Bears. "I remembered looking at that photo and recalling how clean and muscular they had looked. Take a look. There's no bite mark on your arm in that photo. That's when I knew. I hadn't conducted the DNA tests, but I knew what happened. Getting a young black girl pregnant would certainly complicate your plans to run for the presidency, wouldn't it? Mrs. Wilinski might have tolerated your infidelities, but the electorate wouldn't be as forgiving."

The jitters were gone from my belly. I was once again the prosecutor, and I was holding all the trump cards. I could see the fading light in Jim Wilinski's eyes. All that he had worked for, that bright future he had as the leader of the free world, was being sucked down a whirlpool that he was helpless to stop. "Tell me how it happened, Jim," I said. "Did you suggest an abortion and she refused? Is that what started the fight? You gave her the opportunity to end the pregnancy, and she said no. At that point, what choice did a man who wanted to be president have? There was only one option left, so you strangled her. But she was strong and in shape, and she got loose long enough to sink her teeth into that forearm and leave a bright, white scar, didn't she?"

"I played old-school football; you get a lot of bite marks," he said. "It's something you wouldn't know about. You probably never played a game of football in your life."

I knew he hadn't been listening.

From the side pocket of my suit coat I pulled out a plaster cast of Lizzy Love's upper teeth. "Beth Kremer made that cast when we went to Philadelphia to extract the DNA from the fetus. The gap in that scar on your arm is as clear as the gap in her photograph that's hanging on her father's wall. I don't need to press this cast to your arm. I know it's a match, and I'll make sure a jury sees that."

He rested both forearms on the edge of the conference table, a faint smile on his lips. "Having an affair is not a crime. The rest of this is wild-ass speculation on your part. You have no proof that I killed anyone."

"I don't have a photo of you with your hands around her neck, if that's what you mean. But let me ask you this: Did it surprise you that your most loyal henchman, your personal bodyguard, hasn't been around for two days? He hasn't answered his phone, has he? I know that because we have it and you've been blowing it up. Danny Doyle is a big man, but in the end he was weak. He told us everything. You had Majestro and Doyle pick her up that day at the mansion and bring her out to Majestro's house on Piedmont Lake for a fling. Everything was great until you found out she was pregnant. I don't know how the fight began, but I know how it ended—with her lifeless body sprawled on your bed. That's when you called Danny Doyle into the room. Neither of you knew what to do, so you called your fixer—Alfonso Majestro. He told you to wrap a nylon cord around her neck so it would appear that she was a victim of the Egypt Valley Strangler. You had Doyle put the body in Majestro's bass boat and he took it down to the boat club and dumped it under the dock. But you needed more reassurance that this wouldn't come back to haunt you. Majestro told you to call Sheriff Del Brown to make sure he was patrolling the area so he could personally take charge of the investigation. I know that for a fact because you called him on your state-issued phone, and that call log is public record." I held up the last sheet of paper that I had pulled from my jacket pocket. "It's right here. You made the call to Brown's cell phone at eleven-thirty-seven p.m. That's why you hired that moron to run the Bureau of Criminal Investigation and were so protective of him. It was payback for his loyalty and his silence." I took the three sheets of paper, refolded them, and slipped them back into my inside jacket pocket. "The problem was, you relied on Danny Doyle to complete the mission, and as we both know he is not the brightest bulb on the porch. But what choice did you have? The governor of the state of Ohio could hardly be caught driving a bass boat down Piedmont Lake with the corpse of a young black woman, could he? So you sent Doyle, but he dumped the body on the wrong side of the lake. He didn't know Belmont County from Guernsey County, so he dumped it at the first set of docks he came to, which were on the Guernsey County side. You and your brain trust in the next room had to find a patsy to be the Egypt Valley Strangler so you could connect him to the death of Lizzy Love. And you found the perfect foil. Lester Yates. He'd already been tied to the use of a murdered woman's credit card, and you were able to portray him as a white supremacist. No one was going to have any sympathy for him. But just to make sure he got convicted, Majestro set up his inexperienced nephew to be Yates's public defender. Then, D. Kendrick called the sheriff of Guernsey County and said he had arrested the Egypt Valley Strangler, and there was no reason to continue investigating the Love girl's murder—wrap it up and put a bow on it."

"Are you done?" Wilinski asked.

"Almost. When we started investigating this, we thought Lester was arrested to protect someone for the murder of Danielle Quinn—maybe D. Kendrick or Majestro. It took us a while before we figured out that it wasn't about Quinn at all; it was to cover up the murder of Lizzy Love and protect the governor. Lester was the perfect foil because he was stupid and poor and had tried to use Quinn's credit card. He was your sacrificial lamb." We stared at each other for a long moment. "Now, I'm done."

"You will rue the day that you ever crossed me."

"I doubt that. Your days of intimidating anyone are over."

I walked over and opened the door. Three deputies and the Franklin County sheriff, a Democrat who was not about to miss out on handcuffing the Republican governor, entered the office. Within a few minutes, Governor James D. Wilinski had been read his rights, patted down, his thick wrists handcuffed, and led out of the same office tower that only that morning he had dominated with his mere presence.

FORTY-NINE

When the elevator door closed, swallowing the governor and the lawmen, I waved one of the remaining deputies into the governor's office and said, "Please tell the receptionist and anyone else in the suite that they can go home." I pointed at a wall, behind which was the office of Alfonso Majestro. "But not him."

"Yes, sir," the deputy said.

There was a mini fridge built into a kitchenette in the corner of the governor's office. I pulled out a can of ginger ale and snapped it open. "Want one?" I asked Jerry.

"I'm good," he said. I took a seat in one of the chairs in front of a massive desk that had been built from Ohio walnut trees, and watched people file out of the suite. Several were in tears; a few others acted like a fire alarm had gone off. "Aren't you going over to Majestro's office?"

"Eventually," I said.

"What are you waiting on?" Jerry asked.

"Nothing in particular. I'm just letting him swing in the wind for a while—give him some time to consider every borderline felony he's committed over the past seven years."

He smiled, and his lip hitched. "I like your style."

I called Margaret and told her to have my communications staff send the press release to the Associated Press. I sipped my ginger ale. Fifteen minutes passed. It was quiet in the suite. "Ready?" I asked.

"Let's do it."

The deputy was filling up the doorway to Majestro's office. He moved over to let me pass. As I did, I pulled the papers out of my jacket pocket, holding them in my right hand, tapping the palm of my left. Majestro's eyes went immediately to those papers. He swallowed hard. I stopped in front of his desk; Jerry walked past me and leaned against the wall, arms folded, just to Majestro's left and visible in the corner of his eye.

I was no stranger to the look on Majestro's face. During my years as a prosecutor, I had seen it hundreds of times, mostly from white-collar criminals and first-time offenders. It was the look of unadulterated panic, the realization that they were in a situation from which their money and influence could offer no escape. Their mind would race. They would think of ways to correct the problem, to reverse their actions. They wondered if they could get to their bank accounts and run. Leave the state, maybe even the country. They thought of how their names would look in the newspaper alongside a mug shot, and the embarrassment it would cause them and their families. It all ran in front of their eyes, like a movie at fast-forward, and they were desperate for a way to escape.

That was the look on the little ferret face of Alfonso Majestro at that moment. Gone was the cocksure, condescending look of derision he gave me every time we met—that look of smug superiority. It had been replaced with our most primal emotion—raw fear.

Keeping the papers rolled up inside a loose fist, I rested both hands on the front of his desk, leaned in, and said, "Alfonso, Alfonso, Alfonso. How did someone as smart as you get yourself in a pickle like this?"

"A pickle like what?" He worked his dry mouth for saliva. "What the hell is this all about?"

I ignored the question. "Jerry, can you believe this guy was supposed to have been Big Jim Wilinski's fixer, the guy who made all the problems go away?"

Jerry snorted. "He obviously wasn't very good at his job, or they wouldn't have marched Wilinski out of here in handcuffs twenty minutes ago."

Behind his weak moustache, Majestro's lips pulled tight. I grinned and said, "I'll bet your lips aren't the only thing that's puckering up right now. Am I right, Alfonso?"

He didn't answer.

On the corner of Majestro's desk were a photo of him at Piedmont Lake with a trophy bass, a paperweight from some civic group for giving a talk, and a few stacks of paper. With the back of my hand I pushed them toward the edge of the desk and watched as they dropped one by one to the floor, then I took a seat on the edge of the desk.

"So, Alfonso, what was it you were saying to me the other day? Oh, wait, I remember, you said, 'I don't like you, not even a little bit.' Remember that? And you said those other awful things to me, that you didn't trust me, and that I was delusional, and that you were going to personally make sure I was never appointed United States attorney general." I laughed. "That's sort of a moot point given what has transpired in the past twenty-four hours. I'd say the odds of Jim Wilinski getting elected president of the United States are pretty slim." I took the papers out of my hand, pinched the tip with an index finger and thumb, and slowly ran them down the crease. His eyes didn't leave the papers; I thought he might vomit. "Let me tell you something, Alfonso, when I was a prosecutor, I tried to give everyone, even scumballs like you, a degree of respect. I'm not usually the type to hold grudges or take pleasure in the misery of others, but I'm going to make an exception in your case."

"I have no idea what this is all about."

"Sure you do," Jerry said.

"Go ahead, Alfonso, say the name that's bouncing around in your head right now," I said. "Go ahead and say it out loud—Lizzy Love. That's the name, isn't it? But you're thinking, if I say it, Van Buren will know I was involved in helping cover up her murder. Isn't that what you're thinking? See, that's what made me a good prosecutor. I know how criminals think. That's okay, Alfonso, you don't have to say her name; I already know you're involved. And if you think I'm enjoying this . . ." I winked. "You're right. We arrested your old buddy D. Kendrick Brown earlier, and you saw the governor walk out of here with a police escort. They were both indicted by a grand jury this morning. Danny Doyle is in our protection and talking like a man trying to save his own skin. Brown will be the next one to start talking. You know that's true because he's weak and he'll sing like crazy. That's what happens when conspiracies fall apart. The rats start eating one another. You know what that means for you, don't you, Alfonso? It means you're next."

The look on his face told me he believed it.

"I had . . ."

"You had what? Nothing to do with her murder? Is that what you were about to say? That would mean you knew she was murdered, wouldn't it? I've seen a security video of Miss Love getting into your car at the Governor's Residence, and I have a receipt where you bought gas at a convenience store near your cabin. That was the last time she was ever seen alive, and you were with her. You're up to your scrawny little neck in this mess."

"I want to talk to my lawyer."

"I'm sure you do."

Jerry edged in a little closer.

"Where were you that night?"

"I had a date."

"Really? How odd that you would remember so quickly where you were on a Saturday night six years ago. Who was it with? Danielle Quinn?" What little blood that remained in his face drained with the mention of her name. "Oh, wait, that couldn't have been because they had already found her body in Stillwater Creek. That Egypt Valley is quite a dumping ground for unfortunate women, isn't it?"

"I had nothing to do with any of this."

"You delivered that girl to your own lake house. She was murdered in one of your bedrooms, and yet you claim you had no responsibility?"

"There was no crime in taking her there. She was a consenting adult."

"That sounds nice and legal. I have her father's phone number if you'd like to call him and tell him how nice and legal it was. I'm sure that would make him feel better."

"Look, the governor asked to use my cottage for the weekend. He said he needed some alone time to work on some things, so I let him use it. Saturday morning, he called me and said the Love girl was going to help him with some campus outreach, and Doyle wanted to go up and do some fishing, and could I give them a ride to the cabin."

"And you said yes."

"He's the governor; of course, I said yes. I picked up Doyle at his house and the girl at the Governor's Residence. If you saw the security video then you saw her get into my car on her own volition. There was no force. And I bought gas. What the hell? Everybody buys gas. I dropped them off at the cabin and came back to Columbus."

"And you want me to believe that he wanted Lizzy Love, an attractive, twenty-one-year-old college volleyball player, brought out to the cabin to discuss campus outreach. Is that right?"

"That's what he told me, and I did as I was asked. Did I know he was banging her? Of course. He banged a lot of women, but that's his business, not mine."

"Doyle said he called you after she had been murdered and you're the one who told him what to do with the body."

"I have no earthly idea what he's talking about. He called me wanting to know where he could find the keys to the bass boat. I told him where they were. Then he called me a while later because he couldn't find the fishing poles. I told him they were in the shed and where he could find the key to the padlock." I continued to tap the papers against my palm. I said nothing. All you could hear in the room was Jerry's breathing. The silence was uncomfortable for Majestro, which is what I wanted. "I had a date. I have a credit card receipt for the restaurant. We went out for drinks later and I have a receipt for that, too. If that's not good enough, check with the cell phone company. They can tell you which towers my phone pinged during the calls. I was in Columbus the rest of the weekend. I never left, not once."

Majestro looked like he might cry. I looked out the window and saw three television vans setting up for remotes. "The Associated Press must have moved the story," I said. "Do you want to go down and talk to the media?"

He didn't answer. A tiny smile was pursing Jerry's lips. I tapped the papers.

Finally, Majestro asked the question. "Was I indicted?"

"Should you have been?"

"That isn't what I asked."

"No, Alfonso, you weren't indicted. Let me rephrase that. You weren't indicted . . . yet. But if I have any say in it, your day's coming. You're the dirtiest of the bunch."

He sank into his chair, breathing as though he had finished a distance race. "I didn't have anything to do with that," he said. "The only thing you have on me is the word of some guy trying to save his own skin."

"For now. This should be enough to halt the execution of Lester Yates. But it also will reopen the Danielle Quinn investigation, and you never know what we might find."

FIFTY

Nineteen hours before the scheduled execution of Lester Paul Yates.

The head of my legal department, Jim Sanders, was sitting in the lobby of the Tenth District Court of Appeals with a request for a stay of execution in the case of Lester Paul Yates. The court had been notified several hours earlier of the appeal. Before Jerry and I stepped on the elevator, I called Sanders on his cell and said, "File it."

The appeal stated:

- The death of Louise Elizabeth Love has been attributed to the so-called Egypt Valley Strangler.
- James D. Wilinski has been indicted and arrested in connection with the murder of Louise Elizabeth Love.
- D. Kendrick Brown has been indicted for conspiracy in the cover-up of the murder of Louise Elizabeth Love.
- There is substantial evidence available implicating James D. Wilinski and D. Kendrick Brown, both separately and independently, of conspiring to cover up the murder of Louise Elizabeth Love.
- The strangulation death of Danielle Quinn also was attributed to the work of the so-called Egypt Valley Strangler.
- James D. Wilinski and D. Kendrick Brown subsequently conspired to have Lester Yates arrested for the murder of Danielle Quinn as cover for the crime of murder and conspiracy in the death of Louise Elizabeth Love.
- D. Kendrick Brown, acting as the sheriff of Belmont County,

Ohio, subsequently identified Lester Yates as the so-called Egypt Valley Strangler.
- D. Kendrick Brown further stated publicly that Lester Yates was singularly responsible for eighteen murders attributed to the so-called Egypt Valley Strangler, including that of Louise Elizabeth Love.
- In light of the arrest of James D. Wilinski and D. Kendrick Brown, there is now substantial doubt about the guilt of Lester Yates in connection with the murder of Danielle Quinn or any of the women whose deaths were attributed to the so-called Egypt Valley Strangler.

The appeal asked for a sixty-day delay in the execution so that the case against Lester Yates could be investigated further.

It was granted.

After coming down the elevator, I spent much of the rest of the day fielding questions from the media. The arrest of Governor James D. "Big Jim" Wilinski was the lead story on every national news program that night. His lawyer was interviewed and said, "Our attorney general has lost his mind. The absurdity of this charge will be revealed very soon, and Jim Wilinski will walk free and be back on the campaign trail—one-hundred-percent vindicated."

Margaret and the interns worked late. I gave Liberatore my credit card, and she and Donahoe went for Chinese carryout for the fifteen people who would be working well into the night.

I contacted the Ohio Department of Rehabilitation and Correction to find out where Lester Yates was residing. He had been moved out of the tiny cell in the death house and into a single cell at the Southern Ohio Correctional Facility. For his last meal, he had requested a Big Mac, chicken nuggets, and fries. They had already been purchased, and he got to eat them in his cell. The superintendent at the prison told me that Yates was "greatly relieved."

"You think?" I said.

I called Doug Hyde, the prosecuting attorney in Belmont County. He said, "Sounds like you've got yourself a hornet's nest stirred up out there."

"A little bit," I said.

He snorted. "Yeah, a little bit."

"I'd say this puts a pretty dark cloud over the Lester Yates conviction."

"I'd say you're right."

"I'm going to file a motion first thing tomorrow to have the conviction vacated and all charges dismissed."

"If you do, I won't oppose it."

Sanders, my head of legal, was sitting at my conference table eating chicken lo mein out of a paper box with a plastic fork. "I want a motion to vacate the conviction of Lester Yates filed in Belmont County as soon as the court opens in the morning."

"It's already written and ready to be filed," Sanders said.

"Good. Drive down there tonight and get a hotel room. I don't want any screwups in the morning."

The three local television stations asked me to go live for their 11:00 p.m. broadcasts. I agreed. Margaret stayed at her desk, fielding calls from the national media. At 8:00 p.m., I held an hour-long conference call with reporters from several dozen national publications.

At 9:00 p.m., I told Margaret to forward her phone to voice mail and join me, Jerry Adameyer, and Denise Liberatore for some Chinese food at my conference table. It was the first time I had eaten since breakfast; I had pepper steak that I reheated in the microwave. I had just taken my first bite when I heard the distinctive clack of high heels in the foyer. Shelly Dennison was shaking her head as she entered my office.

"I will say one thing for you, Van Buren, you are a model of consistency," she said. "There is absolutely no one on God's earth who can blow up a political campaign like you."

"I am assuming you did not mean that as a compliment," I said.

She sat next to me at the conference table. Margaret eyed her warily. "Take it however you like," Shelly said.

"There's some wor sue gai over here if you're hungry."

"I don't know how you can eat. My stomach is in knots, and I'm not even involved."

She was obviously more involved than she was letting on.

"Look at the bright side, Shelly. At least this time it wasn't my campaign."

Jerry snorted into his orange chicken.

"No, this time you only trashed the campaign of the odds-on favorite to win the presidency. Congratulations. I'm sure the thank-you notes from the Democrats are in the mail."

"Mmm-mmm-mmm-mmm-mmm," Margaret said. "I've said it before and I'll say it again, that boy needs to get right with Jesus."

"If he's smart, he'll get right with a good defense attorney," Jerry said.

Shelly said, "I saw Wilinski's lawyer on the news. He said Wilinski is not resigning or giving up his bid to be president."

"He'll do both within forty-eight hours," I said. "The defense attorney hasn't seen all the evidence against him. Besides, it would be tough campaigning with an ankle monitor, particularly if he can't leave Franklin County." I lowered one eyelid, as though taking aim at Shelly. "You said you didn't think you were going to be that involved in his campaign anyway."

"I'm an optimist," Shelly said. "I was still hoping to get a little piece of the Ohio campaign."

"Let's back up a bit, shall we? A few weeks ago, you said I was going to be your number one priority."

"And you still are. Especially now. This will be the easiest statewide campaign I've ever run. You're going to be the guy who took down Big Jim Wilinski. There are a lot of Republicans out there who hate you right now, but the name recognition alone will get you sixty percent of the vote."

"Good to know."

She picked up a fork from the table and stabbed it into my carton of pepper steak. She shoved a bite into her mouth, then poked the fork my way three times. "Let me throw something at you, Van Buren. With all the notoriety you're going to get over this case, there will be talk about recruiting you to run for governor. You'd be a lock. Are you interested?"

"Amid all this chaos, you're still playing political chess?"

"It's what I do. What do you say? Want to run for governor?"

"Considering my disdain for politics, I can't think of anything I'd rather less do."

"It's the governorship of Ohio. You'd be a national power in Republican politics."

"What do you think, Margaret? Would you want to be the commandant at the governor's suite?"

"If it's all just the same to you, I'm pretty comfy right here," she said.

"I guess we're not interested, Shelly."

FIFTY-ONE

At 9:30 a.m. on August 24, 2007, ninety minutes before he had been scheduled to die by lethal injection, the motion to vacate the conviction of Lester Paul Yates was presented before Judge Michelle Miller of the Belmont County Court of Common Pleas. Fewer than thirty minutes later, Judge Miller granted the motion and it was filed with the clerk of courts. On the morning that he was supposed to die, Lester was cleared of any wrongdoing in the death of Danielle Quinn.

When Jim Sanders walked into my office a few minutes after eleven with a copy of the order to vacate the charges, Jerry and I climbed into his Jeep and headed south on Route 23. From the passenger seat, I telephoned the prison superintendent. Sanders was faxing him the motion and the documents necessary to free Lester. The superintendent said, "It's still going to take us a while to process him out."

"Take all the time you want, but he better be ready to walk out the door by the time I get there," I said. "He's a free man, and I expect him to be treated as such."

Lester had been transferred from the Belmont County Jail to the state penitentiary system in his jailhouse garb. That was all he had worn for the previous six years, and he had no street clothes. When he walked into the lobby of the Southern Ohio Correctional Facility, just twenty feet from freedom, he was still wearing his blue prison-issue pants and shirt, and his flip-flops, which were mandatory for Death Row inmates so they could not hang themselves with shoelaces. The prison's social services director had walked out with

Lester. He said someone from the local Salvation Army thrift store was bringing him some clothes and shoes if he wanted to wait.

He didn't. "These are just fine," he said. "I ain't waitin'. Get me out of here."

I opened the door, and Lester Yates walked up to the threshold and stopped. He smelled the free air, then looked into the parking lot, then down at the step, then to me. All that separated him from the outside world was a three-inch strip of aluminum.

"You don't need permission," Jerry said.

"He's right, Lester. You're a free man."

A little grin creased his lips. For six years he hadn't done anything without the consent of a prison guard. He tentatively stepped outside the building, tapping at the concrete sidewalk with the pad of his foot like someone testing the ice on a pond.

It was one of the saddest things I had ever seen. A man who had been wrongfully convicted walked out of prison after six years and not a single family member or friend was there to greet him or give him a hug. He didn't have a dollar, driver's license, wallet, razor, or a pair of socks. But to Lester's credit, it didn't seem to bother him. As we walked across the parking lot, the flip-flops slapping against his heel, he turned back for a last look at the razor wire. "Glad I'm not in there anymore," he said. I guess when you are a few hours away from being executed and you get to walk out the front door instead, maybe having a crowd to greet you isn't that important.

We stopped at a discount department store in Chillicothe. Surprisingly few people gave Lester and his prison garb a second look. I bought him a couple of shirts, underwear, socks, pants, and some toiletries. We went to a Big Boy restaurant for a late lunch. Before we left, Lester went into the restroom and changed into street clothes, leaving on the tile floor the prison blues of former inmate A333837.

When we got back in the Jeep, Lester asked, "Where we going?"

"Where do you want to go?" I asked.

"Home, I guess."

"Where is that, Lester? Your mother died while you were inside, and your father's in a nursing home somewhere. Is there any home to go back to?"

He thought about that for a minute, then said, "I guess not." He blinked a couple of times, looking perplexed. "I'm not sure what I should do."

Jerry said, "I've got a guest room, Lester. Why don't you stay with me for a couple of days until we figure out what's going to happen next?"

He nodded and said, "That would be nice. Much obliged, Mr. Adameyer."

We had driven a few more miles when he said, "Thanks for these here clothes."

"You're welcome," I said.

"How did all this happen, anyway? How did I get free?"

"A lot of work by a lot of good people."

That seemed to satisfy him. He didn't have any more questions. He sat back in silence, looking out the window and watching as the hills of southern Ohio passed by his window.

FIFTY-TWO

Six days and one hour after the scheduled execution of Lester Paul Yates.

When Herman Fenicks walked into the interview room where Jerry Adameyer and I sat at a table inside the Northeast Ohio Correctional Facility, he laughed and said, "What brings you peckerwoods back up here?"

"We have a little unfinished business with you," I said. "Have a seat. This won't take long. We just have a few follow-up questions."

He pulled out a chair and sat down, an amused look on his face. "Y'all must not have enough to keep you busy."

"I've got plenty to keep me busy, Herman."

"My name's The Rap. Try to remember that. Now, hurry up and ask your questions. It's almost lunchtime."

I opened the manila file folder on the table, pulled out a photograph, and slid it across the table. "Do you recognize this truck?"

"That's my old rig. So what?" He picked up the photo and flipped it back to me. "It looked better when I had it."

"Did you take good care of it?"

"What kind of stupid question is that? Hell yes, I took care of it."

"You should have done a better job of cleaning the inside."

"What the fuck's that supposed to mean?"

"It means we found hair and blood in the cab that belonged to Anne Touvell. We know it was hers because we exhumed her body and compared the DNA."

He said nothing but shrugged his shoulders and swallowed—a telltale sign. He suddenly wasn't so cocky. I'd hit a nerve.

"Anne Touvell. Does that name ring a bell?"

"No."

"It should, but maybe you didn't take the time to ask your victims their names. Or were there so many names that you couldn't possibly remember them all? I'll help you out. She was twenty-one, had that goth thing going—black hair, black lipstick. They found her tied to a tree in the Egypt Valley, strangled, within a few feet of where your truck had engine problems on Egypt North Road." Again, he swallowed hard. "What's wrong, The Rap? You look like you've lost your appetite."

"You've got nothing on me. If you did, you'd have charged me."

"I wouldn't have driven all this way to waste my time. We know you were the Egypt Valley Strangler. There hasn't been a woman killed since you went to prison. You might think that's circumstantial evidence, but I know how juries think, and they'd swallow that in a heartbeat. Now that we have Anne Touvell's DNA in your truck, we're going to start comparing the other samples we found to other victims. I'll put the entire might of the attorney general's office and the FBI on this case. That's going to cost a lot of money and, unfortunately, we're only going to be able to execute you once. So, here's the deal. You kick in to the Touvell murder and tell us about any other unsolved murders that you committed, and you'll do life without chance of parole."

"What kind of deal is that?"

"It's a deal that keeps you breathing. If you turn it down, I'm going for the death penalty."

"No way, uh-uh. I ain't takin' no backdoor parole."

I slipped the photo back in the folder and looked at Jerry. "You said he was smart enough to take the deal."

"I misjudged him," Jerry said.

As I stood, I dropped a business card on the table. "Your call, The Rap. We're heading back to Columbus. If you change your mind, you've got until the end of the day to let me know. Otherwise, all deals are off the table and you're going to be indicted for the murder of Anne Touvell with death-penalty specifications."

"You're bluffing," Fenicks said.

"Bluffing? Really? You think I'm bluffing? Let me ask you this: Have you ever heard of Frankie Simone, Marques "The Meat" Johnson, or Ricky Blood?"

"No. And why should I care?"

"Because they were all men who thought I was bluffing, right up until the minute they got sent to Death Row. Simone and Johnson were electrocuted; Blood died of a lethal injection. They say that's a better way to go, but no one knows for sure because when it's over, you're just as dead." I started toward the door. "Come on, Jerry. Let's leave The Rap alone so he can get some lunch."

As I grabbed the doorknob, Herman Fenicks said, "Wait a minute."

EPILOGUE

One year after the scheduled execution of Lester Paul Yates.

I never got my dog back.

Two weeks after Lester Yates walked out of prison, I saw Liberatore duck into an office in the investigative unit. She was trying to hide from me. "Liberatore!" I said, loud enough that it turned heads in the unit.

She knew what I wanted and yelled back, "You can't take her back now. She's too attached to me."

"She's my dog."

"Please, please, please don't take her."

"So, I get stuck with the three thousand dollar vet bill and you get the dog. Is that how this works?"

She poked her head back into the hallway and smiled, realizing she had won the battle. "Pretty much."

I love that girl's spirit. As soon as she finished law school, I hired her in my legal department. She is going to be a star.

Herman Fenicks was right.

I was bluffing.

I had not one strand of DNA linking Anne Touvell to the truck he had owned. Fortunately, he fell for the feint. Before Jerry and I left that day, he'd signed a statement confessing to her murder and pledged to help us with any unsolved murders attributed to the so-called Egypt Valley Strangler. Jerry and I laughed all the way back to Columbus. The lesson is, if you're telling a lie, say it with conviction.

Fenicks pleaded guilty to Touvell's murder and was sentenced to life in prison without chance of parole. By his own admission, he has been linked to at least nine other murders attributed to the so-called Egypt Valley Strangler. Danielle Quinn's strangulation was not among them; her murder remains unsolved.

Unfortunately, Fenicks became something of a celebrity after it was revealed he was the strangler. He reveled in the notoriety, doing dozens of interviews. Fortunately, sometimes karma is more effective than the judicial system. After a television news show ran a story on the unrepentant Fenicks, a detective in Erie, Pennsylvania, saw the show and began looking at Fenicks in connection with three unsolved strangulation murders along the I-80 corridor. Pennsylvania has the death penalty, and since the agreement he signed pertained only to murders he committed in Ohio, he may still pay the ultimate price.

Let's hope so.

A week after securing the confession from Herman Fenicks, I called Reno Moretti and asked him to meet Jerry and me for breakfast at the Old Alhambra Restaurant in Youngstown. I waited outside the restaurant for him so he wouldn't run when he saw the television vans.

Unbeknownst to him, I had rented a private dining space and called a press conference. "What the hell's this all about?" he asked.

"Just trust me and go with it," I said.

In the room were cameras, reporters, and a special guest: Lester Yates.

I made a brief opening remark.

"A few weeks ago, Reno Moretti was suspended from his job as a guard at the Northeast Ohio Correctional Facility. It was widely reported that the suspension was the result of inappropriate contact with a prisoner. What you didn't know was that Mr. Moretti was working undercover for my office. As a result of his selflessness and incredible detective work, Governor James D. Wilinski and D. Kendrick Brown, the head of the Ohio Bureau of Criminal Investigation, were indicted in connection with the murder of Louise Elizabeth Love. The subsequent investigation also exposed the wrongful conviction of Lester Paul Yates, who is with us today. Mr. Yates was just hours away from being executed before Moretti's diligent work freed him from prison. When political forces targeted Mr. Moretti in an attempt to stop his work and silence him, he quietly accepted both the suspension and the derision of the public and the media, rather than expose and endanger the investigation. Mr. Moretti was singularly responsible for bringing the wrongful conviction of Lester Yates to light. Without this man, Lester Yates would not be alive today."

I presented Moretti with the Stanbery Cross, the award named in honor of Ohio's first attorney general, Henry Stanbery, for meritorious service to the cause of justice. The story of his selfless dedication ran across the top of the front page of the Youngstown *Vindicator* the following day. I also hired him. He works under Jerry as the deputy chief investigator and brings a light heavyweight's attitude to the job. I have a powerlifter and a former world boxing champion heading my investigative unit. It's a beautiful thing.

Danny Doyle was charged with conspiracy after the fact and abuse of a corpse. The conspiracy charge was dropped in exchange for a guilty plea to the other charge. He was sentenced to three years in the state penitentiary, which were suspended in exchange for his cooperation in the prosecution of both D. Kendrick Brown and Jim Wilinski. Doyle received death threats after people in his and Wilinski's native Washington County learned that his testimony would be the linchpin in our case against their favorite son. He is in hiding, awaiting Wilinski's trial.

D. Kendrick Brown went on trial in early 2008 for conspiracy in connection with the death of Lizzy Love. He was found guilty and sentenced to twelve to twenty years in the state penitentiary. He is serving his time at the Marion Correctional Institution, where he was diagnosed with esophageal cancer. He is expected to be indicted for his involvement in the framing of Lester Yates for the murder of Danielle Quinn. However, it is likely the cancer will get him before the prosecutor.

Governor James D. "Big Jim" Wilinski's lawyer was wrong on both counts. The governor resigned his post and withdrew from the presidential race within a week of being arrested. He hired a high-powered defense team from Washington, DC, which has successfully overwhelmed the court in Guernsey County and delayed the start of the trial three times. My legal staff has been helping the locals sort through the miasma of paper that's been filed.

Several months after being charged with murder, Wilinski sat for an interview with *60 Minutes.* He professed his innocence, his mistakes, and his undying love for his wife.

Kathryn Wilinski filed for divorce three days later and moved to Lexington, Kentucky, where she assumed her maiden name and bought a property in an old industrial area that she hopes to convert to a restaurant and microbrewery. Not long after her move to Kentucky, I received a handwritten note that arrived at my residence. In part, it read:

> *I must admit that I was looking forward to being the First Lady of the United States. With that no longer being a possibility, I saw no reason to carry on the charade and put up with his nonsense. It had been a sexless and loveless marriage for a long time.*
>
> *I hope that my behavior at the state fair did not scare you off.*
>
> *My offer still stands. Give me a call.*
>
> *Kathryn*

I have not acted on the offer, as part of me considers it bad form to call on the former wife of a man I'm trying to put in prison. However, I must admit that I have not completely dismissed it, either.

With Brown's departure, Beth Kremer was promoted to superintendent of the Bureau of Criminal Investigation. We remain close, but I have never acted on my feelings because I cannot be sleeping with a member of my cabinet.

Margaret likes Beth and senses the sexual tension between the two of us. When I explained to Margaret that I could not date someone who is a direct report, she said, "Mmm-mmm-mmm-mmm-mmm, what are you thinking? Either fire her or resign, because you should not let that one get away."

We'll see what happens.

I ran unopposed in the primary and, as I predicted, Shelly Dennison is making my Democrat challenger wish he'd never entered the race. I am ahead by double digits. During our last meeting, as we prepared for the stretch run to the election, she said, "We've got our foot on his throat. Now let's grind in the heel."

It was at that moment that I realized she would have made a great Viking shield-maiden but a terrible life partner. I've lost any desire I had to ever share a bed or a life with Shelly. She is beautiful, smart, and dangerous, and that makes her the ideal campaign manager.

Ed Herrick died in the spring at the age of eighty-six. I hope there's an afterlife where he found peace and his daughter.

What do I believe about Alfonso Majestro?

I believe he knew everything about Lizzy Love. However, that puts him in the same boat as Elmer Glick, the Akron drug dealer who I'm sure beat a competitor to death with a shock absorber. Believing and proving are two different things. Majestro was involved in that cover-up from the tips of his little elf feet to the top of his ferret face. I just can't prove it.

While I believe he's a rat of the first order, I don't think he murdered Danielle Quinn. Ordinarily, I don't believe in coincidences, and I find it puzzling that someone like Alfonso was dating a woman who ended up floating in Stillwater Creek.

Danielle was last seen at six o'clock in the morning at the truck stop where she worked. The guy she was talking to did not match Alfonso's description. More likely, she met someone at the truck stop and made a very bad decision. I don't think Alfonso Majestro had the guts or the strength to strangle someone. As Jerry says, no one is immune to a moment of stupidity or a rash decision, but my gut tells me he didn't do it.

I'm never going to tell him that. I'm perfectly content to let him believe I think he killed Danielle and that I want to charge him with her murder.

Let him sweat that out for the rest of his life.

He deserves it.

Jerry Adameyer's offer to allow Lester to stay at his house for a few days has extended to this writing. They've become buddies. I don't think Lester ever had much of a father, and Jerry never had a son, so they both seem to have filled a hole in their lives. They fish the pond behind Jerry's house nearly every evening, and Jerry takes him to a trout club he belongs to in northern Ohio for weekend trips. Jerry paid to have Lester's teeth fixed and bought him a used Jeep to drive to a job he found at a local nursery. He loves the work and has a girlfriend who works in the perennial department.

Jerry put Lester in touch with a lawyer from Akron who is working with the state of Ohio on a wrongful-conviction settlement. It's safe to say the payout will be well into seven figures. Jerry had a long talk with Lester about the money and fiscal responsibility and how the settlement should be turned over to an investment broker to preserve the wealth. Lester said, "Whatever you think is best, Jerry."

Lester doesn't seem overly concerned about the money, and if he's bitter about the years he lost at the hands of corrupt individuals, he doesn't show it. I'm not sure what the future holds for Lester. For now, he's just a guy from Turkey Point who's happy to be alive.

FAVORITE SONS

A NOVEL

ROBIN YOCUM

ARCADE PUBLISHING
NEW YORK

Prologue

My entire professional career has been spent prying secrets out of the accused. When it comes down to it, it's not a complicated job. The path to learning the truth is simply decoding lies and uncovering layers of secrets.

The lies are easy. Every accused in the history of the criminal justice system has lied. Big lies. Little lies. White lies. Monster lies. It's a given. Fortunately, most criminals are not Harvard graduates. It is relatively easy to sort through their statements and pick out the improbabilities and impossibilities. What remains is a semblance of the truth.

It's the secrets that cause police detectives and prosecutors heartache.

Secrets can be fragile. Their structure can be torn apart by a whisper, a faint betrayal into the ear of another. Secrets also can be powerful, for they can control and haunt lives for many years.

In 1983 a woman showed up in the lobby of the Summit County Prosecutor's Office and said she wanted to report a homicide. These were the types of water runs that the new guys got sent on, and as I had been there less than a year I was summoned to the lobby. Her name was Angela Swan and she claimed to have witnessed the homicide. She was fifty-two years old and had deep creases running away from tired, rheumy eyes. As I walked with her to a nearby conference room, Swan nervously rubbed her hands together and said that even at this late juncture, she was feeling guilty about what she was about to tell me.

The homicide had taken place when she was six years old. She had been out with her father, riding in the passenger seat of his pickup truck. He bought her a bottle of pop and told her that he needed to stop and talk to a man. She remembered that he pulled off the road into a parking lot and gravel crunched under the truck tires; bright orange and red leaves adorned the trees. Her dad patted her on the knee and said, "You wait here, sweetheart," then got out of the truck to talk to the man. When the talk turned loud, she strained to look over the dashboard as her dad pulled a pistol from under his jacket and shot the man, maybe in the chest. The blast scared her and she spilled orange pop down the front of a blue and white dress embroidered with butterflies. The gun exploded a second time and a thin line of blood squirted across the windshield. The man fell and her dad fired the gun three more times. She didn't know what triggered the argument or where the parking lot was located. The truck fishtailed and she slid hard against the door as they sped from the lot, gravel pelting the wheel wells, and the panicked look on her father's face brought her to tears. Somewhere on the way home he pulled to the side of the road and wiped the blood from the windshield with his handkerchief, then stuffed it between the steel grates of a storm sewer. When he jumped back in the truck he cupped her face in his hands and said, "Angie, sweetheart, you can never tell anyone what happened today. Not your friends, your teacher, your grandma and grandpa, not even your mommy. It has to be our secret. Do you understand?" She nodded, and had faithfully kept the secret for forty-six years.

When she was young, Angela said she and her dad occasionally spoke in whispers of that day, and each time she renewed her vow of silence. Her dad told her the man he shot was a very bad guy—just like the desperados in the westerns they watched at the Paramount Theatre. It was a great game.

But as she grew older, she witnessed other disturbing actions of her father, which she didn't want to discuss—more secrets. She began to wonder if the dead man had been, in fact, a very bad man.

She wondered who he was, wondered if he had a little girl who missed her father and was tormented by not knowing why he had been murdered. Angela couldn't get it out of her head. But she could never betray her father. Wouldn't even consider it.

Her father had died a week before she showed up in the lobby. Now that he was gone, she felt obligated to report the homicide. Her father's name was Philip Economos. She doubted that anyone was around who remembered the dead man, and didn't know if anyone even cared, but she had to get it off her chest.

Since she didn't know where the shooting had taken place, I went to the library and searched the newspaper microfilm for the fall of 1937, the year Angela Swan was six and the time of year when the leaves would be changing color. On October 13, a story appeared on the front page of the *Beacon Journal* about a man found dead in a roller-skating rink parking lot—shot once in the chest, once in the shoulder, and three times in the back of the head. His name was Willie Backus and he owned the roller rink. He had no criminal record. Neither his lone surviving brother, his ex-wife, nor his only son could shed any light on what may have precipitated the shooting. The reason Willie Backus died, it seemed, was itself a secret that died with Philip Economos.

Angela was a rarity. She kept her secret, smothering the information for forty-six years. Most people can't keep a secret for forty-six minutes. Those who commit crimes without witnesses quite often cannot keep their own secrets. They precipitate their own undoing because they feel compelled to talk. They tell a friend or a girlfriend, who one day becomes a former girlfriend, and soon it is no longer a secret.

I kept my secret, not as long as Angela kept hers, but for a formidable number of years. I didn't tell my mother, or my now ex-wife, or any of the friends and girlfriends who passed through my life. I could never reveal my secret and relieve myself of its crushing burden. To do so would not only have destroyed my life, but the lives of those who were once most dear to me.

Secrets are central to misdeeds, infidelities, and betrayals. Without wrongdoing, there would be little need for secrets. The consequences, whether you're a six-year-old girl with an orange

Nehi, a teenage boy running with his buddies, or a man sworn to uphold the law, may not be realized for decades. There is no way to project to the future and know what those consequences will be. You wait and wonder, not if, but when the rogue asteroid that is circling your life will make its fiery reentry, and with each passing year, the consequences grow, lives become intertwined, and the pain in the chest refuses to subside.

Hutchinson Van Buren
Akron, Ohio
October 14, 2004

PART I

Chapter One

Petey Sanchez was a troubled human being, a stewpot of mental, emotional, and psychological problems manifested in the body of a wild-eyed seventeen-year-old, who cursed and made screeching bird noises as he rode around town on a lime green spider bike with fluorescent pink streamers flying out from the handlebars. Mothers could never relax when Petey was in the neighborhood. He had been banned from every backyard in town, but that didn't stop him from pedaling through the alleys and around the blocks, watching, staring, circling like a wolf on the lighted fringes of an encampment. Occasionally, an angry mother would shoo him off with the gentleness normally reserved for stray curs. "Get out of here, Petey. Go on, git. Go home." He would scream like a wounded raptor and flee, only to return a short time later, circling from a safer distance—pedaling and watching. Crystalton was a little less than two miles long and only about five blocks wide, squeezed hard between the Appalachian foothills and the Ohio River, so even when Petey wasn't in view, he was never far away, a wispy, ubiquitous apparition looming in shadow and mind.

From an early age, I learned the difference between Petey and the other kids who rode the little yellow bus out of town each morning to the school for the handicapped and mentally retarded in Steubenville. To my mother, most of them were objects of pity. There was a girl who lived down the street from us, Sarah Duncan, a frizzy-haired little kid who was cross-eyed, wore bulky, metallic braces on her legs, and struggled to the bus stop every morning, swinging each stiffened leg in an awkward arc. When she passed our open kitchen window you could hear with each footfall the clack of the steel braces and the squeak of the leather restraints, which would cause my mother to sigh, push an open palm to her breast, and say, "That poor little thing." Then, she would turn and glare at me, the corners of her eyes and lips crinkling in anger at my apparent lack of appreciation for the gifts I had been given, and say, without pause for a breath, "You should count your lucky stars that you were born with ten fingers, ten toes, and a good mind. Don't ever let me hear that you were teasing that little Duncan girl. Do you understand me, mister?"

"Yes, ma'am."

"You better. If I hear a word of it I'll knock you into tomorrow."

And she would have. Miriam Van Buren was a sturdy, humorless single mother who meted out discipline to her three children without impunity. She had strong wrists and heavy hands, which I had felt everywhere from the back of my head to my ass. Never mind that my various infractions had never once been for making fun of any handicapped kid. Mom always felt duty bound to forewarn me against potential indiscretions.

But she had no such sympathy for Petey Sanchez, of whom she said, simply, "Stay away from that boy; he's not right in the head."

I didn't need the warning. From an early age I had both detested and feared Petey Sanchez, and bore a J-shaped scar on my chin that I received in the fifth grade after he shoved a stick into the spokes of my bicycle, locking up the front wheel and sending me hurtling over the handlebars face-first into the asphalt parking lot at the elementary school. On our way back from the emergency room my mother stopped by the Sanchezes' to talk to Petey's mother and show the gash that had taken eight stitches to close. When Mrs. Sanchez saw us standing on her front porch with a gauze bandage taped to my chin, she sighed and shook her head, weary of the steady stream of neighbors and police officers knocking on the door with complaints about their feral son. "I'm awfully sorry, Miriam," said Lila Sanchez, a sickly thin woman with train-track scars along the base of her neck from a bout with thyroid cancer. "I know that boy's out of control, but I can't do a doggone thing with him."

As we climbed back in the car, my mother reiterated her early admonitions. "Stay away from the boy." That seemed to be the solution offered by most parents. Unfortunately, staying clear of Petey had its own challenges. He cruised the streets of Crystalton with more regularity than our police department. Throughout elementary and junior high school, if I saw Petey pedaling down the street, or heard his screeching cry, I would duck between houses or hide behind trees to avoid him. If you made eye contact with Petey he would call you a queer and a faggot, his favorite words, and try to run you over with his bicycle.

Petey was the second youngest of the nine children born to Lila and Earl Sanchez, who worked as a coupler on the Pennsylvania Railroad and had lost four fingers and a thumb to his job. The Sanchezes lived at the far north end of town in a paint-starved Victorian house with chipped slate shingles and sagging gutters that was wedged between the Chesapeake & Ohio Railroad tracks and the water treatment plant, where following each heavy storm, effluvium overflowed into the drainage ditch behind their house. They were all skinny, pinched-faced kids with stringy hair the color of dirty straw and the unwashed smell of urine. Petey had a similar look, except he had bad buckteeth that were fuzzy and yellow, rimmed with decay, and foul-smelling. However, the feature that overwhelmed his narrow face was a calcified ridge that ran from the bridge of his nose and disappeared into his hairline, the result of a botched birth during which the doctor grossly misused a pair of forceps. If all this wasn't misfortune enough, his forehead ran back from the calcified ridge, giving his thin face a trout-like quality. This battering of the skull and brain was most likely the genesis of Petey's cocktail of problems. Lila had told my mom that there were times when Petey would roll around on the floor of their living room, sometimes for hours, squeezing his temples between his palms and crying like a fox in a leg trap.

My first introduction to Petey Sanchez was when I was six years old and riding my new bicycle with training wheels down the sidewalk from the house. Behind me, I heard someone making a noise like a police siren and soon Petey flew by me on his bicycle, head tilted upward, mouth agape, howling away. He stopped broadside on the walk, blocking me. I was terrified. He was wearing a dime-store police badge on his T-shirt and carrying a small pad and the stub of a pencil in his hip pocket. Pointing a grimy index finger at my face, Petey slobbered down his chin while admonishing me in a tongue I did not comprehend for a violation I could not fathom. He then pulled the pad and pencil from his pocket, wrote some nonsensical drivel on the paper, ripped it out and handed it to me, then continued down the sidewalk in search of his next traffic violator. When I returned home and showed my mother the "ticket" and told her of my encounter with the strange boy who talked but couldn't say words, she shook her head and for the first time in my life I heard, "That was Petey Sanchez. Stay away from him. He's not right in the head."

Petey's traffic cop antics continued for several years. It seemed harmless enough at first, but after a while Petey started demanding that the young violators pay their fines with whatever change they had in their pockets. Parents complained, but it didn't stop for good until the day Chief Durkin walked out of Williams Drug Store and saw Petey making a traffic stop with a very realistic-looking .38-caliber revolver stuck between his belt and pants.

"Helping me with some speeders, huh, Petey?" Chief Durkin said as he approached Petey and a terrified little girl on the verge of tears.

"Uh-huh," Petey said.

"Did you get the license plate number of her bicycle?" the chief asked, pointing to the rear fender of the girl's bike. When Petey turned his head, Chief Durkin snatched the revolver. Petey screamed, called the chief a queer and a faggot, and lunged for the weapon, which looked realistic because it was, and fully loaded. A highly agitated Chief Durkin put Petey in the back of the cruiser and took him home. "What the hell is wrong with you, Earl, leaving a loaded gun around where a boy like that can get his hands on it?" the chief asked. "Why in hell do you even own a gun? You don't have enough fingers left to pull the damn trigger."

It was one thing after another with Petey. For a while he ran through the streets at night with a black cape, pretending to be a vampire. During another stretch he lurked in bushes and behind fences, pretending to be a tiger, leaping out and scaring young and old, then running off, growling. Twice he got angry with his parents and set his own house on fire, though miraculously the tinderbox was saved both times.

Parents in Crystalton worried that Petey would someday badly hurt or kill another child. Still, most would not reprimand Petey for his misdeeds because they feared he would return in the night and set their houses on fire. Thus, there was a silent but collective sigh of relief among these parents when on the evening of Tuesday, June 15, 1971, a berry picker found the body of Petey Sanchez on Chestnut Ridge.

About the Author

An award-winning former crime reporter with the *Columbus Dispatch*, Robin Yocum has published two true crime books and five critically acclaimed novels. *A Brilliant Death* was a finalist for both the 2017 Edgar and the Silver Falchion for best adult mystery. *Favorite Sons* was named the 2011 Book of the Year for Mystery/Suspense by USA Book News. His short story, *The Last Hit*, was selected for Best American Mystery Stories 2020. He grew up in the Ohio River village of Brilliant and is a graduate of Bowling Green State University, where he received a degree in journalism, which kept him out of the steel mills and prevented an untimely and fiery death.